FICTION BY DAVID HAGBERG

WRITING AS DAVID HAGBERG

WRITING AS SEAN FLANNERY

JOSHUA'S HAMMER

DAVID HAGBERG

TOR®

A TOM DOHERTY ASSOCIATES BOOK
NEW YORK

This is a work of fiction. All the characters and events portrayed in this book are either products of the author's imagination or are used fictitiously.

JOSHUA'S HAMMER

Copyright © 2000 by David Hagberg

A Forge Book
Published by Tom Doherty Associates, LLC
175 Fifth Avenue
New York, NY 10010

www.tor.com

Forge® is a registered trademark of Tom Doherty Associates, LLC.

ISBN-13: 978-0-765-35743-4
ISBN-10: 0-765-35743-7
Library of Congress Catalog Card Number: 00-028803

First Edition: August 2000
First Mass Market Edition: June 2001
Second Mass Market Edition: December 2006

Printed in the United States of America

0 9 8 7 6 5 4 3 2 1

This book is for Lorrel.

**Special thanks to all my friends
at I.R.N.B. You guys are awesome!**

My Father's Daughter

I am my father's daughter . . .
with this armor alone,
I am incredible.

Protected in the shadow of wisdom,
I grew strong of mind.
Guided through the colors of experience,
I grew strong of heart.

Inquiring with forensic precision,
I grew curious and able.
Expounding into understanding,
I grew tolerant and open.

All my fears laid out on the table,
I grew confident of love.
Flaws and foibles brought to light,
I grew to laugh easily.

I am my father's daughter . . .
with this armor,
I am invincible.

—GINA HAGBERG-BALLINGER

THE OPENING MOVES
SUMMER

Behold a pale horse; and his
name that sat on him was Death,
and Hell followed with him.

REVELATIONS 6:8

ONE

A weary and worried Allen Trumble got off the elevator on the seventh floor where he had to submit to a third and final security check. There wasn't a lot of activity in the corridors, but then there usually wasn't except during shift changes. But from the moment he'd entered the front doors he was struck by the underlying tension here, which did nothing to dispel his gloomy mood. What he was bringing to the deputy director of Operations wasn't going to help much; not the CIA and certainly not himself.

The civilian security officer handed Trumble's pass and ID back. "Just down the hall to the right, sir."

"Yes, thank you, I've been here before," Trumble said. But not often and not lately. Most of his seventeen years on the payroll had been spent in foreign postings, most recently as chief of station Riyadh, Saudi Arabia. But it was time to come home now, maybe. His life was beginning to unravel and he didn't really know why or what to do about it, except that a change of scenery might help.

He was an unremarkable looking man of medium height with thinning light brown hair, a slightly stoop-shouldered gait, and puffy features from living for too long in the dry desert climates of the Middle East. But he was an Arabic expert and that's where the work was happening. In fact because he had lived for so long in-country he probably knew more about the region than all but the most senior analysts here. Certainly enough to know that very large trouble was brewing.

But until now he'd also considered himself to be a very lucky man. He had a job that challenged him, a wife who loved him and two children who thought the sun rose and set on their father. All of it going down the toilet. In the past year Gloria had become distant, spending most of her free time watching reruns of American television sitcoms. It was as if she had forgotten what home was like and she was trying to remind herself. Their sixteen-year-old daughter Julie had experimented dying her hair first orange, then pink, but their Saudi neighbors had begun to complain and Trumble had to put his foot down. Julie was still resentful, and she moped around the house speaking only when spoken to, and then in monosyllables. In their twelve-year-old son Daniel's estimation it was time to go home. Most of the people they'd met over there were okay, but they didn't really like Americans, and he was getting tired of it. He wanted a Mickey D's, a real mall, Little League baseball and some new video games. Never mind that he had been born in Baghdad, and had never spent much time in the States. He missed it and he wanted to go home.

The deputy director of Operation's suite was at the end of the hall from the director's office. Trumble hurried down the broad, carpeted corridor, and went inside not at all sure exactly what sort of a message he was bringing home with him. He was the Arab expert, but this time he was out of his depth and he knew it.

"Good afternoon, Mr. Trumble," the DDO's secretary, Dahlia Swanfeld said pleasantly.

"Hello," Trumble smiled, trying to hide his nervousness. "I have a two o'clock with the deputy director." It was one minute before that time now.

"He's on the phone. Shouldn't be long. Would you like some coffee?"

"No thanks. We had a late lunch, McDonald's."

Ms. Swanfeld smiled and nodded. Though she'd never married—the CIA was her life—she sometimes acted like a kindly grandmother. Trumble could feel genuine interest and good cheer radiating from her like warmth from a wood stove on a cold winter's day. He couldn't remember the last time he felt so good.

"How is your family? Happy to be on vacation and back home?"

"It's going to be hard to drag them back to Riyadh. But I think we might be coming home again for Christmas. My folks are insisting on it, and it's hard to say no to your mother, wife and kids. I'm sorta outnumbered."

"I'd like to meet them." The light on her telephone console blinked out and she picked up the phone. "Mr. Trumble is here." She looked up. "You may go in now."

Kirk McGarvey, his jacket off, his tie loose and his shirtsleeves rolled up, was pulling a thick, red-striped file folder from one of the piles on his large desk. Stacks of newspapers and news magazines from a dozen different countries were piled neatly on the floor around him, and a television monitor, the sound very low, was tuned to CNN. The computer monitor on a credenza next to him was on, but showed only the CIA's seal.

"Nice to see you back in one piece." McGarvey got up, came around the desk and shook Trumble's hand. "Gloria and the kids okay?"

"They're out shopping. We need vacation clothes, but God only knows what they're going to buy for me. Whatever it is, though, I'm going to have to wear it and like it."

At fifty, Kirk McGarvey had worked for the CIA for twenty-five years and kept himself in superb condition by a strict physical regimen that included running and swimming everyday and working out at his fencing club whenever he could. He was a hard man, who until he'd taken over the job as DDO twelve months ago, had been the best field officer the CIA had ever known. The fact that he had been a shooter and had killed in the line of duty was widely known. What wasn't so well known, however, was the number of people he had killed, or the tremendous physical and mental toll the job had taken on him and his family.

He was six feet tall, two hundred pounds and built like a rugby player with not an ounce of visible fat on his broad-shouldered frame. But he was a Voltaire scholar and that curious combination—killer, academic and now adminis-trator—seemed to fit him well. He exuded self-confidence, intelligence, honesty and above all dependability. He had never let one of his people down, he had never held any-thing back from them, unless in his estimation they didn't have the need to know, and he was surrounded by a staff of very bright, very dedicated friends who excelled under his direction. There was a comfort zone around him. When you were with McGarvey you knew that everything would turn out okay. All hell might break loose, but you'd come out of it. He'd make sure of it.

His face was wide, handsome and friendly, unless he was being lied to. His motto was: Don't bullshit the troops; tell it like it is, or don't tell it at all.

"Do you want a beer?" McGarvey motioned toward the couch, chairs and low table by the window.

"Sounds good." Trumble set his attaché case on the cof-fee table, dialed the combination and took out his report contained in a thin file folder.

McGarvey got a couple of beers from a small fridge in his credenza and brought them back. He took the report. "Not much here."

"You might want to take a quick read, Mr. McGarvey."

"Mac. But I'd rather hear it from you first. What are our chances?"

"Osama bin Laden is not a good man," Trumble said, opening his beer. His hand shook a little and McGarvey noticed it. "He might be crazy."

"What'd he say to you? What does he want?" McGarvey asked, giving his COS his entire attention.

"Well, he says he wants to talk to someone in authority. Someone higher than a chief of station. It's a good possi-bility that he means to assassinate whoever we send to him, providing he thinks that person is a worthy enough target." Trumble had made the arrangements to meet with the Saudi multimillionaire terrorist in Khartoum, at McGarvey's request. No U.S. intelligence officer had been able to get anywhere near him or his business interests in the Sudan, or his camps in the mountains of Afghanistan, but McGarvey had a hunch that he might be ready to talk. The bad part was that a lot of people here in Washington and in London believed that bin Laden was getting ready to make another spectacular strike again, but no one knew when, where or how. In 1998 more than five thousand people had been hurt and more than two hundred killed when a bomb exploded outside the U.S. embassy in Nairobi. There'd been many other attacks with loss of lives, but Nairobi had been the biggest to date. The general consensus was that there would be a next time and it would be even worse.

"They took my tape recorder before they brought me up to see him, but it really wouldn't have mattered if I'd been able to keep it, because I wasn't with him for more than two or three minutes. He told me that I was the face of evil and that if I were to die then and there, no one would shed a tear."

McGarvey sat back, a dark, calculating expression in his gray-green eyes. Bin Laden hadn't balked at the meeting, in fact he'd agreed to it almost too readily, which meant he wanted something, unless he was stalling for time. It was a possibility they would have to consider. Bin Laden could be keeping them talking while he was getting ready to strike. With the latest information McGarvey had seen and the reason he'd sent Trumble orders to set up the meeting, this time when bin Laden struck it would be worse than Nairobi, much worse than anything they could imagine.

"Did he give you any names, Allen? Anyone in specific who he wanted to talk to?"

"No, just someone more important than me." Trumble shuddered. "The bad part is that he knows more about me than I know about him. He told me to get out or die, but I thought I could push it just a little. Maybe he was bargaining, they do that a lot. So I promised that we'd lift the bounty on his head like you suggested."

"What'd he say to that?"

Trumble looked McGarvey in the eye. "His exact words. He said, 'Your wife's name is Gloria, isn't it? Your children are Daniel and Julie?' "

"Jesus," McGarvey said sitting up suddenly. "Were you followed back to Riyadh?"

"I don't think so. Look, it was just his way of letting me know that his intelligence was at least as good as ours and that he wasn't screwing around. Saving face is everything out there and we are the infidels. He's taken to heart the idea of knowing his enemies. He could have killed me then and there, dumped my body somewhere it would never be found." Trumble shook his head, as if he were trying to shrug off the incident, but he wasn't doing a very good job of it. "He doesn't operate that way, on that small a scale, I mean. If he wants a bigger fish, killing me wouldn't have done him any good."

McGarvey got up and went back to his desk. "Who's your ACOS?"

"Jeff Cook."

"Is he ready to run a station on his own?"

Trumble was a little confused. "He's coming along. I didn't hesitate leaving him in charge. He can handle the routine, although his Arabic is a little weak. The Saudis get along with him okay."

McGarvey picked up his phone. "Dahlia, have Dick come right over and then get me Dave Whittaker." Whittaker was the area divisions chief in charge of all foreign CIA stations and missions. McGarvey held his hand over the phone. "Is he married, any kids?"

"No kids. He's divorced, his wife's back in Michigan, or someplace in the Midwest."

McGarvey turned back to the phone. "Dave, I have a housekeeping job for you, but I want it done on the QT. I'm pulling Allen Trumble and his family out of Riyadh, effective immediately. In fact he's in my office right now, so I want you to send a security detail over there to shut down his apartment and get his things back here."

Trumble was floored, and he started to object, but McGarvey held him off.

"I'm putting his ACOS Jeff Cook in charge for the time being. We'll see how it works out." McGarvey was watching Trumble. "But listen to me, Dave, tell security to watch their step. Allen's apartment could be rigged."

Trumble's stomach flopped. The thought that bin Laden could have ordered someone to booby-trap his apartment had never occurred to him.

"Bin Laden," McGarvey said. "That's what Allen told me, but I don't want to take any chances. This isn't going to turn out to be another Buckley case." In 1985 CIA Director William Casey sent his Beirut COS Bill Buckley back into the field after the U.S. embassy out there had been sacked and his cover blown. He'd been picked up the day he got back. He was tortured and eventually murdered.

Dick Adkins, the DDO's chief of staff, walked in from the adjoining office. Like McGarvey he wore no jacket, his tie was loose and his shirtsleeves rolled up.

"Hi, Allen," he said. "How'd it go in Khartoum?"

"Not very well," Trumble said, and they shook hands. He'd known Adkins for seventeen years, first running into him at the Farm, the CIA's training facility near Williamsburg, where Adkins had been camp commandant. At his welcoming talk to new recruits he'd impressed Trumble as a man who might be short on imagination, but who was very strong on details. The first impression he gave was that of a very steady hand on the helm. Nothing in the intervening years had happened to change Trumble's mind. Adkins was doing the job now that he was always meant to do; acting as precision point man to McGarvey's sometimes maverick tactics.

McGarvey hung up the phone. "I've pulled Allen out of Riyadh and put his ACOS Jeff Cook in charge for the time being."

"I'd just as soon stick with it, if you don't mind," Trumble said. "I've developed a lot of solid contacts in the last three years."

"I do mind," McGarvey said. "Your contacts wouldn't do you any good if you were dead."

"What the hell happened over there?" Adkins demanded.

McGarvey handed him Trumble's report. "Take a look at this, Dick. Bin Laden was playing games with him."

Adkins sat down and quickly read through the report, which ran only to ten pages. When he was finished he glanced up at McGarvey. "Good call," he said quietly, and then he turned his attention back to Trumble. "Did you get the sense that he was actually going to come after you and your family?"

"I don't know. That's not his style. But there were a half-dozen pretty eager looking kids in the room with him, all armed with Kalashnikovs. It would have taken just a word, or even a gesture, from their boss for them to kill me."

"Did you recognize any of them?"

Trumble started to shake his head, but then thought better of it. He had a very good memory for faces, and the station file in Riyadh had an extensive photo archive of known terrorists and their associates. Not only the foot soldiers, but the planners, the bankers, the technicians and anyone else connected with the dozens of various movements and factions in the region. He'd wanted to do a little checking on his own first before he brought it up. He didn't know if he was being foolish, but now he decided was not the time to hold anything back no matter how seemingly meaningless it might be.

"There was one man, older than the others, maybe forty, plain looking, who sat in a corner drinking tea. He was the only one not armed."

"Did you recognize him?" Adkins asked.

Trumble shook his head, trying to place the face as he had done on the way back to the Khartoum airport. "I don't think so. But I got the impression that he might have recognized me. But it was just for a second, and then bin Laden was talking to me."

"Anything in your station files?"

"I looked, but I didn't find anything."

"Okay, it might be nothing," Adkins said, clearly not meaning it. He glanced at McGarvey who was content to let him run with it for now. "What's this number you mention?"

"Bin Laden gave it to me just before I left. It's not a phone number, but it obviously means something."

Adkins handed the report to McGarvey, who looked at it. "He didn't give you any explanation?"

"He said that we'd figure it out."

"What do you want to do, Allen?" Adkins asked.

"First of all I want some solid bargaining points that I can bring back to Khartoum."

"Do you think he'd agree to another meeting?"

"I think so—"

"That's out," McGarvey cut in sharply. "I'm putting you on the Middle East Desk, and if we do set up another meeting it won't be with you, Allen." He and Adkins exchanged a significant look that Trumble caught.

"What am I missing?" he asked.

"Nothing for now," Adkins said. "Do you think that you can come up with a name for this face?"

Trumble wasn't satisfied with the answer, but he let it slide for the moment. "That's the other thing I wanted to try. I'd like to take this to Otto Rencke. We might be able to develop a recognition search program. At least we could narrow down the list of possibilities."

"Good idea," McGarvey said. "You can get Otto started this afternoon. In the meantime what are your vacation plans?"

"That depended on my new orders. We were going to hang around Washington for a couple of days to see the sights, and then if there was time, see my folks in Minnesota."

"Your kids have never really seen the states," Adkins said. "Dan was born in Baghdad, wasn't he?"

"Yeah. But we've been back a few times to Duluth."

"You oughta go down to Orlando. Disney World. It's a little hot this time of year, but after Riyadh it should be a piece of cake."

"They've talked about it."

"That's a good idea," McGarvey said. "Take a couple of weeks, and when you get back we'll have personnel find you a place to live. You'll be looking at some eighty-hour weeks."

"I hate to walk away from this."

"I'm not handing out charity, Allen. You've earned the desk, and right now I need your expertise here, not in Riyadh."

"Yes, sir." Trumble closed his attaché case, and got up.

McGarvey understood his frustration. "There is another factor out there, an important one. But it'll hold for a couple of weeks. Knowing wouldn't do you any good on vacation in any event."

"Just something more to worry about?"

"Something like that."

When Trumble left, McGarvey called down to Otto Rencke to tell him what was coming his way. He also read off the twelve-digit number. "Bin Laden gave this to Allen. Find out what it is, Otto. It's top priority." Trumble was a very good man; intelligent, knowledgeable and sensitive. But he was an academic, and nothing more than an academic, who should never have been given a field assignment in the first place.

"What do you think, Dick?"

Adkins had gone to the fridge for a Coke. "Two possibilities. Either bin Laden is getting tired of hiding out and wants to come back to the real world, or he's stalling us."

"I meant the serial number. If it's what I think it is, we could be in trouble."

Adkins stared out the window, almost as if he was sorry that he was here and he wanted to escape. He was a short, somewhat paunchy man who had fought a weight problem all of his life. He had light, wavy hair and a pale complexion. Sometimes like this morning he looked as if he had been sick for a long time. "Are we going to send somebody else to talk to him?"

"I don't think we have any other choice under the circumstances."

Adkins turned back, his eyes washed out. "Who?" he asked quietly. He knew the answer, but he didn't want to say it.

McGarvey didn't respond. A snatch of something from Voltaire ran through his head. *The problem is that common sense isn't so common after all.* But what good was common sense, McGarvey wondered, in dealing with a madman who'd dedicated his fortune and his life to one thing— killing Americans? All his life he had been witness to some very bright people making the most stupid of mistakes, himself included. He did not want to repeat the errors, especially not this time.

Office of Special Research

Otto Rencke had been trained as a Jesuit priest and professor of computer sciences and mathematics, but he'd been kicked out of the church for having sex with the dean's secretary on top of the dean's desk. His life after that had been one series of scrapes with the law after another, because he was a genius, he didn't respect authority and he thought that he knew more about computers than anyone else in the world, which he probably did. In between troubles he had done some very good and very serious work for the CIA, bringing the Agency into the twenty-first century, and he had worked on a number of projects with McGarvey. But he'd been bored. He'd simply been playing games; with the world, with the projects he'd been assigned, with himself. The fact of the matter was that he had no idea who he was, what was driving him or where he was going. A lost soul, his mother had called him on the day she and her husband had kicked him out of the house for good.

It wasn't until McGarvey became DDO and brought Rencke back into the fold that the forty-one-year-old maverick finally came into his own. He had finally found the one thing he'd been looking for all of his life: a family; someone to love him, someone for him to take care of, to fight for, to be with.

When Trumble walked in on him in his third floor office, he was sitting on top of a table that was strewn with computer printouts, running his delicate fingers through his long, out-of-control, frizzy red hair.

Trumble knocked on the doorframe. "Mr. Rencke?" He'd heard about the assistant to the DDO for Special Research, but he'd never met the man, and until this moment he'd disbelieved almost everything he'd been told as simply too fantastic, too bizarre.

"Bad dog, bad dog. My *father's* name was Mr. Rencke, and he was the baddest dog of all." Rencke hopped down off the table and practically bounded across the room to shake Trumble's hand. He wore faded blue jeans, a dirty MIT sweatshirt, and unlaced black high-top sneakers, showing bare ankles that looked as if they hadn't seen soap and water in a month. But his grip was light, and his wide blue eyes were so intense, so deep, and so utterly warm and filled with intelligence and childlike good cheer, that Trumble couldn't help but smile. "You call me Otto, I call you Allen. Saves a lot of time that way, ya know."

"All right, Otto. I just got in from Riyadh, and Mr. McGarvey thought that you might be able to help me with something."

"The name is Mac, and you're lying. It wasn't his idea, it was yours." Rencke started to hop from one foot to the other, something Trumble had been told he did whenever he was happy or excited about something. "Trumble, Allen Thomas. Born Duluth, Minnesota, 1960. Parents Eugene and Joyce—solid folks. Poli-sci and psych double majors, University of Minnesota, magna cum. Masters in psych,

then the Company recruited you from a fate wor
death in dull, dull, boring hidebound academia. He
grinned, his mouth pulled down on the left. "Hidden talents.
Farsi and a dozen Arabic dialects. You have the gift, and
we're all desperate for gifts, ya know. Married to Gloria
Porter, kids Julie sixteen, Daniel twelve, apples of their
father's eye, tests off the charts in every embassy school
they ever attended."

Rencke stopped in midstream and gave Trumble a
strange, pained look, almost as if he'd suddenly seen something so terrible it was beyond words. "What was he like?
In person, I mean. Bin Laden."

Trumble was at a loss for words. Rencke was overwhelming.

"Come on, Allen, reticence is dull. First thing pops into
your head."

"Gentle," Trumble said, not knowing where that had
come from.

"Gentle?" Rencke prompted.

"Cobra."

"Cobra?"

"Venemous."

"Venemous?" Rencke prompted again, continuing the
word association.

Trumble blinked, knowing exactly what Rencke was
looking for. The only true knowledge, that worth having,
was sometimes to be found only in the subconscious. "He's
a dangerous man because he's smart, he's rich, he's dedicated and he's completely filled with hate. It's his religion,
and he has more followers now than Jesus Christ had two
thousand years ago when he was out among the people
spreading the Word. When he looks at you through those
hooded eyes, he's as mesmerizing as a king cobra."

"Kamikazes in the flock?"

"You can bet on it," Trumble said. "He's got people
around him willing to give their lives for the jihad. Without
hesitation, without even giving it a second thought, except

that they would be gaining an early entry into the gates of paradise."

"Gotcha." Rencke broke out into a broad grin. "That's the guy we're looking for. The unarmed man sitting in the corner drinking tea while all around him the troops were twitching."

"Okay, how do we do it?"

"We're going to generate a 3-D computer model of his face, his build, his mannerisms, anything you can remember no matter how small—just like the old police IdentiKit drawings—and then my darlings will go hunting. From time to time a candidate should pop out of the slot and I'll fax it to you."

"I can stick around—"

"Bzzz. Wrong answer, recruit. The boss says you're on vacation, and this might take some time."

Trumble had to shake his head. Being around Rencke was like being in the middle of a white tornado; it left you breathless and wondering if your feet would ever touch the ground. Trumble had, in the back of his heart, figured that he was pretty smart. But Otto was smarter, a lot smarter than anybody he'd ever known including a couple of Nobel docs at the U. of M. It was almost disquieting. Thank God the man was on our side, he thought.

Rencke started hopping from one foot to the other again. "Do me a big favor, would you, Allen? Just one?"

"Sure, if I can."

"Disney World. Magic Mountain, the roller coaster. Keep your eyes closed the whole time."

Trumble laughed. "Okay, but why?"

"I always wanted to do that," Rencke said dreamily. "When you come back I want you to tell me what color it was. I'm betting red."

TWO

He's a fool." Bari Yousef put the satellite phone back in his bag, a look of disgust on his dark, narrow features. He understood the meaning of his orders. Killing Trumble and his family had to be made into a statement of terror. Strike fear into the hearts of everyone who witnessed the attack, or heard about it, here of all places, at America's mecca for families. But the risks were great.

"You should be careful what you say," Rachid Walid warned. "If we are given an order, then we must carry it out, because he knows what he's doing. We've come this far together, and if we die now it will be glorious."

Yousef knew that nothing was foolproof, but he could think of a dozen different methods to accomplish their goal with a much greater chance for their escape afterward. He wasn't concerned about doing the job, he'd done a lot more difficult things, in Berlin, and Beirut, and Paris, and even in New York. But it was getting away so that they could fight in another place, on another day that worried him. He wasn't an ignorant country boy like so many of the others, he had gone to school for two years at the American University in Beirut, so he could think beyond the moment. He shook his head in frustration.

"Hamza knows his duty," Omar Zawattri said from the back of the van. "He's waiting for us where he should be waiting, just like we planned. He has never failed before.

And by the time the authorities respond we well be a long way from this godless place."

They made a second pass down the Kangaroo 57 row where the Trumbles' rented light-blue Toyota SUV had been parked since nine this morning. If the family followed the same routine as they had for the last four days, they would be leaving the park around 6:00 P.M. to return to their Dixie Landings hotel a few miles away but still on the Disney property.

Yousef checked his watch. It was already five o'clock. "Find us a parking place where we can watch the shuttle bus. We have been given the go-ahead."

Walid, who was driving, glanced over and grinned. Two of his front teeth were missing, and fool that he was he refused to see a dentist in Jersey City where'd they'd lived for the past three years, because he couldn't find a doctor who was also a man of God. He would not have an infidel attend to him. In the meantime, in Yousef's estimation, he looked like an ignorant Bedouin. He had never blended in, which made him dangerous.

Seven hundred meters across the still mostly full vast parking lot, the dimpled silver ball that was the symbol of EPCOT rose sixteen stories into the hazy blue sky. They had been told that small carts took people up inside the globe where at the very top they were given the illusion that they hovered in outer space looking down at the earth. One part of Yousef wanted to disbelieve such fairy tales, but living in America for so long he had seen plenty of other fantastic sights, so that another part of him thought the stories might be true. One of the truck drivers working for their cover company in Jersey City had told them that anything is possible in America, so maybe this was true. But none of it was worth so much as a tiny desert village, because of the godlessness. But that would change, and sooner than any of them expected. *Insha'Allah.*

• • •

Trumble was nearly dead on his feet. Five solid days of being on the go had gotten to him. He sat on a bench with Gloria in the shadow of Spaceship Earth, the EPCOT dome, waiting for the kids to come out. It had been a beautiful week, although the weather was way too humid after the years he had spent in the desert climates. The crowds in the park had been as heavy as Adkins had warned they would be. Kids were on summer vacation, and this was the ultimate family playground. But what surprised him was how efficiently everything was run. Sure there were long lines for every attraction, but the lines moved pretty quickly so that they'd never had to wait much more than twenty or thirty minutes. And another thing amazed him. With all those crowds everyday he'd expected to see a lot of litter, maybe even some graffiti and broken things, or worn-down paint. He'd watched for it, but the entire huge park looked almost brand-new, the same as Magic Kingdom. Perfectly mowed lawns, beautifully arranged flower beds and topiaries. Everything was clean and neat, everybody smiled, everybody was having a good time. It was impressive, and a far contrast to the rigidly defined structure that the Saudis imposed on their people; and it was even worse in the other Islamic countries where they'd lived. He was a Middle East expert, but he decided that he wasn't going to miss living there very much. Coming home was going to be a new start for them.

"A penny?" Gloria asked, contentedly. She'd been a CIA wife for seventeen years, and until recently had always gotten along wherever they were assigned. But Saudi Arabia had gotten to her. He could see that now. She'd taken the news that they were pulling out with a mixture of surprise, and relief, and finally some suspicion. Transfers weren't done so suddenly unless something was wrong. But she'd not made a point of it so far. The only blot on their vacation was the kids. They had been at each other's throats for five days. Nothing was right. There were too many people. It was too hot. They couldn't do what they wanted to do. Julie wanted to spend money on clothes, and Danny wanted to do nothing other than play video games.

He smiled. "A hot shower, clean clothes, one very cold martini, something fishy for dinner—maybe lobster—and two quiet children."

"They'll be okay, Allen. This has been a big change for them. They dreamed about it for so long that now that they're here they can't take it all in."

"Maybe they'll drown each other in the pool tonight and we can start all over again," Trumble said. Gloria laughed at the back of her throat, like she did when she was happy. She hadn't done that for a long time, and Trumble felt a stab of guilt.

"I wouldn't go through that again for all the oil in OPEC."

"Tea in China," he corrected. "At any rate, twelve and sixteen, we're almost home free." He shrugged. " 'Course there'll be college bills, a couple of weddings, grandkids."

Gloria reached over and kissed her husband. "It's going so fast, Allen. I'm glad we're home." She gave him a look that she wanted to be serious now. "Are you going to be okay with this move?"

"It's a promotion."

"You know what I mean," she said. "Are you going to get wanderlust in a few months, reading reports from places we've been—where you think you still belong?"

Trumble thought about it for a moment, then nodded. "I probably will," he admitted. "But it's time for us to come home, sweetheart. And all kidding aside, being with you, Julie and Danny, and being back home like it used to be, beats Riyadh hands down."

Gloria was watching him closely. "You almost said safe. Back home and *safe*."

"That too."

A dark cloud came over her face. "Can you tell me what happened, Allen? Why they won't let us go back even to pack our things?"

"No."

"Were we in some danger over there?" she demanded sharply.

Trumble had never been a very good liar, which was another reason, he knew in his heart of hearts, that he was never a very good spy. An expert, an administrator, an analyst, but not a spy.

"There was a possibility, and I mean a remote possibility, that something might have happened, maybe a kidnapping or something like that. That's why McGarvey pulled us out the way he did."

"How about here? Are we in any danger?"

Trumble looked into his wife's eyes, certain now that their troubles were finally behind them, and told her the absolute truth as he knew it. "Not unless Mickey Mouse turns out to be a rat and bites us."

"We'd have to go back to Magic Kingdom for that—maybe you could ride the roller coaster again," she added coyly.

"I get sick just thinking about it." Rencke had been right; the coaster was red with your eyes closed. Amazing.

He glanced over at the Spaceship Earth exit. The kids were coming down the walk, arguing about something like they'd done all week. The crowds had definitely thinned out since this morning, and most of them looked tired, even their whirlwind Daniel. He'd not raised any objections for a change when they'd headed for the exit. He just wanted to go up in the ball one last time, and had somehow talked his sister into going with him.

"Okay, let's get out of here," Trumble said.

"Sounds good," Gloria agreed. She got up and handed him a couple of the plastic shopping bags. Danny's was the heaviest because he'd bought four glycerine-filled glass globes that contained models of the castle at Magic Kingdom. When the globes were shaken snow seemed to fall all around the castle. He was sending them back to his Saudi friends in Riyadh who'd not only never been to Disney World, but who'd never seen snow. Danny had always been their giver, and Julie was their fashion expert. Until a year ago when their constant bickering had taken on a new, sharper tone, they argued almost constantly, but Danny had always been able to stop his sister short by giving her something out of the clear blue. He used to spend his allowance on her; pierced earrings, watches, and once a twenty-five dollar gift certificate for the big mall in Kuwait City.

"Shut your mouth," Julie was saying, angrily. She was tall and willowly like her mother at that age. "Just shut up."

"Whatever it is, I don't want to hear it," Trumble told them. "We're going back to the hotel now."

"This one you gotta hear, Dad," Daniel said, grinning from ear to ear. He was tall, almost as big as his father. And at twelve he still had some of his baby fat, which his sister chided him unmercifully about.

"Daniel," Julie warned.

Daniel couldn't contain himself. "She's got a bikini, Dad. And she wore it at the pool last night." That was something just not possible in the Middle East.

Julie's lips compressed.

Trumble laughed out loud. "Did she look sexy?"

"Nah, she just looked gross."

"Am I going to get to see this swimsuit?"

"I don't think that would be such a good idea, dear," Gloria intervened.

Outside the gates they were just in time to catch one of the nearly empty shuttle trains. Daniel pulled a small package out of his pocket, and handed it to his sister. She shot him another dirty look, and although she didn't want to open it, she couldn't help herself.

"What'd you spend your money on now?" Trumble asked.

"There was this other girl at the pool. She had an ankle bracelet, which looked pretty cool, but Julie didn't have one." Daniel said it almost shyly.

Julie held up the delicate gold-plated bracelet with a tiny gold Minnie Mouse charm. "What am I supposed to do now, Mother?" she asked plaintively.

"You could try thanking your brother," Gloria said.

Julie looked at her brother, the expression on her face softening, and she shook her head. "Thank you, Daniel," she said.

Danny grinned. "Just don't hang around me and my friends half naked like that. It's embarrassing."

Trumble put his arm around his son's shoulder and pulled him close. "Did I ever tell you that I love you?"

"Ah, Dad." Daniel squirmed.

Julie was misty-eyed. "All the time, Father, and to all of us," she said very seriously, back to her old self.

The shuttle train stopped at the Kangaroo 57-61 rows. They got off with a few other passengers who headed off to their cars. Trumble had forgotten which row they were in.

"Fifty-seven," Gloria said.

Trumble glanced at his watch. It was just six. Tomorrow they were going to Sea World and it was going to be a great day because the kids were finally beginning to settle down. Washington would be pretty good after all, he decided. He might even have time to get back into tennis. Once upon a time he and Gloria had been pretty good, but now he was so out of shape that he didn't think he could last one set, let alone an entire match. Maybe they could get Julie interested in the game—of course, she'd want the best tennis outfits in Washington. And maybe he and Danny could go fishing, or maybe even sailing on the Chesapeake, he'd always wanted to try that.

He heard a car coming up behind them, and he turned as a dark gray van headed way too fast directly at them.

Trumble shoved Danny aside, between parked cars and he raised his hand for the driver to slow down as he tried to reach Gloria and Julie twenty feet back. The van was right on top of them as its side door came open, and he got the impression of a man crouched in the back with a large gun. It was a Kalashnikov, the thought registered on his brain, and an instant later he heard the distinctive clatter of the Russian assault rifle on full automatic.

Gloria and Julie were shoved violently backward, blood

spraying on the trunk lids and rear windows of several cars from a dozen wounds. He simply could not believe what he was witnessing. Not now. Not here. It was impossible!

"No!" Trumble cried out. He spun around and threw Danny to the pavement, shielding his son's body with his own. Some people in the next row stopped short, and a woman screamed. Bullets slammed into the cars, sending glass flying everywhere.

The van screeched to a halt about twenty yards down the row and immediately started back, tires squealing.

Trumble hauled Danny to his feet. "Get out of here, Danny! Run!" He shoved his son toward the next row, then scrambled around the front of the car, blocked for the moment from the direct line of fire. He was moving purely on instinct now, adrenalin pumping through his body, his mind numb by what was happening. This was America. Disney World, the safest place on earth. They were home.

All he could think of were Gloria and Julie. He had to get to them now.

He heard the van screech to a halt directly behind the car he was crouched in front of, and he moved to the left fender where he could see the front of the van. A man sat behind the wheel, looking around wildly as if he expected the police to show up at any moment. Another man ran past the car. Trumble could see him through the windows, a deep, black, sick anger welling up inside his gut. They had come after his family all the way from Saudi Arabia. The bastards! The fucking bastards!

"Dad! Dad!" a little boy shouted in desperation, and in his present state it took Trumble a second before he realized that it was Daniel.

He scrambled back around the front of the car to the other side just as a second man came down the row. He was dark, probably Arab, Trumble thought. The man suddenly crouched down and opened fire with the Kalashnikov, cutting Danny's cries off. None of this was happening. It was all some sort of a terribly bad joke, yet he knew it wasn't so.

The gunman started to swivel around as Trumble leaped

up and swung the heavy plastic shopping bag with Danny's snow globes, connecting solidly with a satisfying thump on the side of the man's head. The bag broke open sending the glass globes flying. The gunman's head cracked open like a soft-boiled egg in a spray of blood, and he was slammed forcefully against the side of the other car, dropping his rifle and collapsing in a heap.

Daniel was down on his back and not moving between the parked cars. The front of his tee shirt was bright red, and a shockingly large pool of blood was spreading out on the pavement. Up the row Trumble could see the bodies of his wife and daughter, and still it made no sense to him. For a heartbeat he was torn between going to them, who he knew without a doubt were dead, or picking up the Kalashnikov and going after the monsters who had done this to his family; now after they had finally begun to work things out.

He turned to the downed gunman as another man ran up from the van, raising his rifle as he came. Trumble knew with utter finality that he had lost, but still he made a try for the rifle lying on the pavement. Something like a freight train slammed into his chest, and an instant later a billion stars burst inside his head as a 7.62mm standard Russian military round plowed through his forehead into his brain.

THREE

Georgetown

Jake's was a glittering restaurant that had just reopened after a terrorist bomb had destroyed it last year, and the al fresco dining area fronting busy Canal Street was even better than before with first-class food, an extensive wine list and French waiters. It was Kathleen who insisted that they have an early dinner here before the symphony at the Kennedy Center, and sitting across from her, McGarvey, ruggedly handsome in his tuxedo, could only marvel at his fantastic good fortune. They had divorced twenty years ago because she could not stand being married to a CIA case officer, but they had finally realized that they could no longer live apart because they loved each other. Being here tonight was going to be a closure, and he hoped a beginning, for both of them. He wanted this to work with everything in his being; and maybe he even needed it for his sanity.

Watching her as the waiter poured their wine, his chest swelled. At fifty she was more beautiful in his eyes than she'd ever been. She wore a black, off-the-shoulder Givenchy evening dress, a string of pearls around her long, delicately formed neck, her blond hair up in back, and the cheap diamond tennis bracelet he'd given her for their first Christmas on her left wrist. On her it looked as if it had come from Tiffany's. She was aristocratic, and when they'd come in everyone had looked at her.

She smiled and raised her glass. "You look gorgeous tonight, Kirk. I think I like you dressed up like this."

He laughed and raised his glass. "That was supposed to be my line. You're beautiful."

She sipped her pinot grigio, then looked at the traffic on the street. McGarvey's car and bodyguard were parked down the block. It was just 6:00 P.M., and still light out, and warm, but she shivered. "I hope you don't mind coming back here."

He put his glass down. "Are you okay, Katy?" He knew exactly what she was thinking, and why she'd wanted to come here. She was trying to erase at least a part of his violent past, which of course was impossible, but maybe being here with him, safe, secure, would help ease some of her fears.

She turned back, a serious expression on her narrow,

finely formed face. "You never told me the whole story. About Jacqueline, I mean. Were you in love with her?"

The question hurt a little, but it was an honest one, and it was something he figured she had to know if they were to put this business behind them. "I thought I was, at least for a little while, but I was sending her back to Paris."

"Why?" she asked, studying his eyes.

"Because I knew that it wasn't going to work," he said softly. "She wasn't going to leave her home, her family, for me, and I wasn't going to leave the Company. Not like that." That drew an almost sympathetic look from her.

"Elizabeth said that she was a good person."

McGarvey smiled sadly. "They got to be friends, but Liz had a tough time of it when we got back to the States."

"She wouldn't talk to me about it, but I knew that the situation was bothering her."

"She wanted you and I to get back together."

Kathleen looked at her hands. She still wore their wedding ring. Even in the bad days, right after their divorce, when she hated him, she'd not taken it off. "I think that our daughter still feels a little guilty about that day, Kirk. But I can't help her unless I know what happened." She was frustrated.

"It's been a year."

"You've not forgotten. You never will. You never forget anything." She'd almost said *forgive*, and McGarvey caught it.

"Jacqueline wanted to get married. I was supposed to quit the CIA, and go back to teaching somewhere."

Kathleen's chin raised a little. "But you were afraid that she was going to get hurt, being around you. That was it, wasn't it? You did that thing for a long time."

"That I did," McGarvey said. He'd been a CIA field officer for twenty-five years, and he'd killed people in the line of duty. A legion of them, whose faces he saw nearly every night in his dreams. There were a lot of grudges out there looking for a place to happen, so he'd pushed the people he cared about away from him; out of harm's way, he'd always hoped. But it had never worked, and it certainly hadn't worked with Jacqueline.

They'd been sitting here almost at this exact spot, having drinks, when he told her that it was no good. That she might as well return to Paris, because it was never going to work out for them. She'd started to cry, and McGarvey clearly remembered holding himself back with everything in his power from reaching out for her hand, and apologizing for being such a bastard. It was for the best, her going home. There was no future here for her. She was a French intelligence officer who'd been sent to keep an eye on McGarvey while he lived in Paris, and she'd fallen in love with him. Too bad for her, too bad for all of them, because she'd followed him back to the States and had gotten herself killed.

McGarvey glanced out at the street. Jacqueline had been on the way out of the restaurant when the black Mercedes came barreling around the corner. Something, some sixth sense, had warned him just in time to hit the deck when the bomb had been tossed out the back window of the car, landing right at Jacqueline's feet. He closed his eyes.

Kathleen reached out and laid a hand on his, her touch gentle.

"There was nothing left of her, Katy. Not a goddammed thing. Nothing even remotely recognizable as human." Elizabeth had come up from the Farm with him, and they were all supposed to go out to dinner somewhere that night. She'd been returning from the bathroom when the bomb was tossed, and McGarvey had managed to pull her behind a table where she escaped the brunt of the massive explosion. Two dozen people had been killed, and twice that many hurt. The visions would not go away.

Kathleen was watching the play of emotions on his face. "You saved our daughter's life, my darling. And you got the people who did that horrible thing, and in the process you saved a lot of other lives. That counts for something, even if you don't want to take the credit."

McGarvey couldn't trust himself to speak. She hadn't

insisted on coming here for herself, she'd pushed him into coming back so that he could deal with it for himself.

Kathleen straightened up. "Time to put it behind you. It's over now." She picked up her wine glass. "To us," she said.

McGarvey wanted to say that the fight was never over; that there would always be some sonofabitch out there with a score to settle, political or religious, or sometimes both, but he raised his glass anyway, and smiled. "To us."

They touched glasses and drank. Her expression darkened for a moment. "I'm sorry I brought it all back for you."

"Don't be. Not tonight," McGarvey said. This time his smile was genuine because he'd managed to push the demons back one more time, and because he had his own reason for coming here tonight.

Her eyes narrowed. "What do you mean?"

McGarvey opened his menu. "If we're going to make the curtain we'd better order something now."

"Something's going on, I can see it in your face."

"I don't know what you're talking about," McGarvey said innocently. Her father had told him once that keeping a secret from his daughter was impossible.

"You do," she said sternly. She had the *I demand* look on her face.

The waiter came and refilled their glasses. "Would you care to order now?"

"Not yet," Kathleen said sharply. "Give us a few minutes."

"Of course, madame."

"What's going on, Kirk?" she asked.

"This may be the wrong place for this. I was going to wait until after the symphony. I thought we'd go someplace for champagne afterward." He was suddenly enjoying himself, but he kept a straight face.

"Is this about work?"

No. It's about us." He took a ring box from his pocket and set it in front of her.

She smiled uncertainly, almost afraid to touch it.

"I can't do anything about the past, Katy," he said seriously. "Neither of us can. It's time now to get on with it." He looked at the little velvet box. "It was my mother's." His heart was in his throat.

She slowly opened the box, and her eyes immediately misted over. She looked up, questioningly, and when he nodded, she took the ring out. It was a small diamond in an inexpensive old-fashioned setting. It was all his father had been able to afford on the salary of an engineer working at Los Alamos on the bomb in the forties. But it had meant everything to his mother, and it meant everything to him now.

"Let's start over again, Katy. Do it right this time. Will you marry me?"

A tender look came over her. "I've always loved you, you know. I never stopped," she said. "But I don't think that I ever loved you more than I do right now." She reached again for his hand. "Yes, my darling, I'll marry you, and this time we'll make it work . . . together."

Chevy Chase

On the way back to Kathleen's home after the concert, they rode very close together like young lovers in the back of the taxi. McGarvey had dismissed his car and bodyguard for the remainder of the evening, and he was glad he had done it. Tonight was personal, anonymous.

At the house she went up the walk to open the door as McGarvey paid the cabby, and when he joined her, she'd already started up the stairs.

"Would you like a glass of wine?" he asked.

"No," she said. "Just you."

He locked up, turned off the hall light, and started up the stairs when the telephone rang. Kathleen answered it in the bedroom on the second ring. He could hear her muffled voice, and when he got to the head of the stairs she came to the bedroom door, a vexed look on her face.

"They're sending your car for you."

"What's happened?"

"It was Otto. He didn't say, except that it was worse than lavender this time."

His heart stopped. Rencke never exaggerated. Lavender was his code word for something very bad. Worst-case scenario.

"I'm sorry, Katy."

"Kathleen," she corrected automatically. "Be careful."

He took her in his arms, and kissed her deeply. "I'll call as soon as I can."

Headlights flashed in the driveway. She shook her head sadly. "You'll never change," she said, and when she saw the look of pain in his eyes it took her breath away. "But I will," she told him.

En Route to Langley

He climbed in the back seat of the Cadillac limousine, and his driver, Dick Yemm, immediately pulled out and headed off at a high speed. "Sorry to bust in on you like this, boss. Mr. Adkins held down the fort for as long as he could until we could get a better handle on the situation."

"Okay, Dick what's the story?"

"Allen Trumble was shot to death about six hours ago down in Orlando." Yemm was a very small, compact man, as rigid and as tough as bar steel, but he was shaking.

It was like a ton of bricks had fallen on McGarvey's head, but he held himself in check. "Do we have somebody with Gloria and the kids?"

"They got them too, along with a couple of innocent bystanders." Yemm viciously cut a driver off and ran a stop sign. "Sonofabitch, boss. Sonofabitch."

The news was simply unbelievable, impossible to digest; it was a random act of violence, like a lightning bolt. Except he knew that it hadn't been random. "What took us so long?" he demanded.

"The Bureau didn't find out that Allen worked for us until after eight, and by the time the duty office made contact with Mr. Adkins it was late. Nobody could believe it. We thought it was some stupid mistake."

Already they were out of Chevy Chase on Western Avenue, their speed topping one hundred miles per hour. Luckily traffic was light. Yemm radioed his position to the duty dispatcher. "Hammerhead is en route. ETA about twenty."

Although Yemm was only a driver/bodyguard, he was the DDO's bodyguard and he kept his ears open. It didn't hurt that he was smart in addition to being tough. He was an ex-SEAL, and he and McGarvey had a lot of history together. For all practical purposes his need to know cut across almost the entire DO. Like McGarvey he was a man who hated bullshit and bureaucracy. He told it like it was. In addition he had given Trumble shooting lessons for requalification last winter, so he had a personal stake.

"What do we know so far?" McGarvey asked, trying to keep his thoughts in order. He had been yanked from Katy's arms back into the real world, and her feel and scent had already faded into that other place in his head.

"Looks like bin Laden ordered it." Yemm's jaw visibly tightened in the rearview mirror. When he was mad he ground his teeth. "There were four of them, AK-47s. Allen wasn't carrying, but he managed to bag one of the bad guys anyway. Hit him in the head with something. The Bureau's Orlando SAC talked to the bastard in the ambulance before he died."

"Do we have a solid ID on him?" McGarvey wasn't going to telephone Adkins because his ADDO had his hands full now, but he needed more information.

"Bari Yousef. Twenty-nine, born in Cairo, came over here in 'ninety-eight. Until two weeks ago he worked as a truck driver for Jersey City Transport, then he disappeared."

The trucking company was under investigation. It was

believed that it was one of a number of possible fronts for bin Laden's operations here in the States. The Bureau's antiterrorist division had been warning for years that bin Laden was going to extend his terrorist attacks to the States. The trucking company and some other enterprises, among them a couple of banks in New Jersey, were thought to be the precursors to something big that was coming. Something that would make Oklahoma City look small. Yemm must have been within earshot in the Ops Center when the connection had been made.

The problem with being DDO was that he got to hear everything, not just the bits and pieces like Yemm. Where Dick was mad, McGarvey was frightened. If the consensus on bin Laden was correct they were going to have the biggest fight of their lives on their hands. This time they were playing with fire. Very serious fire. And a lot of people would get hurt unless the U.S. was very careful in how it responded.

"They were on vacation, boss," Yemm said, angry and frustrated. "Minding their own business. Not hurting anybody. Christ, you know Allen; the man would go out of his way to avoid stepping on a bug."

"Take it easy, Dick. I know how you feel," McGarvey said. "What about the other three shooters?"

"They were driving a Chevy van, stolen in Atlanta four days ago, on a Florida plate that the owner in Tampa didn't even know was stolen until the cops showed up at her door. Some guy and his wife saw what was going down and they called 911 on their cell phone. The van was abandoned about a half-mile from Interstate 4, and nobody else saw a thing."

"How'd we ID Yousef?"

"Prints off his gun. The Bureau ran them and came up with a red flag. The bastard was one of bin Laden's shooters, and he shouldn't have been able to clear customs in the first place. The passport people at Kennedy fucked up."

It was a common occurrence, one of the downsides of a totally free country. As one senior Immigration and Naturalization official told McGarvey, trying to stop illegals coming ashore in leaky old boats was tough enough, but checking people flying in on supposedly legitimate passports was like trying to stop a flood with your finger in the dike.

In the end it was up to the CIA's foreign stations to come up with lists of undesirables, and for the FBI's special units on espionage and counterterrorism to see that the bad guys who did manage to get here didn't do any harm. The CIA and the Bureau were doing a damned fine job, most of their successes never appearing in the media, but the problem was no less impossible than Immigration's.

Now it was starting again, McGarvey thought morosely. In the never-ending battle you won a few, but you lost some too. The Khobar Barracks, the New York Trade Towers, Oklahoma City, the Nairobi embassy, and a host of others to which Orlando would be added.

But this was just the opening move. To what, he wondered. How far would it go this time? He had a very bad feeling that they were going to find out a lot sooner than they wanted to, and once again he was going to be right in the middle of it. Coming to work for the CIA right out of college and Air Force had been just a job, like a military career. Something you did. His parents had worked for the government at Los Alamos and it had been his turn. But after his parents had been killed in the car crash he had been locked into the Company by shackles whose links he had forged himself with his own conscience and sense of fair play. President Truman had a sign on his desk that read: THE BUCK STOPS HERE. The sign on McGarvey's desk read: THE BULLSHIT STOPS HERE.

FOUR

CIA Headquarters

It was 12:25 A.M. when McGarvey, still dressed in his tuxedo, his bow tie undone, reached his office. He'd talked to Trumble five days ago, sending his Riyadh COS and his family on a two-week vacation, and now they were dead. In that time the only thing they'd accomplished was to agree to wait until Allen got back to help with the ops planning for another meeting with bin Laden. Nobody had the least inkling that Trumble was in danger, but it was something that McGarvey knew he should have considered.

But bin Laden didn't work that way; on such a small scale, in Trumble's words. Or at least he'd never worked that way before, and there was no logical reason for him to start now. If he'd wanted Trumble dead, he would have killed him in Khartoum, not waited until the man returned to the United States presumably to report on the meeting, and then taken the risk of killing him and his family in such a public place. Yet he had to keep reminding himself that logical reason might not apply to a man such as bin Laden. Maybe the bastard had finally gone around the bend, really gone nuts. That was a cheery thought.

Dick Adkins walked in from his adjoining office, a stricken, angry expression on his face. McGarvey had seen that kind of look before.

"It came out of left field, Mac."

"Short of keeping them in a safe house, there's nothing we could have done," McGarvey said bitterly. "Hell, the Secret Service can't even guarantee a President's life." He took off his jacket, tossed it on the couch and went to his desk. "I want Jeff Cook alerted to what might be coming his way in Riyadh, and then I want all of our stations and missions to get the word to button down, freeze their assets."

"We did that as soon as we found out. And I called McCafferty over at State to alert our embassies world wide."

"Did we notify the Pentagon?"

"Couple of hours ago." Adkins handed McGarvey a buff-colored file folder with blue edging, denoting urgent attention. "This is what we've come up with so far. The Bureau's Orlando SAC, Scott Thompson, is running the show down there, but Fred Rudolph called a couple of hours ago from his office, so they're on top of it already." Rudolph headed the FBI's Special Investigative Division. McGarvey had a great deal of respect for the man's abilities and judgment. He was a straight shooter; a no-nonsense cop.

"Coffee?"

"Coming up," Adkins said.

McGarvey quickly scanned the file, which didn't contain much more information than he'd already gotten from Dick Yemm, except that the FBI now believed that the Jersey City Trucking Company was no longer a bin Laden front, although it was still owned and operated by Arabs, mostly Egyptians.

Adkins came back with the coffee. "I don't think there's any doubt who ordered the hit or why. I think the Bureau is wrong this time."

"Maybe not," McGarvey said. Bin Laden was on the move, or getting ready to do something spectacular; he was pretty sure of that. But no matter how he looked at it, this killing didn't add up to a bin Laden-ordered hit. "Do we have someone watching Allen's and Gloria's families in Minnesota?"

"I didn't think of that one," Adkins said. "I'll do it now."

"Then call Otto in."

"He's been here all night."

"Okay, send him up." McGarvey picked up the phone and hit the speed dial button for Fred Rudolph's office over at the J. Edgar Hoover Building. "Is everyone else in and up to speed?"

"Since eight," Adkins said, heading for the door.

"Staff meeting in thirty minutes."

"You got it, Mac."

The call was answered on the first ring. "Fred Rudolph." His voice sounded strained. He had graduated summa cum laude with a law degree from Fordham, and had worked for a couple of years with the army's Staff Judge Advocate's office as a special investigator. He'd done the same thing as a civilian for the U.S. Supreme Court and the Department of Justice until he'd signed on with the FBI about six years ago.

"Good morning, Fred. I read your 22:30 fax, anything new since then?"

"You just get in?"

"Yeah."

"It's a bitch, isn't it?" Rudolph said. Sometimes he wished he'd been a banker instead of a cop. "As soon as we got a positive on Yousef we woke up a federal judge and got a search warrant. My people are tossing his apartment right now. We should have something in the next couple of hours or so. But they had a head start, Mac. So unless they get stupid we might come up empty."

The first twenty-four hours, and especially the first six hours of these kinds of investigations were the most crucial. After that they were just picking up the pieces, because if the shooters were professionals they would be long gone by then.

"What's your best guess?"

"Probably Cuba. There were two flights to Havana direct out of Orlando that they could have taken. Scott Thompson's people are looking over the passenger lists, and talking with the baggage handlers and ticket clerks, but both flights are already on the ground in Havana, and won't turn around until morning. As soon as they get back he'll talk to them unless your people can get to them down there."

"We'll work on it," McGarvey promised. "What about the weapon?"

"Except for prints it was clean. No serial number, so it could have been purchased almost anywhere. Ballistics is still working on it."

"How about the van?"

"We lifted some pretty good prints, including Yousef's, but we've come up with nothing on the others yet. Same with hair samples. We're running DNA indentification tests now, but they won't do us any good unless we can get an arrest out of this." Rudolph did not sound optimistic. "What about your shop? Can you tell me what Trumble was up to that made him and his family a target?"

"I can't give you the details, but it involved bin Laden. What can you tell me about Jersey City Trucking?"

"We thought there was a connection, but we ran that operation through a ringer and came up clean last week. There's just nothing there tying it to any of bin Laden's other suspected business interests. Not even remotely."

"I thought they had some kind of a financial arrangement with one of bin Laden's banks."

"For about two months, and that was over five years ago. It's another dead end. Everything about the place stinks, we'll probably close them down under the RICO Act eventually, but there are no terrorists there."

"Except for Bari Yousef."

"We're going to toss the business again, but unless we find something tying Yousef directly to bin Laden through the company, it'll be another dead end. We have to play by the rules even if they don't," he said angrily. "This guy could have been working on his own for some reason, or for somebody else close to bin Laden. It's happened before." Rudolph was silent for a moment. "You would know more about that than me."

"Anything new from INS?" McGarvey asked, sidestepping the comment. It was hard to focus while blaming himself.

"Nothing other than what I've already sent you. Yousef got by them, and so did the other three. It's another angle we're working on. We'll try to find out if anyone else beside him is missing from the business." Again Rudolph hesitated for a moment. "It would be helpful if we could come up with a motive. I mean, are you laying this on bin Laden's doorstep?"

McGarvey looked up as Otto walked in. He waved his special operations officer to a chair. "I just don't know, Fred. On the surface it looks like it, but there's no reason for him to have ordered the hit. If anything it's counterproductive for him. Crazy."

"Yeah," Rudolph agreed. "There's a lot of that going around these days."

"Keep me up to date," McGarvey said.

"It's a two-way street, Mac. Sorry you had to lose one of your people that way. Especially his family."

"There will be a payback," McGarvey said, and he broke the connection. He looked at Otto who was sitting cross-legged on the chair. "You said lavender."

"Hardly any impurities," Rencke replied, almost dreamily. A number of years ago when he was trying to work out the mathematics and physics of a very complicated link between advanced bubble memory systems, he'd struck on what for him was a very simple, but sophisticated notion: how to explain color to a blind person. Using tensor calculus, the same mathematics that Einstein had used for his general theory of relativity, Rencke had come up with a set of equations that he'd tried out on a blind Indian mathematician, who'd made the observation afterward: "Oh, I see." Reversing the process, Rencke developed a method by which he thought of colors to represent mathematical equations that described highly complex real world variables. Lavender was for very bad.

"Are you talking about the man that Trumble was worried about at his meeting with bin Laden?"

"I came up with a dozen candidates I was going to show him when he came back." Otto shook his head in sadness. "But that's not it, Mac. It's the other thing. The bad, bad thing. Bin Laden didn't have Allen killed. At least I don't think so. But one of his lieutenants might have ordered it because bin Laden is probably crazy, and his people want to save their own gnarly hides, ya know."

"Does he want to negotiate, or what?"

"Oh, he wants to talk to somebody, all right. But his troops are passing purple peach pits 'cause they don't know what he wants to do. They're playing with serious fire and they're all wondering if they're going to get their fingers burned big time."

McGarvey felt a cold draft on his neck. "Do you have the proof?" Otto was almost always right, but he had to ask.

Rencke took a diskette out of the thick file he'd brought with him. "When it boots up hit any key."

McGarvey started the disk, and immediately a complicated engineering diagram in 3-D came up on his screen and began to slowly rotate around its long axis. He stared at the device for a long time, his stomach sour, because he knew exactly what it was capable of doing to them.

"I matched the number Trumble gave us with the Russian device."

Sometimes Rencke amazed even McGarvey. "How'd you come up with that?"

Otto grinned. "The FSB is running its own investigation, and I talked to some friends of mine in Amsterdam who hacked the system. That one was missing."

"Why didn't you get in yourself?"

"I wanted to keep it arm's length this time. No telling what the fallout's gonna be."

McGarvey nodded at the obvious understatement. "Where'd it come from?"

"Right where we suspected all along. Yavan Depot."

"Tajikistan," McGarvey said. The former Soviet ground forces special storage depot was located about twenty-five miles southeast of the capital city Dushanbe. It had long been suspected, but never proved, that a small Russian maintenance crew, mostly officers, had been left behind to look after their equipment, for which the independent government received money and kept silent. But money, which was not a problem for bin Laden, was tight in Russia so loyalties had blurred.

"I'm going to need more than this," McGarvey said.

Rencke laid the thick file on the desk. "I made hard copies. I got the names of the four Russian officers under investigation, their contacts, the how and when they got it out of the depot three months ago, the thirty million U.S. they were paid for it, and where it crossed the border at Nizhny Pyandzh into Afghanistan." Otto shrugged. "After that it disappears." His eyes were wild. "But bin Laden has the number, so we know where it showed up."

"Okay, who are these friends of yours in Amsterdam?" It was the news he'd been expecting, and yet it was none the less frightening.

"Just kids," Rencke said. "Their parents were the ones who hacked the system over at Lawrence Livermore in the eighties. Only way we found out about it was because they'd screwed up the payroll section. Wouldn't balance."

"Think they can get back into the FSB system?"

"The Russians aren't spending much on security, but their encryption programs are still pretty good. What do you want them to look for?"

"I want to know what the FSB is doing about this. They sure as hell wouldn't tell me if I picked up the phone and called Kuznetsov." Anatoli Kuznetsov was the director of the Federal Security Service, which was the new KGB.

"They got in that far, they could take the next step." Otto grinned again, which he did whenever he was contemplating doing something illegal. "I can give them a little incentive."

McGarvey gave him a hard look. "I brought you back to help out, not to give away the store."

"Mac, this is worth it, if we can stop the bastard. The

next time out ain't gonna be so pretty. All I'm giving them is an encryption buster. An old one we don't use anymore."

"Okay, so what about the guy with bin Laden that Allen told us about?"

"I came up with a dozen possibilities, but I've gone as far with them as I can without more hard information. A description from another source, something in his hand-writing, maybe a strand of hair, or a recording of his voice. Anything."

"Maybe I can help with that."

Otto's eyes went wide. "Come on, Mac, you're not telling me what I think you're telling me now, are you? Bzz, wrong answer, recruit. Wrong, wrong, wrong."

McGarvey smiled sadly for his friend. Candide once said that optimism is a mania for maintaining that all is well when things are going badly. He'd never been guilty of that frame of mind, or of its opposite, though both were common maladies in Washington. He was going to drop a bombshell in the President's lap, and he hoped the man was up to the decisions he was going to have to start making. A lot of lives depended on it. But Otto was as naive as he was brilliant. One of his failings was trying to keep his friends out of harm's way. Maybe it was a failing they all should have.

The DDO's conference room was a long, windowless space that was mechanically and electronically isolated from the rest of the building, and from the outside world. Anything said or done in the room was completely safe from any kind of eavesdropping. The weakest links were the people who gathered here, and McGarvey knew and trusted all of them. It was all he'd ever had, all he'd ever wanted and worked for—trust. Now that he had it he was afraid of letting his friends down.

When he arrived at 1:25 A.M. all nine of his staff members were seated and waiting for him. They included Dick Adkins, his assistant deputy director of operations; Randy

Bock, chief of Foreign Intelligence which was in charge of espionage activities; Jared Kraus, Technical Services; Scott Graves, Counterintelligence; Arthur Hendrickson, in charge of the Covert Action section, which was responsible for propaganda and disinformation; Raife Melloch, Missions and Programs; David Whittaker, the area divisions chief in charge of the CIA's bases, stations and missions worldwide; Brenda Jordan, Operational Services, which came up with cover stories and legends for field agents; and Otto Rencke.

"Good morning," McGarvey said, taking his place at the head of the long table. "Thanks for coming in, but it's going to be a long night, so take your coffee strong and black."

Everyone around the table was angry and pumped up. One of their own had been murdered. But worse than that, his family had been killed too. They would have no trouble staying awake this night.

"As you know by now, our Riyadh chief of station Allen Trumble, his wife and two children, and two other innocent bystanders were shot to death seven and a half hours ago in the parking lot of Disney's EPCOT in Orlando. This was not a simple drive-by shooting, it was a carefully planned operation carried out by professionals. Our first tasks are to find out who ordered the hit and why."

"I don't think there's any question about that," Adkins said. His eyes were on fire, he looked like an angry pit bull ready to attack.

"I don't agree," McGarvey replied sharply. "So I want all of you to go into this with open minds. There are no foregone conclusions. Clear?"

Heads nodded, but he could see their skepticism and reluctance.

"We're going to generate a SNIE this morning, which I want on my desk no later than 0800." National Intelligence Estimates, which listed targets for the entire U.S. intelligence community, estimates of future international events and enemy strengths, a technical intelligence review, and decisions on which product was to be shared with which

U.S. allies, were usually generated once a week. They came
from the U.S. Intelligence Board made up of the director
of Central Intelligence, the heads of the military intelligence
branches, the National Security Agency, Defense Intelligence Agency, the State Department, FBI, Nuclear Regu-
latory Commission, and Treasury Department. Special
National Intelligence Estimates were done by any of the
agencies on an incident basis. The purpose of the documents was to brief the President and the nation's top policy
makers on whatever crisis the U.S. was faced with. "If it's
a fact, state it. But if it's a wild-ass guess, make that clear
too."

"Where are you taking this, Mac?" Adkins asked. "Because from where we're sitting it looks pretty clear. Allen
met with bin Laden and a week later he was assassinated.
At least one of the shooters had a connection."

"Okay, that goes in the SNIE as your guess, or as a
consensus estimate. The Bureau thinks there's a strong possibility that the other three shooters took a commercial
flight out of Orlando to Havana. I want our resources there
to see what they can come up with. But I don't want anyone
burned trying to get to the air crews in Havana this morning. They'll be back in Miami or Orlando later this morning.

"Fred Rudolph is handling the Bureau's investigation, so
it'll be a good one. But I'm telling you now that he thinks
the Jersey City trucking company where Yousef was apparently employed hasn't been a bin Laden operation for
five years. I want you to keep that in mind.

"I want you to keep a number of other things in mind
too. No one has claimed responsibility for the attack yet,
something bin Laden's followers always do, even if he
doesn't take any of the blame personally. Allen met with
him in Khartoum, so why'd they wait for him to come
home to kill him? And bin Laden told Allen that he wanted
to meet with someone else. Someone with more authority,
which means he might have something on his mind that he
wants to talk about."

"Maybe he just wants to burn a bigger fish," Whittaker said. Trumble's murder had devastated him. His chiefs of stations were family.

"That's a possibility too," McGarvey said. "And I want it in the SNIE. But we've been waiting for bin Laden to pull off something big. I believe he's made his plans, and now he's having second thoughts. He really does want to talk to someone."

"Bullshit, Mac," Adkins exploded. "He's setting up a trap and someone's supposed to walk into it?"

McGarvey didn't mind the outburst. He expected nothing less than complete honesty from his staff, and they gave it to him. "Maybe, maybe not. But if he wanted to lure someone else close enough to take the shot, why kill Allen and his family?" McGarvey shook his head. "Doesn't make any sense."

"Well then, who did it?" Adkins asked, frustrated.

"One of bin Laden's people who might be afraid that his boss is getting cold feet."

"It's a warning?" Whittaker asked. "Is that what you're saying?"

"It could be that they don't want bin Laden talking to us."

"If we lay that on his doorstep, whoever's behind this has to know he'd be risking another missile attack on their camps," Jared Kraus said. "Makes him either very stupid, or a man who knows something that we don't."

"Or thinks he does," McGarvey said. "Bin Laden gave Allen a serial number that Otto has found a match for."

Rencke had loaded his briefing into the large-screen rear-projection television monitor built into the wall at one end of the room. He dimmed the lights and the same 3-D diagram that he showed McGarvey came up. It got everyone's attention, and for the next ten minutes he explained what he'd come up with and what he thought it meant. When he was finished the room was so quiet that they could hear the gentle rush of air through the AC vents. The only thing left showing on the screen now was the engineering diagram of the device.

"I can see why he wants to talk to somebody," Adkins said, subdued. "This might be too big even for him." He tore his eyes away from the monitor. "Who are we going to send . . . ?"

Whittaker interrupted. "That could be a moot point unless we can find him first. Our contacts in Kabul say he's dropped out of sight again. The Taliban aren't saying anything, as usual, but it's possible he's no longer in Afghanistan."

"He's done that before," McGarvey said. "If he wants to talk to us, he'll get the word out when he's ready."

The telephone console at McGarvey's position burred softly. He picked it up. "Yes."

"I'm here." It was the CIA director, Roland Murphy.

"We're just finishing, General. I'll come over in a few minutes."

"Very well."

McGarvey hung up and checked his watch. It was coming up on two. "Okay, we have six hours to put this together. In the mèantime I want our assets and people hunkering down for the moment."

"While trying to find out where bin Laden is hiding out, and who ordered the hit," Adkins said dryly.

"Right," McGarvey said.

"You still haven't told us who you're going to send to meet with him if we can arrange it."

"No, I haven't," McGarvey replied softly. There are truths which are not for all men, nor for all times. Voltaire wrote that to Cardinal de Bernis. He was talking about the Catholic Church, which he despised, but the idea was no different here and now, McGarvey thought, because he was even wondering about admitting the whole truth to himself just yet, except that he had let Trumble and his family down.

• • •

It was one of the worse times in McGarvey's life, because in his heart of hearts he knew that he was to blame for the deaths of Allen Trumble and his family. And he knew that he was going to have to drop a bombshell in the lap of the new President. When he walked into the DCI's palatial office with its view of the river valley, Murphy was on the phone. He poured a cup of coffee, lit a cigarette and took a seat in front of the desk.

Anger would come, he knew, but for the moment it was his job to keep his head on straight so that they could pick up the pieces and avert a much larger, more terrible, even unimaginable disaster from befalling them. He also knew that he would forever look back at this time as a watershed in his own life; a new chapter in his long career in the Company beyond anything he'd ever imagined in his most violent nightmares. The same insistent voice in his head that had told him on countless occasions to get out while he could, to put as much distance as possible between himself and the people he loved and respected so that when the bad guys came looking they would find only him and not his friends, was hammering at the back of his head now. And he had run, more than once; from Lausanne, from Paris, and even from Milford, Delaware where he'd once taught eighteenth-century literature. But it had done no good, because each time the call to action had come he had responded. And each time someone he had cared for had lost their lives. Marta Fredricks, Jacqueline Belleau, even his ex-wife and daughter had almost been killed because of him. Now it was Allen and his family. McGarvey tried to see the good in what he had done, especially in the year since he had been called back to take over the DO, but he was having a hard time focusing.

He could almost hear the distant sound of trumpets; the battle horns; the sounds of men shouting and screaming, bullets flying; people dying because he knew that this one was going to be bad. A call to arms again, like he'd heard for twenty-five years? Or just now this morning an overwrought imagination caused by tiredness and guilt.

He looked at his hands and he could see Allen Trumble's blood on them.

Roland Murphy finished his conversation and put the encrypted telephone down. He stared speculatively at McGarvey for a few beats, then the expression on his craggy, bulldog face softened. "I know how you feel," he said gently. "We're all feeling the same thing. But this was not your fault. Do you read me?"

"Ultimately everything that happens in the DO is my responsibility," McGarvey replied softly. It wasn't a matter of whose fault anything was, that was Washington bureaucratic bullshit. The only thing that mattered right now was making the right response. Already his black mood was being replaced by a quiet anger and determination, but he knew that he would have to be careful not to lash out at everyone around him. It was one of his least endearing character flaws.

"You're right," Murphy conceded. "But don't beat yourself to death over it, because we have work to do. That was Dennis Berndt. We're briefing the National Security Council at nine o'clock." Berndt was the President's national security adviser, and he was no friend of the CIA's, though no one knew why. "They're going to ask some tough questions, and we're going to have to give them some tough answers."

"The SNIE will be ready by eight," McGarvey said. "But attacking bin Laden's camps in Afghanistan again is not one of the answers I'm going to give them." He kept his anger in check and his tone reasonable. "There was no reason for him to kill Allen, and especially not his wife and children. Not now."

"Speculation, Kirk, nothing more."

"Maybe. But there's no hard proof that bin Laden ordered them murdered."

"Slaughtered, you mean," Murphy replied sharply. His anger was bubbling to the surface. Like everyone else at headquarters he wanted to strike back right now at whoever was responsible. Which was a good thing, and something that the President was going to demand, providing they didn't hit the wrong target for the wrong reason.

At sixty-two, Murphy was twelve years McGarvey's senior, although this morning he looked twenty years older than that. In his day he had commanded a tank batallion, and he had earned the nickname Bull Murphy, after the navy's Admiral Bill Halsey, because despite his size he could move quickly and decisively, and like Halsey he had no trouble making straight-ahead decisions. It was quite a combination, an old friend of Murphy's had told McGarvey a few years ago. Watching Roland climbing in and out of tanks was like watching an angry bull that had taken ballet lessons. It was nothing short of awesome. You got out of the way when the man was on the move. But nearly two decades behind a desk had softened his lines, blurred the edges, slowed his body, though not his mind.

"It wasn't his style, you know that. You read Allen's report."

"The bastard thinks he can kill our people and get away with it," Murphy countered strongly. "Well, he's dead wrong, and we're going to show it to him." Murphy had directed the CIA through three White House administrations, and he had never been responsible for the loss of an employee's family. Do the job, but get it done safely, was his watchword. The old cowboy days of shoot 'em outs in Czechoslovakia, parachute drops into Hungary, clandestine jungle training camps in Honduras and arms deals with the Contras were things of the past. Intelligence-gathering in the twenty-first century had become primarily a matter of technical means; electronic eavesdropping, satellites, computers. Shooters like McGarvey had become anachronisms, and Murphy, who had directed many such black operations, had always despised the endeavors with everything in his soul, while at the same time understanding that sometimes violent means were necessary. But he counted this tragic business with Trumble a personal failure. He was ready to turn the clock back. Strike the bastard responsible where he lived.

He glanced at the clock on his desk. "I want you ready at eight-thirty, that'll give us plenty of time to get over to the White House. Since it's your operation you'll give the briefing." He gave McGarvey another speculative look. "Killing one of our chiefs of station is one thing, but his family? That's nothing but terrorism, and bin Laden is the master of it. We're going to teach him a lesson. It's something that the President wants, and it's something I'm going to go along with."

"There's another consideration, General."

"Then you'll have to offer the man an alternative, Kirk. Otherwise we're going to war."

FIVE

The White House

The DCI's limousine pulled up at the White House west gate a few minutes before 9:00 A.M., and the guard waved them through. Both Murphy and McGarvey were well known to the Secret Service. They proceeded up the driveway to the portico where Ken Chapin, the DCI's bodyguard jumped out and opened the car door for his boss.

McGarvey let himself out and stood for a moment looking up at the marine guard at the door. Forty-two presidents before this one had made a lot of tough decisions from this building. Just one year into an administration that was thrust upon him, Lawrence Haynes was going to be faced with a very tough call. McGarvey had the feeling that the man was up to it. At least he hoped for all of their sakes that he was.

"Let's not keep the man waiting," Murphy said, and McGarvey fell in beside him. Together they entered the White House and took the elevator downstairs. They were met by a security detail outside the situation room who checked their briefcases before they were allowed to go inside.

The President had not arrived yet, but already the mood around the long table was somber. Flanking the President's empty chair were Dennis Berndt, his adviser on national security affairs, and Anthony Lang, his chief of staff. They were deep in discussion, but Berndt looked up and gave McGarvey a penetrating glance that was anything but friendly. He looked pissed off, and in the short twelve months of his tenure he'd built a reputation as an easy-to-anger, formidable force to be reckoned with.

On the other side of them were the secretary of defense Arthur Turnquist, secretary of state Eugene Carpenter, attorney general Dorothy Kress, FBI director Herbert Weissman, who had himself just arrived, the chairman of the Joint Chiefs of Staff Admiral Richard Halverson and the National Security Agency director Air Force Major General Thomas Roswell. Murphy and McGarvey took their places next to him, everyone around the table acknowledging them with a nod.

Most of the people at the table were new to this administration, and although McGarvey knew all of them, he didn't know them well enough yet to be able to predict their responses like he had with President Lindsay's staff and cabinet.

Haynes had been vice president when Lindsay had suddenly resigned because of ill health last year. One of Haynes's first promises to the American people was to guarantee their safety by threatening swift and merciless action against any man, organization or government bent on terrorism. He was taking back the fear, and he'd packed his administration with tough, like-minded men and women who were not afraid to make decisions. It was, with some few exceptions, a pleasant change.

Roswell handed Murphy a thin file folder. "These are the latest telephone intercepts from bin Laden's headquarters. I think you might find them interesting."

"What's the upshot?"

"He never returned from Khartoum, and his people are starting to get nervous." Roswell, who looked like a banker with a stern, sometimes sour expression on his round, bland face, had no sense of humor. But he ran his agency, which was three times the size of the CIA, with a lot of creativity. It was said that he played a competent second violin in a string quartet, but that was only speculation because no one admitted to ever having heard him play.

"They know we're listening, it could be orchestrated for our benefit," Murphy said.

"That's what we think," Roswell said unblinking. "But if that indeed is the case, why do it? What is he up to?"

McGarvey handed a diskette to a corpsman to load into the briefing computer. The remote control was on the table in front of him.

"He's not stupid, Tom," McGarvey said. "He's probably figured out that we're going to blame him for this, and we're going to make a response. He's keeping his head down."

Roswell gave McGarvey a hard look. "About what I'd do."

The President came in and everybody got to their feet until he had taken his position. He looked angry, and, like everyone else around the table, tired. None of them had gotten much sleep last night.

"Let's get started, people. We have a busy day ahead of us." Unlike Lindsay, who was tall, thin and "Lincolnesque" as the media called him, this president was built like a Green Bay Packer linebacker, with a massive head, twenty-five inch neck and broad shoulders bulging with muscles. The political cartoonists all exaggerated his physique; in a number of instances they showed him in the boxing ring with captions along the lines that if wars were outlawed in favor of leaders duking it out in the ring, there'd never be any doubt who'd come out the winner. A lot less blood would be shed too.

But as tough as he was, his wife Linda was a kind, gentle spirit. Compared to a young Barbara Bush, she was universally loved by just about everyone in America. As was their beautiful twenty-three-year-old only child, Deborah who had never left home because she was retarded, suffering with a mild form of Down syndrome. From a distance she could be mistaken for a Siberian athlete, or even a Russian haute couture model who had defected to the West. But up close you could see the vacancy in her eyes and in her warm but childlike smile. Haynes was a family man, highly intelligent and honorable, with a squeaky-clean past. Not once in a twenty-seven year political career, which included two terms in the Senate from Oklahoma, had there ever been so much as a hint of scandal associated with him. The media was sometimes frustrated by the lack of juice, but when he'd become President the nation had sighed a collective sigh of relief: Finally we got a good one, with a family we can love and even feel a little sorry for. What made it even better was that Haynes had never capitalized on his daughter's affliction, though he could have done so for political gain. Everyone, even his enemies, respected him for this. In the next election it was expected that he would win by a landslide no matter who was put up against him.

McGarvey passed a stack of leather bound folders around the table. "Mr. President, this is the SNIE that we prepared. I'll make my briefing short this morning, but all of the supporting data and dissenting arguments are included in the folder."

The President held McGarvey's gaze for a long moment then looked around the table. "I want you all to be perfectly clear on one thing. A brutal act of terrorism against American citizens on American soil has been committed. We *will* make an appropriate response. A harsh response."

"Damn right we will," Berndt said.

McGarvey glanced at his copy of the SNIE open in front

of him. He'd had time to briefly scan it on the way over from Langley, but his staff had come up with very little that was new in the past six hours.

"Everyone here knows that our chief of Riyadh station, Allen Trumble, was shot to death along with his wife and children and two tourists down in Orlando yesterday afternoon. In the past fifteen hours we've been trying to make some sense of their murders, and what that act of terrorism might mean for the future." McGarvey closed his SNIE folder. "Mr. President, it's going to be very easy to jump to conclusions, possibly the wrong conclusions, so I'm going to ask everyone to keep an open mind until I'm finished here this morning. It was the same thing I told my staff last night."

He could see the same look of skepticism and anger around the table as he had during his briefing last night.

"Fair enough," the President said, nodding. "You may continue."

"In June I asked my Riyadh station to try to open negotiations with Osama bin Laden," McGarvey said. "I did this for a number of reasons, among them the generally held belief that bin Laden was getting ready to make another strike against U.S. interests somewhere in the world, and possibly even here on our soil." The situation room was suddenly very still.

"In my opinion I thought there also was a possibility that bin Laden might finally be tiring of his life of exile, and might want to go home to Saudi Arabia. He's in his forties now, he has three wives and more than a dozen children, plus family and friends at home. His life in Afghanistan has to be getting old. To date nothing he has done has changed anything, except that we've frozen as many of his assets as we could find, and we've put up a five million dollar bounty on his head. Step by step his movements have been restricted, and even the Afghani Taliban party is starting to get weary of his presence."

"What were you going to offer him?" Berndt demanded. "I never saw such a proposal."

"The operation had my approval," Murphy said softly.

"For starters, the return of his assets, and lifting the bounty. He's said all along that one of the things he wanted was the removal of our forces from Saudi Arabia. We're already talking about doing that, so all that's left would be to broker a deal with the Saudi government so that his family could return home."

"No amnesty," the President said angrily.

"No, sir. Bin Laden would be made to understand that he'd have to face charges for what he has already done. Possibly in the World Court at the Hague. He's a fighter, and he might agree to the proposal because it would give him the forum to tell his side of the story. He'd certainly get the attention of the entire world."

"Well, we know what his response was to that proposal," Berndt said.

"Not necessarily," McGarvey replied, keeping his anger in check. He wanted to tell the NSA to shut up and either read the SNIE or listen to the rest of the briefing before he shot off his mouth. But he couldn't do that.

"All right, Mr. McGarvey, what was bin Laden's response?" the President asked.

"We set up the meeting through our embassies in Pakistan and the Sudan, and Trumble went to see him in Khartoum. It only lasted a couple of minutes, but bin Laden said that he was willing to talk, but only to someone higher in rank than a CIA chief of station. That's the report Allen brought back with him. Along with a serial number."

"Five days later bin Laden had him killed," Berndt said.

"We don't think so," the FBI director said. "The one terrorist left behind was Egyptian, and he'd been in this country for more than three years working for a company that had only a brief association with bin Laden's interests. And that was more than five years ago."

"Oh, come on, Herb, that's a load of crap and you know it," Berndt said. "Maybe bin Laden didn't actually pull the trigger, but he was responsible."

"I haven't heard anything yet to change my mind," Admiral Halverson said angrily. He turned to McGarvey. "You said yourself that the bastard was probably planning something big. Maybe this action was meant to keep us busy, keep our attention and assets focused in one direction while he hits us someplace else."

"Can we pinpoint his location?" Berndt asked.

"The CIA is working on it," McGarvey said.

"Fine," the national security adviser said as if the decision had already been made. "As soon as we have that, we strike him with cruise missiles."

"It didn't work in 'ninety-eight," McGarvey pointed out softly.

"Because of faulty intelligence information," Berndt shot back. "If you do your job right this time, we'll be able to do ours."

"How soon can we be ready to make such an attack?" the President asked Admiral Halverson.

"The *Carl Vinson* and her battle group are already in the Indian Ocean. They could be in striking range in the Arabian Sea within forty-eight hours."

"Is that enough of a force to deliver a decisive knockout punch?"

"Providing we know exactly where bin Laden is hiding, yes, sir. We can put upwards of one hundred fifty cruise missiles on target in under twenty minutes." Admiral Halverson looked at McGarvey as if he were expecting to be challenged. "If need be we can finish the job with air-launched smart bombs."

The President's lips compressed. "Okay, that's an option. Mr. McGarvey, comments?"

"There is another consideration, Mr. President, perhaps the only consideration." McGarvey brought Rencke's briefing file up on the screen at the end of the room. The three-dimensional engineering diagram appeared. "This is the Russian version of our Mark XVII nuclear demolitions device. The serial number that bin Laden sent back with Trumble matches the serial number of a Russian device that is missing."

The entire room was stopped dead. Even the President was at a loss for words.

"We believe with a high degree of confidence that bin Laden purchased it from Russian caretaker officers at the Yavan Depot near Dushanbe, Tajikistan, for thirty million dollars. We think that it was taken across the border into Afghanistan near Nizhny Pyandzh two months ago where it disappeared. Currently the Russian FSB is conducting an investigation to find out what happened."

Everyone around the table stared at the image on the screen. The President was the first to look back at Mc-Garvey.

"This is a nuclear weapon?" he asked, subdued.

"Yes, sir."

"Officially they don't exist," Secretary of Defense Turnquist said uncomfortably.

"They were supposed to have been destroyed," Secretary of State Eugene Carpenter explained softly. Nearing eighty he was the oldest man currently serving in a position of power in Washington. His quiet, studied views were well respected here and abroad, especially in countries like China where old age was venerated. "Do you understand what could happen if you're correct, and this madman has one of the things?" He shook his head because of the enormity of what they were facing. "We have no defense."

"We built a hundred of them," McGarvey said. "We think the Russians built a similar number in the mid to late seventies. Ours were designed at Los Alamos and put together at the Pantex facility in Texas, and so far as I know, Mr. Secretary, they still exist."

"And you're telling us that bin Laden has one of these things?" The President glanced at the diagram again. He was shaken to the core. "What's he going to do with it? Doesn't he need a missile or something to deliver it?"

"No, Mr. President, because it's not a bomb in the conventional sense of the word. It only weighs about ninety pounds, and it fits into a suitcase-size package. They were designed for behind the lines sabotage to take out major bridges, dams, submarine pens and hardened bunkers for fighter aircraft."

"Was it meant to be carried by a man?"

"A strong man, or maybe two of them to switch off. They could sneak up to the target in the middle of the night, hide the package somewhere close to their objective, and then withdraw."

"How powerful is it?"

"About one kiloton, enough to do a very considerable amount of damage wherever it was fired."

"Just how much damage?"

"Mr. President, if it were loaded in the cargo hold of a commercial airplane and detonated over Washington, or New York, or Los Angeles, or any other large city, as many as a million people would die either from the actual blast and heat, or from the aftermath fires, or the long-term effects of radiation poisoning. Roads, schools, government buildings, radio and television stations, telephone towers and exchanges, power plants and distribution centers, satellite antennae—a major portion of a city's infrastructure would be totally destroyed or heavily damaged in just one terrorist attack. It would make the Oklahoma City incident look like a toy popgun."

"Just wait a minute," Berndt broke in. "You don't just walk up to an international airport carrying a nuclear weapon and board the first flight to New York."

"It might not be carried aboard, but it might get through customs disguised as electronic equipment, machinery or even office supplies. And unless it was damaged it wouldn't leak radiation so it'd be invisible to most airport security measures. Even bomb sniffing dogs wouldn't be able to sense it. Nor would our satellites, or NEST (Nuclear Explosives Search Teams) units. It could be moved anywhere around the world almost as easily as a case of beans or a sack of rice."

FBI Director Herbert Weissman shook his head. "We have scenarios in place to deal with anthrax or nerve gas or a dozen other biological and chemical attacks, but not this. Not something this portable."

"Until now there've been tight controls on the things," McGarvey said.

Even Berndt was subdued. "Assuming for the moment that bin Laden has this weapon, and that he can get it here, how is it fired?"

"It's exceedingly simple, sir. Almost foolproof. It can be set off by a simple turn of the key, by a timer, or even by remote control up to a mile away depending on conditions. Or, the signal to detonate could even come from a satellite, one disguised as a simple telephone call."

"Christ," SecDef Turnquist said. "Can we get any cooperation from the Russians?"

"I doubt it, sir," McGarvey said. "They won't even admit they ever built the things, let alone they lost one. They were never included in any of the SALT treaties. Neither were ours, for that matter."

Berndt sat forward, "I think I know what Art is trying to get at. If we can get the Russians to help us, why couldn't we send the signal to detonate the thing right now, while it's still in Afghanistan?"

"No," the President said sharply.

"It's better than taking the risk that the crazy sonofabitch will actually try to bring it here."

The President looked to McGarvey. "It could be anywhere by now, is that right?"

"Yes, sir."

"Somewhere in the mountains of Afghanistan, or in Kabul itself. Or even here in Washington?"

"Yes, sir," McGarvey said.

"Then we're at the bastard's mercy already," Berndt observed. "All the more reason to hit him with cruise missiles as soon as we can. Dead men don't give orders."

The President ignored his NSA, his eyes locked on McGarvey. "You have our attention, Mr. McGarvey. What do you think we should do?"

"Bin Laden wants to talk, so that's exactly what we do."

"Your man in Riyadh tried it, and it got him killed," Berndt pointed out.

"Allen was probably killed on the orders of one of bin Laden's followers. A fanatic. Someone who wants to use the bomb against us."

"But bin Laden doesn't necessarily agree," the President said. "Are you saying that he got it as a bargaining chip?"

"I think that's a possibility we have to consider, Mr. President."

"Okay, who do we send?"

"Me," McGarvey said. It was a bombshell around the table, even to Murphy who saw it coming. As DDO McGarvey was the third most powerful man in U.S. intelligence, bagging him would not only be a major coup for a terrorist such as bin Laden, but it had the potential of harming the U.S. even worse than Aldrich Ames had done. Ames had spied for the Russians in the eighties and early nineties. Because of him nearly all of our deep cover assets in the Soviet Union were blown, most of them assassinated. The CIA still was not fully recovered. "He wants to talk, so I'll go talk to him."

"It's a suicide mission," Admiral Halverson said. "If you're wrong, and bin Laden did order Trumble's assassination, you'd be walking into a hornet's nest." He shook his head. "Hell, even if you're right, and it was one of bin Laden's followers, what would stop him from ordering your death the moment you set foot in Afghanistan?"

"Considering what we're faced with, it's a risk I'm willing to take, Admiral," McGarvey said. "The same risk your people signed on for when they put on a uniform."

The comment stung, and the admiral sat back, chastised.

"I don't think we have any other choice now," Secretary of State Carpenter said in his studied way. "But what would you say to the monster that would make any sort of difference?"

"I'll tell him that we got his message about the bomb, and ask him to turn it over to us," McGarvey said. "I can't think of any other reason he gave the serial number to

Trumble. He wants to make a deal with us. We'll give him back his assets, lift the bounty and try to get the Saudi government to let his family come home. At least that'd be a start."

"We've been over that," Berndt said.

"There's something else he wants. I don't know what it is, but it's something he wants badly enough to agree to talk to us."

"Kill him," Berndt said flatly.

"Another failed missile attack could drive him into using the bomb," McGarvey said. "None of us want that."

"I mean if you actually get close to him, kill the man."

McGarvey went eye-to-eye with the President's national security adviser. "Are you giving me that order, Mr. Berndt?" The room was quiet. "Because if you are, I would like it in writing."

"Dennis, we're a long ways from ordering a suicide mission assassination," the President said. "If we strike his camps with cruise missiles the mission will be to deny him the capability to wage a war of terrorism. We will not specifically target the man."

It was a very fine point, barely within American law, and no one missed it, nor did anyone offer comment. Assassination as a political weapon was not an option, although if bin Laden were to be killed in a missile raid, then so be it.

"How sure are you that he's not simply setting a trap?" the President asked. "It comes down to that."

"If he is, he wouldn't have killed Allen. He would have waited for someone like me to show up. He wants something, and I have to meet with him."

"How soon could you set it up?"

"We'll put the word out, and if he responds it'll be within the week, maybe two," McGarvey said.

"Safeguards?" the President asked.

"We have some limited resources in Kabul."

"Assuming he's still in Afghanistan, how would you get there? Government transport is out."

"Ariana Airlines, through Dubai," McGarvey said. "For

the moment it's the only reliable carrier to Kabul. From there I would expect he'd send someone for me."

The President shook his head. "I don't like this, but I don't see any other alternative under the circumstances."

"No, sir," McGarvey said.

"General?" The President turned to Murphy.

Murphy gave McGarvey an odd, almost pensive look. "He'll have to go in clean. If we try to set something up for him, some kind of a backup, and bin Laden finds out about it, Mac will be a dead man."

The President looked around the table. "Have there been any leaks yet?" To this point the media was accepting the FBI's story that the shooting in Orlando was a case of mistaken identity in a drug cartel war. The eye witnesses said that the shooters were slightly built and dark-skinned, which was a close enough fit to generalize that they were Colombians. Bari Yousef's identity and Allen Trumble's real employer were being kept secret.

"No, sir," Berndt assured him.

"Then we'll keep it that way," the President said. He looked again at McGarvey. "Do it," he said softly.

"Yes, sir," McGarvey said. A whisp of something from Voltaire came to him: I am very fond of truth, but not at all of martyrdom. Before he put himself into the lion's den he would try to even the odds as much as possible. He wanted to stop bin Laden, but he also wanted to make it up to Trumble's family.

The Oval Office

Berndt and Admiral Halverson remained behind as the others filed out of the room. When everyone was gone they followed the President upstairs. On the way in he told his chief of staff to push everything back for another ten minutes, then he went to his desk.

"We can monitor McGarvey's movements into the Afghan mountains, am I correct in this?"

"To within a few meters," Berndt confirmed.

"Okay, if he actually comes face-to-face with the bastard, and if bin Laden so much as farts, I will order the immediate missile attack on his camp once McGarvey is clear."

"Or dead," Berndt said darkly.

The President nodded. "But I'll need an ironclad confirmation of that before we go. Clear?" Berndt nodded. "Admiral, I want the *Carl Vinson* and her battle group moved into position as soon as possible. And we're keeping the lid on this."

"I'll see to it immediately," the admiral said, happy to go into action.

"It's a trap," Berndt predicted. "All he's going to accomplish is get himself killed."

"McGarvey is a capable man. We will give him the chance before we do anything."

"Yes, Mr. President," Berndt said. "Now, what about the funeral for Allen Trumble and his family? We're going to have to stay out of it, officially, if we want the cover story to hold."

The President's eyes went to the photograph on the desk of his wife and daughter. He was doing this for them, he thought. For all Americans, but especially for them. "The CIA will handle it. Whatever they want."

"But, Mr. President—"

The President looked up, an angry set to his jaw. "Allen Trumble was an American hero, Dennis. He will be treated as such." His eyes narrowed. "Let's keep focused. We're facing a madman in possession of a nuclear bomb who has shown a willingness in the past to kill innocent men, women and children. Don't forget it." The President shook his head. "God knows, I won't."

SARAH BIN LADEN

The trumpets blew, and the walls came tumbling down at the battle of Jericho. But in reality Joshua probably used a hammer.

SIX

Kabul, Afghanistan

In the ten days since the President had given his approval to the operation being called Meteor, the mood on the seventh floor of CIA headquarters had gone from one of anger and disbelief to one of quiet acceptance. If bin Laden had the nuclear device, and that was still a big if in a lot of people's minds, then they had no choice except to send an emissary.

McGarvey sat in a window seat near the back of a half-filled shabby Ariana Afghan Airlines 727 inbound for Kabul's International Airport. It was four-thirty in the afternoon, and the flight out of Dubai in the United Arab Emirates was already an hour late. But no one aboard, most of them businessmen, a few of them diplomats from India and Germany, was in any rush to arrive. Afghanistan was not a tourist destination. He'd been thinking about Katy and their last night together. She'd clung very close to him, but she refused to press him for details. He was going out of the country, he couldn't or wouldn't talk about his assignment, and he'd already begun to withdraw to that special place of his where he went to distance himself from his friends and family. She was not a stupid woman, she had an idea where he was going and why. At Trumble's funeral in Minneapolis last week, she'd been impressed to see a tear roll down her husband's cheek, but she'd said nothing about that either, though just now McGarvey realized how hard it must have been for her not to reach out for him, to hold him and console him; tell him that everything would be okay. He probably would have snapped at her, he thought, and she probably had known that too.

He was torn in two directions, as he had been for most of his life. On the one hand he loved his ex-wife with everything in his soul; he wanted them to have a life together. A real life, because he had some alternatives. He didn't have to go out into the field, almost no DDO before him had. In fact he didn't even have to stay with the CIA. He could always go back to teaching Voltaire, maybe back at the small college in Delaware where he'd taught before. Or, he had enough money so that he could retire; they could travel, just be together.

Who the hell am I kidding, he asked himself. He could see Allen Trumble's face in his mind's eye. The man had no names, no conditions.

Elizabeth had come back from Paris for the funeral, and, dealing with her had been even more difficult than her mother, because she was more direct. Word had spread around the DO that bin Laden was on the move and that her father was probably going after him. But no one outside of a handful of people knew the details.

"Otto won't tell me what's going on, and I suppose you're not going to make it any easier for me to find out, are you, Daddy?"

"Just watch yourself, will you, sweetheart," McGarvey said distantly. They were at the airport in Minneapolis to catch her flight back. She'd already said goodbye to her mother who stood a few feet away talking with some of Trumble's family.

"Is there anything you want me to take back to Tom?" Liz asked. She was a pretty young woman of twenty-three with a round face, short blond hair and electric-green, inquisitive, sometimes mischievous eyes. McGarvey pulled himself back to the present.

"Things might get a little dicey in the next few weeks, so keep your head down, okay? Don't take any chances."

She smiled wryly and glanced over at her mother. "What's Mother say?"

McGarvey shrugged. It was none of her business; she was trying to draw him out further. "She's okay."

She nodded. Her mother and father were her world, but they had decided not to tell her they were getting remarried. Not until this was over. "Give 'em hell, Dad," she said seriously, then she gave him a peck on the cheek, waved goodbye to her mother, and headed for the jetway.

He could see her reflection in the glass of the window. I am what I am, he thought. A leopard cannot change its spots. And yet for a brief moment he felt a genuine stab of pain thinking what he was jeopardizing. What he had been jeopardizing all of his professional life.

Below, the mountains spread to a broad plateau and he could see the sprawling city of nearly two million people, and beyond it the international airport five miles to the northeast. Kabul, which was at an elevation slightly higher than Denver's, was obscured by a pale brown haze and looked just as drab and colorless as the gray and brown countryside. After the Russians had pulled out in '89 and the Taliban had taken over, life in Afghanistan had become dreary and brutish. Women had to be covered head to toe, and they could not hold any jobs, not even as medical doctors. It was one of many catch-22s. Women could not be examined by male doctors, and since there were no female doctors, women were never treated for any sickness or injury. The death rate among the female population was becoming horrendous, yet the Taliban ruling party did nothing about it, nor would it allow much of anything to be done by outside agencies. The entire nation of sixteen million fiercely proud people was spiraling downward into a dark age, its borders all but sealed off to the outside world, which for the most part seemed content to allow Afghanistan to self-destruct in civil war.

It was a dark country, McGarvey thought. A brooding place, filled with secrets and repressions and death; a perfect place for a man such as bin Laden and his fanatical followers to wage their jihad against the West.

Coming in, the American-built airport looked like any

other around the world; long paved runways, a large fairly modern terminal and control tower, maintenance hangars, warehouses. But there were very few jetliners on the ground, and only a handful of cars and a few trucks in the parking lot. Definitely not right for a city this size; it was as if the place were holding its breath, waiting.

He closed his eyes as they touched down with a jolt and a sharp bark of tires, putting his family and that life completely behind him. Divorcing himself completely from one life of normal routines, for the other more dangerous existence in which the slightest misjudgement, the tiniest error, the briefest hesitation at the wrong time, the most innocuous miscalculation could cost him his life. It was a self defense mechanism, an instinct for survival in which he fell back on a set of skills that he'd honed over twenty-five years in the business; automatic reflexes, an almost preternatural awareness of his surroundings and the dangers they held. When he opened his eyes again, the transformation was nothing less than startling. Had the French businessman seated next to him been watching he would have sworn that his seatmate on landing was not the same who'd flown from Dubai. But then the only differences were in McGarvey's cold, gray-green eyes, and in the way he held himself; loosely erect, yet like a coiled spring ready to strike. He was back in the field.

McGarvey's only luggage was a small overnight bag and a laptop computer in a leather case, both of which he had carried aboard. Bags in hand, he followed the line of passengers across the tarmac into the customs hall of the terminal. Armed military guards seemed to be everywhere, and unlike the security people in many airports he'd flown to or from, these men looked as if they meant business. They were alert, their attention constantly shifting from passenger to passenger as if they expected an attack to come at any second. Nothing sloppy here, McGarvey thought.

When his turn came he laid his bags on the low table in front of a uniformed customs inspector and handed over his passport. The man looked up comparing the photograph to McGarvey's face.

"Wait here," he said, and he walked off to a military officer who was talking on a phone at a standup desk. When the officer was finished the customs inspector handed him McGarvey's passport.

The customs hall was a long, narrow room with windows facing the parked airplane, several doors leading to offices, a set of large swinging doors through which incoming baggage was brought in and a pair of turnstiles leading to a corridor marked: TO TERMINAL in Arabic and French. A top line of print that had probably been in Russian was painted out. A pair of armed guards, Kalashnikovs slung over their shoulders, flanked the exit. They were checking everybody's entry cards.

The military officer examined McGarvey's passport and CIA-forged visa stamp, looked over at him and then made another brief phone call. When he was finished he came over with the customs inspector. Neither of them smiled, though the military officer didn't seem as nervous or as belligerent as the inspector, and his British-accented English was much better.

"What is the purpose of your visit to Afghanistan?"

"Business," McGarvey said. Out of the corner of his eye he could see that one of the soldiers at the turnstiles was watching them.

"This is a diplomatic passport. What sort of business?"

"Actually I've been sent over by my government to inspect our old embassy building."

The officer's thin lips compressed beneath his luxuriant dark mustache. "Open your bags."

McGarvey did as he was told, and the officer rifled through the clothes, which included a pair of soft boots and bush jacket. He pulled out a toiletries kit and looked through it, then picked up a small leather pouch.

"What is this?"

"A camera," McGarvey said.

The officer handed it to the customs inspector. "There are no cameras permitted in Afghanistan." He turned his attention to the computer. "Switch it on."

McGarvey did it, and Windows 98 came up on the LCD screen. A few seconds later the icons appeared. He brought up the file manager and clicked on one named: EMB-K. A picture of the U.S. embassy in Kabul was displayed.

The officer was impressed despite himself. He gave McGarvey an appraising look. "You will need permission from the Ministry of Security before you can inspect this building."

McGarvey held his gaze for a beat, then nodded. "I understand."

"You will also be required to have an escort."

"Yes, sir."

"Take everything out of your pockets."

McGarvey complied, laying his ballpoint, wallet, handkerchief, comb, several hundred dollars and change, penknife and satellite phone on the counter.

The officer eyed the money, but picked up the phone which was about the size of a pack of cigarettes. "What is this?"

"A telephone."

"Portable phones are not permitted in Afghanistan," he said, and he handed it to the customs inspector.

"In that case I'll stay right here until the next flight leaves, and I'll be on it."

"It is the law." The officer straightened up.

"You have my camera, but I'll keep my phone." McGarvey took a hundred dollar bill from the pile and slid it across the counter.

"What is the meaning of this?" the officer said, recoiling.

"It's for my telephone permit," McGarvey said with a straight face. "It's the same in most other countries. The money goes to your Ministry of Communications. It's a licensing fee, do you understand?"

The military officer motioned sharply for one of the guards to come over. "Search him."

McGarvey spread his arms and legs, and the young bearded soldier quickly frisked him. When he was finished he stepped back and shook his head. McGarvey noticed that the hundred dollar bill was gone.

The tension in the hall was very high. Some of the other armed guards, seeing that something was going on, had unslung their rifles. Most of the other passengers had already cleared customs and were gone, but the few who were left behind looked over, then quickly averted their eyes. No one wanted to get involved.

After another few seconds, the officer took the satellite phone from the inspector and laid it down on the counter with McGarvey's other things. "A car and driver will take you directly to the Inter-Continental, Mr. McGarvey. Do not leave the hotel until you are given permission to do so. It is *you* who must understand."

It was the mistake McGarvey had waited for. He'd not mentioned the hotel, nor was it listed on his travel documents. Bin Laden's reach was still in place with the Taliban religious government.

"Yes, sir."

The customs inspector filled out an entry permit, inserted it in McGarvey's passport and laid it on the counter. He and the military officer watched as McGarvey gathered his things, closed his bag and computer and headed for the turnstiles. He could feel every eye on him. But he was here in Kabul at bin Laden's sufferance, and for the time being no one would interfere with him.

A filthy, battered Mercedes taxi was waiting outside the terminal for him when McGarvey emerged into the glaringly bright sunlight. There wasn't a cloud in the crystal-clear blue sky. The haze he'd seen from the air was not noticeable here on the ground. It was very hot, nearly a hundred degrees, but very dry, and the air smelled like a

combination of burned kerojet, diesel exhaust fumes and
something else, like burning charcoal in a backyard bar-
becue. A dusty, ancient, foreign smell with strange under-
tones.

On the drive into the city, made long because the roads
were not very good, and because the young cabbie took his
time, McGarvey caught his first good look at Kabul, which
had been heavily damaged in the civil war and continued
fighting since the Russians had left. The sprawling city,
nestled in between rugged, treeless mountains was com-
posed primarily of what looked like adobe huts and other
small buildings hidden behind mud walls. They passed over
the Kabul River several times, coming into the city center,
but at this time of the year it was more like a muddy, dried-
up creek or open sewer than an actual stream. Nearly everything was old, ramshackle and run-down, even in a part
of the city center he was able to see as they passed. Most
of the bomb damage had not been repaired, and in some
places the rubble hadn't even been cleared from the streets
and the cabbie had to maneuver around it. On either side
of Bebe-Maihro Street were rat warrens of kiosks, shops
and stalls along narrow dirt streets. It was Sunday afternoon, but traffic was very light, not many people out and
about. McGarvey got the impression that people were hiding behind the walls of their compounds, waiting for something, or perhaps simply existing one day to the next. He'd
never been to a place that seemed so cheerless, so devoid
of life, so filled with dark foreboding, and the hairs at the
nape of his neck bristled.

Coming in he had caught a glimpse of the old U.S. embassy building, but from a block away he could not see any
real damage, though he spotted a military jeep and at least
two soldiers out front.

Pushunistan Square at the city's center seemed mostly
intact, the four-story government buildings in reasonably
good repair, though everything he'd seen so far that wasn't
shot up or broken was in bad need of paint or at least a
good cleaning. There was more traffic here, and the parking

areas in front of the buildings were filled with battered Russian cars from the seventies, a few older-model American cars and a number of Russian and Chinese jeeps.

A few minutes later the cabbie pulled into the driveway of the Inter-Continental. He turned around and gave McGarvey a shy, warm, toothless smile. "Mista, you will pay in American dollars?"

There was no official exchange rate between the afghani and the dollar, and in fact most of the economy now was based on what little foreign currency there was available. McGarvey handed the kid a twenty dollar bill, which seemed to make him happy. He held out another twenty.

"Is there a decent restaurant somewhere nearby?"

The cabbie took the question very seriously, and after a couple of seconds, he nodded and smiled again, then took the money. "This hotel has very good food. The very best. You should stay here. You can get alcohol, and they have television."

"Right," McGarvey said, and returned the young man's smile. An Afghani might slit your throat because you were the enemy, but first he would make sure that you were happy and that he hadn't offended you. Honor was just as important to them as their pride, which was intense.

The Inter-Continental, which had been one of the only decent hotels by Western standards in Kabul, was now the *only* hotel for Westerners. Once upon a time it had been among the best public buildings in the city, but despite obvious attempts to keep up, the hotel was run-down and even shabby.

The lobby was deserted, and the only clerk at the long reception desk had a long, sad face behind his thick beard, as if he were getting set at any moment to burst into tears apologizing for the sorry state of the hotel. McGarvey signed the registration slip with his own pen. His gold VISA card was refused and the clerk would only accept two hundred dollars in cash for one night, being vague about payment for the remainder of McGarvey's stay, which was supposed to be for five nights.

"We have a most excellent restaurant on the third floor," the clerk said earnestly. "It is open tonight from eight until the curfew at ten." He seemed suddenly very proud. Like the cabbie, he wanted to please. He handed McGarvey the key for 411.

"Can I make a telephone call from my room?"

The clerk looked at him as if he was from another planet. "Where do you wish to call?"

"The Ministry of Security."

"Oh," the clerk said, relieved, and he grinned. "In the morning you can make arrangements for your call."

But he wouldn't be here in the morning, and the clerk knew it.

"Are there any messages for me?"

"No, there are no messages," the clerk said. "Mista, why don't you stay here in this fine hotel tonight. You will see that our hospitality is very good. You will enjoy your stay with us. Guaranteed. Eat some good food, get some good rest after your long journey. These things are very good for you."

"Thank you. I'll do just that." McGarvey picked up his bags and crossed the lobby to the single elevator that was working. The other two had OUT OF ORDER signs in Arabic, French and English posted on them.

As the door closed, McGarvey looked back at the reception desk in time to see the clerk in heated discussion with three other men, these in military uniforms, who'd evidently been waiting in back. One of them was the military officer from the airport customs hall. At the last moment the officer looked up and his eyes met McGarvey's. Even at a distance of a hundred feet the expression on his face was clearly bleak. McGarvey might be an important guest of Osama bin Laden, who himself was a guest of the Taliban, but he wasn't welcome.

McGarvey's room was small but more or less clean, although there was only one pillow on the large bed, and only one hand towel in the bathroom. But there was plenty of hot water and half a bar of very strong disinfectant soap.

It was nearly nine o'clock by the time he had cleaned up and had a cigarette on a small balcony that looked toward the city center. Already the temperature had dropped to the high sixties, and it was still going down.

He went downstairs to what had once been a good restaurant. Two thirds of it was blocked off by wooden screens, and none of the handful of patrons bothered looking up as he walked in and was immediately seated alone at a window table by an old man in a dirty apron who kept staring at him.

The only items available on the menu were a stew of vegetables, lamb kebabs and the flat bread called nan. There were only two bottles of Heineken left, according to the waiter, and each cost eleven dollars for which McGarvey had to pay cash on the spot. But the beer was cool, and the food was warm, plentiful and very good.

At ten o'clock sharp the waiters came out with the checks, and cleared the tables in a big hurry, although not everyone had finished eating. It was the law, McGarvey's waiter explained. In any event it was time for all good and pious people to go home for their evening prayers before bed.

Back upstairs McGarvey changed into khaki trousers, a thick turtleneck sweater over a tee shirt, thick socks and desert boots. He put a few packs of cigarettes in his bush jacket and laid it over a chair, then opened his computer on the bed. He removed the six small screws from the laptop's back panel with his penknife, and took out his Walther PPK and one spare magazine of ammunition. He resecured the back panel, cycled the weapon's ejector slide several times to make sure it worked smoothly, reloaded the gun, and then dropped his trousers and taped the gun and spare magazine high on his inner thigh.

When he was finished he took his cell phone out on the balcony where he lit a cigarette. Someone would be coming for him tonight, there was little doubt of it after the way the cabbie and desk clerk had treated him. The only questions were: who was coming for him, how thorough would their search be and how far up in the mountains was bin Laden's encampment?

He hit the speed dial, the phone took a couple of seconds to acquire the proper satellite, and the call went through. It was eleven at night here, and although the city was lit, it was mostly in darkness, as was the surrounding countryside. It was two in the afternoon in Langley. Two different worlds, McGarvey thought. One of simple insanity, and the other, more complex, but just as insane. There were no absolute truths.

His call was answered on the first ring. "Oh, boy, am I ever glad to hear from you," Otto gushed. "They didn't take your phone. That's good."

"I gave them the camera so they wouldn't come away empty-handed," McGarvey told him. It's exactly what they figured would happen, and he had no need of the camera in any event.

"Has anyone made contact with you yet?"

"No, but I think it'll be tonight."

"Standby, I'm going to calibrate," Otto said.

Because of the curfew there was no traffic on the streets, but McGarvey was surprised that absolutely nothing was moving downtown, not even military vehicles. Otto was back a minute later.

"You're at the hotel. West side. Looks like twelve meters, plus or minus one, above ground level. Fourth floor?"

"Four-eleven," McGarvey confirmed. He rubbed his left side where he had lost one of his kidneys a few years ago in an operation that had almost cost him his life. The cavity wasn't so empty now. Six months ago McGarvey had quietly implemented Otto's idea of surgically implanting a small GPS homing chip, not much larger than a postage stamp including its long-life battery, in every CIA field officer's body. The GPS chips were uplinked with the National Reconnaissance Office's Jupiter satellite system that had been ostensibly put up to monitor military communications over India and Pakistan. But the satellites were steerable, and in fact could be positioned to receive the GPS chip signals from almost anywhere in the world. It could be seen as a provocative act from the right point of view, just like a police informant wearing a wire, but already it had proved its worth, especially in Iraq.

In one instance infrared KH11 satellite surveillance had spotted three Special Revolutionary Guard troop trucks heading out of Baghdad at high speed toward a suspected chemical weapons development laboratory that a CIA field officer was in the process of penetrating. Word had been sent to the agent to get out, and he'd made it with more than a half hour to spare. Without the GPS chip to locate his actual position Ops would never have known where he was, and word for him to pull out would not have been sent. He would have been captured or killed.

The chips were not meant for administrative personnel; there was a certain danger of complications from the operation because of the batteries. But McGarvey had one implanted in his side because what was good enough for his field officers was good enough for him. And despite his promises to Kathleen, and to himself, he knew deep in his soul exactly who and what he was. He was not ready to retire from the field for good, and probably never would be. It was like a narcotic, intelligence work; or, according to a number of good men who had gone before him, like a religion. You had to take it on faith that what you were doing was good and right. Once you went down that path there was no turning back. At least that's how he'd felt then; he wasn't as sure now.

"How is it over there?" Otto asked.

"Dark," McGarvey replied. "Anything new on the shooters?"

"They showed up in Havana, just like Rudolph thought they would, but then they disappeared, like you predicted. Chances are they're already on their way back. The big question, kimo sabe, is where is *back*?" Otto hesitated a moment. "But there's another problem coming your way."

"The *Carl Vinson*?"

"Correctamundo. The battle group is already in the Gulf of Oman, though nobody is admitting it to us. Could be they're planning an end run."

"Not until I'm out of here," McGarvey said, wondering if he really believed that himself. "Take it to Murphy, I want my back covered."

"Will do," Otto said. "But there is some good news in all this. Liz went back to Paris and started making a lot of noise, so Dick had Dave Whittaker pull her back here. They put her down in Ops."

"She's not cleared for Meteor."

Otto chuckled, happily. "She's the boss's daughter, you can't keep anything secret from her."

There was no use fighting the inevitable, McGarvey told himself. And there was nothing he could do about it now. "Okay, keep an eye on her."

"Dick Yemm is on it. After Allen and his family, nobody is taking any chances around here." Again Otto hesitated. "Oh, and Mac, congratulations."

"For what?"

"You know," Otto said playfully. "I think it's great, that's all. Just super, ya know." He meant Mac and Katy getting back together.

"Thanks," McGarvey said, but he didn't know if he meant that either. He'd always managed to keep his family and personal life in a separate, very secure compartment when he was in the field. Looking across the dark city toward the even darker, bleak mountains, he was sorry that his secret place had been reopened. He suddenly felt very vulnerable, and very much alone out here.

"Watch yourself, Mac."

"Right," McGarvey said. "You too."

SEVEN

Out of Kabul

McGarvey had been on the go for two days, catching only snatches of sleep here and there, mostly on airplanes, but he didn't feel too bad yet. It was a few minutes after midnight when he stubbed out his cigarette in the overflowing ashtray. He'd been sitting in the darkness by the window looking down at the deserted street since he'd gotten off the phone with Otto, trying to clear his mind of his family.

A dark blue Volkswagen van appeared around the corner a block away, drove directly to the hotel and pulled into the driveway, disappearing under the overhang. From his position he could not see if anyone was getting out and coming into the hotel. But after a minute when the van did not drive off, he turned away from the window, switched on the bedside light, and put on his bush jacket.

He slipped the safety chain off and opened the door. The elevator was on its way up. His bag was repacked and sitting on the bed with the laptop computer. He pulled the chair away from the window, placed it in the circle of light and sat down, crossing his legs. The first few seconds of encounters like these were always the most dangerous because no one knew what to expect. He was offering them no surprises; sitting in plain view, his hands resting on the arms of the chair, his door open. No threat, no menace, no confrontation here.

The hotel was very quiet. He could hear the elevator

arrive and the shuffling of several people coming down the hall.

Afghani mujahedeen, warriors of God, were as a rule a kind, but trigger happy-people, made that way because of more than twenty years of continuous fighting since the Russians had invaded in '79 and the ongoing civil war that had been raging since the Russians finally pulled out in '89. Be careful with them, Mac, his DO briefing team had warned him. If you make a threatening move, if you piss them off, they're going to shoot first and beg your forgiveness later. If you don't make it in one piece bin Laden might throw a fit, but he won't blame his own people, he'll blame you, and expect that if we're serious we'll send somebody else who knows their customs.

They don't separate their religion from their politics, and they don't understand anybody who does. So watch yourself on that score too.

But if you show a weakness, any sign of it, they'll jump on that too. Push them, and they'll react violently. Make a mistake about religion, and they'll pop off. Cower, and they'll run you over.

Otto had walked in on one session, and he hopped from one foot to the other. "You gotta act like you know something they don't, just like stroking my computers, ya know. That's the secret."

A husky figure dressed in Russian combat boots, baggy trousers and some sort of long, dirty tunic over which he wore a long vest, appeared in the doorway. He was armed with a Kalashnikov rifle, and his face was covered by a dark balaclava. He swept his rifle left to right, then charged into the room. Two others similarly dressed appeared in the corridor behind him.

"You Kirk McGarvey?" he demanded. His English was heavily accented, and he sounded young and angry, perhaps even frightened.

"Yes, I am. I've been waiting for you."

"Okay, you stand up now, Mista CIA."

McGarvey got slowly to his feet, keeping his hands well

away from his body. "Is bin Laden nearby, or do we have a long way to go?"

One of the others in the corridor handed his companion his rifle and came into the room. A fourth, very slightly built figure came to the doorway, and stared at McGarvey, only his eyes visible behind the mask.

"Arms out, legs out," the unarmed mujahed ordered.

McGarvey did as he was told, and the young man quickly frisked him. But he missed the gun and spare magazine taped to McGarvey's thigh. He stepped back. The small one in the corridor motioned to the bag and laptop case on the bed. The mujahed quickly went through the bag, pocketing the phone and lingering for a minute at the computer, his fingers carressing the keys. He looked up. "You will show me how to use this, mista?" he asked diffidently.

"That depends on how you treat me," McGarvey said with a straight face. It was like dealing with children in a toy store. Only these were armed and dangerous children who could lash out and kill him without a moment's hesitation or thought.

The one holding the rifle on McGarvey laughed as if the comment was the funniest thing he'd ever heard. "Maybe if we treat you like a prince you will give it to us?" he asked, his voice heavy with sarcasm.

"What would you do with a computer?"

"Send email," the mujahed replied nonchalantly as if it was something he did every day.

"What about my phone?"

"No portable phones in Afghanistan. It is not allowed."

"If you damage it I will expect payment," McGarvey warned sternly. "I have respect for my possessions, I expect the same from you."

The mujahed flicked his rifle's safety catch off.

"Whoever carries my telephone will be responsible for its safety," McGarvey insisted, not backing down.

The small mujahed at the door said something, his voice so soft as to be barely audible. But the warrior with the phone handed it to him without hesitation.

The one holding the gun on McGarvey safetied his weapon, and insolently stepped aside. "We go now," he said sullenly.

McGarvey got the impression that something was going on between them; some power struggle between the one holding the gun and the slightly built mujahed at the door, which made an already volatile situation even more dangerous.

"What about my bags?"

"I'll take them," the one who'd frisked McGarvey said.

McGarvey walked out of the room and down the corridor to the waiting elevator, two of the mujahedeen in front of him, and two, including the sullen one, behind him. Downstairs, the lobby was illuminated by only one dim light behind the registration desk. No one was around, but he got the impression that they were being watched. When they got outside, McGarvey looked up at the perfectly clear sky. Because there were so few lights in the city the stars were brilliant, and because of the elevation it seemed as if he could reach up and touch them. There were no sounds in the city. None of the usual sirens you always heard in large metropolitan centers at this time of night; no rumbling trucks or buses, no airplanes flying overhead. Not even any wind tonight, and the air smelled of burning charcoal mixed with a sweeter, fresher, more fragrant odor of gardens, maybe fruit trees in blossom, or flowers. Pleasant smells.

McGarvey's bags were put in the back of the van, and he was waved into the middle seat. One of the other mujahed climbed in behind the wheel, the slightly built one in the front passenger seat. The other two got in the back seat behind McGarvey, once again sandwiching him in so there was no possibility of him causing any trouble. They gave him a filthy balaclava and motioned for him to put it on. It occurred to him that his escorts weren't hiding their identities from him, but from someone they expected to encounter tonight. Perhaps a police or military patrol. The city was officially under curfew until four in the morning.

"When we are stopped you will do no talking," the sullen one in back said.

"Whatever you say."

"This is important," the driver said. "Your life is in danger, and we must protect you. So you do as we say. Understand?"

The truce between bin Laden and the ruling Taliban religious party still ran deep. Bin Laden had left his family and his businesses in Saudi Arabia in 1979 to help the Afghanis fight Russians. He'd been wounded several times, and he had gained the reputation of being a very brave, very fierce fighter. He was a hero of the people, much respected, especially in the countryside and small villages, but even his welcome was finally beginning to wear out. Afghanistan was an insular country that wanted as little to do with the outside world as possible. They wanted to tend to their own lives, which centered around Islam, and they simply wanted to be left alone. But bin Laden's terrorist jihad around the world had brought unwanted attention to the Taliban for continuing to harbor him. It was one of the reasons, McGarvey thought, that he was so willing to open a dialogue with the U.S. If he was forced to leave Afghanistan he needed someplace to go. The logical choice would be his home in Saudi Arabia. But that would take U.S. influence; in fact it would probably take a great deal of pressure on the Saudi ruling family just to talk about it, and bin Laden knew it. If they were stopped by a police patrol a fiction could be maintained that the cops didn't recognize anyone in the van. It was a truth through the back door. But if McGarvey showed his clean-shaven face, or if he spoke, it would be obvious that he wasn't an Afghani, and the police would have to do something about him. So the only logical solution out of such a dilemma would be to shoot him and dump his body alongside the road. Not a perfect solution, but one that everyone could live with if they had to. An American came to Afghanistan, despite warnings from his own State Department, and bandits or opposition forces had kidnapped and killed him to embarrass the Taliban. It happened all too frequently to foreign visitors. Even bin Laden could claim that he wasn't responsible. Someone had gotten to McGarvey before his people could reach him and guarantee his safety.

"I understand," he said. He pulled on the balaclava.

"Very good, mista," the driver said, and they pulled out of the hotel's driveway and headed north the way McGarvey had come in from the airport. He looked back and caught a glimpse of a face in a third floor window of the hotel, but then they turned the corner.

All the cars parked at the government buildings were gone, only a blue-and-white Fiat police car was left beside the fountain in Pushunistan Square. But nobody seemed to be in it, and they went around the traffic circle and hurried up Bebe-Maihro Street. Like thieves in the night, McGarvey thought. They were tense, and no one said a word. But Kabul had always been the most dangerous place in all of Afghanistan because it was a crossroads between the West over the Khybar Pass, and Islam. The city was straining at its ideological seams, and could burst at almost any moment given the slightest provocation. No one in the van wanted to give them that.

The mujahed driving the van wasn't as slow as the cabbie had been this afternoon, and they passed the road to the airport fifteen minutes after leaving the hotel. A Russian-built BDRM-2 armored scout car was parked just off the highway, the Afghani white flag hanging limply from its whip antenna.

The slightly built mujahed said something to their driver, who immediately slowed down, pulled off the opposite side of the road and stopped twenty-five yards from the scout car. Again his voice was so soft that McGarvey couldn't catch the words or even the tone of voice.

The scout car's turret came around and its 7.62mm PKT machine gun slowly depressed to a point directly at them.

"Say nothing, mista," one of the men in back warned. "Do not move."

The slightly built one said something else to the driver,

then got out of the van and headed across the highway as a man dressed in a military uniform climbed out of the scout car.

"Fool," the sullen one in back whispered harshly in English, which struck McGarvey as odd.

The mujahed and officer met halfway in the middle of the highway. For a full minute it seemed as if they just stood there, but then the officer pointed at the van, and the mujahed shook his head. He took something out of his pocket and handed it to the officer. They stood there for another long minute, and then the mujahed turned and slowly walked back to the van, the officer not moving from his spot.

The way the slightly built mujahed moved also struck McGarvey as off; lightly on the balls of his feet, as if he was a ballet dancer, or as if his boots were a couple of sizes too small and he was getting ready to bolt at any moment.

He climbed in the passenger seat, motioned for the driver to go, and then glanced back at McGarvey. For a brief moment their eyes met, and McGarvey suddenly knew what had bothered him, and the realization was staggering.

There was no traffic, and the mujahed drove at a steady sixty miles per hour in silence, leaving McGarvey to sit back, his eyes half-closed, as he tried to convince himself that he was wrong.

The highway was perfectly straight, but ran in ever rising undulating waves higher into the mountains. A hundred miles or so to the northwest was the Hindu Kush mountain range, which was the western extremity of the Himalayas. A no man's land of some of the highest peaks in the world; snow-covered, treeless, where rock slides and avalanches dominated the upper slopes, while Afghani and Russian-sown land mines dominated the approaches. A little farther north the forces opposing the Taliban waged their war of independence for a bleak country that had not seen any real peace since Genghis Kahn. A strange land of harsh, man-killing contradictions in which Osama bin Laden, himself a man of many contradictions, had found his manhood, his God and his war.

There was nothing in the dossiers on the man that McGarvey had studied that gave any clue as to what had happened during the ten years he had been here fighting Russians. But something must have happened to him, because coming into Afghanistan he'd been the son of a billionaire father loyal to the Fahd family, and when he came out he'd become a religious fanatic and terrorist bent on kicking the royal family out of Riyadh, removing all foreigners from the Arabian peninsula and killing Americans whenever and wherever he could.

It was here in the mountains that he had set up his headquarters from where he ran his worldwide businesses and attacks. Voltaire had written that to succeed in chaining the multitudes you must seem to wear the same fetters. Bin Laden wore the same clothes, ate the same food and lived the same hard life as the people he led. And they were willing to follow him to the death.

Looking at the back of the head of the mujahed in the front passenger seat, McGarvey thought that he was beginning to understand at least one aspect of bin Laden. The man might appear to be insane, but he was not a fanatic; on the contrary he was probably a realist who was perfectly willing to use whatever resources were available to him, no matter what the Qoran and his God had to say about it. If he had the bomb it made him the most dangerous man on earth, because given the right push he would not hesitate to use it.

A half-hour after they'd passed the military checkpoint near the airport, McGarvey glanced out the window. In the distance ahead he spotted the green and white rotating beacon of Bagram Air Base. It had been built by the Russians during the war, for air operations around the capital city. Now the Taliban used it for what few military aircraft they had operational—a few French-built Mirage fighters, a number of MiG-21 Floggers and a few Russian Hind attack helicopters—and for the headquarters of their military high command. They also had a prison there just off the end of one of the runways, but to this point the CIA had almost no hard intelligence on the place. What few people the Company had managed to send out there had simply disappeared, and had never been heard from again. A hard place, in a harsh land.

A few miles farther on the van suddenly slowed down and turned onto a narrow dirt road that wound its way down a sharply sloping hill, across a shallow, rocky stream, then back up behind a low hill to a copse of gnarled trees. The partially bombed-out ruins of a large stone-and-mud house were hidden beneath a latticework of wooden poles supporting a thick tangle of grape vines that were in full leaf.

It was obvious that no one lived here, but the van stopped on a slight rise, its headlights flashing against what once was the front entrance of the house. They caught a glimpse of three small windows whose blue shutters seemed as if they'd been painted just yesterday. The middle shutter was open. The driver said something in Dari, Afghan Persian, and the slightly built mujahed apparently agreed, because they continued the rest of the way down to the house. The open shutter was a signal that this place was safe.

The driver doused the headlights and drove around to the back of the house where a dark brown, mud-spattered, late-model Land Rover was parked in the shelter of an extension of the grape arbor. He pulled up beside it, and a minute later five mujahedeen came out of the house, Kalashnikovs slung over their shoulders. They all wore balaclavas, and at least to a casual observer they could pass for McGarvey and the four who had taken him from the hotel. One of them was even wearing a bush jacket, and another was slightly built.

Without a word, McGarvey, his bags and his four escorts transferred to the Land Rover. The five from the house got into the van and drove off. He sat in the back seat between two of his escorts, but the driver made no move to start the engine.

The windows were down and the night had become very cold. A light breeze had started from the north and they could smell the snow from the distant peaks.

McGarvey lit a cigarette, and the driver turned around and looked at him, so he passed the pack around. When it came back it was empty.

"How much longer do we have to wait here?" he asked.

"Not long," the driver said, contentedly drawing on the American cigarette. "If there is trouble at the checkpoint we will hear the gunfire."

"Not from this distance. That has to be sixty or seventy kilometers."

"It's only five kilometers to Bagram. Sometimes there is trouble, but only sometimes."

McGarvey had misunderstood. The van was not returning to Kabul as he had thought it would. It was continuing north as a probe to see if the highway was blocked. The five who had gone ahead were risking their lives to make sure that McGarvey's group got through.

"What if they're stopped?" he asked.

"There are other routes. But this way is faster."

It was exactly as McGarvey thought. However they got him up to bin Laden's camp, it would not be by the main route. "How much farther do we have to go?"

The driver started to answer, but the slightly built mujahed, the only one not smoking, said something and he turned away.

"The sooner I see him, the sooner the fighting will stop. That's why he wanted the meeting."

"The struggle will not end until all *feringhi* are dead, *Insha'Allah*," the sullen one beside McGarvey shot back angrily. It was the word for foreigners with a rude connotation.

"Is that what you want now—paradise?" McGarvey asked, pushing the man. He wanted to find out just how tight bin Laden's control was on them. "If you want Paradise that badly, why don't you put a gun in your mouth and pull the trigger? Save us all some trouble."

The mujahed yanked a Russian army-issue PSM pistol from inside his vest, pointed it an inch from McGarvey's head and pulled back the hammer.

"Mohammed," the slight mujahed warned softly.

The mujahed's aim didn't waver, but his eyes flicked to the front seat. McGarvey reached up, grabbed the man's wrist and jammed his thumb between the hammer and the rear of the slide, making it impossible for the pistol to fire. He twisted the gun right, then sharply left breaking the man's grip and pulled the gun away from him.

"The next time you point this toy gun at me, I'll take it away from you again, shove it up your ass and fire all eight rounds." McGarvey eased the hammer down and handed the gun to the momentarily stunned Mohammed who looked as if he wanted more than anything else to slit McGarvey's throat.

He took the pistol and held it so tightly that even in the dim starlight McGarvey could see that the man's hand had turned white.

The slight one from the front said something in Persian, and after several long seconds Mohammed slowly put the gun away. He stared at McGarvey a little longer, and then threw his head back and laughed almost hysterically, his hands now gripped tightly around the barrel stock of the Kalashnikov resting between his knees.

McGarvey figured that the man was insane, and he was going to have to keep a tight watch on his back for the remainder of the mission. The mujahedeen were very quick to take offense, and very very slow to forgive or forget, but they admired courage. And bin Laden's control was anything but complete.

The night remained deathly still except for the light breeze. After another ten minutes the slightly built mujahed gave a nod. The driver started the engine and headed slowly back to the highway by the same dirt track across the narrow stream that they had taken to get here.

Mohammed sat forward, cradling his rifle and staring at McGarvey, while the mujahed on McGarvey's right watched out the window.

They stopped on the slight rise just before the highway. In the distance across a flat plain the air base was only partially lit. The airport beacon was still flashing, but the runway lights were out and most of the low, hulking buildings were dark. But there were lights showing on what appeared to be guard towers and tall fences even farther in the distance, which McGarvey took to be the prison.

Nothing moved in either direction on the highway for as far as they could see, nor were there any signs of movement or lights in the sky. If there were an opposite side to the civilized world this was it. Dark, hidden, bleak, a perfect place for a man such as bin Laden. A desert scorpion in its nest ready to strike out with its poison.

The driver headed down the steep track then back up the deeply rutted path to the highway. He turned north and accelerated before he finally turned on the Rover's headlights. They were so bright after they'd gotten their night vision that they were partially blinded for the first couple of minutes.

Passing the road to the air base they spotted several military vehicles parked just inside the gates about a half-mile away. The guardhouse was lit up, but they saw no signs of movement, nor was the Volkswagen van anywhere to be seen. This seemed to encourage McGarvey's captors so that as they sped north into the night, putting the base miles behind them, the mood in the Rover got increasingly lighter, the tension melting away. They started to laugh and talk, obviously relieved. They had passed two hurdles, and looking toward the not-so-distant mountains, McGarvey could feel the biggest hurdle of all approaching: Osama bin Laden and his madness.

Something else from Voltaire came to his mind; something he'd written an entire chapter about in the book he'd been working on for nearly ten years.

Voltaire had almost no regard for governments, especially their institutions and bureaucracies. But he understood that governments were not buildings and monuments alone, but were made of people. Voltaire wrote that if a man wanted to obtain a great name, and be the founder of a sect or an establishment, it helped to be crazy. Be *completely* mad, he said.

"But be sure that the madness corresponds with the turn and temper of your age. Have in your madness reason enough to guide your extravagances; and do not forget to be obsessively opinionated and obstinate. It is certainly possible that you may get hanged; but if you escape hanging, you will have altars erected to you."

Was that it, McGarvey wondered. Was bin Laden looking for an altar; some last act that would go down in history as so tremendous, so heinous that he would never be forgotten?

EIGHT

Into the Afghan Mountains

They passed through the deserted streets of a good-sized town called Charikar about 2:30 A.M. The only evidence that the place wasn't devoid of life were lights here and there behind the walls of compounds, and a few cars and trucks parked off the narrow streets. There was nothing that looked even remotely like an open hotel or restaurant, although in the city center there were several official-looking buildings in front of which were parked some army vehicles.

Charikar was the provincial capital of Parawn and was the scene of a substantial Russian effort to keep the puppet communist regime in power during the war. In a true Afghan tradition, the mujahedeen never fought in the city until near the end. Instead of confronting the Russian troops, the Afghani warriors manned an extensive series of ditches and tunnels that completely surrounded the place. Russians found it almost impossible to move in or out without heavy casualties. The communists said that they controlled the city. But the mujahedeen sentiment was as simple as it was direct: Do the men in prison control the prison?

His escorts did not seem nervous passing through the town, and McGarvey figured that the farther out of Kabul they went the less influence the Taliban had on the people, and the more bin Laden's sympathizers were welcome. Listening to the talk flowing around him in Persian it occured to him that if they had been high strung before, they were relieved and even happy now. Even Mohammed seemed to lighten up.

A few miles north of the city they crossed a stone bridge over a raging mountain river, and ten minutes later they pulled off the highway and bumped along a narrow, extremely rocky track that wound its way west and, as far as McGarvey could tell, south, back toward the river. The mountains were all around them now, and the early morning hour was very cold; perhaps in the high thirties.

At one point the driver stopped the Rover and shut off the headlights. They sat in silence for a full five minutes to let their night vision come back, and then started off again. Now the track rose so steeply in places that the driver had to switch into the low range of four-wheel drive, and even then the going was nearly impossible at times.

For a couple of thousand yards they followed what was probably a donkey path, very slowly, a fifty-degree slope rising on their right, and a shear cliff that dropped three hundred feet down into the river on their left. They could hear the low-throated roar and feel the tremendous power of the water rushing through the narrow gorge below, and even the mujahedeen seemed respectful of this place.

Gradually the walls of the steep cut began to widen, until

they came dramatically out to a long, rising valley, the end of which rose suddenly toward a pair of snow-capped mountains that were probably still twenty-five or thirty miles away. The hills on either side of the valley were covered with brush and small trees in dark irregular patterns like long waves on a barren sea.

The path ended, finally, and the driver had to pick his way to the northwest toward a cut at the base of the valley, negotiating around the larger boulders, but driving over everything else with back-jarring bumps. It seemed as if they were at the top of the world here in this valley, even though the mountains rose far above them. The scale was impossible to accept.

A half hour later they crossed a wide, shallow stream, and turned north again, following its twists and turns, and finally after a long loop that ran with the contours of the hills, they came to the bombed-out ruins of a small village. Only a few mud and stone walls were left intact. Shattered bricks, splintered wooden poles and trees and glass and pottery shards littered the entire settlement. Even before the bombing—probably by the Russians if this had been a mujahedeen stronghold, McGarvey thought—this place had to have been a very mean spot in which to subsist. And yet as they came from the south he could see that the river went directly through the middle of the town where patios had been constructed, villagers could sit in the mornings with their tea, or in the late afternoons for their prayers beside the flowing water. He also picked out the remnants of several small fields of corn mostly gone to seed now, and perhaps a half-acre of grapevines in what was once a well-tended vineyard. There'd probably been goats and chickens and all the other basic necessities of a simple Muslim life. Laughing children playing in the dusty streets, old men talking Islam in the *chai khanas*, tea houses, while their veiled women went about their chores floating through the village like ghostly figures; seen but not seen except behind the walls of their homes.

They parked on the far side of the village in the ruins of

a barn. The driver shut off the engine, got out and walked back about twenty yards to a clearing where he studied the sky to their south for a minute or so. When he came back he pulled off his balaclava and stuffed it in a pocket. He was just a kid, maybe sixteen or seventeen, with a thin mustache, scraggly beard and wide, dark eyes beneath finely drawn eyebrows.

He said something in Persian.

"In English, Farid," the slightly built mujahed said. "For our guest."

He took off his balaclava, and McGarvey saw that he had guessed correctly back at the checkpoint. The mujahed was a young woman, not a man, with fine features, high, delicate cheekbones, a clear complexion, full, rich lips and dark, almond-shaped eyes that were alive with simple amusement.

"The sky is clear. No one follows." Farid's accent was very strong.

"We have only two hours to make our first camp," the woman said. "We'll have to hurry." Her voice was soft and cultured, she'd been educated in England or perhaps Europe, or at the very least tutored by someone very good. She turned and looked back at McGarvey. "You knew when we stopped at the airport, didn't you?"

"I wasn't sure," McGarvey said. "It had to be very dangerous for you to come into Kabul, and then to talk to that officer."

She shrugged matter-of-factly. "My father expects it of me. He's a religious man, Mr. McGarvey, but he is a Saudi, and modern."

"Are you Osama bin Laden's daughter?"

"I am Sarah, his oldest child."

The CIA had little or nothing of any substance about bin Laden's family. He knew nothing about her.

Mohammed, who had taken off his balaclava to reveal a heavily pockmarked face under a thick salt-and-pepper beard, was angry. He scowled, and then said something in Persian to Sarah. He wasn't as young as McGarvey thought he was from his voice. Sarah shot back a reply, her left eyebrow rising. He mumbled something else under his breath, and then climbed out of the car and stalked off.

"Not everyone has come to an equal understanding. But we can hope, *Insha'Allah*," she said regretfully. She opened the door, then reached across to roll up the driver's window, grab the keys and hit the door locks. "We have a long distance to travel before dawn, so we must leave now."

Farid and the other mujahed, who looked almost as young, pulled camo netting over the Rover making it practically invisible from the air even during the day. Sarah walked over to where Mohammed was waiting, his Kalashnikov slung over his shoulder, and she said something to him. It was obviously a conciliatory gesture. He towered menacingly over her, and for a brief moment McGarvey thought he was going to strike her down. But then he looked away insolently. She reached out and touched his arm, and he stepped back as if he was getting ready to strike again. His hand reached for the pistol in his tunic, but Sarah stood her ground, and after several seconds he withdrew his hand.

She came back, pulling a round felt cap on her head, and stuffing stray strands of black hair inside it. She got her rifle from the other mujahed, named Hash, slung it over her shoulder, then came over to where McGarvey was standing just outside the barn.

She studied his face as if trying to read something from his expression. Her own expression was one of concern and weariness, as if she was tired of the struggle. And yet he could see clearly stamped on her face a fierce determination and pride.

"Have you come here to assassinate my father, Mr. McGarvey?" she asked directly, without guile.

McGarvey shook his head. "Just to talk," he said. He was already beginning to admire the young woman.

"About what?"

"We want the killing to stop."

She nodded her understanding. "Then I think that you must have a great deal to say."

"I do. But am I going to be wasting my time?"

She thought about that, and took a moment to formulate her answer. She was being very serious. "My father is not the monster you in the West think he is. But he is a very hard man, as the Russians found out." She smiled wistfully. "He too wants peace, but an honorable peace."

"Will he listen to me?"

"Listen to an infidel?" she asked rhetorically. Then she cocked her head and pursed her lips. "Do you believe that the prophet Isa was God? You call him Jesus."

"I didn't come here to talk about religion."

"Then your task will be doubly hard. For us, Islam is life."

"I understand."

Sarah gave him an odd, thoughtful look. "I don't know if you can. But I hope so."

McGarvey motioned toward Mohammed who had hunkered down and was looking out across the valley toward the mountains as he smoked a cigarette. "What about him?"

Sarah followed his gaze. "He is an Afghani, and maybe he is already too old to change. I think he is a spy for the Taliban."

The admission of a weakness in bin Laden's armor was extraordinary, and McGarvey wondered if she had told him that to get some kind of a reaction, or merely because she was young and naive. He didn't think she could be much older than eighteen or twenty.

"Why not send him away?" McGarvey asked.

This time Sarah laughed out loud, the sound soft and throaty. "Better to have a spy you know in your midst, than one you don't watching you from a distance."

Farid and Hash had taken four bundles from the back of the Rover. They put McGarvey's bag and laptop into one of them, and the mujahedeen, including Sarah, shouldered the heavy loads.

"I can carry some of that," McGarvey said.

"You have your work to do, we have ours," Sarah replied.

They headed north from the village along the base of the foothills that stretched up the long valley, Sarah and Farid in the lead, with McGarvey in the middle as usual, and Mohammed and Hash bringing up the rear.

Within the first fifty yards they fell into an easy, loping gait that for the first mile or two seemed unnecessarily slow. But as the floor of the valley continued to rise toward the distant mountains, sometimes hardpan and rock-strewn, at other times swampy, the ground muddy, McGarvey could feel the altitude in his lungs and his legs. He was in excellent physical condition, but he had to wonder how long Sarah and the others could keep up the pace, and if he could match it.

They spoke very little on the trek, though from time to time Farid would look back over his shoulder at the sky to the south and then shoot McGarvey a glance to make sure he was okay. He smiled each time and gave the thumbs-up sign.

Sarah was very small, maybe five-feet-two, and slender. Although her pack was as big as the others, and she carried a rifle and a bandolier of ammunition, it was she who set the pace, never once faltering or slowing down.

Around 3:30 A.M., the village already several miles behind them, they turned to the northwest into a steep arroyo down which a narrow stream bubbled gaily. They climbed for twenty minutes until the defile took a turn to the right, putting the valley below them out of sight for the first time. At a small flat spot beneath a long rock overhang that would protect them from the air, Sarah stopped and took off her pack.

"Five minutes," she announced. She took a Russian-made canteen from her pack and filled it in the stream. The others did the same.

This place had been used as a rest stop before. McGarvey could see the disturbed sand, and farther back beneath the overhang someone had built small campfires. The rocks were blackened and the overhead was dark with soot.

Sarah came back and offered him a drink from the canteen. The water was sweet and cool. Simple pleasures were the best, the line came to him from somewhere, and he smiled at her. "Thank you."

"How are your legs?" she asked.

"I'll live. Is it much farther?"

She glanced at the defile, then back east. The sun rose here around 4:30 A.M. this time of year, and the tops of the distant mountains were already turning pink. "Another twenty minutes. But it is very steep."

"Is your father's camp nearby?"

She shook her head. "We have to stop for the day. It's too dangerous for us to travel. But we'll get there by tomorrow morning."

Mohammed and the others were still at the stream and out of earshot. "Dangerous for whom?" he asked. "Not the Taliban, you have a spy with you."

"I believe you call them Keyhole satellites." She gave him a bemused look. "I think they might be watching us because of you."

Actually the satellites' infrared detectors could pick up the heat signatures of human bodies better at night. But the KH11 and -12 series were in positions just now to watch the ongoing troubles in Yugoslavia, and one to watch a possible treaty violation in Antarctica. He didn't tell her that.

McGarvey offered her a cigarette, but she declined. He lit one for himself. "Do you miss Saudi Arabia?" he asked.

The question startled her. She started to say something, but then changed her mind and shook her head. "I was born in the Sudan," she said at length. "But I've never been to see my father's family." She lowered her eyes. "Have you been to Riyadh?"

She was holding something back, as if she were frightened. "Several times," McGarvey said.

"Mecca?"

"Once."

She looked up, a sad smile on her pretty face. "Then you have seen more than I have seen."

"We can change all that," McGarvey said.

"I hope so," she replied. "Before it's too late."

"What do you mean?"

She drew herself up suddenly realizing that she had said too much. "It's time to go now."

McGarvey wanted to reach out to her, to take some of the load of the world she was evidently carrying off her shoulders. Maybe in the early days in the Sudan when her mother had taken care of her while her father fought Russians here in Afghanistan, she'd had a normal life. But since moving here to be at her father's side her life had to be anything but normal.

They shouldered their packs and followed the stream upward. Almost immediately the going became very difficult as the walls of the defile narrowed and rose sharply to a ridge a couple of hundred feet higher. A small waterfall tumbled from a rocky ledge, splashing on the rocks below, sending a mist rising into what developed into a thickening fog as they climbed.

All conversation became impossible because of the strenuousness of the ascent. For the next fifteen minutes McGarvey's world was reduced to the next foothold below and handhold above. The fog closed in so completely that he could no longer see the base of the slope or the ridge. The rocks were slippery and they had to take extreme care with each move lest they lose their footing. If they started to fall they would not be able to stop themselves, and it would probably kill them.

The sky behind them was turning light now, and McGarvey sensed an urgency in the others that had not been there before. Sarah and Farid began to outdistance him, and then two mujahedeed below pressed him so that he had to speed up, take chances and unnecessary risks.

His body needed rest, but thoughts were bouncing

around inside his head at the speed of light; how much longer he could continue, exactly what he was going to say to bin Laden, hoping Kathleen wasn't worrying too much about him, and that Liz was safe.

Afghanistan and the people he'd come in contact with so far were about what he'd expected from his briefings and the dossiers he'd read. But he'd not gotten the sense of isolation from his readings that he felt at this moment. He could have been on a desert island, or in the middle of Antarctica, completely cut off from civilization. Afghanistan had always been a difficult place, but now that the Taliban were mostly in control, and trying to make the country into an Islamic fundamentalist's paradise, you could get killed simply because the hairs on your arms ran the wrong way. If you were a devout Muslim, and washed yourself for the five-times-a-day prayers, the hairs on your arms would all point down toward your wrists. If a man walked to the side of the road and urinated standing up, he could be shot to death on the spot. Muslim men always squatted to pee.

It was crazy to the extreme. But he was back in the field, in one of the most isolated countries in the world, where a single wrong move could cause his death, to talk a madman out of using a nuclear weapon to kill Americans. Maybe Dennis Berndt had been right. Maybe he should just say the hell with all the talking, and simply kill bin Laden the first moment an opportunity presented itself.

He reached for the next handhold and pulled himself up, the muscles in his arms starting to shake.

He had to believe that this path wasn't the only way to bin Laden's camp. It would be impossible to bring supplies on a regular basis this way. And although his location would be secure, his comings and goings would be severely restricted. They'd taken this route to make it impossible for McGarvey to ever find his way back. Coming up from the valley they'd passed any number of arroyos that looked exactly like this one.

Of course with his phone and the GPS chip imbedded in

his body he could easily pinpoint his exact location. But they didn't know that, and he would have to make sure they didn't find out.

A series of natural stone steps angled steeply to the right, and suddenly McGarvey was over the top where Sarah and Farid were already heading along a path around a broad pool. Mohammed and Hash came over the top and the three of them followed as fast as they could.

The sun was just appearing over the far wall of the valley behind them when they reached a much larger rock overhang than the one below. Sarah had already dropped her pack, and she hurried alone along the water's edge until she disappeared in the fog twenty or thirty yards upstream.

"There will be no trouble from you now, Mista CIA," Mohammed warned.

He and the two other men dropped their bundles but carried their rifles down to the pool. Stripping off their outer clothing and boots and socks, they hurriedly rinsed their hands, mouths, noses, faces, forearms and feet three times. Then, completely ignoring McGarvey, who watched from beneath the overhang above the pool, they knelt down on their vests, faced southwest toward Mecca and began the first of their five daily prayers.

At this moment McGarvey knew that he could pull out his gun and kill them all. They were as vulnerable now as a mother was during the act of giving birth; their conscious thoughts were turned inward to the task at hand; to Allah and to the belief that some day Paradise would be theirs. A Muslim believed that life on earth was nothing more than a reflection, a mirror image, of their real lives in heaven, so whatever they did here was holy.

McGarvey sat down cross-legged in the sand and watched the three men pray. Sarah had gone off by herself because Muslim men and women did not pray together, it was forbidden by the Qoran. But as he watched he wondered where and how it had all gone terribly wrong for so many of them. Why the jihads and fatwahs, the acts of terrorism, the senseless killings, the endless wars, the intolerance that led a man like bin Laden to contemplate using a nuclear weapon against innocent men, women and children? He didn't know if even Islam's most religious leaders could answer that simple question, and yet it was probably the most important question they'd ever been faced with. One that he had come here to ask bin Laden.

Stop the killing, there was no need for it. A strange thought, he had to admit to himself, for an assassin to entertain. But he could not ignore reality.

He got up and went deeper under the overhang where the three mujahedeen by the pool could not see him, and untaped his pistol and spare magazine from his thigh. He pocketed the magazine and stuffed the gun beneath his bush jacket in his belt at the small of his back.

When he came out again Sarah was returning from upstream, and the three men were putting on their boots. Mohammed watched her pick her way down the rocky path, and then looked up at McGarvey, his face screwing up in an expression of deep hatred.

Sarah was refreshed, as if the march and hard climb this morning had been nothing to her. When she and the others came up to the campsite she smiled wistfully. "It's too bad you don't know what you are missing, Mr. McGarvey."

"I'm happy for you that you have your faith," McGarvey said.

"I think it's not very different for you." She was serious now, her round face radiant, her dark eyes wide and earnest, filled with a deep, almost sensuous expression. "First came Abraham and Moses, then Isa and finally Mohammed. All on the same path to Allah. We're all traveling together."

"Or should be," McGarvey said.

Hash and Farid had gathered some wood and they were starting a campfire. They looked up curiously.

"Insha'Allah," Sarah replied softly.

"Yes, God willing."

Mohammed, who had been standing a little apart, watching and listening, said something sharp in Persian.

"Don't blaspheme," Sarah told him reasonably, and she

waited for an argument. When it didn't come she nodded in satisfaction. "We'll have something to eat now, and then get some rest. Maybe we'll catch some fish this afternoon for our dinner."

Their breakfast was nothing more than some very strong black tea and the flat bread called nan. It was quite good and filling, but not satisfying. Mohammed took his meal down to a flat rock beneath the branches of a small tree at the water's edge, and turned his back to them. McGarvey thought about trying to talk to him, but he didn't think it would do any good. The man was like a volcano, or a time bomb, ready to explode at the slightest provocation. There was nothing McGarvey could say to him that would make the slightest difference. They could have come from different planets. They had no real common language, the very meanings of the words they used were completely different for each of them. Mohammed was a man like many others McGarvey had met in his career, filled with an unreasoning hate through which nothing could penetrate.

Even Farid and Hash sat slightly apart from Sarah, and while she was eating they avoided looking directly at her as much as possible. There were other subtle things going on between them as well; in the way they spoke to her, deferentially, but with a slightly irritating delay every time they answered a question or followed an order. When they did speak to her, they would look at each other first for support. Sarah was bin Laden's daughter, and therefore she was a very important personage in their world. But she was a woman, and their strong Islamic upbringing made it almost impossible for them to deal with her on an equal, let alone superior, basis.

Still another subtle layer to the situation was the very fact that bin Laden had sent his daughter to help fetch McGarvey. It was a clear message that he was a modern man after all, whereas the Western media portrayed him as a rabid Islamic fundamentalist whose only mission in life was to kill the infidels.

McGarvey looked inward for a brief moment and he could see Trumble's face. Allen had protested being pulled out of Riyadh and brought back to Langley, and yet McGarvey had read a measure of relief in the man's eyes. Something had been going on in his life that he hoped coming home would help. Sending families over there was a double-edged sword for the CIA. On the one hand a wife and children provided a stabilizing influence on the field agent, even lent them a sense of legitimacy. On the other it was usually the agent's families who cried uncle first. When that happened families came apart, and the agent's effectiveness was diminished. There was a high rate of divorce in the Company, and a disturbingly high rate of suicide.

"Tell me please about Disney World and EPCOT," Sarah said, bringing him out of his thoughts. "Have you been there?"

McGarvey looked at her, trying to gauge what she really wanted to know; if she'd brought this up now to tell him that she knew about the killings of Trumble and his family. But all he saw was a naiveté; a genuine interest, even eagerness. No cunning.

"Not for a long time," he said. "But how about you? There's one just outside of Paris."

"I've never been to France," she said. She exchanged a glance with Farid.

"Well, your English is good, you didn't learn it in Yemen or the Sudan, did you?"

"I had tutors."

"Haven't you ever been out of the Middle East?"

She smiled wistfully. "I was allowed to attend school in Switzerland for just one year when I was quite young. But then my father wanted me to come home, and my mother agreed that it would be for the best."

"Then you know at least a little about the West," McGarvey said.

"I was watched very closely," she said. "And I was never allowed to go off campus with the other girls."

McGarvey knew what it must have been like for her. She'd been a rich man's daughter, with bodyguards watching her every movement. It was a wonder that bin Laden had allowed her even that much freedom.

"My daughter went to school in Switzerland," he said.

Sarah's eyes lit up. "Tell me about her, please. Does she watch MTV?"

"I don't know, but I suppose she does," McGarvey said laughing. "Have you seen it?"

"In Switzerland, but there are no televisions here." A look of frustration crossed her pretty features. "Does she wear pretty clothes?"

"Sometimes."

"Dresses."

McGarvey nodded.

"Makeup?"

Again McGarvey nodded.

"She doesn't listen to her father then," Hash said sadly.

"How old is she?" Sarah, still enthused, asked.

"Twenty-three."

"Does she have a job? Does she earn her own money?"

For some reason McGarvey thought about Allen Trumble's daughter, wondering what she would have grown up to do. Follow in her father's footsteps like Liz was following in his; like Sarah following in her father's? "She works translating Russian into English, and she's become pretty good with computers."

"She is like a Sabra woman then," Sarah said as a statement of fact. "The Americans, like the Israelis, have at least that much right. Their women are allowed to be mujahedeen." She looked again at Farid and Hash, who averted their eyes. "That is not possible here. Yet."

"Or ever will be," Mohammed said darkly at the entrance to the overhang. He was seething with rage. If he was a Taliban spy, Sarah's talking so openly to McGarvey, let alone that she had spent time in the West, thought women

should have rights, and wore no veil to cover her face, was
a major insult to his religious, and therefore political, beliefs. If they'd been in Kabul now she would have been
arrested and very possibly put to death, bin Laden's daughter or not.

Sarah flipped her left hand at him, another Islamic insult,
and he reacted as if he had been slapped, but he said nothing.

"It is time to get some rest now," she said. "We'll leave
at dusk if the sky is clear of the enemy."

"I'll take the first watch," Mohammed said, and he turned
and walked off.

McGarvey slept fitfully until noon on the rough wool blanket they provided for him. Instead of warming up, the fog
persisted and the day remained chilly and damp. When he
opened his eyes Sarah and the others were leaving the shelter of the overhang with their Kalashnikovs.

He sat up. "Is there trouble?"

"It's time for our prayers, Mr. McGarvey," Sarah answered softly. "Go back to sleep."

When they were gone, he got up and went to the entrance
where he could just make out the misty figures of the three
men by the pool. Sarah had already gone upstream.

Watching them rinse their bodies in the Islamic ritual he
was once again struck by the contradictions of their religion
and their war of terrorism. When they knelt down to face
Mecca and began their prayers he wondered what they were
thinking about, or if, as the Qoran instructed, they were
giving themselves completely to the moment and to their
God.

When they were finished Farid and Hash came back up
to the campsite, but Mohammed remained behind. They
passed McGarvey without a word, and curled up in their
blankets.

Mohammed turned and looked up river in the direction
Sarah had gone. McGarvey stepped a little farther back into

the relative darkness of the overhang so that the mujahed would have to come halfway up the hill in order to see him standing there. But Mohammed never looked up, instead he unslung his rifle and started up stream.

McGarvey checked Farid and Hash. They were already dead to the world, their blankets drawn over their heads so that only their noses poked out. Taking care not to wake them he crept out of the campsite and went down to the water's edge. He hadn't noticed on the way up, but now he could see that the stream had been partially dammed to form the pool, meaning this was a regular stopping place. From the air it would look natural; only from up close could you see that someone had piled rocks across the stream. A narrow but well-used path skirted the edge of the river.

He followed the path for about thirty or forty yards until it angled away from the stream and disappeared into a thick tangle of brush and tall grasses. He stopped to listen, but the day was silent except for the soft gurgle of the creek off to his left.

Pulling out his pistol he headed slowly into the thicket, careful to make as little noise as possible, stopping every few yards to listen.

The path took an abrupt turn back to the left, and plunged down into a water-filled hole about twenty feet across. He could see footprints in the mud on the high side of the depression, and he followed these, coming again to the river's edge in another thirty yards. Trees and even thicker, taller brush and grasses hung over the water so that McGarvey had to duck low to make his way through.

Somewhere just a few yards farther upstream, a man said something low, and urgent in Persian, which was followed almost immediately by Sarah's equally low and urgent reply.

McGarvey could not understand the language, but he knew from the tone of their voices that something was wrong. He pushed his way through the last few feet of tangled brush until the path opened to a narrow beach along another, much smaller pool than the one below at their campsite.

Mohammed, his back to McGarvey, stood at the water's edge. He was a few feet away from Sarah who'd been bathing in the pool. She was completely naked, crouching in a defensive posture in ankle-deep water. Mohammed's rifle was leaning against a rock along with her rifle and clothing, fifteen feet away. He must have sneaked up on her when she was swimming.

He suddenly lunged, and she couldn't get out of the way fast enough. He caught her arm and yanked her roughly onto the beach where he pawed her breasts.

She didn't scream, but she snarled something at him in Persian. He pulled back a hand to hit her, and she raised her slender bare arm to ward off the blow.

The angle and the light were bad, but McGarvey raised his pistol and fired one shot, hitting Mohammed in the back of the hand, the wound erupting in a splash of blood. The shot echoed sharply off the wall of the cliff across the stream, and Mohammed bellowed in shock and pain. He let go of Sarah's arm and pawed inside his vest for his pistol as he swung around like an angry bull.

"I'll put the next one between your eyes," McGarvey shouted.

Mohammed's hand hesitated. Sarah said something to him in Persian, and he turned his head slightly so that he could see her and still keep an eye on McGarvey. Blood dripped from his wounded hand, but no artery had been hit. He was shaking with a barely suppressed frenzy.

"It was a mistake," Sarah told McGarvey. She edged farther away from Mohammed, then straightened up, her slight figure almost boyish. "I should not have been here like this," she said. Mustering up as much dignity as she could she turned her back on them, walked back to her clothes and started to get dressed.

"Are you okay?" McGarvey asked. Since the airport checkpoint he had a feeling that something like this might happen.

"Please go now."

"What about him?"

Sarah put on her baggy trousers, and pulled her shirt over her head. She turned and McGarvey could see that she was crying. "It was my fault," she said in a very small voice. "But Mohammed has respect for my father so nothing will be said."

McGarvey's heart went out to her. She was tough on the outside, but she was younger than Liz, still just a baby girl in a very wild and difficult world.

"Harlot," Mohammed said in English, and McGarvey's finger tightened on the trigger.

Sarah turned away in shame without replying.

"Take the gun out of your pocket and throw it on the ground," McGarvey said in a measured voice. "Very carefully now, or I'll kill you."

Mohammed didn't hesitate. He got the pistol out of his vest and tossed it up on the beach. McGarvey walked over, picked it up and put it in his pocket. He released the hammer on his own gun, switched the safety on and stuffed it in his belt at the small of his back.

"You will have to sleep sometime, Mista CIA," Mohammed warned. His eyes were like a feral animal's.

"How would you explain it to my father?" Sarah demanded, turning back once again. She had gotten her emotions in control. She picked up Mohammed's rifle and brought it over to him. "We have a long way to travel. This is very important."

Mohammed snatched the gun from her, and for a second it seemed as if he was going to hit her with it, but then he slung the rifle over his shoulder. "He shot me, how are you going to explain his weapon?"

"Did you expect him to come here unarmed?" Sarah demanded.

"It's Hashmatullah's fault for not searching him better at the hotel."

"Mr. McGarvey will hand over his gun to me before I take him to my father. Your wound is a stupid accident."

"What about mine?"

McGarvey took the pistol out of his pocket and tossed it to Mohammed who had to scramble to catch it with his good hand. "Like I told you before. If you pull it on me I'll take it away from you, shove it up your ass and empty the magazine."

Farid and Hash came crashing out of the bushes in a dead run, their rifles at the ready. They pulled up short in confusion, not sure what the situation was.

"Everything is okay," Sarah told them.

"We heard a shot," Farid said, eyeing McGarvey suspiciously. Then he noticed Mohammed's wounded hand, and he raised his rifle at McGarvey.

"It was an accident," Sarah said. "I want you to take Mohammed back and bandage his hand. Then we're going to leave."

"Not until dark," Hash objected strongly.

"It's a risk we'll have to take," Sarah said. "You heard the shot, maybe somebody else has."

McGarvey stepped aside to let Mohammed pass, and when he was gone with the other two, Sarah pulled on her boots and shouldered her rifle.

"If my father learns the truth he will not thank you," she said. "I have brought shame to him, and somehow you managed to come here with a gun."

"What Mohammed did wasn't your fault."

She looked at him, her eyes unreadable now, but it was as if she'd aged suddenly into a mature woman. "Did you come here after all to assassinate my father?"

"Just to talk," McGarvey said.

"Very well," Sarah nodded. "Then the sooner I bring you to him, the sooner you can talk. In the meantime you will be safe. You are our guest." She smiled sadly. "It is a matter of honor, especially among the Afghanis."

NINE

Osama bin Laden's Camp

Bin Laden's camp came as a surprise to McGarvey, the size of it, nestled in a high mountain valley, with conical nomad tents, mud and brick buildings, a dozen or more army vehicles parked under shelters and a Russian Hind helicopter, its rotors tied down, beneath camouflage netting. It looked more like his military base at Kunar than an isolated hiding spot.

It was early evening but still light by the time they finally topped the last rise above the camp and stopped. Their forced trek through the afternoon had been made in complete silence. This time Mohammed was in the lead, with Sarah in the rear from where she could keep an eye on him. They'd stopped only once to drink water, eat more nan and a handful of grapes that Hash produced from his pack, and once again for late afternoon prayers. Afterward McGarvey passed the cigarettes around, their talk friendly as if nothing had happened.

Sarah took a small walkie-talkie out of her pack and radioed something in rapid-fire Persian. A few seconds later she got a reply.

"They're surprised we're here so early," she said. "Please give me your gun, Mr. McGarvey."

Mohammed watched closely, a strange, dreamy look on his face as if he had been biding his time, and very soon now he would get to act. McGarvey took the gun from his belt, checked to make sure the safety was on, and handed it to Sarah.

"Do you have any other weapons?"

"No."

She handed the Walther to Hash. "Put this with his other things. I'm making you responsible for their safe return."

Hash glanced at Farid, then nodded and put the gun in his pack. "Ali will want to inspect the computer."

"I'll tell my father," Sarah said. Mohammed started to object, but she silenced him with a glance, and he turned away sullenly.

Sarah was no longer friendly and curious. Now she was brusque and businesslike. On the trail they had become travelers together. Now I'm the enemy, McGarvey thought. The infidel come from the other side of the world at her father's summons. But he was a very powerful, dangerous American, which made her father's authority even all the more encompassing.

Gone too was the eye-averting shame from the incident at the river. She was once again Osama bin Laden's daughter, and therefore an important power among these men even though she was a woman. And power was one thing that mujahedeen respected and greatly admired.

The camp was two hundred feet below them, down a very steep, rocky hill. The path switched back and forth so that it was another half-hour before they reached the floor of the valley and crossed another shallow stream. McGarvey picked out a dozen armed men, their rifles at the ready, peering out of doorways and tents. Two men had been working on the helicopter, but they too picked up weapons and watched the incoming procession. He also spotted a microwave dish concealed beneath camouflage netting halfway up the steep hill on the other side of the narrow valley. From the air this place would look like just about any other mountain village, or perhaps the encampment of nomads. There were even a few camels hobbled behind a tent sixty or seventy yards downstream.

Security seemed very tight, as McGarvey figured it would be. But except for the few mud and stone buildings, this place could be dismantled and moved out within a few hours. Secrecy, mobility and utterly devoted followers had kept bin Laden a free man and alive all these years. There would be a road leading out of here, but in an all-out emergency bin Laden could be whisked away in the helicopter, leaving his people behind to fight a delaying rear guard action.

Despite all that, however, the camp had the look of permanence. He spotted garbage dumps indicating that people had been living here for a long time, possibly a year or more. Were they getting tired of always being on the run, he wondered, or did bin Laden feel safe up here?

A broad path wound its way through the middle of the camp, past the helicopter and some trucks. Without a word, Mohammed and the other two mujahedeen headed over to a low stone building, leaving McGarvey to continue with Sarah. On the other side they started up the steep hill, only this time there was no path; nothing to mark that this was a well-used route to anywhere.

McGarvey was tired of climbing up and down mountains, he was hungry and he was dirty, and now that he was this close he couldn't put Allen Trumble and his family out of his mind. If a nuclear weapon, even a small one, went off in New York or Washington or any other major U.S. city, there would be tens of thousands of Allen Trumbles and families. For what? That was the question he wanted to ask bin Laden. Why?

McGarvey had killed in the line of duty; he wasn't proud of it, but he'd never taken the life of an innocent person, and that was the difference between him and men like bin Laden. It was that aim of terrorism that he could not get.

Terrorism had never furthered any cause. Never.

"Here," Sarah said, stepping aside.

Two armed majahedeen sat fiercely in the shadows behind a pair of large boulders that flanked the narrow entrance to a cave. A tall, slender man with a long, graying beard, thick lips and dark melancholy eyes stood in the relative darkness just inside the opening. A Kalashnikov was slung across his chest, and he held a cane in his left hand. He wore a white head covering and white flowing robes. He was barefoot but he wore a bush jacket against the chill mountain air.

"Good evening, Mr. McGarvey. I am Osama bin Laden," the man said in English. His voice was soft, his accent British, but there was an underlying tension there, a tightening of his mouth, the corners of his eyes.

"Good evening," McGarvey said. He did not offer to shake hands, but he felt that bin Laden was waiting for it, taking his measure.

"Salaam alaikum," Sarah said deferentially. "Hello Father." They embraced warmly, but then he gave her a stern, disapproving look that nonetheless could not hide his obvious love and pride for her. He was clearly vexed.

"Salaam alaikum," he said. Peace be to you. "It is nearly time for prayers. We will talk later."

"Yes, Father," she replied, lowering her eyes. She turned without looking at McGarvey and headed back down the hill into the camp. Bin Laden watched her go, a wistful expression on his face that curiously made him seem very human, even vulnerable at that moment. His daughter was his weak link, as daughters were for many fathers.

"Children can sometimes be trying," McGarvey said.

Bin Laden's eyes zeroed in on McGarvey's, his face suddenly filled with barely controlled hate and contempt. It was like being next to a volcano that was ready to explode any second. "They are our future."

"All the worse when young lives are cut short unnecessarily," McGarvey shot back. He was not willing to back down. That's not why he had come here. The sonofabitch was responsible for killing a lot of innocent people.

"But then there are casualties in every battle. The goal is to avoid the larger war."

"We got your message, that's why I'm here."

"I thought you might find it of some interest—"

"You got our attention, all right," McGarvey cut him off. "There's a contingent in my government who are chomping at the bit to send the marines in here to wipe you off the face of the earth. There wouldn't be a whole hell of a lot of people who'd so much as blink if it happened."

"I didn't ask for this war," bin Laden replied angrily. The guards flanking the cave entrance clutched their rifles. "My people did not create the situation. We would have been content to live the way we have always lived. But you wanted your precious oil and you didn't care who you destroyed to get it. Nor did you hesitate to invent nuclear weapons and use them. Your government, McGarvey, not mine."

"Are you trying to tell me that blowing up our embassies and killing or hurting thousands of innocent men and women is the solution?"

"Your government thought so in 1945 at Hiroshima and Nagasaki."

"Give me a break," McGarvey said. "That was at the end of a very long war that we did not start. And as far as oil goes your own people are the ones who are profiting the most. Your own father made his billions because of it."

Bin Laden's hands went to his rifle. "Maybe I'll kill you here and now, and send the bomb anyway."

"Maybe you will," McGarvey said. "Maybe that's your plan, lure us out into the open one at a time and shoot us and our families down. Then send the bomb to blow up another one of our embassies, or maybe you're crazy enough to try to get it to Washington and blow up the White House. Then what? Do you think that we'll suddenly fold up our tents and go away? Are you that naive? Have you lived up here in the mountains for so long that you don't know who or what you're dealing with?"

"A great many people would die."

"Yes, they would," McGarvey said. "And not just Americans. We would strike back. The loss of lives on both sides would be terrible and unnecessary. It could even spell the end of Islam; certainly the end of your fanatical movements. Which is the real reason that you called me out here, and why I came." McGarvey spread his hands. "The ball is in your court, pal. Either shoot me or let's go inside and talk this out. Maybe we can figure out how to save *everybody's* daughters."

A play of emotions crossed bin Laden's face, most of them impossible for McGarvey to read because of the vast cultural and religious differences between them. Bin Laden professed that everything he did was in the name of Allah. McGarvey on the other hand was an agnostic. He'd been so close to death so often that he could not believe in some afterlife in which half the people went to Paradise and the other half went to hell. If there was a God, he had decided early on, it rather than He had to be a force simply of creation. What was left was a dependency on civilization; on the good will of men, on the rule of law. Men were gregarious by nature. They formed villages, and communities, and finally states and nations, all predicated on the beliefs that being together was better than being alone; that the whole was greater than the sum of its parts. And that the strong protected the weak. When religion spoke to the issues of the afterlife that was one thing, in McGarvey's estimation. But when in the name of Jesus during the Crusades, and Allah nowadays in the struggle between Islam, Judaism and Christianity, innocent people were killed, that was another, reprehensible thing. The first gave comfort, the latter tore down civilizations.

Bin Laden looked up at the sky to the northeast where the sun was just touching the tops of the not so distant mountains. "It is time for prayers," he said. There was anger, some fear, perhaps even some pain and something else in his eyes. Something that went even beyond the simple knee-jerk hate of the ordinary terrorist. Bin Laden was anything but a simple man.

"And talk," McGarvey said.

Bin Laden nodded. "Yes." He stepped aside, allowing McGarvey to go ahead of him into the cave. McGarvey had the fleeting feeling that he was stepping into the maw of a monster from which escape was utterly impossible.

A narrow, dark passage ran about fifty feet back into the hillside where it opened to a chamber at least forty feet in diameter. From this place and others like it scattered throughout the mountains of Afghanistan, bin Laden managed his war against the west with a very effective hand. But it was just a cave, after all, and the people living in it nothing but animals.

The main chamber was dimly lit with hissing gas lanterns. Shadows played on the tall ceiling that sloped toward the back where another narrow opening led even farther back into the hill. Wall hangings were afixed to the rocks, the floor was covered with thick Persian rugs and along one curving wall dozens of cushions were laid out in a semi-circle around a large cast-iron brazier on which live coals glowed. The chamber was warm, which was a welcome relief from the chill air outside, but not smoky because air funneled from the back of the cave and out the passageway.

From farther inside McGarvey thought that he could hear the muted hum of men in conversation, and perhaps computer printers; and over the charcoal smell perhaps the distinctive odors of a great deal of electronic equipment. He could not hear a generator running, but it would be outside somewhere, under camouflage netting.

A tripod held a video camera pointed at the arrangement of cushions where the light was a little better. A cable snaked from the camera along the wall where it disappeared down the dark passage.

On the opposite side, prayer rugs had been laid on top of the carpets, beside which was a wooden stand that held a large ceramic bowl filled with water. Several small towels were neatly folded and lying on the floor.

Bin Laden motioned to the bowl. "Cleanse yourself," he said. He laid his rifle next to one of the cushions and waited patiently.

The water was warm and scented and felt good, although a hot shower and a couple of beers would have been better. This was Arab hospitality. Bin Laden was watching him with an odd, almost ascetic smile. A Muslim warrior would slit your throat if you were his enemy, but if you were his guest he would first treat you kindly. It was a matter of Islamic honor.

A pair of men brought fresh water and switched bowls. When they were gone, four armed mujahedeen came in and quietly hunkered down in the shadows, their rifles between their knees. One of them was playing with the safety catch.

Bin Laden indicated a spot for McGarvey to sit, and he graciously poured tea. "It is time for my prayers." He gave McGarvey a baleful look. "Don't make any sudden moves, your actions might be misunderstood."

"The odds are in your favor."

"They usually are."

Bin Laden made a point of seating McGarvey within reach of the rifle he'd laid on the cushions. I'm the boss and I'm confident, his actions said.

McGarvey sipped the strong tea as bin Laden went through the Islamic ritual washing, then kneeled on a prayer rug facing southwest, and began his prayers, softly repeating the *Sura Fatihah*, which was the opening chapter of the Qoran, eight times.

> Praise be to God, Lord of the Universe,
>   The Compassionate, the Merciful,
>   Sovereign of the Day of Judgment!
>   You alone we worship, and to You alone
>   we turn for help.
>   Guide us to the straight path,
>   The path of those whom You have favored,
>   Not of those who have incurred Your wrath,
>   Nor of those who have gone astray.

To succeed in chaining the multitudes, you must seem to wear the same fetters. The line from Voltaire ran through McGarvey's head. Bin Laden was a common man here at this moment, but he was a major figure among Islamic fundamentalists, and had been ever since the ten-year war against the Russians. He was a Saudi rich kid, but he'd come to Afghanistan to help the freedom fighters, putting his money and his life on the line for them, and everybody loved him.

He had been bright, soft-spoken, gentle—except to the Russian invaders—even pious and helpful. But all that had changed by the time the war was over and he came back home. He had become a rabble rouser. He wanted to pull the Saudi royal family from power, install an Islamic fundamentalist government and go back to the old ways. The best ways. He wanted to get rid of all foreigners from the entire Gulf region, especially Americans, and he wasn't afraid to tell anyone who would listen that he thought Americans should be killed whenever and wherever possible, and with any means at hand.

Watching him praying, the words gentle, McGarvey tried to fathom what had happened here to change the man so profoundly. War changed people, but not like that. Something drastic had happened to him here; something so terrible that he had changed from the son of a multibillionaire construction boss who would inherit everything to a terrorist content to live in caves and eat unleavened bread so that he could kill Americans.

The U.S. had supplied money and arms to the Afghanis, and presumably bin Laden had come in contact with some of the CIA's field officers out here. It was a reasonable assumption. But McGarvey had found nothing in the record about any meetings; no contact sheets, no incident reports, not even a fleeting mention. It was almost as if the records had been erased or had been altered. Or as if bin Laden himself had purposely avoided contact with the CIA.

Whatever had happened out here during the war was a complete mystery that only bin Laden knew.

Though he denied it, bin Laden had been implicated in dozens of bloody incidents against Americans; the embassies in Kenya and Tanzania, the Khobar Barracks attack, the slaughter of fifty-eight tourists at the Valley of the Kings near Luxor and the bombing of the American-run National Guard training center in Riyadh, the capital city of his own country.

And now this. The biggest one of all. The attack everyone in the West had been holding their breath waiting for. And still McGarvey could not understand why. Where was the sonofabitch coming from?

McGarvey took a closer look at the way bin Laden was kneeling, the way he leaned forward to touch his forehead to the rug. There was something wrong with him. He moved like he was in pain. Was that it, McGarvey wondered. Was it that simple after all? Was bin Laden sick, maybe even dying?

Bin Laden got slowly to his feet with the aid of his cane, a satisfied, almost happy look on his face that was in total contrast to just a few minutes ago. His eyes looked distant, almost as if he was on drugs, and he moved very carefully. He came over and sat down on the cushions, the rifle between him and McGarvey. "It had to have been a long and dangerous trip for you," he slurred.

"Like I said, we got your messages." He could see that there was a pallor to bin Laden's skin, and a slight tremble in his right hand as he picked up his tea.

"I did not order the killings of Mr. Trumble and his family. I don't work on such a small scale." His matter-of-fact tone was chilling, almost irrational.

"We identified one of the killers. He worked for you."

Bin Laden dismissed it with a slight hand gesture, as if it was nothing of importance. "Trumble was a fool, and perhaps some people who believe in the jihad took it into their own hands to silence him."

McGarvey stiffened. "I could silence you before your guards had a chance to stop me."

Bin Laden smiled sadly. "You are not a martyr. That's not why you came here."

"Lives, even so few as four of them, are very precious to us."

"Do you think that life is any less precious to me?" bin Laden replied mildly. "Do you think that I don't weep each time blood is shed?"

"Soldiers are one thing, innocent women and children are something different."

Bin Laden shook his head. "In this world there are no innocents," he said blandly.

"Your daughter included?" McGarvey shot back, and he waited for a reaction. He wanted to get to the man where he lived.

Bin Laden's face darkened, and McGarvey could see the obvious struggle he was going through to regain control. By degrees the same look of peace and contentment as before settled back into his eyes. His face relaxed, and the line of his mouth softened. "Women have a special place in our culture."

"They do in ours too," McGarvey said. "But I don't think the Taliban are in complete agreement with you."

Bin Laden seemed to think about that for a moment. "This has never been anything more than a temporary arrangement."

His daughter was his weak point. Maybe he felt a little guilt because in a secret part of his soul he wished that Sarah was a man. And maybe even more guilt because he couldn't provide a normal life for his family so long as he remained in hiding here in the rough mountains.

"Your daughter is a very special woman," McGarvey said. "It took great courage for her to come for me in Kabul."

Bin Laden shrugged, but McGarvey could see the pride in his eyes. "She is a foolish girl at times."

"I worry about my own daughter. Sometimes she takes unnecessary chances. She's headstrong."

"But then you taught her to be that way. You are a headstrong man."

"I wonder if we would worry less if they were men instead of women."

"The worry would be no less, merely different," bin Laden said. "This is a difficult world in which we live, difficult times. Dangerous."

"Which is why I am here," McGarvey replied.

Bin Laden looked at him like a snake might look at its dinner. "Perhaps it was a mistake, this meeting."

"We're here to avert a disaster," McGarvey said, careful to keep his tone and manner neutral. He felt as if he was teetering on the edge of a deep abyss, the slightest misstep or wrong word would send him over the edge. "It's time to stop the killing."

"What then? What if we come to an agreement?"

"Your family could go home."

"Saudi Arabia?"

"Yes."

Bin Laden's reaction was masked, but it was there: despair. "Not until American forces leave the Peninsula," he said mildly.

"We're talking about that in Washington. You know about it."

Bin Laden became serious. "If the kingdom returned to its Islamic roots it might jeopardize your precious oil resources." He was testing.

"We get oil from Iran, and will from Iraq once they agree to let us take a look at their weapons production facilities." McGarvey put his tea down. "We don't have a problem with your religion, except when you hide behind it to kill people."

"Bay of Pigs, Vietnam, Grenada, Panama Canal." Bin Laden watched McGarvey for a reaction. "We have our faith, Mr. McGarvey. What has driven you to ethnically cleanse your native population? Deny your blacks their rights?" He smiled disparagingly. "Ruby Ridge, Waco. The list is nearly endless. Tell me what fine principle you follow." His eyes narrowed. "Christianity?"

"The terrorist's litany," McGarvey said. "Okay, do you want to take them one-by-one? Are we going to compare what we did as a nation a hundred fifty years ago, knowing what we knew then, to what you're doing now, with what you know now? The Bay of Pigs and Vietnam were colossal mistakes on our part, but putting aside your cynicism about the West, we truly believed that the Cubans and the

South Vietnamese wanted their freedom from oppressive government. We lost, and look at the systems they have now."

Bin Laden was finally beginning to come out of his stupor, and he was getting agitated. "Are you trying to bait me?" he asked. "Freedom?"

"That's right," McGarvey retorted. "Why else do you think I would have come up here like this? But while we're at it let's check out the immigration numbers to countries like the U.S., England, France and Canada compared with Iran, Iraq and Libya—all fine religious nations." McGarvey measured distances between himself and the guards, and between himself and bin Laden's rifle. "The Qoran is a wonderful holy book, but nobody is beating down the doors to Dar-al-Islam, especially after guys like Khomenni twisted it so out of all recognition."

"Blasphemer," bin Laden shouted. His guards brought their weapons up in alarm, not sure what was happening except that their boss was mad.

McGarvey girded himself to make a try for the rifle. "That's your title," he said. "And you earned it. Your hands are bloody with it."

Before McGarvey could make a move bin Laden grabbed the rifle, his movements suddenly very precise, very crisp. He switched the safety off and pointed it at McGarvey's chest, the muzzle only a few inches away. His face was filled with an insane light now. Either his lethargy had been a sham or he'd suddenly snapped out of it. There was no way of telling.

His guards jumped to their feet and pointed their rifles at McGarvey.

"Did you bring me here to kill me? Is that what all this is about? Or do you want to let your family go home? Get out of these mountains. Stop the jihad before it gets totally out of hand." McGarvey sat forward. "Once you cross the line—the nuclear line—there'll be no way home. Not for you, not for anyone connected with you. But we have a chance to stop the madness once and for all."

Bin Laden regained control by degrees. But his face remained a mask of hate. "Killing you would give me more pleasure than you can imagine." He said it so softly that only McGarvey could hear it.

"I would be replaced."

"Not in your daughter's heart."

McGarvey was momentarily taken aback by the intimacy of the statement. He slowly shook his head. "No, not in my daughter's heart," he admitted. "But she knows that I came here to broker a peace agreement with you. If I have to die at least it will have been for a good cause."

"A noble sentiment for a CIA assassin."

His movements very slow, very precise, McGarvey poured two glasses of tea. He picked up one and offered it to bin Laden. "We got your message. I'm here."

Bin Laden hesitated, not wanting to give up his anger. But finally a look of conciliation, even a hint of defeat, crossed his face. He was tired again, wan, drawn out, as if the brief outburst had sapped his strength.

He switched the safety on, casually laid the rifle aside and took the tea. "All American forces would have to immediately leave the Arabian Peninsula."

"That would take some time, and my government would want safeguards in place against further trouble from Iraq."

"We would deal with that situation in our own fashion."

"It would have to be a mutual agreement."

"Oil," bin Laden said.

"Yes, oil," McGarvey replied. "Your family would be allowed to return home to Saudi Arabia."

"But not me."

McGarvey shook his head. "We can lift the bounty from your head, but the best that we could try for would be a trial in the World Court at the Hague."

"On what charges?" bin Laden demanded. It struck McGarvey as bizarre, almost surreal that bin Laden could ask such a question.

"International terrorism."

"It's war."

"Not to the people you killed," McGarvey said.

Bin Laden stared at him, a complex play of emotions across his lined, expressive face. "There can never be peace between us so long as your government supports Tel Aviv."

"That's not likely to change anytime soon, and I think you know it," McGarvey said. "But at least there can be an agreement between us. It's as far as we're willing to go."

Bin Laden smiled faintly, and stroked his beard. "Your military is already in the process of leaving Saudi Arabia. The bounty on my head is of no real consequence because the Taliban protect my interests. And my family would never agree to leave my side."

"But you would not have to remain in hiding," McGarvey countered. He couldn't tell if the man was toying with him, but it was possible. This was all some macabre game to him.

"What would I have to give you in return?"

"The bomb whose serial number you gave Allen Trumble."

Bin Laden sat calmly, not moving, waiting for McGarvey to continue.

"At first we didn't know what the number meant, in fact it took us several days to figure out that it came from a weapon that's missing from the Russian military depot at Dushanbe. Once we had that you had our complete attention."

Bin Laden smiled again, almost coyly this time. "Does your President believe that I would use this device against Americans?"

"I wouldn't be here otherwise. We would have done something else."

"A serial number and the actual device are two different things. Having the one does not guarantee having the other. I may be lying to you."

"We think not."

"Perhaps I brought you here as a diversion, to give me

time to place the bomb somewhere effective. My bargaining position would be stronger."

The origin of evil has always been an abyss, the depth of which no one has been able to sound, Voltaire had written. McGarvey thought that no one in the West had any idea who bin Laden really was. We had deluded ourselves into believing that he was nothing more than another Islamic fundamentalist waging a holy war against the infidels. Just like in the thirties when we had deluded ourselves into thinking that Hitler was only interested in righting the wrongs of the Versailles Treaty, and gaining *Lebensraum* for his people.

"What else do you want?" McGarvey asked, keeping his voice even. Maybe Dennis Berndt and the others had been right. Maybe this *was* an exercise in futility that was going to get him killed.

"I can see what you are thinking, but you are wrong. I am a simple man who wants nothing more than an Islamic peace for my people."

"Why did you give Allen Trumble the serial number? There has to be something else that you want, something other than what we've already talked about."

"There is," bin Laden said. "But it is not an impossible condition." He pursed his lips. "It's possible—"

A short, slightly built man, wearing the baggy trousers, long vest and head covering of a mujahed came in from the back. He waved the four soliders to their feet and came directly to bin Laden. He wore a white-and-blue striped fringed scarf over his face so that only his eyes were visible.

"We have a potential problem," he said, looking at McGarvey. He spoke English.

"What is it?" bin Laden asked, instinctively reaching for his gun.

"I'll show you." He motioned for McGarvey to get to his feet. "In the center of the room."

McGarvey hesitated. He had no idea what was going on, but he knew that he was in trouble.

The man with the scarf pulled out a gun. "If need be I'll put one in your right knee. If you're ever allowed to get out of here alive, the return trip would not be pleasant."

McGarvey had the feeling that he'd heard the voice before. Something in the British accent, in the intonation of certain words, seemed familiar. Unlike the others who were armed with Russian weapons, this one held a Glock 17, certainly powerful enough to take off a knee.

He motioned with the pistol.

McGarvey stepped around the brazier and went to the middle of the chamber. The armed guards watched him closely.

"Spread your arms and legs," the man ordered.

McGarvey did as he was told. "I've already been searched."

"Yes, I know. I found out how you brought your gun through airport security, and past our people. Very clever." Hash had mentioned that a man named Ali would want to inspect the laptop. This was the same man?

Ali laid his pistol down next to bin Laden, took what looked like an electronic security wand used at airports from his vest and came over to where McGarvey was standing. He found the spare magazine of ammunition in McGarvey's bush jacket and took it. Then he slowly moved the wand over McGarvey's entire body. Just above the belt line on McGarvey's left side the device emitted a high-pitched squeal.

He stepped back. "Take off your jacket and sweater."

Bin Laden and the guards watched with interest as McGarvey stripped to the waist. Coming here with the GPS chip had been a calculated risk, but Technical Services had assured him that its power was so low, its frequency so high and its bandwidth so narrow that it was virtually undetectable. They were wrong, McGarvey thought bitterly.

His torso was marked with the scars from several bullet wounds and other injuries, plus the removal of his left kidney. The expression in Ali's eyes was unreadable, but he studied McGarvey's body for a long beat.

"You've lost a few battles."

"Some."

Ali ran the wand over the kidney scar and the device squealed. "Even more clever."

"What is it?" bin Laden asked softly.

"Mr. McGarvey has been fitted with a global positioning system transmitter. Surgically implanted where he once had a kidney. It's the latest thing in the CIA."

McGarvey measured distances between himself and the guards, and to where bin Laden was seated. If any sort of an agreement was dead, he would have to kill the man before the bomb could be delivered and set off. But the guards had kept a clear field of fire. If he made a move they could shoot him without fear of hitting their boss.

"Then they know that he's here."

"Not here in the cave, there's too much rock above us. It blocks the signal. But they certainly followed his movements through the mountains."

Ali was close enough that McGarvey could grab him. But unless the man was very important to bin Laden, the guards might not hesitate to shoot anyway.

"What do we do with him now?" Ali said, keeping his eyes on McGarvey. "A bullet would destroy the device, that's for sure."

"Nothing's changed," McGarvey said to bin Laden. "We can still make our deal. That's why I came."

"Why did you bring such a thing here?" bin Laden demanded.

"To pinpoint your exact location," Ali answered before McGarvey could speak.

"That's right," McGarvey said. "We have ships standing by in the Gulf waiting for word from me. You didn't think I was going to come here unprotected did you? You have your armed guards, I have my cruise missiles. But think it out. Nothing has changed. You made me an offer, and I'm going to take it back to my government."

Ali walked back and got his pistol. "We need to leave

immediately," he said. He cycled a round into the chamber and pointed the gun at McGarvey.

Bin Laden said something to him in Persian, and he looked back, vexed.

"The signal is picked up by satellites. There's enough of them in orbit so that there's always at least three above the horizon."

"Then they know for sure that he's in this camp," bin Laden said, switching back to English. "But the signal cannot penetrate this cave, you're sure about that?"

"Absolutely."

"If he were to be taken down into the camp, the signal would reappear in their monitors, is this also correct?"

Ali nodded impatiently. "What are you getting at Osama?"

"They know exactly where we are. If they wanted to attack they could do it at any time."

"That's right."

"But Mr. McGarvey is a very important man to them. They wouldn't attack us while he's still here. *While the device he is carrying in his body is still here.*"

Ali looked at McGarvey with renewed interest. "Do you still want to send him home?"

"Yes," bin Laden said. "Maybe he actually did come to offer us a deal as he claims, and not merely to lead a missile attack."

"Keep me here, and let me telephone the President—"

Bin Laden dismissed McGarvey's suggestion with a gesture. "No, you will return to Washington."

"As soon as he leaves the camp, they'll attack," Ali warned.

"No," bin Laden said, supremely confident.

"But they'll track the GPS chip."

"That's correct," bin Laden said. "Mr. McGarvey will leave tonight, but the device will stay here with us. So long as it's here, the CIA will think Mr. McGarvey is also here, and they will not attack. Simple. It gives us maneuvering room."

TEN

In the Afghan Mountains

McGarvey looked for a way out on the way down the hill into the camp. The two mujahedeen escorting him were wide awake, ready for trouble. The camp seemed deserted, yet he could feel a hundred pairs of eyes on him; watching, waiting for him to make a move. He looked over his shoulder, back up at the cave opening. If anyone was standing there they were lost in the deeper darkness. The stars were very bright and large; somewhere up there a series of satellites had picked up his signal as soon as he'd emerged from the cave. Back home they knew that he was on the move again. His exact position was pinpointed to within a couple of meters. There was no telling what they made of the fact his signal had cut out during the hour he'd been under cover, but somebody had probably figured it out. At least he hoped so, because if they thought he was dead, the GPS chip destroyed, they would order the missile attack. That would be the worst possible thing they could do right now. There was no doubt, not even a lingering suspicion, that bin Laden had the nuclear weapon and would use it if they couldn't come to some kind of an agreement. A missile attack now would not kill bin Laden so long as he remained in his cave. And if they missed there would be no going back. If for no other reason than that, he couldn't leave now. He felt cornered.

At the bottom they passed through the silent camp. Just beyond the helicopter a mujahed was hunched in front of a low, mud-brick structure of the type very common in Afghanistan, used for everything from sheltering humans and animals to storing equipment and supplies. When they got closer McGarvey saw that it was Mohammed, and he was grinning maniacally.

He said something to the guards escorting McGarvey. One of them grunted something in reply, and then they pushed a heavy wool curtain covering the doorway back, and prodded McGarvey inside.

The single, low-ceilinged room, lit by a couple of kerosene lanterns, was equipped as a crude emergency hospital. One of the lanterns hung over a narrow table that was draped with a none-too-clean sheet. A tray with a few surgical instruments, gauze pads and tape was laid out on a small cart beside the table. A man in a long white gown, a bandana tied on his head, was pulling on a pair of rubber gloves. He gave McGarvey an interested look and said something to one of the guards.

McGarvey stepped back a pace and calmed down. He considered his options and his chances.

"The doctor says that if you promise not to make trouble for him, he will allow us to wait outside."

Overpowering the two mujahedeen was possible, but then what? He had two choices: He could try to get back to bin Laden and kill him. Or, he could do as he was told. Let them take the chip out of his body, and then somehow find his satellite phone to call off the attack. Even if the operation wasn't botched, the chip would go off the air within twenty-four hours after the delicate battery hit the open air.

The clock was about to start running, and he didn't have many choices left.

The doctor said something.

"You are not to worry. The procedure will be sterile if we wait outside," the mujahed said. "It is for your safety."

McGarvey nodded.

Mohammed was at the doorway, the blanket pushed back, and he was practically licking his chops.

"Tell the doctor that I won't make trouble. But I want to be awake during the operation."

The mujahed said something to the doctor, who shrugged indifferently, and then nodded.

"And keep Mohammed away from me," McGarvey said sternly. "If he comes in here I'll kill him."

One of the guards glanced at Mohammed and then looked back, grinning. He was enjoying himself. "No one will bother you in here. Tonight."

"Okay," McGarvey said. He unbuttoned his bush jacket and laid it on a chair. Next he took off his sweater, laid it on top of his jacket and spread his hands to show the guards he was offering no resistance. The doctor said something, and the guards left the room, letting the wool blanket cover the opening.

The doctor had taken a needle out of his bag, and filled it with something from a small bottle. "Loosen your trousers, and lay facedown on the table. I'll give you the injection. It's just lidocaine."

"You speak English," McGarvey said, surprised.

"I was educated in London," the doctor said indifferently. "You might become lightheaded, but you won't feel any pain."

McGarvey undid his belt and the top button of his trousers and climbed up on the table. It smelled strongly of disinfectant, which was a good sign.

The doctor swabbed alcohol on a spot on McGarvey's left side and gave him the shot. "It'll take a couple of minutes for the drug to begin to work." He palpated the area on and around the kidney scar. "You've had this kidney removed, and the implant is in the cavity, is that correct?" Before McGarvey could answer, he probed deeper with his fingers. "Ah, yes, here it is, just a few centimeters under the skin."

McGarvey looked over his shoulder as the doctor swabbed an orange disinfectant around the area of the scar tissue. He tossed the swab into the bucket and took a scalpel from the table. McGarvey tensed up.

"Turn your head, you're tightening your muscles," the doctor said. He probed the area with his fingers, but McGarvey could only feel a dull pressure, the area in his side was already numb.

"Why didn't you stay in London?" McGarvey asked.

"Because they took my license from me," the doctor said curtly. McGarvey could feel a tearing sensation in his side. Although there was no pain he knew that he was being cut. It was a disquieting sensation.

"I was fixing gunshot wounds, without reporting them. The authorities would rather have let them die," the doctor explained, as he operated.

"Terrorists," McGarvey snarled. His stomach did a slow roll.

"That's what they called them. But they were very brave men."

"Who liked to kill innocent women and children."

Out of the side of his eye McGarvey saw the doctor toss the bloody scalpel into a small tray, then select a pair of curved forceps. He could feel his warm blood trickling down his side beyond where the lidocaine injection had taken hold. That too was an unsettling sensation.

"Why did you come here then, better pay?"

The doctor laughed humorlessly. "I'm a Muslim, Mr. McGarvey, and this is where the jihad is being fought." There was a sharp tearing deep in McGarvey's side and he winced. "Be still," the doctor ordered, sharply.

It felt as if his muscles were being pulled inside out, and another very sharp pain rebounded up to his chest and shoulder, making him catch his breath involuntarily. He grunted.

"There, I have it now," the doctor said. The GPS chip was about an eighth the size of a credit card, but a little thicker. It was clamped in the bloody tines of the forceps. The doctor went to place it in the tray, but he missed and the chip and forceps fell to the floor, hitting the edge of the metal bucket. "Damn," he muttered.

The clock was running. The batteries would go bad in

twenty-four hours. But if the chip had been damaged it might already be off the air.

The doctor used another pair of forceps to pick up the chip. He held it over the tray and poured some alcohol over it, than laid it and both pair of forceps gently on a white towel. As far as McGarvey could see it wasn't damaged.

"You should not have come here, Mr. McGarvey," the doctor said brusquely, taking the first stitch.

"Neither should you have." McGarvey could not feel the needle pricks, but he could feel a deep ache in his side that went all the way up to his collarbone. Even if the chip was already off the air the President would wait at least twenty-four hours to order the attack. Murphy would see to that. Or at least McGarvey hoped he would. But Dennis Berndt was a power in the White House; the President had complete confidence in him. He might convince Haynes to attack immediately, and considering the risk that they were facing, McGarvey could hardly blame them if they did.

"I'll give you a shot of antibiotics against a possible infection, but when you get back to Washington have someone look at this."

That was nothing but a circular argument. He considered asking bin Laden to give back his satellite phone, or at the very least let him use the communications equipment here to call the White House. But the man was crazy, and there was no telling how he might react to such a request, especially since McGarvey had come here with the GPS chip implanted in his body. The U.S. military knew the exact position of this camp, and McGarvey might confirm that bin Laden was here and go ahead with the attack.

His only chance now was to get out of the camp as soon as possible and hope that his escorts brought his telephone with them. Short of that he would have to make it back to Kabul and somehow find a way to call Washington.

The doctor finished closing the small wound. He bandaged it, cleaned up the blood, gave McGarvey a shot and helped him sit up.

"When can I expect your bill?"

The doctor gave McGarvey an owlish look from behind thick glasses. He didn't see the humor. He took off his gloves, tossed them in a bucket and handed McGarvey his sweater.

"Bin Laden is sick, isn't he," McGarvey said. He carefully pulled on his sweater, the simple effort causing sweat to pop out on his forehead.

The doctor turned his back to McGarvey, took the bandana off his head and began untying his gown at the back.

"I think he might be dying," McGarvey pressed. "What is it? Cancer?"

The doctor turned on him. "Don't push your luck," he warned. "All your fancy gadgets and satellites and military hardware won't save you if he wants you dead. This is Afghanistan, Mr. McGarvey, and you have no idea what that really means."

"Are you giving our guest a geography lesson, Dr. Nosair?" bin Laden said from the doorway. He came in with the two mujahedeen who had escorted McGarvey from the cave. If anything his face looked even sallower than before, and it wasn't just because of the kerosene light. The effort of coming down the hill had visibly tired him.

"The sooner this man is gone from here, the better I'll feel," Dr. Nosair said.

"Is he fit to travel?"

The doctor gave McGarvey a critical look. "I've seen our men march for three days with untended bullet wounds. This operation was nothing by comparison. When the anesthetic wears off he'll be in some discomfort, but it shouldn't slow him down much."

Bin Laden held out his hand. The doctor picked up the chip and gave it to him. "To an Afghani farmer this is magic," bin Laden said, studying the device. "It may well be, because now the satellites believe that I am Mr. McGarvey." He pocketed the chip and smiled at McGarvey. "And you have suddenly become one of us. A nonentity."

"What now?" McGarvey asked.

"The good doctor is right, of course. The sooner you are

away from here the better we will all feel. You'll leave immediately, back the same way you came."

"Do we have a deal?"

"I think that we have the beginning of an agreement," bin Laden said. "When President Haynes announces in the United Nations the withdrawal of all foreign troops from the Arabian Peninsula, the retraction of the bounty on my head, and the opening of negotiations with the Saudi government for the repatriation of my family, the first steps will have been taken. We will see it as a sign of good faith."

"What about the rest of it?"

"If all of that comes to pass you have my word that I will make no further moves against the West." Bin Laden was suddenly stern. "But only under those conditions, make that perfectly clear to your President."

"It still leaves the most important reason I came here," McGarvey said evenly. He was thinking of Allen and his family. The bastard was still bargaining for lives, and he was enjoying it.

"When the announcement is made, we will talk again about that and about another matter. You have my word on that as well."

"Don't make the mistake of underestimating us. If you go back on your word we will come after you personally with everything in our power."

Bin Laden smiled benignly. "I am not afraid of death, Mr. McGarvey, are you?"

"I'm respectful of it."

Bin Laden gave him a long, appraising look. "*Insha'Allah*," he said, and he turned to go.

"We want the other three men responsible for the attack on Allen Trumble and his family. That's going to be a part of the deal."

"I'll think about it. But now it's time for you to leave. I'll be waiting for your President's reply. Tell him not to delay."

• • •

McGarvey looked at his watch as he emerged from the crude hospital, and he was surprised to see that it was only a few minutes after 10:00 P.M. After all that had happened he'd only been in the camp for a couple of hours. The anesthetic would wear off soon, but for now he felt okay except for the lack of sleep, proper food and the dull ache that seemed to have settled somewhere just below his left shoulder. He'd been in and out of so many hospitals in his career that he knew what to expect, and he knew how his body was going to react, how much strength he had in reserve, how fast he could move and when to husband his strength so that he'd have something left if and when he needed it. Which was going to have to be very soon if he was going to stop the missile attack.

Hash and Farid, packs slung over their shoulders along with their Kalashnikovs, waited in the darkness. Mohammed, also carrying a pack and a rifle, stood a few feet away, the same crazy look as before on his broad peasant's face. They were to be his escorts back to the Rover parked in the village, and then back to Kabul. But whatever instructions bin Laden had given them about McGarvey's safe passage were going to be ignored by Mohammed. McGarvey could see it in the man's eyes. Mohammed was obviously itching to get out of the camp where somewhere in the mountains there would be an accident.

McGarvey glanced up at the entrance to the cave in the hillside. Bin Laden had the nuclear bomb hidden somewhere, perhaps even here. That was the *only* consideration now; getting it back.

"Who has my things?" he asked.

Mohammed raised his pack a couple of inches off his shoulder, but said nothing. His eyes were wild.

"We'll go now, mista," Hash said.

"I want to see my things first," McGarvey said. "I don't trust this bastard. He looks like a thief."

Hash said something, and Mohammed opened the bundle and dumped the contents in the dust. McGarvey's pistol and spare magazine of ammunition were wrapped in an old rag, but the laptop computer and telephone were missing.

"Where are the rest of my things?"

"The computer stays here. Ali has it," Hash said apologetically.

"What about my telephone?"

Mohammed took it out of his pocket, then laughed uproariously. "I'll give it back to you in Kabul, you'll see."

Hash and Farid in the lead, with Mohammed bringing up the rear, they headed single file through the seemingly deserted camp. But as before McGarvey could feel dozens of pairs of eyes watching from all around. There was no sign that they were getting ready to break camp and go to ground somewhere else, but that could happen as soon as he got out of sight, and it would only take them a couple of hours to bug out.

They crossed the shallow stream at the far side of the camp and started up the steep switchbacks to the crest of the hill two hundred feet above. McGarvey climbed slowly, stumbling from time to time as if he was having a great deal of difficulty. The only way he was going to get his phone back was to kill Mohammed. And with three-to-one odds he needed every advantage he could get, including instilling a false sense of security in them.

Halfway up, McGarvey stopped to catch his breath. He looked down the way they had come, and across the camp to the facing hill. For a second he thought he might be seeing the glow from the tip of a cigarette about where he figured the cave entrance might be. But then it was gone, though he could well imagine that bin Laden himself, or perhaps the man called Ali, was there watching him leave. Ali fit the general description that Trumble had given them of the man sitting silently in the corner at the Khartoum meeting. And bin Laden had been respectful of his opinions. Perhaps he was bin Laden's chief of staff. It was a possibility.

They reached the top of the hill twenty minutes later, and McGarvey stopped again for a minute to catch his breath. The moon was just coming up over the distant mountains, casting a malevolent orange glow on the snow-covered peaks. The doctor was correct about one thing; this was Afghanistan, and no one in the West had any real idea what that meant. The entire country was in chaos; the pressures of the modern world with its dazzling technologies clashing with the centuries-old insular traditions that had either defeated or swallowed every invader ever to cross the Khyber Pass. Even the Russians, with their brutality in the field, had failed to conquer the Afghanis. And there was a lot of doubt that the Taliban, with their fanatical interpretation of the Qoran, would be successful either. A strange place. A fitting place for a man such as bin Laden with his jihad and hatreds.

"Ready?" Hash asked respectfully.

"Yeah," McGarvey said, and they started down the narrow, rocky path when a dark figure suddenly materialized out of the shadows behind some boulders.

Hash and Farid pulled up short and reached for their rifles when the figure said something in Persian, and scrambled up onto the path. It was Sarah.

"I'm coming part of the way with you," she said in English.

"Your father will forbid this," Mohammed told her, angrily.

"Very well. We will wait here until you return to camp and tell him."

"I will use the radio—"

"That is forbidden except for an emergency," Sarah warned sharply. "Or do you wish to disobey not only me, but my father too?"

Mohammed was fuming, but after a beat he shook his head. Maybe there would be two accidents, McGarvey thought. And he wondered if bin Laden knew just how unstable their situation was here.

Sarah carried a short-stock version of the AK-47 slung over her shoulder, the muzzle pointed to the ground. But she had no pack. She fell in beside McGarvey and for the first half-mile or so they moved through the night in silence.

A light breeze had come up, and although it was very cold McGarvey was sweating. The lidocaine had completely worn off and besides the ache beneath his shoulder, there was a very sharp pain in his side from the incision. It was like a toothache, only worse, and he could not completely put it out of his mind. That, and Mohammed's presence at his back, made him edgy. The clock was still running.

"I'd like to ask you a favor," McGarvey said, finally breaking the silence.

Sarah gave him a quizzical look. "What?"

"Mohammed has my things, I would like to have them back."

She shrugged. "When you get back to Kabul. He's been told."

"I'd like them now."

"No," she said. "I have my orders too. We all do. You will have to wait until Kabul." She looked into his face. "I'm sorry Mr. McGarvey. I know about the electronic device that you brought with you. Its significance was explained to me. And it was explained that you must not communicate with your people until you are a long way from here. I think we will be moving from this camp. It will make us all feel better. Safer. Do you understand?"

McGarvey nodded. "We want the killing to finally stop."

"Then I hope you are able to convince your President of this when you get home."

They walked for a long time in silence, the night bitterly cold. McGarvey settled down, concentrating on the march because there was nothing else he could do for the moment.

"Now that you have meet my father, what do you think?" Sarah asked innocently at one point.

The path had dipped below the crest of the hill that overlooked the camp, and it started back up again, the slope gentle at first, but steadily rising. What few trees were here were stunted and gnarled in the thin topsoil. At this altitude they were just below the treeline. McGarvey took a long time to answer. Bin Laden was a monster, but to Sarah he was her father.

"I think that he's getting tired of hiding here in the mountains," McGarvey said. "He wants to go home."

"Wouldn't you?" She smiled wistfully. At that moment she looked like a tomboy, and McGarvey was reminded of his own Liz at that age. "Was the operation painful?" she asked.

"A little, but I'll live. What did your father say about the—incident?"

Sarah stole a glance over her shoulder. Mohammed was far enough back so that he was out of earshot if they spoke softly. "He didn't say anything. I think he is disappointed." It was a very tough admission for her to make.

But it wasn't your fault. If that's what the Qoran is teaching you it's all wrong. "The Taliban are fanatics. But do you suppose they would condone what he tried to do to you?"

"Probably. But sometimes it gets confusing."

"Welcome to the club," McGarvey said. He felt sorry for her, and he wondered about her mother, and her father's other wives and all the siblings. Dinner at the bin Ladens' would be quite a spectacle, if such mixed eating arrangements were possible in a fundamentalist's household.

She looked at him questioningly. "Club?"

"I meant it's the same for everybody. Nobody has all the answers, especially not young people."

She picked up on that with eagerness. "Tell me more about your daughter. Aren't you afraid for her safety because of all the violence in America?"

McGarvey stifled a laugh. "The newspapers have some of it wrong. They like to exaggerate." He swept his arm around the wild mountain scenery. "This isn't exactly a safe haven. And for you Kabul must be even worse."

The comment hurt her. She lowered her eyes. "We don't chose to stay here."

"If you could leave Afghanistan where would you like to go? Riyadh? You have family there."

"London," she said without hesitation. "I'd like to go to school there. My English is good enough, I think."

"Your English is very good."

"I would like to study in school in London, and in the evenings I would go out to see plays, and attend grand openings, and eat in restaurants with my friends. On the weekends we might go driving in the country, maybe go swimming where it's permitted. I would like to see the ocean, and the English Channel. Maybe we could go to Paris through the tunnel on a very fast train." She half closed her eyes happy for that moment. "We wouldn't always eat at McDonald's, there are other places. Places where I might be able to wear a dress, makeup, nylons. And there would be magazines, and television." She smiled. "And movies." She gave McGarvey an excited look. "Does your daughter do all of that?"

"That and more," McGarvey said.

"Does she obey everything you tell her?"

This time McGarvey did laugh. "No. She's a lot like you."

Sarah's face fell and she averted her eyes. McGarvey had said the wrong thing again. "It's against the Qoran for a daughter to disobey her father. It brings great shame to the house."

"It's the same in America, but we're just a little more tolerant of our children," McGarvey said gently. "What would you study in school?"

"Construction engineering and economics so I could continue my father's businesses."

There it was again, McGarvey thought. "You don't have any brothers to take over?"

"They're all too young, and besides I already know more about the business than they do."

"School takes time, maybe four years."

Sarah shook her head adamantly. "I could learn everything I need to know in one year. Maybe less if I studied hard."

McGarvey felt like a heel manipulating her that way, but they needed hard information. If bin Laden was dying, and didn't have much time left—which apparently he didn't from the things Sarah was saying—then he was getting desperate now. He'd gotten hold of a nuclear weapon and he meant to use it as a lever to assure his family's safety.

"Then what, after you finish school?" he asked. "Would you make your headquarters in Riyadh?"

"Maybe," she said breezily. "Maybe Yemen, or the Sudan. Of course my family has interests in a lot of places. Germany, Brazil, Japan."

"The United States," McGarvey suggested.

Her moods were mercurial. "Did you know that the original McDonald's is in Downey, California?"

He had to smile. "No, I didn't."

"It is. I'd like to go there to see it."

Western culture was infectious. A lot of people, her father included, thought it was a disease to be stamped out, or at the very least, to be contained. He didn't think she spoke like this with him.

"But first there has to be peace," McGarvey said. "The killing has to stop."

She gave him a sharp, shrewd look. "To you my father is a terrorist. To us he is a warrior for justice, just like you claim you were in Kosovo."

"Helping Muslims."

"Yes, that surprised us at first," she admitted. "But it was just a matter of influence. Washington over the rest of the world."

"Do you really believe that?"

"What else can we believe?" she shot back. "The list of people you have dominated either with your military or with your economics goes on and on, and there's no end in sight."

"Do you think that your father has the answers by killing innocent people?"

"There are no innocents in the world."

It was the same circular argument used by terrorists around the world. On the one hand they claimed to hate the United States government, but not the people. Yet their mission was to kill those people. What they couldn't—or wouldn't—understand, they attacked; what they couldn't build, they destroyed. And they had no tolerance for any view but their own. The author Salman Rushdie had to go into hiding for years because of something he'd written.

Two hundred years ago Voltaire wrote that more than half the habitable world was still peopled with two-footed animals who lived in the horrible state approaching pure nature, existing with difficulty, scarcely enjoying the gift of speech, scarcely perceiving that they were unfortunate, and living and dying almost without knowing it. Nothing much had changed since then, McGarvey thought. The real problem was that the United States had the audacity to live well and to show the rest of the world what it was missing.

They fell into a troubled silence as they continued up to the saddle in the mountains that formed a pass. They'd crossed over it on the way up here, and it was the highest point on the trip. From there it would be downhill to the resting place at the stream, and below that the long valley leading down to the village where the Rover was parked.

McGarvey could see that Sarah was puzzled. She was trying to reconcile the things he had come here to represent with what her father had taught her. On the one hand she wanted to go to the West to see with her own eyes what it was all about. While on the other hand she wanted to believe that *everything* in the West was bad. But it was hard for her to understand how music, and fashion, and light and life were evil, while the mountains of Afghanistan and what they were doing from here was good. She was mature enough to understand that what she was being told wasn't necessarily all true, but she was still young enough so that she couldn't make up her own mind. Part of that was the culture into which she'd been born, repressive to women, but a large part of it was that she was still just a kid.

There was some snow on the path for the last hundred yards or so, but the wind was blowing strongly enough that their footprints from earlier were already gone. A long, ragged plume of snow was blowing from the top of a distant mountain, lit by the bright moon so that it looked as if there was a forest fire raging up there. The scene from the top, looking both ways toward the valleys on either side was primordial. There were no lights, no roads, nothing to suggest that people lived up here, or ever had come this way except for the snow-covered path they stood on.

Sarah took Mohammed a few yards farther along the path and they had a long conference while McGarvey smoked a cigarette.

When she was finished she came back, leaving Mohammed looking even more sullen than before.

"Mohammed understands that you are bringing a very important message back to your President from my father," she said. "No harm will come to you. He knows that he would have to answer to all of us if it did."

"Thank you," McGarvey said.

A faint smile creased her lips. "But don't provoke him, Mr. McGarvey. Men such as Mohammed are creatures of—passion."

It was an odd thing for her to say, but then she was a young woman of very great contrasts because of her unbringing.

"I'll behave myself." McGarvey returned the smile. He put out his hand.

She hesitated, but then she shook his hand, hers tiny and cool in his. "Goodbye," she said. "Allah go with you."

"And with you," McGarvey said.

ELEVEN

Bin Laden's Camp

The beam of a flashlight bounced off the narrowing walls of the cave, and a moment later Osama bin Laden, stoop-shouldered, shuffled into sight. He stopped and leaned heavily on his ornately carved wooden cane, a gift from Sarah, and shined the light back the way he had come. He held his breath to listen for sounds of footsteps behind him. But the tiny chamber he'd come to was silent, as were the passageways behind him. He couldn't even hear the sounds of the generator lost behind millions of tons of solid rock.

He turned back, and played the flashlight beam into the narrow grotto that they'd discovered at the extreme end of the system of caves. It was at a higher elevation than the rest of the chambers, and was completely free of water. Cold, but dry as a desert, yet he thought that he could feel heat coming from inside. He shivered in anticipation.

The Americans had come as he knew they would. First the ineffectual fool from Riyadh, and then the man from Washington, who was a much more dangerous adversary than they'd ever faced, if Ali was to be believed. And his chief of staff *was* to be believed; the man never made a mistake. Never. He was a heathen, but a very useful tool. Do not blame the rapier for its penetrating insensitivity, it's not the sword that kills the enemy, it is the hand that directs the thrust.

He stooped so that he would not hit his head on the low roof and entered the inner chamber. About ten meters long and barely three wide, the grotto was nothing more than a passageway deeper into the mountain. But it stopped at a solid wall of rock. There was little or no airflow back here, and the air smelled ancient, indicating that there was no other way in or out except by the series of passages from the front.

For all of his life bin Laden had been surrounded by people; sometimes by his enemies, but for most of the time by his friends. But he'd always felt desperately alone. Five times a day at his prayers, and then at night with sleep that usually came only after a very long struggle, he was isolated with his own thoughts, which for the most part centered on dreams of hate and especially absolution, a concept he'd never really understood as a young man, but one that had become increasingly important to him as he grew older, and especially in this last, horrible year.

Except for a fiberglass case about a meter and a half on a side and half that deep, which rested on a slightly larger wooden crate, the chamber was empty. Bin Laden hesitated for a minute or so at the entrance, his light playing on the container.

In the beginning the struggle had seemed so simple to him. It had never been about religion, at least not in the sense that Westerners thought it was. Islam, Judaism and Christianity were fundamentally the same; they all believed in one God and the same prophets. It was a matter of interpretation, and a matter of living within a religion. The Jews blamed everyone else for their problems, as they always had, and they arrogantly believed that they, and they alone, were the chosen people. They wanted to take over their corner of the world, which in reality had always belonged to the Arabs, and they were willing to murder anyone who stood in their way. He hated them with everything in his soul. The Christians, on the other hand, led by the Americans, only paid lip service to their religion. For them the one true God was money. Their only aim since the Crusades was the rape and pillage of the world. In some ways even more important than the need for oil was the need to dominate the entire planet. To do this they were engaged in the systematic poisoning of the world with their industrial pollution, their technology and worst of all with their warped ideas. The struggle, in bin Laden's estimation, was for nothing less than the minds and souls of Muslims to practice their lifestyle wherever they lived.

Lately, however, he had begun to question the methods he had used in the jihad. Every blow he'd struck had turned out to be nothing more than a pinprick. Bows and arrows against tanks. Valiant, but meaningless.

But it was difficult, and maybe even impossible, for him to let go of the hate and fear and even shame that he had carried deep inside of him for so long.

He closed his eyes for a moment. The woman's name was Lynn Larkin, and she worked for the CIA as a field agent, though her being in Afghanistan was insanity. Most of the time she hid her identity as a woman as she went from the site of one firefight to another, bringing the latest intelligence information on Russian positions and troop movements to the freedom fighters. When she was in Kabul she wore the proper clothing, and although there were rumors, no one knew for sure that Lynn Larkin, the woman in Kabul, was the same person as Lawrence Larsen, the CIA spy in the field.

It was during the battle for Charikar that bin Laden came head-to-head with her. He wanted to attack the city because he had a gut feeling that the attack would be successful. The troops he was leading had had no clearcut victories in several months, and they were beginning to question the Saudi rich kid's abilities as a battlefield commander. The CIA, however, advised against the attack. The city was too well fortified. The Russians had secretly brought in extra troops and heavy guns over the past several days in anticipation of just such an attack.

"You'll get yourself and your men killed if you go in there now," the woman insisted.

She was right, and bin Laden was wrong. In the attack he'd lost eighteen out of twenty of his men, and would have been killed himself except that the woman had crawled across a hundred meters of no man's land in the middle of the night, and half-dragged, half-carried him back to safety.

"You stupid fool," she said, bandaging his wounds. In the fight she'd lost her hat, and her blond hair fell around her ears and forehead revealing who she was.

Bin Laden remembered the deep, deep shame he'd felt at that moment. The other two men who'd she'd brought back started to laugh, and something snapped inside of him. He pulled out his pistol and shot both of them in the head, killing them instantly.

Lynn Larkin reared back and struggled to reach her gun as bin Laden turned his pistol on her and shot her point-blank in the face.

Before morning he burned her body, and then walked twenty kilometers to the nearest enclave of freedom fighters where he told them that the CIA had betrayed them, and that the Russians weren't their only enemy. The Americans in fact were worse.

He opened his eyes. A slight sheen of sweat dampened his forehead from the pain of his illness, and from the pain of his humiliation.

He approached the container, dragging his left leg behind him. The legend stenciled on the top cover was in English. Written below that was MADE IN CHINA. That brought a smile to his lips. Life was a matter of interpretation, he'd come to understand in the last year. It was nothing more than a mirror reflection of their everlasting existence in heaven; a wonderous gift not to be taken lightly. It was to be appreciated, to be honored. He'd sometimes seen that idea reflected in the eyes of his wives and children, but he'd never seen it so strongly and so fiercely proud as he saw it in the eyes of Sarah.

He closed his eyes again, and his lips compressed in pain. How to reconcile the jihad with her smile? How to understand Mohammed Toorak's brutal attack on her body? Or McGarvey's actions at the river. *Believe in me and I will be your salvation.* Sarah had been wrong to expose herself so wantonly. But Mohammed had twisted their religion to justify his animal lust. And McGarvey had acted . . . how, bin Laden asked himself. Like a father? Would he have done the same thing if it had been McGarvey's daughter? It was a question that he could not answer, because Sarah was much more than just a daughter to him; when he looked at her it was as if he were looking into the mirror image of himself.

Of all his children she was the only one who had remained at his side without question since his name had been linked to terrorism. Even when he said publicly that all Americans should be killed whenever and wherever they could be found, she did not turn away from him. Never once had he seen a questioning look in her eyes for something he'd said or done. She was his flesh and blood by birth, but she was also his flesh and blood by word and deed, right down to the bottom of her heart and soul.

When she was twelve in Khartoum, bin Laden had called her to his sitting room to punish her. Her brother, Sa'lid had caught her reading a years-old issue of an American teen magazine called *Tiger Beat*, and brought the magazine to their father.

When she came into the room she bowed her head, but there was a look of defiance on her face. Bin Laden held up the magazine.

"Is this yours?" he demanded.

She raised her eyes. "Obviously," she told him, her voice dripping with sarcasm.

For a moment a black rage threatened to blot out his sanity. But then he regained his control. "Where did you get it?"

She said nothing, but she didn't look away.

"You will answer me."

She shook her head.

"What did you expect to learn from this filth?" he demanded, "Tell me at least that much."

"The truth."

"The truth," bin Laden muttered. He was amazed. "What truth?"

"There are no Godless heathens in that magazine. No murderers of Muslims. No Jews. Only children like me having fun—"

"Stop!" bin Laden roared. "You know nothing about the truth." He threw down the magazine, picked up the long, whippy willow stick lying beside him and went to her. She looked up at him, no fear, only rebellion in her eyes. "You will tell me the name of the person who gave you the magazine."

"No, Father," she said.

Bin Laden pulled her around by the arm, and struck her in the backs of her legs with the willow stick. She took a half-step forward, but she did not cry out.

"The name," he said, but she did not answer him, so he struck her again on the backs of the legs, and then on her buttocks, and back, and legs again. He was crazy with rage and with fear that he was losing the most precious thing in his life to the very system he had dedicated his life to destroying.

She was wearing a white chador. Bin Laden's upraised hand stopped in midswing. There was blood on her back. He let go of her arm and stepped back, aghast at what he had done to his child. In the name of Allah, he had hurt her.

She looked up at him. "I'm not afraid of the truth, Father," she said in a very strong voice. "Are you?"

He lowered his hand, and let the willow stick fall to the floor. "No, child, I am not afraid of the truth," he answered. An overwhelming shame for what he had done, and tenderness for his daughter came over him. He wanted to protect her, and all he had done was cause her pain.

He held out his arms for her, and without a moment's hesitation she came to him and he held her close.

"I'm sorry, Father," she sobbed.

"Don't be," he comforted her. "But I want you to be wary of the truth—or what *seems* to be the truth—until you are old enough and wise enough to recognize lies for what they are."

"Yes, Father," she said. "I'll try."

Bin Laden opened his eyes. Nothing was ever more clear to him than his love for his daughter, then or now. Yet at this moment he felt as if he was seeing everything with a crystal purity, something never possible before. Years ago the infidel British philosopher Bertrand Russell said that for centuries we've been told that God can move mountains, and a lot of people believed it. Nowadays we say that atomic bombs can move mountains and *everybody* believes it.

What did he believe, bin Laden asked himself. What was the truth this time? The gates to Paradise were never more bright, but the path never more dark.

Laying his cane aside, and awkwardly holding the flashlight under his right arm, he undid the four catches at the corners of the container, removed the top cover and laid it on the floor. He unfolded the thick rubber and fabric covering, exposing an inner aluminum cover. This he unlocked with a four-digit code on a keypad. The panel swung open, revealing four metal catches, which he slid back, releasing the top of the case. He pulled this off with some difficulty because it was heavy, and set it on the floor.

He was sure that he could feel the heat coming off the exposed mechanism now, even though he knew it was just his imagination. In this state the nuclear weapon was perfectly harmless; cool to the touch, leaking no radiation, impossible to accidentally detonate, and just as impossible to detect by any means other than disassembly.

Most of the device was shrouded by sealed covers, only some brightly colored wires came together in neatly bound thick bundles to the control mechanism, which was about the size of a hardcover book, attached to the lower right corner of the inner case. A display screen with room for twelve digits and symbols topped what appeared to be the keypad for an advanced scientific calculator. The first code activated the control circuitry. The second code determined how the weapon was to be fired: by a direct timer with as much as a thirty-six-hour delay; by a remote control device that could, depending on conditions, be effective up to five miles away; or by an incoming signal to the weapon's on-board satellite receiver. The frequency, duration and built-in code in the remote firing signal could be determined by the weapon's keypad.

Complicated, but exquisitely failsafe and simple. Once the weapon was activated nothing could stop it.

Bin Laden's eyes strayed to the metal identification plate to the right of the keypad. On it was stamped the serial number and the factory where the bomb had been assembled.

The irony would have been sweet, he told himself. And this would have been only the first of many blows. But he was getting tired of the fight, and he felt a deep sense of awe and even dread standing this close to so much power. He was going to have many difficulties convincing the others of his change of heart. But in time they too would come to see the wisdom of his decision.

He reassembled the bomb case, making sure that all the locks and catches were firmly in place, then picked up his cane and headed back. Deep down he felt a sense of failure, and yet he was looking forward to the new challenge. He didn't have much time left so he would have to work hard to convince a skeptical world that all he wanted was a Muslim peace. And he would have to work even harder to control his hate, which at times threatened to block out all reason and sanity. But it could be done, because it had to be done.

The grotto was nearly a half-kilometer into the mountainside, so it took him almost ten minutes to make his way to the front chambers. It was two in the morning and everyone but a few guards were down for the night. He felt a little sorrow for his men, most of whom would have nowhere to go after he quit. Some of them would probably join the rebels in the north to fight the Taliban. But for many of them there would be nothing. They would be disappointed, even angry, but it could not be helped.

"Insha'Allah," he murmured softly. He switched off the flashlight, pocketed it and shuffled down the final tunnel to the opening in the hillside. He needed fresh air after the confines of the cave.

The two guards outside were wrapped in blankets against the chill night air. When bin Laden appeared they started to get up, but he waved them down.

"All is quiet tonight?" he asked.

"Yes, sir," one of them replied.

They were safe here, yet bin Laden, out of long habit, studied the brilliant sky for the fast moving pinpoint of light from a satellite passing overhead, even though he knew that the next one wasn't due for another two hours. They'd learned to time their movements by the satellite passes, and schedule their most important work for when the skies were overcast and the satellites were blind.

Someone came out from the medical hut and started up the hill. Instinctively bin Laden stepped back inside the cave, his eyes narrowing as he watched the man approach. But then he recognized it was his chief of staff and he relaxed.

Ali Bahmad, whose voice had oftentimes been the only one of reason, had surprisingly been against opening negotiations with the Americans. He predicted it would lead to more trouble than they could imagine. His predictions were disturbing, all the more so because Bahmad had worked in the West, and he knew the Western mind as well as any Muslim could.

As bin Laden watched Bahmad make his way up the hill he realized that after eight years he really didn't know his chief of staff as well as he should. Brilliant, highly trained, capable, efficient, but as cold as the winds off the high peaks of the Hindu Kush. And yet bin Laden had seen Bahmad do so many little kindnesses for the few children in the camp, and especially for Sarah. She was smitten by him because he had lived in the West and wasn't afraid of it like so many others here. They would sometimes sit for hours talking about London and Washington where Bahmad had once been stationed with the British Secret Intelligence Service.

Bin Laden had also listened to Bahmad play the violin; his long, delicately thin, perfectly manicured fingers caressing the strings as if they were a woman's thighs. Yet for all his talents, including combat training, and his ruthlessness—it was he who had ordered and engineered the killings of Allen Trumble and his family—Bahmad could have passed for a shopkeeper almost anywhere in the world. His skin was pale, his English perfect, and his mannerisms Western. Quiet, mild, even studious looking, he was very short, with plain features, a round undistinguished face, balding, with a slight paunch, he posed no threat to anyone.

Born of an Egyptian mother and a Yemeni father, he was in his forties now, but he came up the hill with the grace of a gazelle, his movements like everything else about him, surprisingly swift and sure.

He'd been educated at the American University in Beirut, but after his parents had been killed in an Israeli bombing raid, he'd slipped out of the city to work with a PLO cell. After a couple of years of killing silently in the night, he came to the attention of Yasir Arafat who recognized not only his unique intelligence and special skills, but his burning drive and utter fearlessness. Bahmad was the perfect soldier.

Two years after that, he showed up suddenly at Oxford on beautifully forged papers with a solid background, where he studied for and received his degree in Middle East studies. He was recruited by British intelligence right out of school, and for a few years he worked in London as an analyst. In the late eighties he was sent to the U.S. on an exchange program to work for the CIA and National Security Agency, generating Middle East position papers for the National Security Council.

But then he resigned, and quietly slipped back to Lebanon and Arafat when he felt that some uncomfortable questions were about to be asked of him. Besides, he admitted to Arafat, he felt that he could do more for the PLO than simply pass along intelligence information.

The fact of the matter, Arafat told bin Laden, was that Bahmad wanted to kill people. He *needed* to kill, perhaps as a retribution for his parents' murders.

But because of the Camp David Accords and other agreements, Arafat's position on the West began to soften, and he no longer had need for men such as Bahmad. The feeling was mutual. It was then, after the Russians had pulled out of Afghanistan, and the Soviet Union had disintegrated, that bin Laden had quietly recruited him. Since that time Bahmad had been the mastermind behind every terrorist attack that the West blamed on bin Laden. But his planning had been so good that no Western police agency had ever been able to come up with solid proof that bin Laden had been behind any of the attacks. Nor did any Western intelligence agency know about Bahmad's connection, or even his existence: His death had been faked in an Israeli raid in Lebanon.

Bin Laden stepped out of the cave as Bahmad reached the entrance. "You're up late tonight."

"So are you," Bahmad said mildly. "Your toy is still safe?"

Bin Laden nodded. "Is everything all right?"

Bahmad glanced at the guards, his expression bland, as if he was a tailor measuring them for suits. "It's a good thing for us that I didn't destroy McGarvey's satellite phone as you ordered. He's going to need it. The transmitter we took out of his body no longer works."

Bin Laden's jaw tightened. "What happened to it?"

"The stupid doctor admitted he dropped it on the floor."

"The American monitors will believe that it has malfunctioned, either that or it's out of range, its signal blocked. Where is the problem?"

"The problem is, Osama, that there is a third possibility they may be considering," Bahmad said cooly. "McGarvey may have been killed, his body destroyed and the transmitter with it. But the exact location of this installation has

already been pinpointed to within a couple of meters." He shrugged. "They know exactly where you are, and for whatever the reason McGarvey is no longer a consideration for them. Do you see where I am taking this?"

"He came here to bargain with me, not lead an attack."

Bahmad smiled slightly. "It was really quite brilliant of you to give them that serial number. It got their attention. But now they will do anything to stop you from using it. If they believe McGarvey is dead, they'll try to kill you."

"Send someone after McGarvey."

"I already have. But the transmitter has been down four hours now, I think that we should leave immediately, at least until we get word that McGarvey has made his call."

"Do you expect me to scurry off someplace else to hide?" bin Laden demanded.

"That's exactly what I'm suggesting."

"I'll go back to my quarters—"

"McGarvey's device transmitted the exact coordinates of this very spot. Their smart bombs are accurate enough to come right down the tunnel. You would die, and the cave would be sealed for all time."

"Send Sarah to me, we'll talk."

"Sarah is gone," Bahmad said.

"Gone? Where?"

"She was worried about Mohammed, so she decided to go with them at least part of the way."

"And you let her go?" bin Laden roared.

Bahmad was unmoved. "You have very little control over your daughter, what do you expect of me?" His expression softened. "If something were to happen here tonight she's better off away from the camp. I sent one of my men after them. He'll get word to McGarvey and bring Sarah back here."

Bin Laden looked up at the sky. If the Americans attacked tonight the jihad would already have been lost. Any further talks between them would be impossible. The only thing left would be retribution. A strike or strikes so devastating that no American would ever feel safe again. So devastating that the American government would have to retaliate with all of its might, with every means at its disposal. It would finally be a war that bin Laden knew he could not win.

He shook his head. "I don't think the Americans will attack us so soon. They take time to think about actions like that. Talk them over with their military commanders, and maybe some key Congressmen. When your man gets word to McGarvey he can make a telephone call to the CIA to let them know he has not been harmed." Bin Laden spread his hands and smiled. "You see, there is no problem."

"Are you willing to bet your life on it, Osama?" Bahmad asked.

Bin Laden nodded without hesitation. "Yes, I am," he said. *"Insha'Allah."*

CIA Headquarters

DCI Roland Murphy put down his White House phone and looked up as the connecting door from the deputy director of Operations office opened, not at all surprised to see Otto Rencke standing there, his wild red hair flying everywhere. It was coming up on 6:00 P.M. "I haven't heard anything new, but you already know that."

"Oh, boy, I think they're getting set to make a big mistake," Rencke gushed. "They've got some of the right reasons, but the wrong interp. They're not looking close enough, ya know."

"By they, I take it you mean the White House," Murphy said. He'd seen Rencke in one of his "moods" before, but nothing quite like this.

"The National Security Council. They're on their way over there right now. You gotta stop them, General."

"I just got the call myself, Otto. We're going to have a teleconference in ten minutes, and the President's going to want my best recommendation."

"I want seventy-two hours," Rencke said.

Murphy shook his head. "I don't think they'd give me twelve. Mac is off the air, and unless you have something for me, we have to assume that he's dead and the chip has been destroyed. You've seen the data."

"All right, forty-eight hours then. At least long enough for Mac to get back to Kabul. Someplace where he can call us."

"If he died four hours ago, they'll be getting set to move out of there. The President wants to hit the bastards right now. Show them that we can move fast when we want to."

"You don't understand, General, Mac is still alive." Rencke was deeply distressed. Murphy didn't know what Otto was going to do, but when geniuses suddenly started getting excited and raising their voices, you listened.

"You have ten minutes to convince me."

Rencke came around the desk, and Murphy moved aside so that he could get to the computer. Otto brought up an action file that moved in slow motion. Along the bottom of the screen was a time-elapsed bar starting forty-eight hours ago. Displayed on the screen was a detailed map of the section of Afghanistan northwest of Charikar. It was constantly shifting to keep a small red icon that was moving through the mountains centered, and the time bar filled in.

"Okay, they take him from the Inter-Continental, and they head north past the airport, where they stop once—" Rencke looked up. "Probably a military patrol. But no problemo, they're bin Laden's boys. Around Bagram they stop for awhile."

"Another checkpoint," Murphy suggested.

"They switched cars," Rencke said. "After they made the second stop, Mac's transmitter moves about five meters to the west, but at a direct ninety-degree angle to the line it was moving in."

"I don't understand."

"When a car makes a turn, even a sharp turn like at an intersection, there's a radius of curve. Cars just don't turn on a dime like people do."

"You're saying that they stopped the car, Mac got out and walked over to another car, which took off in the opposite direction twenty minutes later."

"Right. And now you know what I'm looking for here. The anomalies that tell us something," Rencke said. "They head north after that, past the air base, and then northwest, but very slowly now. They're off the highway and probably off even dirt roads. They're in the mountains."

"Then he goes on foot," Murphy said.

Rencke used the mouse to speed up the sequence until about eight hours ago. With a few keystrokes he brought up a topographic overlay so that they were seeing elevations as well as the simple north-south orientation.

"This is bin Laden's camp," Rencke said. "We've had one satellite pass to confirm that there're a lot more people down there than you'd expect to see in a nomad camp." Rencke looked up. "Anyway, the only reason nomads go up into the high mountains in summer is for grazing land." He grinned like a kid. "But they screwed up this time."

"What do you mean?"

"No goats," Rencke said. "Lots of people, a couple of big animals, maybe camels, a couple of horses, but no goats."

The analysts over at the NRO had missed that one, but then Otto wasn't working for them. "All right. In the next couple of hours Mac's signal disappears once, reappears less than an hour later, then disappears for good. What's your take on that sequence?"

"Look at the overlay," Rencke said. He sped up the sequence. The icon moved down into the valley, and then back up the hill on the other side where it disappeared. "Bin Laden's den of iniquity. He invites Mac in for a bite to eat and a chat. But something happens in there, and Mac's signal suddenly reappears." Rencke looked up again. "Too soon, too soon, General, don't ya get it?"

"They weren't in there for very long."

"Exactamundo. Bin Laden tells us he's got a nuclear weapon and he wants to parley. But they only chat for a few minutes? Wrong answer, recruit. Something went haywire in there, and you just gotta ask yourself what that might be, ya know."

Rencke hit another couple of keys and the screen was suddenly split, the new half showing a pair of squiggly lines moving left to right, traces on an oscilloscope. "Okay, this is a recording of Mac's uplink with our satellite. The top line is before he went into bin Laden's cave, and the bottom line is when he came out."

Murphy studied them. "Are they different?" he asked. "Because if they are I don't see it. They look the same to me."

"Did to me too, at first," Rencke admitted. "So I put both signals through a spectrum analyzer." He brought up a new display with two sets of signals running left to right. This time it was clear that the bottom signal was slightly different from the top one. It looked as if the spikes had shifted a tiny amount to the right.

"It's a phase shift, actually. But the guys downstairs are big time for sure that this wasn't caused by low battery strength, or a component's tolerance variation in the chip. This was an induced shift." Rencke grinned like a kid at Christmas. "I told them to try a metal detector, like we use downstairs at the front door, on one of the test chips." He brought up a third trace, which exactly matched the one directly above it. They were identical. "Bingo," Rencke said. "They got wise to something, ran a metal detector over Mac, and found it."

Murphy looked at the screen in amazement. Rencke wasn't afraid of taking an idea and running with it wherever it might go, unlike just about all of official Washington. He didn't give a damn about his job, his only concern was for McGarvey's safety. Murphy looked away from the monitor. "All you're telling me is why they killed him, Otto. I'm sorry—"

"Another wrong answer, recruit. That's two in a row." Rencke restored the map with its overlay and started the time bar again. "Okay, he moves out of the cave and down the hill into a hut." Before Murphy could ask how he knew it was a hut, Otto pulled up a second overlay on the map. This one was a screened down image taken of the camp by one of the satellites. The position of the icon exactly matched a small building. "That picture was taken later, but the positions match up," Rencke said. "A few minutes later the signal disappears for good."

"So they took him inside a building and killed him," Murphy said.

"No, sir. An earlier picture shows a man in a white gown entering the building. A doctor. That's a medical hut. They took Mac in there to remove the chip. Then they destroyed it. Don't you see? Mac is still alive."

Murphy let out a pent-up breath. "Is that it, Otto?"

Rencke realized that he had not made a good case, and his expression dropped. "General, I know he's alive. I can feel it in my gut."

"I understand. But that doesn't alter the fact that we're dealing with a madman who apparently wants to play games with us over a nuclear weapon. A man who is responsible for the deaths of hundreds, maybe thousands of people including Allen Trumble and his wife and children."

"Give him a chance—"

"I'll present this to the President, but he's not going to buy it, Otto. He'll want more."

"But we need time, General. Goddammit, we have to give Mac more time before we go charging in."

"Is there any way that you can get through to him on his satellite phone?"

Rencke shook his head. "I tried, but he's still got it switched to the simplex mode—send only. He's in a position where he can't call out, and he doesn't want an incoming."

"Or he's dead," Murphy suggested softly.

"He's not," Rencke snapped. He looked desperately over at the White House phone that connected directly with the President. "I could pull down the entire White House communications center so that the order couldn't go out."

Murphy said nothing, though he suspected that Rencke was probably not exaggerating.

"I could even get into the fleet's command and control system so that they couldn't so much as fart let alone launch a cruise missile."

"I imagine you could."

"I could shut down this entire town, and it'd be easier than you can possibly imagine."

"I'm sure of that too, Otto," Murphy said tiredly. "I'll try to buy us as much time as I can. But I don't think he'll listen to me unless you come up with something more convincing. There's just too much at stake."

Rencke gave Murphy a bleak look. "Tell them not to miss. Because if they do, and bin Laden survives, he'll come after us with a vengeance."

Murphy nodded. "Don't say anything to his wife or daughter, okay?"

"Yeah," Otto replied glumly. "Whatta bummer."

CVN 70 *Carl Vinson*

The eastern horizon over the Arabian Sea was starting to show the first hints of a cloudless dawn when the battle group commander, Admiral Steph Earle, the Duke of Earl, put down the telephone on the bridge. He'd had a five-minute conversation with the President of the United States. There was absolutely no doubt in his mind about the mission.

He turned to the *Carl Vinson*'s skipper, Captain Robert Twinning. "Final Justice is a go, Captain. You're free to launch on your command."

"Aye, aye, Admiral," Twinning said. He reached for the growler phone.

"Give 'em hell, Bob," Earle said.

Twinning looked up and grinned. "That bastard'll never know what hit him."

TWELVE

In the Afghan Mountains

They reached the first stopping point at the pool above the waterfall just as dawn reached the upper peaks. Hash and Farid, who had taken the lead, had talked in soft tones during the all night trek, but Mohammed in the rear had not uttered a single word. McGarvey had watched for an opening, but it was useless. In order to get to his phone he would have to kill all three of them. But he had needed their help to get this far. Looking around now at the somewhat familiar surroundings he was sure for the first time that he could find his way back to the Rover, and then down to Kabul from here.

They had stopped a couple of times to eat some nan and drink cold tea, but they'd been anxious to get down from the snow and cold in the high passes, so they hadn't lingered long.

They had made good progress, and providing that the chip was still working, McGarvey figured they might even make it into Kabul before the twenty-four hours were up. He'd been counting on that up until now, because there was no other choice. Nothing would give him more satisfaction than going head-to-head with Mohammed, but he didn't want to hurt the other two. There was no reason for it.

Despite the operation and his lack of sleep he felt surprisingly good, and with the morning sun his spirits were somehow bouyed up. It might be possible after all to avert the worst disaster the U.S. ever had to face.

"We'll rest here for one hour," Hash said, and Farid nodded his approval.

"Sounds good to me," McGarvey agreed.

Mohammed laid down his pack and went down to the river to fill the canteens as Hash and Farid gathered some wood and started a small campfire. They worked together with a quiet efficiency at something they had done many many times before. Wherever bin Laden had recruited them from they were truly Afghani mountain men now; a fiercely proud, self-sufficient people whose strength seemed nearly boundless. They were as comfortable here as an American teenager would be at a mall back home. The cultural gap was almost beyond bridging. Yet, sitting on a rock and smoking a cigarette as he watched them work, he was struck again by the contradictions Sarah was facing, which somehow made her seem fragile. She was as tough as a woman in this culture had to be, and yet there was a tender side to her that was painful to observe. He'd seen it in her eyes when he was telling her about food and fashions in the West, and especially about his own daughter, Elizabeth. And in the way her father had so peremptorily dismissed her at the cave entrance after her ordeal. No love there, or at least no outward signs of it, and her eyes had dropped in disappointment and resignation. If it had been Liz in the same situation, McGarvey knew that he would have given her a hug, told her that she had done a terrific job, and would have taken Mohammed apart piece by piece.

Another line from Voltaire came to him: He who is merely just is severe. Was that part of bin Laden's ethic up here in the mountains? Was he looking so hard for a Muslim justice that he couldn't allow himself the tender emotions of a father?

For a time he had considered the idea that the incident at the upper pool had been staged. But he decided against it. The look of self-righteous anger on Mohammed's face, and Sarah's fear and shame had been genuine. No acting there. Mohammed had been trying to rape her. So why the hell hadn't bin Laden done something about it? The cultural gap was vast, but goddammit, being a father was the same everywhere, wasn't it?

"How are you feeling now, mista?" Hash asked. The climb down to the valley wouldn't be easy, but after that it'd get better. McGarvey had thought about that last climb all the way back from the camp. The wound in his side ached, and his left shoulder continued to give him trouble, but his legs were still fine. Fencing did that for him.

"If we get something to eat first, I'll be okay," McGarvey said. "Unless you're planning to starve me to death."

Mohammed, who had come back from the river, laughed uproariously. It reminded McGarvey of the wildlife films he'd see in which hyenas laughed as they circled in for the kill. Mohammed was waiting for the excuse, any excuse to go head-to-head with him.

"We've got plenty of food, you'll see," Hash said. He gave Mohammed a nervous look. "Pretty soon you'll be home and everything will be A-okay."

Farid put two tin pots of water on the fire to boil. Into one he threw a handful of black tea, and into the other a couple of handfuls of brown rice and bits of something that might have been dried lamb or maybe fish. Almost immediately it began to smell good, and McGarvey decided that he had been gone from home way too long. Then the dark thought came to him that Allen Trumble had probably felt the same thing when he got back to Washington with his family.

"It's time for prayers," Mohammed told them. He and the other two went down to the pool to wash up, and this time he took the bundle containing McGarvey's gun with him.

McGarvey watched them for a couple of minutes, looking for an opening, some way to separate Mohammed from the others and kill him. But at least for now that was not possible.

He sat down on the soft sand, his back against a rock and started to put together exactly what he was going to tell Murphy to stop the attack. That came first, but when he got back to Washington he would be facing an even tougher challenge; convincing the President and his National Security Council, and especially Dennis Berndt, that bin Laden did not want to use the bomb, but would if he was pushed.

He closed his eyes for a moment, and he saw the bloody GPS chip falling from the doctor's hand. He could hear the metallic clink as it hit the edge of the bucket. Until he was back in Kabul and his telephone was returned to him, the chip was his only link with the CIA. He hoped that it hadn't been damaged. If it had malfunctioned God only knew how the President was reacting.

Bin Laden's Camp

Talking with McGarvey had been in some way more disturbing to Sarah than Mohammed's nearly successful attempt to rape her. Had he succeeded he would have been sent back to Kabul, but she would have borne the brunt of her father's rage, and that of all the mujahedeen. She should not have insisted on going to Kabul in the first place. She had no business out in the mountain wilderness alone with four men—one of them an infidel. And she should not have bared her body so wantonly. She had no modesty. She could hear the words coming from her father's lips. It was a sentiment that would be shared by her mother and especially her younger brothers. She'd brought dishonor to the House of bin Laden, and no deed of hers could ever erase the stigma.

It hadn't been like this in Switzerland. She'd been watched very closely of course, but she'd been allowed to read books, attend classes with the other girls, watch television. It was wonderful. Free. Easy. Happy. Relaxed. And yet if she had known then what she would have to come back to, she wondered if she would have gone to Switzerland in the first place. Or, once she was there, if she wouldn't have run away, to London or Paris or Rome, somewhere they could not find her. Where she could have started a new life.

Topping the last rise above the camp at the same moment the sun appeared between a pair of snow-covered peaks far to the east, she pulled up. The return trip had taken longer because she had been lost in thought, struggling with a host of new emotions and new ideas. She'd also been delayed for a few minutes when she'd spotted someone coming up the trail toward her. She'd hidden herself in the rocks until she got a good look at the man as he passed, recognizing him as one of Ali Bahmad's special soldiers. She had debated following him to find out what he was up to. But in the end she decided that she'd done as much as she could, and it was time to get back.

McGarvey's presence had been so disturbing to her because he had given life to her most secret dreams about someday leaving the mountains for good. He was the first American man she had ever met, and certainly the first Western man she'd ever spent any length of time with. He was older than her own father, and she had no romantic illusions about him, or at least not many—he had seen her naked—but he had turned her head with his easy attitude and relaxed self-confidence as completely as the most ardent suitor could ever do.

The camp below was dark, and it struck her all at once that it was horribly dreary and isolated. Despite her strong will, and her deep faith in her religion and in her father, she began to cry. She didn't close her eyes, nor did she wipe away her tears, she simply stood looking down into the camp and wept, her shoulders unmoving, her back ramrod straight. She couldn't remember the last time she had cried, but it must have been when she was a little girl in Khartoum. Nor could she remember what it had felt like. But now a great sadness came over her like a thick blanket of fog falling into a deep valley, obscuring everything. She didn't know what she was thinking at that moment; she was just feeling sad, lost, depressed, melancholic. She wanted her mother. She wanted someone to have tea with, someone to brush out her hair and braid it, someone to listen with a sympathetic ear. But her mother had returned to Khartoum in secret two months ago and there'd been no mention of when or if she was coming back.

McGarvey had been ready to kill Mohammed. She had seen it in his eyes, and in his deep anger. He wasn't ashamed of her, nor had he blamed her for the attack. He had simply been a father protecting a girl. Squeezing her eyes shut she could imagine her father at the pool, see his flashing eyes on her, and on Mohammed. She could see his disappointment in her, his scorn, his anger. But at her, not Mohammed. As hard as she tried, however, she could not imagine her father doing what McGarvey had done for her. And she felt guilty for wanting such a thing. Ashamed. Sad.

But she loved her father with every fiber of her soul. As long as he stayed here in the mountains she would remain with him. Gladly. Wherever he was, that's where she would be. She did not feel complete except when she was at his side. Nor could she feel warm except in the glow of his approval. Which was why she was having such a terrible time of it now.

McGarvey coming here was the worst thing that had ever happened to her. She didn't think she would ever get over it.

The sun began to feel warm on her face as she started down the steep switchback trail. It was almost time for morning prayers and, afterward, bed. There were moments when the five-times-daily ritual seemed too much to bear, but this morning she felt a great need for the comfort of Allah. Repeating the *Sura Fatihah* forty times each day was an intensely personal connection between her and God that sometimes made her forget everything except the moment. She needed that surrender now more than she had ever needed it before.

By dint of great willpower, Osama bin Laden began to clear his mind for the morning ritual as he came into the main chamber. He felt an overpowering sense of doom and a strong, almost desperate need for the comfort of prayer. His plan had to work if he was going to be allowed to make his final hajj to Mecca and then to Medina. It was the last condition he was going to impose on his enemies before he turned over the bomb, and it was an absolute.

He had been nothing more than God's warrior, and he found himself now longing for the peace of Paradise. There had never been any innocents in the struggle, it was something they didn't understand in the West. Nor did they understand that when an infidel died he simply went to hell for a period until his soul was finally cleansed by the fire. Then the gates of Paradise would open even for him. In the end they all would become brothers in one; all children of a merciful God.

Ali Bahmad came into the chamber and stood respectfully in the shadows without speaking until bin Laden noticed him.

"Yes?"

"Your daughter has returned."

"Alone?" bin Laden asked softly. He was relieved.

Ali Bahmad nodded. "She's coming down the hill now."

"Thank you for letting me know. After prayers have her come to me."

"As you wish."

"What about Hamed? Have you heard anything from him?"

"He passed Sarah on the trail. But she was on the way back so he didn't stop." Bahmad explained. "She hid from him."

Bin Laden suppressed a smile. His daughter was independent, for which he was both proud and fearful. "When he reaches the others I want to know."

"Very well," Bahmad said, and he turned to leave as a tremendous explosion shattered the early morning silence. It had come from down in the camp, and for a millisecond bin Laden wanted to believe that there'd been an accident in the fuel storage pit across from the helicopter.

A second explosion, then a third and a fourth shattered that illusion. McGarvey had not come here with a deal! He had been sent with his GPS chip to find this camp and guide the missiles to it!

Bahmad had already turned and was racing up the tunnel to the entrance, as three guards clutching their Kalashnikovs came running from the back.

Bin Laden grabbed his rifle and half-limped half-raced after Bahmad as so many explosions ripped into the camp that it sounded like continuous thunder. They were Tomahawk missiles; he well remembered the sound, like an incoming jet airliner, followed immediately by a very sharp slap as the burst shoved a wall of compressed air outward followed immediately by a mind-numbing blast.

Sarah was out there. Bin Laden was sick with fear and impotent rage. The Americans had always fought by their own sense of rules; fair play they called it. They had never gone after a man's family, or even after an enemy leader, only the soldiers and weapons. It wasn't supposed to be this way.

Bahmad lay on the floor of the tunnel just within the entrance, watching the attack. Dozens, maybe more, of the missiles rained down on the camp, the bright flashes lighting up the entire valley even brighter than day. Bin Laden could think of nothing other than his daughter. She was down there, her body naked to the devastation falling all around her.

Bin Laden stepped around Bahmad's prone figure, when his chief of staff reached up, grabbed a handful of pant leg and pulled him back.

"Get down, you fool!" he shouted over the terrible din.

Bin Laden batted Bahmad's hand away with the butt of his rifle. "Get everybody out of the cave, I'm going after my daughter."

"You'll get yourself killed! They're targeting the camp not us up here!"

The three guards came from behind and tried to drag bin Laden back from the entrance. He swung his rifle viciously catching one of them in the face, pushing him back against the other two.

"You know what to do," bin Laden snarled at Bahmad, and he stumbled outside as the missiles continued to fall on them, one after the other; sometimes in pairs, sometimes so many at once they could not be counted.

Keeping as low as he could despite the terrible pain in his knees, bin Laden scrambled down the steep hill into the maelstrom, as he searched the far side of the camp and the opposite hill for his daughter. It was hard to make sense of what was happening. The bright flashes and concussions made it nearly impossible to think. The helicopter was already destroyed, as were many of the buildings. Debris rained down in an area at least four hundred meters in diameter. Dust filled the air, and black, oily flames shot a hundred meters or more into the cloudless sky from the cache of fuel that had been dug into the ground and covered by camouflage netting.

He had fought for ten years against the Russians in these mountains, but he'd never seen anything as bad as this. He wanted to strike back, raise his rifle and lash out at the monsters who were doing this to them. But he was helpless.

At the bottom of the hill, he started through the bombed-out buildings, his right arm over his head to protect himself from the dirt and rocks and brick and steel falling all around him, when a bright flash/bang erupted directly in front of him. He was thrown back by a blast of hot air that felt like a brick wall. As he fell he could hear or sense pieces of metal softly whispering past his head like a thousand jagged pellets from a huge shotgun.

He'd lost his rifle when he'd been thrown back, and his head boomed as if he was inside a kettle drum when he picked himself up and started forward in a daze. At that moment the missiles stopped coming. In the deafening silence he thought he could hear men crying out, some of them screaming in agony. Three of them appeared from behind a low brick wall, all that remained of one of the buildings, and started toward him, blood streaming from dozens of wounds.

Too soon, the thought crystallized in his brain. He desperately waved his men back. This was just a pause in the action, the missile attack wasn't finished. There would be a second round.

Others were pulling themselves out of the rubble when he spotted Sarah, the mangled stump of her left arm spurting blood, stumbling across from where the helicopter had been. He was instantly gripped with such nausea and fear that for a brief moment he was unable to move, when a missile struck fifteen or twenty meters behind her, throwing her body forward in a spray of rocks and debris and blood.

More bombs fell around them now, all through the camp, in a rolling thunder that hammered off the hills. Staggering forward, totally oblivious to the destruction around him, bin Laden reached his daughter's body and fell to his knees beside her.

Her right leg was shattered, a big rock was embedded in her right shoulder, and her face was a mass of cuts and torn flesh. But she was still alive. There was still some awareness in her dark, pretty eyes.

"My Sarah," bin Laden whispered as the missiles continued to rain down on them. He knew that she couldn't hear him, but her eyes lit up in recognition.

"Father," she mouthed the word, blood welling from her mouth.

Bin Laden, tears streaming down his face, gently cradled his daughter in his arms. Not this one, he prayed. Please God, not Sarah. But it was useless. She was going to die here and now, and no power on earth or in heaven would save her. No miracle would be enough.

He looked into her eyes as he held her, watching her life run out, feeling it in the unnatural looseness of her muscles.

"Peace, my little one," he said. *"Insha'Allah."*

Sarah's face went utterly pale, and blood stopped bubbling out of her mouth at the same time the last missile struck a hundred meters away, destroying the nomad tent.

Bin Laden threw back his head and screamed a cry of anguish from the bottom of his soul, while in another compartment of his brain he could feel his heart already hardening for the terrible task that lay ahead of them.

THIRTEEN

The White House

President Haynes glanced at the clock when the direct line from the CIA chirped. It was 10:05 P.M. Waiting with him in the Oval Office were his national security adviser Dennis Berndt and his chief of staff Tony Lang. He'd been in a blue funk all evening, ever since he'd agreed to the missile attack on bin Laden's mountain camp. "This isn't a war game, Dennis," he'd peevishly told his NSA earlier. "Real people are going to get killed up there."

"Sometimes things like this have to be done, Mr. President," Berndt had replied.

The problem was that he saw no other way out of the gravest situation the U.S. had faced since Pearl Harbor. The President put the call on the speakerphone. "Good evening, Roland."

"Good evening, Mr. President," Murphy replied, tiredly. He sounded resigned. "The attack just got over, and it looks good. From what we're seeing the camp was completely wiped out. There won't be many survivors."

The President looked at his advisers. "Was there any indication of a secondary nuclear explosion?" It was something he'd worried about.

"No, sir. My people tell me that even if we had hit the

package, it would not have caused a detonation. But we're putting a drone on target now to check for radiation."

"No accidents this time?" the President asked. "We didn't hit anything we weren't supposed to hit?"

"No, sir. There's nothing in the near vicinity of bin Laden's camp," Murphy assured him. "We're putting together the damage assessment now. Should be ready in a couple of hours once we get the data back from the drone. I can bring it over to you tonight."

"That's not necessary, Roland. It's too late for any sort of an announcement tonight in any event. I'm scheduling a news conference for eleven in the morning. If you can get over here by nine it'll be plenty of time."

"Yes, Mr. President."

"I'm sorry about McGarvey, he was a brave man. What he tried to do for us out there was very courageous. But he never really had a chance."

"You're probably right, Mr. President."

"I'll call his wife—"

"Mr. President, why don't we wait on that until morning," Murphy said. "I haven't told his daughter yet either."

"You can't think there's still hope."

"McGarvey's come out of tough situations before. He's a survivor. Let's wait."

Berndt was shaking his head in disgust, and for some reason it irritated the President and he shot him a dirty look.

"Okay, General, we'll hold it until morning," the President agreed. "But I want you to know that if there's any sign that McGarvey's still alive I'll give you anything you need to get him back. Anything."

"Thank you, sir. I appreciate it."

"Try to get some sleep, Roland. Tomorrow is going to be a long day."

"You too, Mr. President."

In the Afghan Mountains

McGarvey crouched in a depression above the path waiting for them to come after him. As soon as he'd heard the first batch of what sounded like incoming jets down in the valley he'd slipped away. He knew what they were, but Mohammed and the others had jumped up and run down river to the cliff to look.

It was just his bad luck that they'd had the presence of mind to take their weapons with them. But he had managed to grab Mohammed's pack and get out of there before they came running back. As soon as he'd found a suitable vantage point from which to defend himself, he'd retrieved his gun and spare magazine of ammunition from the bundle of filthy, stinking clothing, blankets and food. The gun was oily and gritty from something that had gotten all over it, but he pumped a couple of rounds out and the mechanism worked okay.

McGarvey watched the path carefully, as he considered his options. He was pissed off, but his anger would have to wait. For the moment his biggest challenge would be saving his own life and then somehow getting out of Afghanistan. The time for talking had ended when the first cruise missile had struck. If bin Laden had survived he would use the bomb. There was no doubt about it. Their only hope now was to stop it before it got to the States.

For that he needed a phone to warn Otto, and to work out a means of getting out of the country. That's providing he could first survive the three-to-one odds he was facing now, and then make it down to Kabul without running the car off the mountain cliffs.

He thought about trying to reach Pakistan over the mountains, but that would be next to impossible without guides and provisions. And it would take far too long. Because of the missile attack they no longer had the luxury of time.

What the hell were they thinking? They could have

waited for at least a couple of days. He didn't want to get into a firefight with his mujahedeen. He was outnumbered and outgunned. But he didn't think Mohammed was going to simply give up and scurry back to camp. The man had a score to settle and it was going to be here and now.

McGarvey raised his head a couple of inches above the rim of the depression in time to see Farid dash up the path and duck behind a large boulder. They were about five hundred yards from the camp, just beyond the copse of trees and the pool where Sarah had almost been raped. The stream tumbling over the rocks just below the path made a lulling sound, but from farther up he could hear the deeper-throated roar where it fell down a series of cataracts.

"We have to go back now, mista," Farid called up.

McGarvey studied the path and the rocks and brush below it. He could make out the flash suppressor on the end of Farid's rifle, but he could not spot the other two mujahedeen.

Farid suddenly leaped up and darted another ten yards up the path, throwing himself into the ditch. A second later Hash sprung from the trees and keeping low raced to the protection of the boulder Farid had just left. He leaped up and fired a sustained burst into the rocks and boulders about twenty yards farther west from McGarvey's position, the gunfire shockingly loud in the narrow defile, bullets ricocheting all over the place.

They knew that he was up here somewhere, and they were trying to draw him out to pinpoint his position. He was at a triple disadvantage; they not only outnumbered and outgunned him, but these were their mountains. They were just as at home here as McGarvey was in Paris or Washington.

Except for the sounds of the stream a stillness descended over them. The problem was Mohammed. He was out there somewhere too, and between the three of them they had probably hatched some sort of a plan.

He checked over his shoulder, but so far as he could tell nothing moved on the steep, rock-strewn slope that rose four hundred feet to the top of a hill studded with scraggly wind-bent trees.

They wouldn't want to stick around here too long. It was the one weakness in their plan. They knew that they had to get back to the camp as soon as possible to see what had happened, help with the wounded and pack up what remained to bug out. Unless Mohammed forced them to stay until McGarvey was dead they might not come after him if he doubled back, climbed down to the valley and made it to the Rover.

He dumped the contents of Mohammed's pack on the ground and hurriedly searched through the greasy, filthy clothes for the car keys or anything else he could use, while keeping an eye on the path below. There was nothing for him among the mujahed's meager possessions. It was Farid who had driven the Rover, so the keys would either be in his backpack at the camp by the pool, or with him in a pocket. If he could make it down to the Rover he would find something to pop the ignition lock and hot-wire the starter.

Farid jumped up and fired a burst into the hill to the west of McGarvey. An instant later Hash fired another sustained burst walking his shots east. McGarvey had to duck down and cover his head as the shots hammered the rocks directly below him. Too late he realized that they knew where he was hiding and they were pinning him down. He looked over his shoulder when a rifle muzzle was jammed into the side of his head.

The firing from below suddenly ceased and Mohammed laughed wildly. Blood dripped from the filthy bandage on his wounded hand, and his face was cut up from flying rock chips. "I warned him about you," he shouted triumphantly. "But he wouldn't listen." He stepped back a little, the rifle never wavering from McGarvey's head. "Put your gun down. Get to your feet."

McGarvey carefully laid his gun on a flat rock and got up, spreading his hands out to either side, letting a calmness come over him. Mohammed's eyes were red and they kept flicking from McGarvey to the path below. He held the Kalashnikov in a white-knuckled death grip. His clothing was dirty and ripped from his climb up the hill over the rocks. The butt of his pistol had worked itself half out of his vest, the hammer snagged on the corner of a pocket. If he tried to pull it out in a hurry it would catch. "So now what? Are you going to take me back to bin Laden?"

"You're not going to leave this place alive."

"That would be a very big mistake—"

"You didn't come here to talk," Mohammed shouted.

"That's not true."

"Where else did your missiles hit, mista?" Mohammed demanded. He was working himself up.

"I don't know," McGarvey replied calmly.

"Liar," Mohammed snarled. "Come up here now," he called down to Hash and Farid.

McGarvey figured he had only a couple of minutes before the other two got up here and then the odds against him would be impossible. He smiled. "I'll tell you what, Mohammed. If you turn around right now and get the hell out of here I won't kill you."

Mohammed was surprised and then enraged. He poked the rifle muzzle sharply into McGarvey's chest. It was a mistake.

"Just go, and you'll live to fight another day," McGarvey said, in an infuriatingly relaxed tone. "But if you poke me again I *will* kill you. For Sarah."

The mujahed's face turned purple. "Slut," he shouted wildly. He pulled the rifle back, his left hand on the stock, his wounded right hand near the trigger guard, and he swung the heavy butt at McGarvey's head. McGarvey ducked the blow and drove his shoulder into the man's chest, knocking him off his feet. McGarvey yanked the Kalashnikov out of Mohammed's hands and spun around.

Hash and Farid were halfway up the hill, aware that something was happening above them, but not quite sure what it was.

McGarvey fired a couple of rounds over their heads, and

they hit the ground, scrambling for cover. Mohammed was clawing for his pistol. McGarvey turned back to him. "You can still leave here alive."

Mohammed got the pistol out of his pocket, fumbled for the hammer and raised it. McGarvey shot him once, the bullet plowing into his forehead.

Not necessary, McGarvey thought with disgust. Yet this was one killing he knew that he would never regret.

Hash and Farid started firing wildly up the hill, the bullets whining off the rocks all over the place. McGarvey dropped down into the protection of the depression and waited until they stopped shooting.

"Mohammed is dead," he called down to them. He got his pistol and stuffed it in his belt. "I didn't order the missile strike, and I mean you no harm now." He ejected the Kalashnikov's magazine and checked the rounds. There was one in the chamber and seven in the clip. "Go back and tell bin Laden that we can still work a deal. The missiles were a mistake. My government thought I was dead."

McGarvey checked over the rim of the depression. One of the mujahedeen was directly below him, the other had moved back about fifteen or twenty yards to the east. They were trying to box him in, get him in a crossfire. Whatever their previous orders had been they meant to kill him now.

He popped up and fired three shots at the man crouched behind the rocks below him. The other one jumped out of hiding and started up the hill. McGarvey calmly switched aim and squeezed off two shots, the second catching the man in the side, knocking him down. "Goddammit," he muttered, pulling back. It was senseless.

A silence fell over the defile again, and except for the burbling stream there were no sounds.

"It's only you now," McGarvey called out. He crawled over to Mohammed's body, took the PSM pistol, then crawled back to the rim. "We can stay here and fight it out, or you can go back to the camp."

"I can't do that, mista." It was Farid. McGarvey recognized the voice, and he sounded frightened.

"Yes, you can," McGarvey said. He checked the load in Mohammed's pistol. There was one in the chamber, and eight in the magazine. "I didn't want to shoot Hash, but I had no other choice."

"You brought the missiles."

"No, I didn't. My government made a mistake. I was sent here to stop the killing, and we can still do that if you tell bin Laden that I'll make it right when I get back to Washington. Something like this won't happen again. You can give him my word."

"Liar," Farid shouted, and he fired several rounds up the hill.

"Shit," McGarvey said. He rose up and emptied the Kalashnikov on the rocks where the mujahed was hiding then ducked back. "Sooner or later one of us is going to get lucky," McGarvey said. He laid the rifle aside and picked up the Russian pistol. "Since I have the high ground it'll probably be me."

The defile was silent again.

A minute later McGarvey cautiously rose up so that he could see where Farid was hiding. Nothing moved. He rose a little higher, but he still couldn't see any sign of the mujahed down there.

"Farid," he called.

There was no answer.

He swept his eyes across the rocks and path. Hash was still lying where he'd gone down, but to the west McGarvey was just in time to see Farid keeping low and moving fast then disappear over the crest of a hill.

McGarvey lowered the pistol and allowed himself to come down. Now it begins, he told himself morosely as he stared at the empty path back to bin Laden's camp and listened to the pleasant sounds of the stream.

Bin Laden's Camp

Bin Laden, with his daughter's bloody body in his arms, her long dark hair hanging loose, made his way slowly through the camp. His two dozen remaining mujahedeen parted respectfully for him as he passed, then gathered behind him in a funeral march.

As the procession started up the hill Ali Bahmad, dressed for travel in khakis, came back to the cave entrance, a two-way radio held loosely in his left hand. He glanced into the sky to the east. An unmanned reconnaissance drone had passed over the camp fifteen minutes ago to assess the damage the missile strike had caused, and at this moment the CIA's spy satellites were looking down on them, passing their high-resolution real-time images back to Washington. Bahmad had once even stood in the National Reconnaissance Office's operations center, and had been shown a tiny part of what the machines were capable of. It was nothing short of miraculous.

At the bottom of the hill bin Laden stopped to gather his strength for the climb. Although he clearly needed help no one came forward out of respect for him. This was a task meant only for a grieving father, and his followers had more love for him at this moment then they'd ever had before. The experience was almost religious, Bahmad could see it in the way they stood, heads up but in silence.

A pall of smoke hung over the valley, and flames still rose from a dozen fires, including the one at the fuel dump, which would probably burn all day and into the night. The drone had come in low enough to get clear pictures of everything not under cover, and the satellites were capable of very sharp infrared imaging. The Americans knew what damage their strike had caused, and more importantly who had survived.

Bahmad had warned Osama that this might happen. He had advised either using the bomb as it was intended to be used, or get rid of it. "But don't try to bargain with him," he'd cautioned. "Once they know that you have it they won't stop until you're dead and the bomb is either destroyed or in their possession."

Time to leave now, he told himself. Not only from this camp, but perhaps from these mountains and even from the jihad. Bahmad had toyed with the notion of slipping away ever since bin Laden's agents had gotten their hands on the bomb. But something inside of him had made him stay. Like a moth drawn to a flame he had been seduced by the power of the device. In one act of terrorism they could finally strike fear into the hearts of every Westerner who'd dared to come to the Middle East with their insatiable appetite for oil; with their infectious culture and ideas that were far more dangerous than any deadly virus. He could finally strike a decisive blow for the deaths of his parents that had scarred his soul more deeply than even he could admit to himself. They had been his entire world. He'd been a shy, delicate boy whom his parents had protected. When they were killed by the Jews he'd almost drawn inside of himself, into a nothingness, into a deep depression from which he knew he would never have survived. Instead, his heart had turned to stone, and he had begun the long fight against Israel and every nation that supported it that would, he understood on a pragmatic level, not end until he was dead. But the fight had been glorious at times. And there was still one more blow to be delivered, if bin Laden could be kept from going completely insane and ordering the impossible.

The procession started up the hill at the same moment the radio squawked softly.

Bahmad stepped closer to the cave entrance for better radio reception. "Yes," he answered.

"There is trouble," Hamed came back.

"Is McGarvey dead?"

"No."

"Where are you now?"

"At the cataracts."

That was a spot on the path about a kilometer above the first rest area before the valley. Bahmad worked to keep his anger in check. "What happened?"

"I'm not sure. But there was a fight and he killed Mohammed and Hash. Farid just showed up, he's with me now."

"Was McGarvey wounded?"

"Apparently not," Hamed replied.

Bahmed who had picked his inner circle very well, had complete faith in Hamed. "He's probably on his way to the Rover. Stop him before he reaches it. Whatever you must do, kill him, is that clear?"

"Yes, sir," Hamed said. "Is everything all right up there?"

"No," Bahmad said softly. He pocketed the radio, and took out his phone as bin Laden reached the cave opening. Their eyes met, but he could read nothing in bin Laden's other than a father's despair. Bin Laden turned to his followers who were gathered a few meters below.

"Final justice will be ours," bin Laden shouted, his voice surprisingly strong.

Bahmad stepped back out of sight and pushed the speed dial button for a number in Kabul.

"No American will be safe from our wrath. When we strike it will be in the infidels' homeland."

It was what Bahmad had expected and feared most. Bin Laden *was* crazy and he meant to take them all down with him. But there were plans. Possibilities. Even targets, because he had been working on the problem for several months now.

"No one will ever forget," bin Laden shouted.

The call was answered on the second ring. "Hello."

"Do you know who this is, Colonel?"

"Yes, I do," the man said in a guarded voice. In the background Bahmad could hear a great deal of commotion. "We're still trying to find out where the missiles hit. Was it you?"

"Yes, it was. We're leaving here in a few hours, but there's something you must do for me."

"Listen, the Shura is finally going to demand that he leave Afghanistan. All foreigners are going to be expelled within the next forty-eight hours for their own protection. The rioting has already started down here. We can't have this any longer. You must make him understand!" The Shura was the ruling council.

"We do understand, and we are leaving," Bahmad said, keeping his voice reasonable. "But there is one last thing that you must do for me."

The phone was dead for a moment. Bin Laden was quoting the Qoran, his voice like Bahmad's, clear, calm, unhurried. He was a teacher instructing his eager pupils, a shepherd showing his flock the way.

"What do you want?"

"The American Kirk McGarvey may be on his way back to Kabul in the Rover."

"You should have killed him," the army colonel said bitterly.

"We tried but failed," Bahmad admitted. "He is a very resourceful man. If he reaches Kabul I want him killed. At all costs. Do you understand me?"

"Who is he?"

"Just a CIA field agent. But he came here for one purpose only, to kill Osama. For that he has to die."

"Was his mission a success?"

Bahmad was looking at bin Laden. "No, it was not," he said. "Will you do this one last thing for us?"

"Yes," the colonel said without hesitation. "If he gets this far he will die. I guarantee it."

"Thank you," Bahmad said and he broke the connection.

"The walls of Jericho will come tumbling down," bin Laden told his people. "But this time there will be a hammer—Joshua's hammer—swung by an Islamic fist for all the world to see and respect. *Insha'Allah*."

Yes, Bahmad thought. *Insha'Allah*. God willing.

ELIZABETH MCGARVEY

Vengeance is mine;
I will repay, saith the Lord.
ROMANS 12:19

FOURTEEN

In the Afghan Mountains

McGarvey searched Mohammed's body, finding three full magazines for the Kalashnikov. He had to decide if he should take them and the rifle or continue without the extra weight.

It would take the rest of the day for Farid to make it back to the camp, and depending on what he found there, possibly another half-day to bring reinforcements back with him. It wasn't likely that everyone had been killed in the missile raid, and if bin Laden had survived he would go all out to stop McGarvey from leaving Afghanistan alive.

If there were other more direct routes to the Rover they would take those in an effort to intercept him. If that failed they might alert the military in Kabul to be on the lookout for him. It meant in reality that he only had a few hours' head start, time enough for Farid to reach the camp, so he had to travel light.

He set the magazines aside and found his satellite phone in another pocket. The low-battery indicator light was on. Mohammed had evidently been playing with it. But it didn't matter as much now, because the damage had already been done.

He entered the security code and then hit the speed dial button. After a minute the phone acquired a satellite and the call went through. He looked at his watch. It was after midnight in Washington, but if Otto wasn't in his office the call would automatically be rolled over to his cell phone or his apartment. It was answered before the first ring was completed.

"Oh, wow, Mac," Rencke shouted excitedly. "I knew you were alive! I just knew it!"

"Okay, settle down, Otto. I'm in one piece, but I'm going to need some help getting out of the country, and I want to know what the hell is going on there."

"Are you someplace we can come get you?" Rencke asked, all business.

"I'm still in the mountains, maybe ten or twelve miles from bin Laden's camp. If everything goes okay I should be in Kabul sometime tonight, my time."

"That might not be the best place right now. They're already rioting down there. The Taliban is behind it, of course, it wouldn't have started so fast otherwise. You'll never make it back to the hotel."

McGarvey glanced up the path, and stopped to listen for a moment. Had he heard something? "I don't have any other option," he said, deciding he hadn't heard anything after all. It was just his nerves. "How about our old embassy? If I can get to it is there a place I can hide out?"

"That's where the rioting is starting to concentrate. But the ambassador's old residence is a possibility. It's in your laptop."

"I don't have that anymore," McGarvey said. "But I think I can find the place, and if there's only the two caretakers I should be able to get in easily enough."

"The Taliban have given all foreigners forty-eight hours to get out of Afghanistan. I'll try to arrange something with one of the embassies. You might be able to get out with one of their staffs."

"How about our own people? There has to be some Americans here."

"A few UN observers, a handful of Red Crescent people and maybe a couple dozen businessmen. But they're leaving on commercial airlines to Dubai, the same way you came in."

"With the rioting that's going to be dangerous for them,"

McGarvey suggested. "The Taliban would have to provide an escort, something I don't think they'll do."

Rencke picked up on it immediately. "We can send a C-130 with a few marines to provide security. The President said he would do whatever it takes to protect our people. But the Taliban know your face, so unless you can come up with a disguise and new papers they'll never allow you to get on that plane, marines or no marines."

"I'll work something out at this end," McGarvey said. "Just get the transport aircraft here and I'll get aboard somehow. Try Riyadh, it'll be quicker."

"I'm on it."

"I'm not even going to ask why the attack was launched so fast. But what about damage assessments? How badly did we hurt them?"

"We flattened the camp, Mac. But there're survivors, and nobody thinks any differently. When your chip went off the air they wouldn't listen to me. Even Murphy tried to delay the attack."

"It was Berndt."

"Bingo," Rencke said. "I did some checking. He worked for the SecDef a few years ago, and guess what one of his primary responsibilities was? Final target approval for our raids into Kosovo and Serbia. He took the heat for a lot of the mistakes we made over there, and he blamed it on the Agency for giving him bad intelligence. Especially in the Chinese embassy thing."

McGarvey knew there had been something like that in the national security adviser's past, but he'd never had the time to look into it. In all other respects Dennis Berndt was doing a good job for a President whom the country loved and respected. It was the one issue that blinded him from doing an otherwise almost perfect job. "You'd better have Murphy get over there and brief them on what's coming our way. Unless we killed bin Laden he'll come after us."

"We're still working on that part. But we might not be able to come up with anything conclusive. If he's alive he'll have to show himself before we can know for sure. Either that or use his cell phone. If we get lucky and pick up one of his calls we'll have him."

"He has the bomb, Otto, and unless we can give him another way out he's going to use it against us."

"The big questions are where and when."

"In the States and damned soon."

"Oh, boy," Rencke said after a moment. "Was he willing to go along with the deal?"

"I think so," McGarvey said tiredly. "But now he'll blame his actions on us. He's going to claim that he tried to work with us in good faith, but that we tried to assassinate him."

"We did," Rencke said softly.

"Yeah."

"Do you think that he'll go after the President?"

"I think that's too specific a target even for bin Laden. But he's going to bring the bomb to the States."

"Maybe it's already here."

McGarvey had given that possibility some thought. "I don't think so. It's just a gut feeling, but if the bomb was already there he would have been more aggressive because his position would have been stronger. Do what I want right now, or suffer the consequences right now. He never acted that way."

"If that's true then it gives us a little time," Rencke said. "That's something. What about his staff? Did you see the guy Allen told us about?"

"Yeah, his name is Ali, but I never got a look at his face, only his eyes. He knew about the chip and about our satellite schedules, so he's well connected."

"I'll have something for you to look at and listen to when you get back. Maybe he's a key."

"Let's hope so," McGarvey said. "Because we need one." The phone cut out momentarily, but then reacquired the satellite.

"Mac . . . ?"

"I'm back. My batteries are almost flat. I want you to

talk to Dick Yemm and have him keep an eye on Katy and Liz until I get back."

"Do you think they'll be a target?"

"I can almost guarantee it," McGarvey replied bitterly. "Call Fred Rudolph and have the Bureau's antiterrorism people keep their heads up. Adkins can work with him. I want all of our assets worldwide on this right now. Nothing else takes priority. And I mean nothing."

"Gotcha."

"I want a new SNIE developed and on the President's desk within twelve hours. As soon as I get out of here I'll send you more information. The INS will have to be in the mix, because there's no way of knowing how the bomb is going to be delivered. But every airport, seaport and border crossing will have to be watched much closer than normal, twenty-four hours a day.

"That still leaves a lot of holes, ya know," Rencke said bleakly. "We can't put a fence around the country, it's too late, and it wouldn't work anyway."

"I know it, but we might get lucky, especially if bin Laden is alive and he makes a move."

"That would be the wrong thing for him to do, and he's gotta know it," Rencke said. "If I were him I'd go to ground somewhere and keep my head down until it was over. Maybe for a long time afterward."

"I think he's dying, Otto. Maybe cancer."

"We could offer him medical help."

"He'd never take it."

"Desperate men make desperate decisions," Rencke said softly. "Shit, Mac, what a mess."

"It's going to get a lot worse," McGarvey said. "I'll call you from Kabul."

McGarvey pocketed the phone then hurried over to where Hash lay in the rocks in a large pool of blood from the gaping wound in his side, and quickly searched his body. Besides a couple of magazines of ammunition there was nothing much except for a rusty knife, a waterproof tin of matches and a filthy scrap of rag he'd used for a handkerchief. No car keys.

It seemed like a long time since he had eaten anything decent and he was very tired. The wound in his side throbbed painfully. He scrambled down to the path and took it back to the rock overhang, stopping just long enough at the stream to splash some cold water on his face. The packs were lying next to the campfire, but neither of them contained the car keys. He took one of the full canteens, slung it over his shoulder then grabbed a couple of pieces of nan from one of the bundles, stuffed them in his pocket and headed around the dammed-up pool to the waterfall.

The cliff dropped about three hundred feet to the head of the steep arroyo that wound its way with the stream down to the floor of the valley. McGarvey stopped at the edge to catch his breath. The morning chill had given way to a gloriously sunny day. Down in Kabul it would be very hot, but here the mountain air was cool and sweet. But there was death all around. Rivers of blood had been shed in Afghanistan over the past thousand years or more. And there was no end in sight.

Chevy Chase

Elizabeth McGarvey awoke in a cold sweat, disoriented and not exactly sure where she was for the first few moments.

She'd been having the familiar dream again in which she was at a mall carrying around a bottle of perfume she wanted to buy for her mother's birthday. But she couldn't find a cashier. She was a teenager still in junior high school, and she had just enough money to the penny to pay for the perfume. Her mother had been on her case about spending her allowance as fast as she got it. It was something that her father would never approve of. He'd been gone long enough from their lives that she had begun to fantasize about him. Whenever she found herself in a situation she would try to think what her father would say or do. This time she had saved her money, which would make him proud, and she was buying a good bottle of perfume, which would make her mother happy. She couldn't lose except that she couldn't find a cashier.

She found herself at the main exit from the mall, the bottle of perfume still in her hand. For some reason she thought she might be able to find a cashier outside in the parking lot; maybe one of them coming to work. The moment she stepped outside, however, sirens began to blare, and two policemen, guns drawn, came running after her, shouting for her to stop or they would shoot. That's when she spotted her parents. Her father had come back and he was standing in her mother's driveway. They were having a teriffic argument, and no matter what she did to get their attention they were ignoring her. She figured if she could get across the street her father would know what to do; he would straighten out the mess, give the policemen the money for the perfume and send them back to the mall. But her mother was saying something to him in that maddeningly calm voice of hers, and her father was just standing there taking it, and she knew she would never be able to reach them until it was too late, though she wanted nothing more than their love and for them to be proud of her.

The house was quiet. Elizabeth looked at the clock radio on the nightstand as it switched to 12:21 A.M., and her heart began to slow down. She was in one of the spare bedrooms down the hall from her mother. She was safe. Nothing could hurt her here. And yet she was frightened.

She got up, used the bathroom without turning on the light, then put on a robe and went to her mother's door. Her mouth was gummy from too much wine. She hesitated a moment, then knocked softly.

"Elizabeth?" her mother's voice came softly from within.

"May I come in?"

"Of course, dear."

Her mother, dressed in a bathrobe sat in one of the chairs by the window that looked out over the country club's fifteenth fairway. The window was open. Elizabeth could smell the night grass smells from the golf course and hear the sprinkler systems at work.

"I didn't mean to wake you," Elizabeth said. She came to the window and looked outside. The sky was partly cloudy, but it was a moonless night and despite the glow of Washington's lights she could see a lot of stars. The same stars, she thought, that her father might be seeing. But then she realized that in Afghanistan it was already morning. No stars. The thought made him seem even more distant to her.

She looked back. Her mother, her face still unlined and beautiful even without makeup, was watching her. "I couldn't sleep."

"Neither could I," Kathleen said. "Are you okay?"

Elizabeth sat down beside her mother. "I was having a bad dream."

"About your father?"

"And you," Elizabeth said shyly. She'd never told her mother about that dream.

"The shoplifting one?" her mother asked, and Elizabeth's mouth opened. Her mother smiled gently. "Close your mouth, dear. You sometimes talk in your sleep."

Elizabeth looked at her mother closely for the first time in a long time. There *were* lines at the corners of her eyes and full lips, but her eyes were clear and startlingly bright even in the starlight. There was a calmness in her expression, a peacefulness that overrode even a hint of fear. She'd been in this position before; waiting, wondering when the phone would ring with the news. Her husband was in harm's way, and although he'd always managed to somehow survive, there was always that possibility that even his skill and luck would finally run out. She was steeling herself for it, as she had before, only this time it was different. This time she wanted him to come back. She wanted to know that he was safe and that she would have him back in her life at least for a little while until he went off again on another assignment.

Elizabeth saw all of that in her mother's face, and understood now how much hell her mother had somehow endured over the past twenty-five years. A very large wave of love washed over her and she reached out for her mother's hand.

Kathleen smiled gently. "A penny," she said.

"I was just thinking that I love you and Daddy. But I never knew just how much until right now."

Kathleen's eyes glistened and she looked away. "Dammit."

"It's what he does, Mother. It's who he is."

Kathleen turned back, her delicate nostrils flared in a flash of anger. "He's very, very good at it. But he's a stupid man because he won't admit to himself how many people are dependent on him. They're going to suck him dry until there's nothing left."

The outburst left Elizabeth speechless, but her mother always had the ability to surprise her. On the surface she was nothing more than another well put together post-Junior League society woman. In reality she was one of the major behind-the-scenes fundraisers for a dozen charities and major organizations, among them the American Red Cross. She had the ability to mingle with the wealthy and talk them out of significant amounts of money before they realized what had hit them. She was as intelligent, well bred and knowledgeable as she was beautiful.

"It's true," Kathleen said. "You work in the Directorate of Operations now, so you've seen your father's file, and I suppose there are stories you could tell me. But I have my own stories too. I've seen what the job has done to him over the past twenty-five years. I don't think anybody knows where it will end, least of all your father."

"He'll never go back to teaching," Elizabeth said with a little anger. She was afraid she was hearing her old mother now, the one who had driven her husband away.

"Don't give me that look, Elizabeth. I'm not asking your father to quit for my sake. But he'll destroy himself unless he can finally learn how to depend on someone other than himself."

"He has Otto and Dick Adkins and the rest of his staff."

Kathleen shook her head. "I mean emotionally. The difference between your father and me, is that when I get hurt I want to be surrounded by people I love. But when he's hurt he's like a dog who runs under the nearest porch to be alone so that he can lick his wounds."

Elizabeth understood exactly what her mother was saying, because she'd always been torn both ways herself; wanting to run home to her mother for sympathy, while at the same time wanting to be left alone to nurse her own wounds. It was one of the messages from her dream, she supposed. She wanted to get to her father so that he could take care of the policemen chasing her, yet she could never reach him. Her subconscious was telling her to work out her own problems. How else could her father be proud of her?

They sat for a while in silence, looking out the window at the golf course. The windows on this side of the house were Lexan plastic because of the occasional stray ball. Her mother didn't seem to mind; she'd lived here for a long time and she was a member of the club.

"Where did your father go this time?"

"Afghanistan," Elizabeth answered without hesitation.

"Is he going after bin Laden?"

"Just to talk."

"Is he still there? Have you heard anything yet?"

Elizabeth shook her head. "Nothing yet, but he's carrying something that allows us to know where he is at all times."

"I thought the chip was only for field officers," Kathleen said, but then she smiled wanly. "That was a dumb comment, I suppose."

Elizabeth said nothing.

"How is Todd Van Buren these days? I haven't heard anything about him lately."

"We're going to dinner on Friday," Elizabeth said, feeling a sudden warm glow. Van Buren was an instructor at the CIA's training facility in Williamsburg. He'd saved her life on a mission that had gone sour last year. Since then they'd had a slowly developing relationship. Van Buren was a little too macho and Elizabeth was a little too independent. It was something that they recognized in each other, and in themselves, and they were working on it. He was the first man Elizabeth had known who could compare to her father. They were big shoes to fill, in her estimation.

"When your father gets back to Washington invite Todd out here for dinner." Kathleen smiled. "Unless you're not ready for that yet."

Elizabeth had to laugh. "It would scare him half to death, but it would be cool to see how he handled it."

Kathleen laughed too. "I think it will frighten your father just as badly." She studied her daughter's face for a long moment or two. "I'm afraid for you in the business."

"There's hardly any kind of a job without a risk, Mother. And I'm not going to live in a cotton-lined box."

"I don't mean physically, though that frightens me. I'm talking about what it's eventually going to do to you. Your father is a wonderful, kind, caring, giving man. I love him. But there's a hard, cynical side to him because of what the CIA has made him do. Sometimes being around him is like biting on tinfoil." Kathleen smiled sadly, and reached out and brushed a strand of hair off her daughter's forehead. "I don't want that for you. There's nothing wrong with being soft and feminine. You can even accomplish it without being weak and stupid."

"You've proven that, Mother," Elizabeth said, warmly.

The telephone rang. Kathleen flinched, but then took the portable phone out of her bathrobe pocket and answered it. She'd been expecting the call. "Hello."

Elizabeth watched her mother's face for some sign of what kind of a call it was.

"Yes, I understand, Otto. Thank you for calling." Kathleen's face was perfectly neutral. "I know that you can't go into the details, but how soon before you know when he's out of there and safe?"

Elizabeth's heart skipped a beat.

"Thank you," Kathleen said. "As a matter of fact she's here with me now. I'll put her on." She gave the phone to Elizabeth. "Otto's heard from your father. He's safe for now."

Elizabeth took the phone. "Thanks for calling, Otto," she said. "Is he still in-country?"

"About ten miles from bin Laden's camp. He's going to try to make it down to Kabul sometime tonight, and we're sending a C-130 and some marines to pull him and some other Americans out. The White House will have to put some pressure on the Taliban government, but that can be done."

"What's going on? Why can't he fly out of there commercially the same way he came in?"

"Oh, wow, Liz, I don't know if you want to tell Mrs. M. this, but the President's holding a news conference around eleven. Your father's chip went off the air yesterday and the President ordered a cruise missile strike on bin Laden's camp."

"Goddammit—"

"Wait, Liz. We tried to delay the strike until we were sure what was going on up there, but the White House was convinced that your father was dead, and their only option was to hit bin Laden as hard as they could."

"But my father's okay?"

"For now. But the Taliban are probably waiting for him to show up in Kabul, and there's rioting all over the city. The Taliban have given all foreigners forty-eight hours to get out of there, so it's a little confusing."

"What about our assets on the ground?"

"We have a couple of people at the old embassy, but that's where a lot of the rioting is concentrated. Dave Whittaker will try to reach them to see if they can do anything to help, but for now it's up to your dad."

Kathleen got up and went into the bathroom, leaving Elizabeth alone for the moment.

"Did we get bin Laden?"

"Nobody knows yet. There was a lot of damage, but there were survivors. The NRO is working on the updates, so we'll just have to wait."

"My father will be okay," Elizabeth said, more for her own benefit than Rencke's.

"He's made it this far, he'll make it the rest of the way, Liz. He's tough."

"That he is," Elizabeth said. "I'll get dressed and come in."

"Maybe you want to stay with your mom."

"I'll be there in a half-hour."

"Okay, but Dick Yemm is on his way out there, so tell Mrs. M. to sit tight for now."

"Whose idea was that?"

"Your dad's."

"I see," Elizabeth said. She broke the connection as her mother came back. They exchanged looks and that was enough.

"I'll put on the coffee while you get dressed," Kathleen said. "But I want you to keep me informed."

FIFTEEN

National Reconnaissance Office
Langley

There wasn't a day went by that Major Louise Horn didn't miss her old mentor Hubert Wight. But six months ago he'd been promoted to lieutenant colonel and reassigned to Air Force Intelligence Operations in the Pentagon. She was moved up to his old slot as chief of photographic interpretation at the NRO's Operations Center attached to the CIA's headquarters (renamed the George Bush Center for Intelligence). She wished he was here right now. A lot of the downloaded satellite images she was looking at were indistinct because of a pall of smoke that still covered bin Laden's camp. What looked like the remains of a burned-out truck in one photograph turned out to more likely be the corner of a building in the next, and perhaps a storage depot of fifty-gallon oil drums in another. His eye was always sharper than hers, and he had the uncanny ability to pick out some little detail that cleared up whatever mystery they were trying to unravel. It was unrealistic, but several times this morning she had seriously contemplated picking up the phone and asking him to drive out.

He used to have a miniature gallows and noose on his desk. Everybody knew that it signified what would happen to anyone who made a serious mistake and bounced it upstairs without double checking. Their customers, besides the air force, CIA and National Security Agency, were the President and his National Security Council. They were the big dogs, the ones who set national policy. It was a heavy responsibility that Louise was feeling this morning because she wasn't sure what she was seeing. When he left, Wight had given her the gallows for her desk.

She was hunched over one of the big light tables in the dimly lit Interp Center above the Pit where a dozen computer terminals were arranged in semicircular tiers facing the main display. The screen, ninety feet wide and thirty feet tall, showed the real-time positions and tracks of every U.S. intelligence-gathering satellite in orbit. What those satellites looked at was controlled from the consoles.

The first series of shots they had downlinked during the missile strike were clear enough to make a snap judgment. The camp had been almost totally obliterated. Based on the first look, Louise had sent out the preliminary damage assessment over her signature, complete with a dozen of the best photographs and her interpretation of them.

She stubbed out a cigarette in an overflowing ashtray and

immediately lit another. Chain-smoking was a bad habit she'd been trying to break for the past year. And she had done pretty good until last night. She had graduated third in her class at the Air Force Academy. She had wanted to fly jets, but at six-five with an IQ of 160 she was too tall and too smart to be a fighter pilot. She belonged here, and she loved her job, eavesdropping on the entire world. It was a voyeur's playground, and Louise was nothing if not curious. But what she was looking at now wasn't squaring with her first assessment. The camp had been heavily damaged, there was no doubt about that, but there were more survivors than she had first suspected. In fact her count was already up to eighteen, and still rising, while her earlier prediction had been for only a handful.

The Far Eastern Division morning supervisor Lieutenant Mark Hagedorn came over from the processing lab with a fresh batch of 100cm × 100cm transparencies. A third of them were marked with red tabs, indicating that they were infrared-enhanced. "Hot off the press, Maj," he said. Hagedorn had graduated last in his class at the Academy, but he had the same gift as Colonel Wight. He was able to "see" things. Although his smartass attitude was almost unbearable at times, every supervisor he worked for, including Louise, wished they had a dozen of him.

Louise looked up. "What did you bring me?" Hagedorn was only a couple of hours into his shift, but already his uniform looked as if it had been slept in.

"The navy's gonna be pissed off." Hagedorn laid a couple of the transparencies on an empty spot on the light table. "Unless I've been playing with myself too much and I'm going blind, I think that's bin Laden in the lower right quadrant."

Louise moved a large magnifying lens over the first photograph and studied the image in the lower right corner. It was definitely a man, and definitely dressed like bin Laden. His face was turned to the left, showing his profile. He was looking at a light bloom toward the center of the camp. Louise moved the magnifying lens, but she didn't need it to see that what she was looking at wasn't a fire or a secondary explosion; it was a missile strike.

She looked up.

"That was the second-to-the-last hit," Hagedorn said. "But I wasn't satisfied with the first shots, so I ran these through again, and played with some light values. The flashes from the HE warheads tend to fuzz out a lot of the details."

Louise turned back to the transparency. "How sure are you that this is bin Laden?"

"The computer was about seventy-five percent with the first, but we hit near a hundred percent with the second."

Louise switched to the second image, and this time the figure had thrown back his head and seemed to be shouting something up into the sky. There was no doubt in her mind that she was looking at a very-much-alive Osama bin Laden.

"That one's after the last strike, so there's no doubt that the navy missed him," Hagedorn said.

Louise cleared the other transparencies off the light table, and Hagedorn spread the rest of the pictures he had brought in sequence. "You've enhanced all of these?" she asked.

"Had to, because we weren't seeing diddly squat through the smoke, most of which incidentally came from burning diesel. Probably hit their fuel storage area. And the chopper was putting out a lot of smoke too."

Louise took her time studying each of the photographs that had been taken at two minute intervals after the attack had ended. The camp was flattened, nothing she was seeing changed her earlier assessment about that. But there were a lot of survivors. She counted at least two dozen, maybe more. But most disturbing was the fact that bin Laden had survived.

"He's carrying something," Louise said.

"Somebody," Hagedorn corrected. He laid out three infrared-enchanced transparencies, and it became immediately apparent that bin Laden was carrying a human form.

In each succeeding image the heat emanating from the body was fading.

Louise looked up. "Whoever it is was killed in the raid."

"That's what it looks like. The million dollar question is who. I mean bin Laden loves his men and all that, but he had a gimpy leg and he's not about to dive into the middle of a missile raid and pick up just anybody."

Louise went back to the photograph in which bin Laden had gotten to his feet. She could see that he was carrying somebody. She switched the magnifying lens to the next image showing him heading toward the middle of the camp, and then the next three, a cold knot beginning to form at the pit of her stomach. She looked up again and Hagedorn was staring at her.

"I think I'm going to show these to somebody who might know what they mean."

"Your old friend the colonel?" Hagedorn asked.

Louise shook her head. "You wouldn't know him. He's next door in the DO. Name is Otto Rencke. But first I want you to enhance everything we've downloaded so far. I don't want to make a mistake."

CIA Headquarters

Rencke went over to Murphy's office. Dick Adkins and Dave Whittaker were already there with the general who'd just returned from his home in Chevy Chase. "He's alive and on his way to Kabul," Rencke told them triumphantly.

Murphy was rocked to the core. "Was he hurt?"

"His phone was going bad so we didn't have much time. He was ten or twelve miles outside of bin Laden's camp, and he figured that he could make it down to Kabul sometime tonight, his time. Another ten or twelve hours."

"Then what?" Adkins asked. "And what the hell happened to his chip?"

"He didn't say about the chip, but he's going to try to make it to the ambassador's old residence," Rencke said.

"I'll see about getting our people over to him," Whittaker said, but he didn't sound so sure. "They're under siege at the old embassy so it's going to be a problem for them."

"Okay, assuming that he gets that far without running into a Taliban military patrol or the crowds, getting him out of the country isn't going to be a piece of cake," Adkins said.

"We're not going to leave him there," Murphy said firmly. "What do you have in mind, Otto?"

"There's maybe fifty Americans in Kabul right now, and they have to get out too. It'd make sense if we sent a C-130 from Riyadh to pick them up."

"It's likely that the Taliban are looking for him," Adkins said. "If he's spotted they'll never let him get close to the airport, let alone get aboard—even if the Taliban do let us fly in."

"Mac said that if we could get a C-130 in there he'd get aboard," Rencke countered, keeping his temper in check.

"I don't know how," Whittaker said.

"If Mac says he can do something, then we'd better believe him," Adkins flared. He turned to Murphy. "I can get the plane, that's no problem, but we'll have to put pressure on the Taliban government to give us flight clearance."

"I'll call the President right now," Murphy said. "He promised that if we found out that Mac was still alive he'd give us whatever we needed to get him out in one piece."

"I'll get Jeff Cook started. He can pull some strings, and with any luck by the time the C-130 approaches Afghani airspace we'll have the clearance," Adkins said, and he picked up the phone.

Murphy glanced at the clock. It was coming up on two. "The rest is going to be up to Mac, although I don't know what the hell the President is going to say to them."

"We only hit bin Laden's camp," Whittaker pointed out. "It's not as if we hit an Afghani civilian target. There's nothing else up there."

"There's more," Rencke said as Murphy reached for the direct line phone to the White House.

The general stopped.

"Mac told me that there's no doubt now that bin Laden has the bomb."

They all looked at him, the office suddenly very quiet. It was their worst fear. The reason they had sent McGarvey into what they all thought was a suicide mission.

"If he wasn't killed in the raid he'll use it against us."

"Do we have anything new from the NRO?" Murphy asked, subdued.

"Not yet, but they're working on it. The NSA is monitoring the usual lines of communications he's used in the past, but unless we get lucky we might not know for sure until it's too late."

"Until it's too late," Murphy repeated softly.

Rencke nodded glumly. "Mac wants a SNIE developed for the National Security Council by first thing in the morning. I've already called Fred Rudolph and told him what might be coming our way, and INS will have to be notified asap. Mac wants all of our assets worldwide put on alert, because the only way we're going to stop this shit is if somebody spots him." Rencke shook his head. "Oh, boy, this is the big one. If bin Laden is alive, and he wants to get a nuclear weapon to the U.S. and set it off, he'll do it."

"We're pretty good too, Otto," Murphy said.

"Yeah, but if he's alive he's gotta be seriously pissed off, ya know? He's gonna be one motivated dude."

Adkins put the phone down. "Jeff will arrange the C-130, but they'll need formal orders. They'll have to fly down the Gulf to avoid Iranian airspace, but the real problem is going to be Pakistan. The President will have to talk to them for over-flight permission. As it is Jeff figures that the one-way air distance is around sixteen hundred miles. But if they have to fly another route, over India let's say, it'll take twice as long."

"Can we make contact with Mac?" Murphy asked Rencke.

"No, his phone is still on simplex. But he said that he would call again once he got to Kabul. We have until then to come up with something for him. He'll need an ETA."

"We will, Otto," Murphy said seriously. "You have my word on it."

Adkins and Whittaker got up. "We'd best get to it then," Adkins said and they left.

Rencke got to his feet. "We can't leave him stuck there, General."

"We won't," Murphy said. "What did Kathleen say when you told her."

Rencke looked like a startled deer caught in headlights.

"I know you called her," Murphy prompted gently.

"She's a tough lady, but I thought she should know what's coming down," Rencke said defensively.

"Maybe we should send someone out to be with her."

"Already done, General," Rencke said. "And Liz is on her way in right now. I'm putting her in the loop."

"Good idea," Murphy agreed. "If you hear anything else let me know. But we *will* get him out of there. And we *will* stop bin Laden."

"Yes, sir," Rencke said, but he didn't seem to be very convinced about the second part.

Bin Laden's Camp

"We will talk now," bin Laden said. The morning was surreal, almost like a nightmare of hell. The sky over the camp was still filled with smoke. The distant mountains, usually crisp in the clear air, were obscured. Below there was a lot of frantic activity as their remaining mujahedeen cleaned up the missle damage, buried their dead and sifted through the rubble for anything usable. Although the order to pack up and leave had not come yet, everybody knew that they could no longer stay here. If the Americans suspected that anyone had survived, which they surely did by now, they might mount another attack. Even if they didn't, however, there was little or nothing left here except for the facility inside the cave. There were other camps, other caves that had not yet been pinpointed.

Bin Laden was numb with fatigue and grief. He wanted to run away and hide somewhere until it was time to die. His body was on fire, his left leg ached from the bone cancer eating at his hip and pelvis. Strange thoughts and visions kept popping into his head like lightning flashes, there for one brilliant split second, and then gone. He'd actually managed to do his midmorning prayers, lingering over each word, savoring each as if it were a sip of blessed ice water in the middle of the hot desert. But when he was finished he did not feel the same refreshment of spirit that he usually felt. Sarah, the light of his soul, was gone, and the only thought that allowed him to hold onto even a small portion of his sanity was that he would soon be joining her in Paradise, if indeed she was there. The Qoran said nothing about women in heaven. But Allah was just. He would not abandon her. He could not.

Bin Laden closed his eyes for just a moment, seeing the missiles raining down on them, feeling Sarah's lifeless body in his arms.

"As you wish," Bahmad said softly. He had read most of that from bin Laden's body language. He watched the struggle the man was going through with some sympathy because he had been there himself.

Sarah's body, completely wrapped in linen, lay on a prayer rug in the middle of the main chamber. When it got dark they would burn it. Bahmad was brought back to the funeral for his parents. He'd felt an impotent rage that he'd tried to quench all of his life. But now, though he wanted to feel some sadness for the girl, that part of him was already burned out. Sarah had been a wonderful girl; a daughter that he'd never had, never would have. They had talked often about life in the West, and she'd hung on everything he told her. And yet he still could not feel the loss. All he could feel now was a little sympathy for bin Laden, and the stirrings of anticipation for what might be coming next.

Leaning heavily on his cane, bin Laden walked back from the entrance and settled wearily on the cushions in front of the brazier. A young mujahed brought him tea, and then bin Laden dismissed him and the other guard standing by. They looked nervously to Bahmad who nodded, and they went out.

"We must leave here, Osama," Bahmad said, joining him on the cushions. Bin Laden poured him a glass of tea with shaking hands.

"Soon," bin Laden said. "But for us there will be different paths."

Bin Laden's manner and speech were formal, which was worrisome to Bahmad. The man was coming unglued. There was a holy zeal in his eyes. He'd seen the same look in the eyes of mujahedeen about to go off on suicide missions with ten kilos of plastique strapped to their chests. "I have always followed your orders faithfully."

"Yes, you have. And now I am sending you out on one last mission."

"Are you asking me to throw away my life?"

Bin Laden shook his head. "No, my old friend. But you will have to be very clever to walk away from this one. And where you will go afterwards will be up to you. Once your assignment is completed, you will be on your own." Bin Laden managed a small, coy smile despite his obvious physical and mental pain. "I think that you miss London."

"There are some aspects of life in the West that I have enjoyed," Bahmad admitted. "But no place might be safe for me if you want me to do what I think you want."

"Are you a mind reader?"

"No, a loyal servant."

"Of me, or of the cause?" bin Laden asked sharply. He glanced at Sarah's body.

"I've never known the difference."

Bin Laden might not have heard him. "It will be another burden for her mother to bear. So many burdens, so much pain. But she understands the jihad." He looked back in anguish. "She must!"

"The most difficult pain for a mother to bear," Bahmad offered gently. He thought about his own mother who had been mercifully spared that pain, though she had endured others. Because of the West.

A silence fell between them. The hiss of the gas lanterns was the only sound to be heard. After the missile strike the quiet was almost shocking.

"Kirk McGarvey must not be allowed to leave Afghanistan alive," bin Laden said after a minute. "Have you received word from Hamed?"

"I gave him orders to kill McGarvey, but he is out of radio range now, so there is no way of knowing if he succeeded until he returns."

"What if he reaches Kabul?"

"I have made arrangements."

"There must be no mistakes."

"Not this time."

Bin Laden nodded his satisfaction. "Sarah told me that she and McGarvey spoke about his daughter. She works for the CIA."

"She also mentioned it to me. But we knew about his background."

"Her name is Elizabeth."

"Yes."

"I want you to kill her," bin Laden said in a gentle voice. "After Mr. McGarvey, she will be your first priority."

Bahmad hid his surprise. "There is no reason for that, Osama," he said carefully. "Her father came here on a dangerous mission to find you and lead the missile attack. Killing him can be viewed as an act of war. Killing his daughter will be taken as nothing more than a senseless act of vengeance."

"You had Trumble and his family killed."

"That was to send the CIA the message that we were serious. It guaranteed that someone such as McGarvey would come."

"Will you do it?" bin Laden asked simply.

"Killing her would be a criminal waste of time and resources. Every American law enforcement agency would go on a worldwide alert of such intensity that no place would be safe. She is an innocent—"

"There are no innocents," bin Laden raised his voice. "You will show them that. You will teach the entire world."

Bahmad lowered his eyes. Not out of deference, but because he knew what else was coming. He'd known for several months, the realization coming to him on the day he learned about the bomb, about bin Laden's illness and about the final deal bin Laden had wanted to make with the West, with the nuclear weapon as the ultimate bargaining chip. He'd known that negotiating could not succeed. And he'd begun to work out a plan that he'd sincerely hoped he would never have to implement. Nevertheless he had started putting things in place in the U.S., renewing old contacts there and in London, Paris and Berlin. Phone calls, promises, threats. The only surprise now was going after McGarvey's daughter. It would present certain problems.

"Will you do it?" bin Laden asked again.

"Yes."

A new, even more intense light came into bin Laden's eyes. "Then there will be the final act of retribution," he said softly. "Joshua's hammer."

When the realization had come to him that they would use the nuclear weapon in some way to strike against America, Bahmad had gone searching for the right target at the right time. An air burst over Washington during a joint session of Congress would certainly never be forgotten so long as there was a civilized world. Nor would it be forgotten if the bomb were to be detonated in front of the White House, killing the President and his staff. An air burst over the financial center in New York would disrupt the Americans' capitalist hold on the world, as an airburst over a small Midwestern town would disrupt the average American's feelings of safety and invulnerability; the bomb at the Murrah Federal Building had done just that to the nation, though on a much smaller scale. But he came finally to the notion that what would strike the most fear in Americans' hearts would be an attack on what was most precious and sacred to them: their children. He had not foreseen Sarah's death, nor had he envisioned going after Mc-Garvey's daughter. But he had come up with a plan to do the one thing that would not be forgotten in a thousand years. Thinking about the plan he had devised, he could see that there was a certain symmetry between it and what bin Laden had ordered him to do. Sarah had been murdered by the Americans. In retaliation bin Laden wanted Mc-Garvey's daughter assassinated, and he was now ready to use the nuclear weapon.

"This will be very expensive," Bahmad said. "Not only in terms of money, but in terms of men."

"This will be my last blow. Time is running out for me." Bin Laden gave him a sad, knowing smile. "But I think you already guessed."

"Cancer?"

Bin Laden nodded. "Unless there is a miracle I have one year." He looked at Sarah's shrouded body. "I want America to feel the same pain I am feeling at this moment."

"If we do this thing your name will not be respected," Bahmad warned. "You will be vilified not only in the West, but among Muslims as well."

Bin Laden's gaze hardened. "But I will be remembered."

"Indeed you will."

Bin Laden thought about it for a long time, and when he looked up once more his resolve was as clear on his face as his pain. "How do we proceed?"

"Give me a minute and I will show you." Bahmad got up and went to his sleeping quarters off the operations center near the back of the cave. He lit one of the gas lamps and went to a four-drawer file cabinet, which he unlocked. The room was austere, only the bare rock floor, a small cot, a writing table and the file cabinet. There was nothing on the walls, no photographs or pictures; no rugs or vases, nothing to mark that anyone had lived here on and off for more than a year. But since Beirut, Bahmad had been a man who carried all of his decorations and mementoes in his brain.

He took a thick manila envelope out of the top drawer and relocked the file cabinet. He'd been an avid reader for a long time, a habit he had developed in England working for the SIS. Part of his job had been to read all the newspapers, journals and magazines coming out of the Middle East, and read transcripts from television and radio broadcasts, as well as from intercepted military and diplomatic traffic. He'd developed an insatiable appetite for news of what was going on in the world. Here in the mountains it had been fantastically difficult to keep abreast of what was happening in the outside world, but he had managed to have a weekly package of newspapers and magazines from around the world brought up here. And he consumed all the international news as it was presented, with different spins in the major newspapers of a dozen different countries. He had time to think, to plan, to let his mind soar wherever it would; to make connections where seemingly there were none; to make associations where none were apparent; and to draw out scenarios based on what he had learned.

Holding the envelope containing his planning details, he wondered why he had taken this notion as far as he had. Most of his ideas were just that, *nothing* but ideas. Way too fantastically difficult or even horrible to consider. But this idea had stuck with him, for some reason, and the operation would be his very last. With bin Laden dead, however, Bahmad would be set financially for the rest of his life. If he could pull this last thing off and get away, he had the numbers for a dozen of bin Laden's secret off-shore bank accounts worth somewhere in the neighborhood of three hundred million dollars. Enough to last any man a lifetime in luxury. And with bin Laden gone there would be no one to come after him.

Returning to the main chamber where bin Laden was waiting, Bahmad stopped a moment in the corridor. One last time he asked himself if he should go through with this. The idea was so monstrous that it had taken even his breath away when it had come to him. But years of hate had burned out whatever conscience he'd ever had. Yasir Arafat had fed into it, used it, just as bin Laden had, so that now even the bizarre seemed ordinary to him. Human life did not mean to him now what it had when he was a child.

The problem, he thought, walking into the main chamber, would be fitting the plan with Elizabeth McGarvey's assassination. For that he would need a diversion, and even before he sat down beside bin Laden it came to him; the entire thing in perfect detail, and he smiled. It would only take a few more phone calls and a transfer of some funds to the proper accounts.

"I see that you have already given this some thought," bin Laden said.

"Yes, I have." Bahmad opened the envelope and took out several articles that he had clipped from the *New York Times, Washington Post* and *San Francisco Examiner* three months ago. He handed them to bin Laden.

"I will read these later—" bin Laden said, but then a photograph of a pretty young woman in the lead article caught his attention. He drew a sudden, sharp breath and looked up, a sense of wonder on his face.

"She would be the target," Bahmad said.

Bin Laden's mind was racing a thousand miles per hour. "But not the President?"

"Not necessarily."

"Not the President," bin Laden said forcefully. He studied the photograph. "I want him to feel the same grief I am feeling. A father's grief when his daughter is killed in front of his eyes. It must be done that way."

"The target will be Deborah Haynes, the President's daughter."

Bin Laden sat back and closed his eyes. "You would use a nuclear weapon to kill one person?"

"No, there would be many others. Perhaps two thousand, probably even more than that."

"Tell me."

"The President's daughter is mildly retarded, which makes the fact of *her* innocence without argument. America loves her as they love their President. Every father can have sympathy for the family. For what they will go through. But America is also very proud of her. Besides being beautiful, she is talented. She is a gymnast and a long-distance runner."

Bin Laden opened his eyes. "I didn't know that."

"Three months from now, in September, Deborah Haynes is going to take part in the International Special Olympics in San Francisco. After the opening ceremonies in Candlestick Park, she, and perhaps as many as fifteen hundred other handicapped runners, is going to compete in a half-marathon. From the park she'll cross the Golden Gate Bridge and head to Sausalito, but she'll never get that far. Joshua's Hammer will be aboard a ship passing beneath the bridge. At the moment Deborah Haynes is in the middle of the bridge the bomb will explode."

For just a moment a touch of sanity crossed bin Laden's face and he looked away, his eyes coming to rest on his daughter's shrouded body.

"There'll be no going back to the old ways for any of us," Bahmad warned.

"It will be no mere footnote in the history books," bin Laden said softly. "Unlike Sarah's murder." He turned back. "Where will you go afterwards?"

"I have a place in mind," Bahmad said. The money he already had would be sufficient to gain him the safe haven. And once he had raided bin Laden's accounts, he would buy a large ranch inland. He'd thought about raising horses, perhaps even sugarcane. Legitimate pursuits. He would never be able to travel again, but then with what he had in mind there would be no need. He would trade his career as a terrorist for one of a gentleman farmer.

"When we leave here we will never see or hear from each other again."

"Where will you go, Osama?"

Bin Laden said nothing, and after a few moments of silence, Bahmad nodded.

"It's just as well that I don't know. But we need to be gone from here within the next twenty-four hours, no longer."

"Do you have a plan for transporting the bomb to California?"

"Yes, but for that I will need your help. Four of your most trusted mujahedeen need to move it out of here, and your international connections to get me a cargo ship."

A sudden understanding dawned in bin Laden's eyes. "It's why you insisted on camouflaging it in that package. It will be—"

Bahmad held up a hand. "No one must know about this except for us, Osama. Not your mujahedeen who will transport the device, and certainly not the ship captain or his crew." He took the newspaper articles from bin Laden's hand, and dropped them onto the live coals in the brazier. The paper flared up, and Bahmad took the rest of the planning documents, maps, photographs, notes and timetables out of the manila envelope and fed them to the fire too. Lastly he dropped the envelope into the flames. He knew everything by heart.

They watched in silence until there was nothing left but ashes, which Bahmad stirred with a small wooden-handle rake.

"Insha'Allah," bin Laden said.

Bahmad held his piece. But no, he thought. In this instance he didn't believe that Allah or God would play any part, because this act would be too bloody even for them.

SIXTEEN

The White House

Ladies and gentlemen, the President of the United States."

The President's press secretary Sterling Mott stepped aside and the Washington press corps got to its feet as President Haynes strode purposefully into the map room and took his place at the podium. He'd brought no notes, and when he looked into the television cameras his manner was stern but forthright.

"Here's a man with a clear conscience," the AP political analyst said to the ABC newswoman seated beside him, which elicited a chuckle.

"For several years the United States has offered a five million dollar reward for the capture of the Saudi Arabian terrorist, Osama bin Laden," the President began. "Since the bombing of a Saudi National Guard Post in Riyadh in 1996 in which five Americans were killed, bin Laden has been directly or indirectly tied to numerous other terrorist acts in which hundreds of Americans and thousands of other innocent civilians were brutally killed or injured."

The President paused. "Dahran, Kenya, Tanzania and even New York City . . . bin Laden has waged his war of terror against the West—against specifically the United States and all Americans—for a very long and bloody time.

"In 1998 he made it perfectly clear to the world that it was every Muslim's duty to kill Americans and our allies, both civilian and military, wherever and whenever possible.

"Under the banner that he calls Al Qaeda, or the Base,

he has systematically recruited three kinds of people—those who were failures and had nothing else in their lives, no jobs, no families, no prospects for the future; those who love Islam but have no real idea what the Koran teaches; and finally those who know nothing but fighting and killing—professional terrorists.

"In August of 1998, President Clinton ordered missile strikes at bin Laden's camps near the town of Khost in northeastern Afghanistan, and at a bin Laden-financed chemical weapons factory in Khartoum. All the targets were heavily damaged or completely destroyed, seriously affecting bin Laden's ability to wage his war of terrorism against us."

The President paused again to gauge the effect that his words were having.

"Although bin Laden escaped personal injury, we thought that such an attack would make him think twice about continuing what he calls his jihad—or, holy war. But we were mistaken.

"Over the past months our intelligence agencies have been engaged in what we thought was a meaningful dialogue with bin Laden. We acted in good faith, agreeing to lift the bounty on him, to negotiate with the government of Saudi Arabia for the repatriation of his family, and certain other considerations that we felt would put an end to the killings.

"Bin Laden responded in a very clear, very concise and very deadly manner. Two weeks ago, gunmen, under the direct orders of bin Laden, shot to death a State Department employee, Allen Trumble, his wife and two children along with two bystanders in the parking lot of EPCOT Center in Orlando, Florida."

That got everybody's attention and two dozen hands shot up, but the President held them off.

"I ordered the Federal Bureau of Investigation to withhold the essential facts of the attack until we were certain who was behind it. When we had concrete evidence laying the crime on bin Laden's doorstep, we continued to withhold the announcement while we considered an appropriate response."

A heavy silence fell over the room. All eyes and cameras were on the President.

"Yesterday, after a week-long series of meetings with my National Security Council, I ordered our armed forces to strike at bin Laden's primary camp in the mountains of Afghanistan, eighty miles north of the capital city Kabul."

The announcement answered the questions about anti-American rioting in Kabul that had begun this morning. Until now the White House had stonewalled the issue.

"In addition to the incident in Orlando, our intelligence services confirmed the strong likelihood that bin Laden was planning another, even more deadly attack against Americans on U.S. soil. I cannot share all the details with you at this time because of national security concerns, but we believe that if such an attack were brought against us the loss of lives would be staggering. It would be a far worse tragedy than anything bin Laden has engineered to date."

The President was grim-faced. It was clear to everybody watching and listening that he had been forced into ordering the attack. It was something abhorrent to him. And yet he was being firm. During his campaign he'd promised the American people that he would take back the fear. And this was the first necessary though painful step in that direction.

"The mission was a success," he continued. "Preliminary reconnaissance aircraft and satellite photos indicate that the terrorist camp was obliterated. Wiped from the face of the earth. There was no loss of American lives, nor were any civilian targets damaged or destroyed. This was a surgical strike."

The President looked directly into the television cameras. "I made it perfectly clear when I was hired for this job, and I will make it perfectly clear again: The United States has a zero-tolerance policy toward all acts of terrorism against Americans, wherever they may be, and against the monsters who perpetrate them. There is, and will continue to be, no safe haven for terrorists anywhere on earth. Strike at us, and we *will* find and destroy you. And that is a promise."

In the Afghan Mountains

Sunset was in another twenty minutes at 8:27. McGarvey had gone without proper rest for more than forty-eight hours, and he didn't know how much longer he could keep it up.

The worst part had been climbing down the steep cliff beside the waterfall. He'd almost lost his footing several times, and when he finally reached the lower camp his legs had shaken so badly he had to stop for ten minutes before he could go on.

Twice making his way down the arroyo to the valley he'd stumbled on rocks and nearly broke an ankle. Afterward, however, the going was much easier and he had allowed himself the luxury of a cigarette and a drink of water.

The day had been very warm, but now with the sun behind the mountains to the west the temperature was dropping fast. There wasn't a cloud in the sky, but a strong wind blew down the valley and he could smell the snow on the upper peaks. Just thinking about what this valley would be like in the dead of winter made him shiver, and he picked up the pace.

Already he was behind schedule. The climb down the cliff and through the arroyo had taken much longer than he thought it would. He tried jogging, but after a hundred yards or so he was winded because of the altitude, and he felt a very sharp, painful stitch at his side, so that he had to slow down. The feeling he'd had at the top of the cliff that someone was behind him—perhaps Farid had turned around and come back after all—had finally faded. He stopped several times to look back, but each time he saw nothing. No movement of any kind. He could have been on a deserted planet.

As he walked he thought about Sarah. If she had taken

her time getting back to the camp she would have missed the attack. But if she had hurried she would have been caught in the middle of it. Then her only hope would have been to get inside the cave. Either way if she had survived it would have been a terrible blow for her. Everything her father had taught her about Americans would have been proven true. They were not to be trusted, their word was as godless as their society.

However badly we hurt them up there, the surviving mujahedeen would be tending to their wounded. McGarvey knew from the last time bin Laden had been hit that his people would be gone from that location within twenty-four hours.

But they would be sending someone for him. Of that he had little doubt. And if they came he would have to kill them. The time for negotiating had passed.

He spotted the outlying stubble of the abandoned cornfields, and the outlines of the bombed-out buildings in the village, and he picked up the pace again. It was possible that there was another, faster path down from bin Laden's camp; the route they had taken might have been only for his benefit. Even now he thought that he would have a hard time retracing his steps. Every arroyo looked almost exactly the same from the valley floor as every other one.

With darkness coming he angled to the west up into the hills above the valley. He reached a spot from where he could look down into the village, and held up. Nothing moved below. From where he crouched in the scrub brush he could make out the barn where they had parked the Rover, and even a bit of the camo netting. On the other side of the village he could see the wide stream meandering down the valley. And above him, at the crest of the hills, there was nothing.

He settled down to wait until it was completely dark, his back against the trunk of a short, gnarled tree. If someone was down there now, the advantage would be theirs until nightfall. He wanted a cigarette, but the breeze was at his back and would carry the smoke down into the village.

Instead, he ate a piece of nan and drank some water. The little bit of food helped, but every bone in his body ached, and one of the stitches from his operation had opened and the wound was seeping blood.

This mission could have succeeded if the missile attack hadn't been carried out. Yet from the President's point of view there wasn't any other choice, especially with Berndt constantly in his ear. When the chip went off the air they had to assume the worse, that McGarvey was dead. Now, if bin Laden had survived, the battle was going to be on his terms, and it would very likely end in disaster.

He toyed with doing the totally unexpected. If he turned around now and headed back up to bin Laden's camp he might possibly make it before daybreak. But even if the camp hadn't been dismantled and abandoned by then, actually finding bin Laden and putting a bullet in his brain would be next to impossible. McGarvey had turned the problem over in his head, trying to come up with a scenario that made sense in which he could get back there, find bin Laden, kill him and then get free again. But each time he came up against several brick walls, not the least of which was his exhaustion. Spending the night and the entire day hidden in the mountains before he went in wouldn't do much good either. Without supplies his condition would worsen.

He drifted off, thinking about Katy and Liz waiting for him back in Washington. They would be worried, because Otto couldn't keep a secret from Liz, and she in turn would have told her mother what was going on. But it was no good thinking about them for now. One step at a time. It was all he could do.

He woke twenty minutes later, the night almost pitch-black except for the starlight. He was deeply chilled and it took several seconds before he could loosen his muscles enough to simply stand up.

The village was nothing but indistinct shadows and angles. As he picked his way down the hill he took out his gun, and by feel made sure the action still worked smoothly and the safety catch was off.

He reached the cornfields ten minutes later, still stiff and cold despite the exertion. When he got to the first building to the north of the barn where the Rover was parked, he stopped in the deeper shadows to watch and listen. The only sounds were the gurgling of the nearby stream and the wind in the hills above him. It would only take a minute or so to pop the car's ignition switch and hot-wire it. If he didn't run into any trouble on the way out of the mountains he figured he could reach the Taliban checkpoint near the airport before dawn. From there it would be anyone's guess what he might encounter. But if he got that far he would have at least a chance of getting out of the country.

He slipped around the side of the building and worked his way through the rubble, holding up every ten yards or so to watch and listen. It was quiet. It did not look as if the camouflage netting covering the car had been disturbed. It was going to be good to sit on a soft seat with back support and the car's heater for a change. He couldn't remember then last time he'd been this cold or strung out.

Farid came out of the barn, a Kalashnikov slung over his shoulder, and nervously lit a cigarette.

McGarvey held perfectly still in the darkness, his stiff, aching muscles totally forgotten for the moment. There was another route back after all and Farid had taken it. But had he returned alone? McGarvey didn't think that Farid would have had time to return to the camp and then get back here, even if there was a shortcut. The only other possibility was that someone else had started out after him.

If that were the case then this was a trap. But McGarvey wondered if he was simply being paranoid. Rather than face bin Laden's wrath for failing, Farid may have decided to come back on his own hoping to get a jump on McGarvey when he showed up at the car. But he had to assume the worst.

After a few minutes Farid tossed the cigarette away and went back into the barn.

McGarvey stepped out of the deeper shadows and hurried to the rear of the building, taking care not to stumble on the loose rocks, bricks and pieces of wood lying everywhere. Most of the back wall of the barn was gone. Farid had climbed up on a pile of rubble and was looking toward the north, the same direction McGarvey had come from. Had he been standing there earlier there was a good possibility he'd seen McGarvey coming in.

It was very dark back here. An entire army of mujahedeen could be hidden in the village and they would be invisible.

McGarvey stepped inside the barn and ducked down behind the Rover. Flattening himself on the dirt floor he looked under the car. He could see the rubble pile that Farid was standing on, but so far as he could tell no one was crouched waiting on the other side.

He got up and crept to the back of the car, and checked outside. There was nothing there. But he knew that it was distinctly possible that this was a setup. The problem was that he could not stay here all night waiting for something to develop.

He moved to the other side of the Rover, then keeping his eye on Farid, he took several steps closer and raised his pistol. "You should not have come back," he said softly.

Farid spun around, a guilty look on his face. But he did not look frightened, nor did he try to reach for his rifle. His eyes flicked to something behind McGarvey.

All that took only a split second. It *was* a trap.

McGarvey jumped up on the hood of the Rover and rolled to the other side of the car as a burst from a Kalashnikov rifle raked the floor where he'd been standing.

He hit the dirt floor on his right shoulder, brought his gun around and fired two quick shots at Farid's retreating figure as the mujahed disappeared around the corner outside.

Whoever had fired from the door had come from the other side of the barn. He was moving cautiously around the back of the Rover. McGarvey looked under the car, saw a pair of boots and fired, hitting the man in the ankle.

McGarvey jumped up as the mujahed cried out in pain. The man was staggering backward, trying to keep his balance while he tried to bring his rifle to bear. McGarvey rushed around the back of the car, batted the rifle aside with his free hand, and crashed into the mujahed, sending them both sprawling to the ground outside the barn.

McGarvey jammed the muzzle of his pistol in the mujahed's throat just below his chin. If he pulled the trigger the bullet would crash into the man's brain, and he knew it. His struggles stopped immediately.

"How many others did you bring with you?" McGarvey looked up to make sure that Farid hadn't come around from behind the barn.

"Six," the mujahed grunted.

"Including Farid?"

The mujahed hesitated a fraction of a second. It was enough to tell McGarvey that he was lying. "Who sent you? Was it bin Laden or Ali?"

"Screw you."

"I didn't come here to lead the missile attack. I came to make a deal." McGarvey took the rifle from the mujahed and tossed it aside. "I won't kill you if you give me your word that you and Farid will return to the camp."

The mujahed shouted something in Persian as Farid came around the corner of the barn. McGarvey rolled left and fired three shots as Farid brought his rifle up, all three of them hitting the young man in the chest and driving him backward.

McGarvey turned around. The mujahed he had wounded in the leg had reached his rifle and he was snatching it out of the dirt as McGarvey fired one shot, catching the man in the temple, killing him instantly.

Farid was still alive. He was struggling to pull a pistol out of his vest, but he was too weak to do it.

McGarvey got up, walked over and crouched down beside him. Blood covered his chest, and bubbles were forming over the lung shot. His face was deathly pale, flecks of foamy blood on his lips. He was a dead man and he knew it.

"I didn't want to kill any of you."

Farid whispered something in Persian.

"This should never have happened to you. To any of you, but the killing and terrorism has to stop. No more jihad."

Farid was very young, and as McGarvey watched the life drain out of his face, a great sadness came over him. Along with it he thought about Sarah, sincerely hoping that she had come out of the missile attack okay, and about his own daughter who, because of her father, had almost been killed three times. A waste, all of it was a terrible waste. The sins of the fathers were to be suffered by the sons. Only now McGarvey was afraid that the daughters would somehow bear the brunt.

Farid whispered something else in Persian, and then was still.

"Goddammit," McGarvey said, and he sat back. "Goddammit to hell."

CIA Headquarters

The CIA was on emergency status. The most effective deputy director of Operations that the Company had ever known was stuck in badland and all the stops had been pulled to get him out of there.

Adkins had temporarily assigned Elizabeth as acting assistant to Otto Rencke, who had set her up at a computer terminal in his offices. She was working on flight plans from Riyadh down the Gulf and across Pakistan to Kabul, the most direct route, and the one that made the most sense, considering what her father was facing. But she was also working out several alternative routes, including one that passed through Indian airspace, and the much longer way, northwest through Syria and Turkey, then straight east over the former Russian republics of Armenia and Azerbaijan, across the Caspian Sea and then Turkmenistan.

The Russian route, as she thought of it, would be tough. Flight clearances might take days, if they were ever given, and there would have to be a refueling stop somewhere. In addition, that route put the flight path over northern Afghanistan where the rebels fighting the Taliban had Stinger missiles. They were shooting down anything that came within range.

Elizabeth sat back and pushed a wisp of blond hair off her forehead. She hadn't had much time to worry about her father all day, but relaxing for a moment she tried to envision what he was going through, and it sent a shiver up her spine.

Waiting was infinitely more difficult than doing, she decided. In the field, on the run, you were too busy to spend much time worrying about what might happen. The adrenalin was pumping, inner reserves were kicking in and everything you'd learned in training and from previous missions—the good ones as well as the bad—became foremost in your mind. When your survival was at stake, your focus tended to be sharp. But sitting here waiting, wondering, fretting, was the pits.

Rencke came in from a staff meeting at 5:30 P.M. Elizabeth jumped up. "We've got Pakistan," he said, dumping an armload of file folders and computer printouts on his already-overflowing conference table.

"Thank God," she said. "When do they get airborne?"

"They left fifteen minutes ago."

Elizabeth's eyes went automatically to the half-dozen world clocks on the wall. The one for Kabul read 0500. Rencke knew exactly what she was thinking.

"It'll be broad daylight when they touch down," he said. "Around ten in the morning, his time. But there wasn't much else we could do, Liz. The airport closes down after dark. Besides, they have to think he'd want to make a try under cover of darkness. This might throw them a curve."

"It might also make it impossible for my father to even get close to the airport, let alone make it to the airplane."

"The longer he stays there, the greater the risk he faces,"

Rencke started to hop from one foot to the other, but stopped. "Oh, wow, Liz, I'm really scared. But your dad's pretty smart, he'll figure it out. And he's tough too."

Her heart softened. "Okay, Otto, take it easy. How do we get the ETA to my father?"

"When he gets to the ambassador's old compound in Kabul he's going to call me."

"You said that his phone battery was low. What if he can't call?"

Rencke looked even more forlorn. "There's no phone in the compound, I checked. But even if there was he'd have to go through their international exchange, and the Taliban control every call out of the country."

"Could he get to one of the other embassies?"

"He might." Rencke shook his head in frustration.

Elizabeth tried to put herself in her father's place, think what he might do. "Maybe he could rig up a battery charger."

"There's no electricity to the house. No water, no sewer, nothing."

"I thought there was someone living there, like caretakers."

"So did I. But right now there're only a couple of Taliban guards stationed outside." He brightened a little. "One good thing, all the rioting is concentrated downtown at our old embassy for now."

"For now," Elizabeth repeated glumly.

"He's got to get out of there, Liz, and he knows it. There's too much at stake now. We need him back here or we're going to be in some very big shit."

This was something new. She looked at him. "What do you mean? What else is going on?"

Rencke was getting agitated again. "This is eyes-only shit. The big enchilada. It's why your dad took the chance going over there in the first place."

"What is it?"

"Oh, shit, Liz. Oh, goddam shit." Rencke suddenly stopped moving. "It's lavender again. It's bin Laden, he's got a nuclear weapon and he wanted to give it to us, but the missiles ruined that deal. Your dad was going to talk him out of it. That's the real reason he went over there."

Elizabeth was stunned. "I thought it was about Allen Trumble."

"That too. But unless we nailed bin Laden in the raid, he'll be coming after us big time, and your dad is the only one who knows him well enough now to figure out what he's going to do and how to stop him."

"Where'd he get it?"

"The Russians. It's just a demolitions device, around a kiloton, but it's real little. Eighty pounds, fits in a suitcase. It could do a lot of bad stuff to us."

The telephone on Rencke's desk rang. He whipped around and snatched it up. "What?" he demanded.

Elizabeth was numb. She hadn't any inkling of the real reason her father was going over to meet with bin Laden. She'd known that something big was in the wind, but not what. This news was simply staggering.

"Five minutes," Rencke said, subdued. He broke the connection and called the security desk downstairs. "This is Rencke in the DO. Major Horn is coming across from the NRO's Photo Interp Section. Give her a pass and have an escort bring her up here as soon as she arrives."

"Who's Major Horn?" Elizabeth asked.

Rencke went to his conference table and started taking everything off it, stacking the files and printouts in untidy piles against the wall. "She's a friend," he said distractedly. "A very bright friend." He stopped and gave Elizabeth an owlish look. "She says we have some serious trouble coming our way. And Louise does not exaggerate. Never."

Elizabeth helped him clear the table. "What kind of trouble?"

"She's bringing over some satellite shots." He stopped again. "But she sounded scared, Liz. I've never heard her like that."

"I don't know what else can go wrong," Elizabeth said.

"Plenty," Rencke told her.

. . .

Louise Horn got to Rencke's office a few minutes later, a big leather photograph portfolio under her arm. She looked as if she hadn't slept in a month. "Hi," she said, almost shyly.

Rencke introduced her to Elizabeth, and they shook hands.

"You're Kirk McGarvey's daughter, aren't you?" she asked.

"Yes. I'm working with Otto for now."

Louise and Rencke exchanged a worried but warm glance. "Well, wherever your dad is right now, he's going to want to know about this," she said. She took a dozen 100cm × 100cm photographs that had been made from the transparencies, and spread them out in sequence on the conference table. "These are mostly enhanced KH-13 images of bin Laden's camp before, during and after the missile raid." She handed a large magnifying glass to Rencke.

"What am I supposed to be seeing?" he asked.

"Upper right quadrant, first three shots. There's someone coming down the hill into the camp from the south. That's a few minutes before the missiles hit."

Rencke studied the photographs for a minute. "Could be Mac's escort coming back."

"We figured that was one possibility," Louise said. "We don't have any establishing shot showing him leaving, but assuming he wasn't there during the raid . . ." She trailed off and looked at Elizabeth. "Sorry, but this isn't going to get any easier, I'm afraid."

"That's all right," Elizabeth said. "I'm here to do a job just like everybody else."

"He wasn't there," Rencke said. "I talked to him via satellite phone."

"Okay, maybe his escort then, or one of them." Louise directed his attention to the next series of shots. "Lower center this time. There, below the helicopter, you can see the figure. The next is the heat bloom from a missile strike."

Rencke studied the photo. "Right on top of him."

"Not quite, but close," Louise said. "You can see in the next two shots that she's down, but primarily intact."

Rencke and Elizabeth looked up. "She?" Rencke asked.

Louise nodded tiredly. "We weren't sure at first, so I had my people go back and re-enhance every image we downloaded from the get-go. Then I pulled up bin Laden's package."

Rencke moved ahead to the next photographs, which he studied for a long time. When he looked up he handed the glass to Elizabeth. "Bin Laden is alive."

Louise nodded. "I hope they don't shoot the messenger, but somebody's got to tell the navy that they missed."

Elizabeth bent over the table and studied the images, especially the last few, which showed bin Laden carrying the body of a woman, her long black hair streaming nearly to the ground. "Who is she?" Elizabeth asked, looking up.

Louise took two more photographs out of the portfolio. One was a blown-up and enhanced section of one of the satellite photos, showing the face and neck of the body in bin Laden's arms. The second was a file photograph of a young, beautiful woman dressed in traditional garb, except that her face and hair were uncovered. They were the same woman.

"Sarah bin Laden. His daughter."

It hit Elizabeth all at once. "My God, I know her."

"How? Where?" Rencke demanded.

"I don't know, but her face, it's so familiar to me."

"The Bern Polytechnic," Louise said. "I checked the records, she was there one year the same time you were. I wondered if you would remember her."

"She was younger than me, I think, but we might have had a couple of the same classes." Elizabeth looked up in amazement. "I remember her because she always had bodyguards around her. Some of the other girls thought it was cool, but I thought it was a pain in the neck." She looked at the photograph again. "She was sorta quiet, and very smart. But she was never allowed to go into town, or on trips with us. I remember that, because we all thought it was sad, you know. The poor little Arab rich kid."

"Well, our missiles killed her and not bin Laden," Louise said.

"Adkins has to see this," Elizabeth said, a cold fist closing around her heart. Bin Laden would be insane with rage now.

Rencke's brain was going a mile a minute. "The President has to be informed," he said distractedly. He focused on Louise. "Good job, kiddo," he said softly. "But you'd better stick around, there's gonna be some questions."

"I figured as much," she said. "I'll be next door in the Pit if you need me. Maybe we can come up with something else. The weather over there is still on our side." She glanced at Elizabeth. "Too bad about his daughter."

"He's going to come after my father," Elizabeth said.

"I think you're right," Louise replied. "But from what I understand, your dad is a pretty tough dude himself." She smiled. "It's not over so don't count him out yet." She turned back to Rencke. "When you're ready for a break give me a call. We can go over to my apartment and I'll fix us some supper."

"I'll call you," Rencke promised, but he'd already lifted the phone to Dick Adkins.

SEVENTEEN

To Kabul

McGarvey pulled off the side of the highway and got out to check under the hood. An armored scout car was parked a couple of hundred yards away at the road to the airport.

They might be looking for a Rover, but they were expecting an American. McGarvey had taken the time to pull Farid's clothes over his khakis and sweater. He wore a cap, and although he was clean shaven he'd wrapped a cotton scarf around his neck and chin. It might be unclear to someone passing, or to someone standing beside the road exactly who or what he was.

The trip down the valley from the bombed-out village, and the path along the river cliffs in the dark had taken him much longer than he expected. It had already been light when he'd passed Charikar. Stopped now beside the road he was seeing a lot of traffic, most of it big trucks bringing food into the city from the countryside.

By now Farid and the other mujahed would be missed. Someone else might have been sent to find out what had happened, and each hour that passed the likelihood that the Taliban in Kabul had been notified increased exponentially. It was important that he get to a place of relative safety very soon so that he could get a few hours' rest, and hopefully something to eat and drink. He was at his extreme physical limit. He was having trouble concentrating on what he was doing, trouble keeping in focus.

He closed the Rover's hood and got back behind the wheel. A couple of cars and a broken-down old bus passed him, none of the drivers slowing for the checkpoint. In the rearview mirror a minute later McGarvey saw what he had been looking for. A convoy of what appeared to be at least six large trucks lumbered down the highway, a cloud of blue-gray exhaust trailing behind them.

He put the car in gear and waited until the lead truck was almost upon him, then suddenly gunned the engine and pulled out in front of it. McGarvey glanced in the rearview mirror in time to see the driver shake a fist at him as the distance between them closed alarmingly fast. He stomped the gas pedal to the floor and the Rover shot out ahead, at the same moment the scout car's turret hatch opened, and a man popped up.

He was a soldier, McGarvey could see that much as he

got closer, and he was speaking into a microphone. Seventy-five yards away, the turret started to move as a plume of diesel smoke blossomed out of the exhaust stack, and the scout car lurched toward the highway.

McGarvey checked the rearview mirror again, and then slowed down so that the lead truck was once more right on his bumper. The scout car crew had spotted him and they were going to try to intercept him. But they had to know that if they fired there was a good chance they'd hit the truck right behind him too. At the very least they would cause a tremendous accident that would probably end up with a lot of casualties, ruined food supplies and a traffic jam that would be snarled for most of the morning.

Thirty yards out the muzzle of the main 14.5 mm heavy machinegun came around to point directly at him, and the scout car stopped just off the highway's paved surface. It would be like shooting fish in a barrel. There wasn't the slightest chance that the gunner would miss. McGarvey could see that the soldier in the turret was an officer, and he was frantically speaking into his microphone while gesticulating for McGarvey to pull over.

A string of several cars and a couple of trucks was coming out of the city. The officer turned and spotted them as they were nearly on top of his position. He bent down and shouted something through the open turret. At the last possible instant the cars flashed past the scout car as McGarvey, the six trucks directly on his tail, also passed, and the moment to open fire was gone.

McGarvey breathed a sigh of relief, and allowed himself to relax for just a minute. The first problem, getting past the airport checkpoint, was solved, but now he was faced with the even larger problems of getting into the city, ditching the car and making it on foot to the ambassador's old residence compound. Then he would have to get inside past any guards that the Taliban might have posted because of the riots, and somehow deal with the two caretakers. They were there to protect American property so he could not harm them. Yet they were in fact employees of the Taliban government so they wouldn't hesitate to try to arrest him, which might end up becoming his biggest problem this morning. But he needed food and drink and rest, and he needed it very soon.

He gradually sped up, putting more distance between himself and the convoy of trucks. He kept a sharp eye for military vehicles, and he kept checking the sky to make sure they hadn't sent a helicopter gunship after him. If they did that he wouldn't stand a chance out here in the open.

He couldn't help but think about Sarah bin Laden. In another time and place she could have gone to London for her education, and could have eventually taken over the family's business interests. He had no doubt that she would have been good at it, because she was bright and she had proved how adaptable she was by existing in Afghanistan disguised as a mujahed. He could see her in a private jet flitting from one world capital to another, attending high-level business meetings; informing her business opponents, with an arched eyebrow, that they had no conception of what truly difficult negotiations could be like. She'd been there, seen that, done that.

The city gradually enfolded him like a dirty pair of trousers. Low, mud-brick buildings on either side of the highway gave way to larger and thicker concentrations of walled compounds, and rat warrens of hovels rising up from the floor of the river valley into the arid, treeless hills overlooking the city.

Unlike the day he came in from the airport when the streets were all but devoid of life, traffic this morning was fairly heavy, and the marketplaces, as he approached the city center, were filled with shoppers. Out this early, he suspected, to beat the summer heat.

As best he could remember from studying the maps and files he'd brought with him in his laptop, the ambassador's residence was not too far from the old embassy, which was on Ansari Wat in the northeastern part of the city called Wzir Akbar Khan Mena. He'd seen the embassy on the way in from the airport and he had a fuzzy idea how to get from it to the residence. But Otto warned him that the anti-American rioting was concentrating around the old embassy. No one would expect him to walk into the middle of a demonstration, but it might be his safest bet for now.

In the distance ahead he spotted a roadblock. Several army trucks and jeeps, and at least one armored car blocked the main road. He slowed down. The officer at the airport checkpoint would have radioed that the Rover had passed him and was on the way into the city. They were waiting for him, and he looked for someplace to ditch the car.

The main street was filled with people, and as McGarvey got even closer he realized that the roadblock had been set up not to catch him, but to allow the crowd to get across. Off to the right, in the direction the people were moving, was the old American embassy. What he was seeing was more people being directed toward the demonstration. Like most of these riots it was being choreographed by the government, and they had their hands full. It gave him the advantage for the moment.

A block away he pulled into a narrow side street that wound its way past a series of shops, a lot of them closed, and some three- and four-story European-style structures that looked like apartment buildings.

He came to a large park ringed by apartment buildings. At one end of the park was a mosque, its minaret rising into the cloudless, pale blue sky. The traffic was very light now, and what few people were on foot seemed to be heading up toward the embassy.

McGarvey drove slowly down an alley between buildings and found a parking spot beside an old Mercedes and a small Fiat delivery van. He got out and walked back down the alley to the street, then crossed the park, pulling the scarf over his mouth so that only his nose and eyes were left uncovered.

When they found the Rover they would have no idea where he had gotten himself to. It was unlikely that they would believe he had headed into the crowd around the old embassy. They might think that he was trying to make it to another embassy, or even out to the airport, anywhere but toward the heart of the anti-American disturbance.

A block beyond the park, down a pleasant, tree-lined street of upscale private homes, all of them protected behind tall brick walls, he heard the noise of a crowd and he guessed that he was getting close to the embassy. There were no street signs back here, and the only people he saw was a band of young men a couple of blocks away down an intersecting avenue.

He stopped to get his bearings.

He figured that he had to be within a half-mile of the embassy, which put him somewhere in the vicinity of the ambassador's residence. If he had his laptop finding the place would be easy. But he remembered that it was at the end of a short dead-end street, behind which was a two-block-square neighborhood of weavers' workshops and retail stores. Before the Taliban had taken over, and even before the Russians had started their war here, the area had been a busy one, catering mostly to foreigners with money. Afghan rugs and carpets had been one of the major cottage industries in the city. Dealers from all over the world had come here to pick up bargains for resale in their stores in all the major Western cities. All that was a thing of the past, but the workshops were still in business, or at least some of them were according to the State Department report he'd read. And some carpets still found their way out of the country. He headed to the right, away from the noise of the crowd.

Two blocks later he came to the dead-end street. There was a Russian jeep parked in front of the compound's main gate. Two men in uniform were lounging back, their feet propped up on the open doors. Nothing was happening here and they were obviously bored and inattentive.

McGarvey stepped back out of sight around the corner. Behind the walls a Georgian mansion rose four stories, its windows shuttered. The house could have been directly transplanted from a fashionable London neighborhood. It looked out of place, which was typical of a lot of American installations around the world. Most U.S. ambassadors did not speak the language of their assigned country, and many of their embassies and residences stuck out like sore thumbs. It was a holdover from a more arrogant colonial period.

He turned around and walked to the last intersecting street he had passed and followed it, coming to the rug weavers' district. The streets were quite narrow, as they were in the other traditional working class areas of the city. Not a single person was about, and all the shops and houses were closed, some of them boarded up. The neighborhood had the feel of abandonment, fallen on hard times.

McGarvey made his way to a small, boarded-up shop that he figured was directly behind the ambassador's compound. Nothing, not even a dog or a scrap of paper, moved on the street, nor did he spot anyone looking out a window or a doorway at him.

The scraps of wood nailed over the door were mostly rotten, and came away easily. McGarvey stacked them on a nearby pile of trash, then, checking one last time to make sure that he wasn't being observed, kicked the door in, the old, soft metal lock disintegrating with the first blow.

He slipped inside and closed the door. The light filtering in from outside was enough for him to see that he was in an empty shop. Piles of trash and scraps of lumber were scattered about. Beyond the front room, he could see directly to the back of the shop where sunlight streamed in through the cracks in a boarded-up window.

McGarvey jammed a piece of scrap wood against the door, which would hold it shut unless someone else put their back into it, then went to the rear of the shop and looked out through the cracks in the window boards. A narrow, garbage-strewn alley separated the rear of the buildings from the brick wall of the ambassador's compound. There were no guards in sight.

The back door was beneath a set of narrow stairs, and was secured only by a flimsy bolt. He slipped it off and stepped out into the alley, the stench from the open sewage ditch instantly assailing his nostrils. Human waste lay in piles, and the almost completely decomposed body of a dog or some other small animal lay half-buried under a slimy mass of rotting garbage. It was all he could do in his present condition to keep from throwing up what little he had in his stomach.

The wall ran at least thirty or forty yards in either direction, and was ten feet tall. But some of the bricks were missing and a lot of the mortar had fallen out of the joints so that scaling it would present no problem. He picked his way carefully across the filthy alley, and climbed to the top of the wall so that he could see inside the compound. The house was toward the front of the property, and back here was a five-car garage, a lot of trees, an overgrown tennis court, the net gone and big holes in the wire fence, and what probably had once been a large vegetable garden. There was no sign that anyone had been in residence for a long time. Everything was run-down and gone to weed. All the rear windows of the house were shuttered, and there were no tire marks in the driveway leading from the front. Nor was there any trash. If there were caretakers here now, he decided, they were uncommonly tidy for Afghanis.

With the last of his strength he levered himself up over the top of the wall, and dropped down into the garden on the other side.

It was silent. He could not even hear the noise from the demonstration. For the moment he felt that he was as safe here as he could be anywhere in Kabul, and he let a little of the tension drain away as he crossed behind the tennis court and made his way to the back of the mansion.

There were several doors, one of them obviously leading down into a basement, another for deliveries into what was most likely the kitchen and pantry area and another from a broad porch. McGarvey tried the delivery door. It was locked as he expected it would be. He put an ear to the door and held his breath to listen. There were no sounds from within. Not even the sounds of running machinery such as a refrigerator or freezer motor. The house was dead.

He took his jacket off, wrapped it around his pistol, then averted his face and fired one round into the lock. It jammed when he tried it, but then came free in his hand, and he let himself inside.

He found himself in what had been the laundry room. There were hookups for two washers and dryers, but the appliances were gone, and the cabinets on the walls were empty. All the cupboards and shelves in the large pantry beyond it were also empty, as were the walk-in cooler and freezer in the adjoining kitchen. Nor did the kitchen sinks work. Everything, including water had been shut off.

There was nothing here. The Taliban caretakers had stripped the place bare of just about everything useful. The chairs and table were gone, and even the spot where a large industrial range had stood was bare.

Very little light came through the shutters, so that the interior was mostly in shadows. It was somehow eerie. The dining room was empty, and standing in the spacious stair-hall he could see that the living room and library had been stripped too. He leaned against the stair rail and lowered his head for a moment to catch his breath. There was nothing here for him other than a relatively safe haven for as long as he could last.

There was a mouthful of tepid water left in the canteen. He drank it and then went upstairs. All the rooms were bare. Even the pictures on the walls and the rugs on the floors had been taken. In a rear bedroom on the top floor, he sat down with his back to the wall, laid his gun on the floor beside him and took off the filthy scarf and cap.

McGarvey felt drained. What anger he had toward bin Laden had faded into the background for the moment. He wanted to lay his head back and sleep. He touched his side where the chip had been cut and his fingers came away bloody. He had to get back to Washington. Too many people were depending on him. He wasn't going to simply give up here and wait to pass out from weakness, or for some bright Taliban officer to send soldiers here to find him. He wasn't built that way.

McGarvey got out his satellite phone. The low-battery indicator glowed steadily red, and when he hit the speed dial button, the numbers came up on the tiny screen, but after a few seconds the display flashed a string of six Es, indicating that no satellite had been acquired.

He cleared the screen and tried it again with the same results. The battery was simply too low. He laid his head back and closed his eyes for a second. Without the phone he had no way of finding out if the Taliban government had been convinced to allow the American military to send in transportation for its citizens, or when it was due to arrive at the airport. He would somehow have to find another phone. Short of that he would have to try to get to the airport and wait until the plane arrived. But the chances of pulling that off without getting caught were even more impossible.

His eyes opened. Temperature. Batteries were affected by it. In the winter when it was freezing, car batteries went flat. Maybe the opposite was true.

He removed the small battery pack from the phone, lit his cigarette lighter and held it a couple of inches below the plastic case. Within a couple of seconds the plastic began to melt. He pulled it away from the flame until it cooled down a little, and then waved it slowly back and forth over the lighter, pulling it back whenever the plastic began to melt again. After a couple of minutes the battery pack was getting too hot to handle, so he put it back in the phone. This time the low-battery indicator did not come on.

He hit the speed dial button, the numbers came up and a couple of seconds later the phone acquired a satellite and the call went through.

Rencke answered it on the first ring. "Oh, boy, Mac, am I ever glad to hear from you. All hell is breaking loose—"

"There's no time for that, my phone battery is almost dead. Is a plane coming for me?"

"We got the clearances . . ."

The low-battery light began to flash and the phone lost

the satellite for just a moment, but then got it back.

". . . C-130, but you don't have much time," Rencke was saying.

"What time will it be here?" McGarvey demanded.

"Ten o'clock your time. This morning, Mac—"

The phone lost the satellite again, chirped once and then went completely dead. Not even the numbers remained on the display, and the keypad no longer worked.

McGarvey looked at his watch. It was already well after seven, which left him less than three hours.

In the Afghan Mountains

Bin Laden came out of the cave a few minutes after 7:30. He was disguised as an ordinary mujahed; no fatigue jacket, no white robes, not even his cane, so that if a satellite was watching there'd be no positive identification. He'd often traveled this way, only this time he would not be coming back. Two mujahedeen came up the hill as he started down, but he refused their help.

"Did Ali leave?" he asked, taking care not to stumble. The pain in his hip and legs was excruciating. There was nothing left of the camp. Even the last of the fires had finally burned down.

"Last night with the others," one of them replied respectfully. Bin Laden couldn't seem to remember his name. But it didn't matter.

At the bottom they climbed onto horses that had survived the attack and headed down the valley, along the stream. The Taliban military unit at Bagram was sending a helicopter to a rendezvous point about ten miles away for him. The same way Ali got out. And from there bin Laden would be flying by private jet to Khartoum. It was the last act of cooperation from them. It had been made clear that he would never be welcome back. Regretful but necessary, the mullah had told him by phone last night.

The pain from riding on a horse was much worse than

it was walking, but he had taken an injection of morphine just before he'd left the cave, so it was bearable, though the drug somewhat muddled his thinking and his ability to speak or keep in focus.

As he rode, his thoughts drifted back and forth between Sarah and the bomb. At times the two were mingled together. Sarah's body had been consumed by fire, as the President's daughter would be consumed in an awful fire. It was just. The retribution would be terrible, but necessary. His only fear was that something would go wrong. Bahmad might be blocked from entering the U.S., some of his carefully laid plans and preparations might go awry, or worse he might get himself arrested and under questioning reveal everything. But Bahmad was better than that, he would never allow himself to be captured alive. Even if he was he didn't know all the details. He knew that the bomb was coming to California aboard a ship, but he didn't know which ship. Not yet. Not until everything else was in place.

Bin Laden realized that he had drifted off. He opened his eyes as they came down into the broader valley that ran along the base of the mountain range. Far to the east four of his mujahedeen who had left last night were heading as fast as they could travel for Pakistan, the bomb wrapped in burlap, strapped to the back of a horse. They had no idea what they were really carrying, they only knew that it was of supreme importance, and that their lives depended on getting safely to Peshwar where they would hand it over to two of bin Laden's most trusted agents.

"Are you all right, Osama?" one of his mujahed asked respectfully. "Should we stop here for a rest?"

Bin Laden looked at him with love. He was just a young boy, as most of them were. He shook his head. "There will be time for rest later."

The two mujahedeen exchanged a worried glance. Since Sarah's death in the missile raid he had not been himself. He had changed in some not-so-subtle way that none of them could define. It was troublesome.

Bin Laden let his thoughts soar like an eagle down the

valley to the four men heading east with the bomb. He could actually see them on horseback. They were boys, and they could go on like that day and night. Good boys. Dedicated. Religious. They understood the jihad at a deeper, more visceral level than anyone in the West could comprehend. They felt God not only in their hearts, but in every fiber of their beings.

Last night they had brought the nervous pack animal up into the cave where the package was waiting for them, and listened as bin Laden explained the importance of their mission. "You will take this to men who will transport it to Mecca where it will be buried in a place of honor," bin Laden told them.

He rubbed his hand along the horse's muzzle, then touched the hem of the burlap covering the bomb. He could almost feel the warmth emanating from it.

The four mujahedeen watched him, their eyes wide. They were impressed because they thought that they were being ordered to carry the remains of bin Laden's daughter home for burial. They were suddenly filled with a religious zeal and an overwhelming love for bin Laden. "We will not fail you," Mohammed's brother Achmed promised. His grip tightened on the strap of the Kalashnikov rifle.

"Of course you won't," bin Laden said. *"Insha'Allah."* He embraced each of the four men, and then watched as they led the horse out of the cave and down the hill where they mounted their horses and headed off into the darkness.

His thoughts came back to the present, and tears filled his eyes. He was seeing these mountains for the very last time. Leaving the mortal remains of his beloved Sarah forever bound with the Afghan soil. It was a pain more unbearable than that of his cancer. He began to recite to himself the opening chapter of the Qoran, peace coming very slowly to his soul.

Kabul

The morning was in full bloom, the sky crystalline clear. From an opening between the slats of the shutters covering a window in a front bedroom, McGarvey looked down at the quiet street. The two soldiers were still parked in front, so no one suspected he was here yet.

He felt detached, somewhat distant because of his fatigue, but he had to keep his head. He had to think his way out of this. Coming here he'd formed a vague plan of overpowering the caretakers and stealing their clothing and identification papers. He figured that with such a disguise he might be able to get out to the airport. From there he would have to improvise. But with the C-130 on the tarmac, and a line of anxious Americans pushing to get aboard, he thought he'd have a better than even chance.

That was no longer possible, there were no caretakers here. He had to come up with another plan no matter how improbable. Out there he had a chance, and he had faced worse odds before.

He went to the back bedroom where he retrieved his phone, the cap and the scarf and headed downstairs to the back door.

When the American military transport came in for a landing, the airport would be cleared of all other traffic. The Taliban would not want to create an incident that might cause a military retaliation. This was bin Laden's fight now, and they would want to stay as distant from it as possible. The C-130 would land, taxi to the terminal, pick up its passengers, then taxi back to the end of the runway for takeoff. If the Taliban were waiting for him they would have to logically assume that he would try to make it to the terminal and somehow bluff his way aboard. Their attention would be concentrated there, wanting to get the plane loaded and away as quickly as possible.

Peering out the laundry room door at the backyard, the

first glimmerings of a plan came to him. It would be all or nothing, and would depend on timing and luck. But he decided that it was his only real chance for getting out.

He pulled on the cap, wrapped the scarf around his neck and slipped out the door and hurried past the tennis court to the wall.

The bricks were in much better condition on this side, so it took him three running attempts to reach the top and pull himself over. He dropped down into the sewage-clogged alley, crossed the ditch and let himself back into the empty rug merchant's shop.

He had to stop for a couple of minutes to catch his breath. The slightest exertion was difficult, and scaling the wall had used almost all of his reserves.

The narrow street in front was still deserted. Nothing seemed to have changed in the half-hour he'd been inside the ambassador's compound, which he found was odd. But he couldn't dwell on it now. Stealing another car was a possibility he was going to have to consider. But if no one had discovered the Rover yet using it one last time might pose less of a risk.

His luck ran out when he left the shop and started down the narrow street.

Dozens of men suddenly materialized out of the shops and homes up and down the street. Some of them were armed with clubs, but none of them were in uniform, nor did he see any guns.

McGarvey stopped, and held his empty hands out. An older man with a long white beard, wearing a leather apron, shouted something at him in Persian. Some of the others murmured angrily. McGarvey put his hands over his ears, showing them that he was deaf.

The old man pointed to the shop that McGarvey had just come out of and shouted something else. They thought he was a thief. He shook his head and again held out his empty hands to show them that he had taken nothing. He took a step forward and the old man backed up warily. They were just ordinary people trying to protect their neighborhood in troubled times. Had they been interested in politics they would be demonstrating at the old American embassy.

More people were coming out of their homes and shops into the street behind him, ringing him in. Soon it would be impossible to move two feet let alone break free. It had to be now.

He shook his head and walked directly toward the old man. He didn't think he had much to fear from these people once he got away from here. They might report a religious crime to the Taliban, but they probably wouldn't go to the government to report a suspected thief. They would deal with it in their own way by running him off.

The old man and those around him backed up, and when it looked as if McGarvey wasn't going to stop, they parted for him.

He shook his head as if he was disgusted as he passed through them, and without breaking stride or looking back he headed down the street the way he had come in. Once he reached the corner and got out of the neighborhood he figured he would be okay. But the crowd was becoming agitated, the men shouting something, arguing with each other.

Ten feet from the corner rocks and bricks began to rain down around him, one of them hitting him in the shoulder. Covering his head, he bolted, and a huge cry rose up behind him.

He almost made it to safety, but as he turned down the side street a brick smashed into the side of his head, driving him to his knees and temporarily blacking out his vision. A wave of nausea rose up from his gut causing him to retch as he got unsteadily to his feet and stumbled away as fast as he could move. He was dizzy, moving mostly on instinct, and the day was suddenly very dark, his vision reduced to a narrow tunnel directly in front of him. But there were no more rocks, and at the next corner he looked back. In the distance, what seemed to him to be a mile away, the crowd had stopped just at the edge of their district as he hoped they would. The last he saw of them they were shaking their fists and clubs.

There was a huge knot on the side of his head just above his right ear. When he explored it with his fingers it was extremely tender to the touch, but there was no blood. As he walked, he wrapped the scarf around his mouth and nose, and gradually his vision began to clear.

Down several intersecting streets he could see road blocks and more people heading in the direction of the embassy, but no one noticed him heading in the opposite direction, or if they did, nobody seemed to care.

The Rover was where he had left it, parked between the battered Mercedes and the Fiat van. But he approached carefully to make sure that it had not been staked out. As far as he could tell, however, there wasn't a single soul around.

He got behind the wheel, touched the starter wires together and the car's engine came immediately to life. He backed out of the parking slot, drove out the alley and headed down the street to the main boulevard that led to the airport.

To the south on Bebe-Maihro Street, toward the city center, there seemed to be roadblocks, military vehicles and soldiers everywhere, directing the thousands or perhaps tens of thousands of people heading toward the embassy. Traffic was being diverted away from the barricades, and was already backing up.

To the north, in the direction of the airport, the road was clear, but that was the direction they'd be expecting him to come. There was only one main road to the airport, and it would be heavily guarded until the American transport aircraft came in, picked up its passengers and departed.

Airports were very large places, however. They sprawled across hundreds of acres of flat countryside. There might be only one road to take passengers to the terminal, but there would have to be several access roads for cargo deliveries, fuel and aircraft repair supplies, and for maintenance vehicles to have access to the ILS lights and electronic aids.

McGarvey headed straight across the broad boulevard, and found himself in another section of narrow, winding streets that sometimes opened to broad avenues lined with apartment buildings, or parks, or other districts of crafts-men—wool merchants, tin- and coppersmiths and even goldsmiths. Like the other areas of the city he'd seen this morning, most of these shops were closed, some of them boarded up, others with steel mesh security shutters low-ered over their windows and doors. The anti-American demonstrations had turned into a national holiday of sorts.

He worked his way generally north and east, sometimes finding himself stopped by dead-end streets and having to backtrack several blocks before he could find another way. It was like being a rat in a maze. At one point he came around a corner into the middle of another large crowd of people and official vehicles, their blue lights flashing. He jammed on his brakes. But it wasn't a roadblock as he had feared. A large building that might have been a warehouse was on fire. Flames and smoke shot several hundred feet into the sky. Firemen using antiquated equipment poured water into the building, while on the other side of the street dozens of men had formed a bucket brigade and were dous-ing down their own shops and houses in a frantic effort to stop the flames from spreading. No one noticed him as he backed up and hurried off in the opposite direction.

The houses and shops and other buildings began to thin out about the same time the pavement ended. The streets continued in some places only as narrow dirt tracks. He came around another corner, and the track abruptly stopped at a tall chain-link fence topped with razor wire. For several long seconds he gripped the steering wheel and simply stared at the fence as he tried to catch his breath. His vision had gone blurry again, but when it began to clear he real-ized that he had reached the airport. Directly across from him, perhaps fifty or sixty yards away, was what looked like the main east-west runway. He could make out the white lights along the paved surface. In the distance to the right he could see the markers at the end of the runway. Straight across was a line of maintenance and storage hangers, and in the far distance to the left were the control tower and terminal.

His heart skipped a beat. Pulling away from the terminal was the distinctive, squat shape of a C-130 Hercules transport. McGarvey checked his watch. It was already past nine o'clock. It had taken him two hours to come this far, but the airplane was almost an hour early.

In minutes his last chance to get out of Afghanistan would be at the end of the runway and lined up for takeoff. He needed to find a way to get out there, or at the very least signal to them.

As the C-130 majestically started up the long taxiway, McGarvey threw the Rover in reverse, backed around and spit gravel as he raced through the labyrinth of narrow, bumpy tracks. This far from the city center the dwellings were little more than crude adobe brick hovels. But there were people around, most of them farmers tending small fields or herds of goats. Some of them looked up in astonishment at the speeding car, others didn't bother.

He got lost several times and had to backtrack so that he could keep the airport perimeter fence in sight. The C-130 was nearly to the end of the runway by the time he reached a gate. There were no guards, but the gate was secured with a heavy chain and thick businesslike padlock.

He jumped out of the Rover, drew his pistol and fired three shots into the lock. The bullets fragmented on the hardened steel and ricochetted dangerously around him, but the lock held.

The Hercules had reached the end of the taxiway and was turning onto the runway as McGarvey popped the Rover's rear lid, pulled the spare tire out of its compartment and found the tire iron. At the gate he jammed the tool into one of the links of the chain and tried to pry it open. The tire iron bent, but the chain held.

A pair of Russian jeeps, their lights flashing, were racing

directly up the runway from the terminal, directly for the nose of the C-130 as the pilot gunned the four Allison turboprop engines.

McGarvey tossed the tire iron aside, jumped back into the Rover and backed up twenty yards. He slammed the transmission in drive and floored the accelerator. The heavy car shot forward, slamming into the gate, shoving it backwards nearly off its hinges.

The C-130 was lined up now and starting to roll, as McGarvey backed up again, dropped the transmission into four-wheel-drive and jammed the pedal to the floor. He hit the fence with a bone-jarring crash. The big Rover climbed up and over the mangled gate, finally breaking free with a horrible screeching of metal. Immediately the oil pressure indicator began to drop and hot oil started to spray out from under the hood.

He shifted to drive, never taking his foot off the accelerator, bumped over the last few yards of grass up onto the runway and headed after the accelerating C-130 while flashing his headlights.

He tore the scarf and hat off and tossed them aside. The Rover's engine started to bog down as the temperature needle climbed into the red and pegged. The C-130 began to pull away from him.

"Goddammit," he shouted.

He started to look for a way out of the airport, when incredibly the rear loading deck of the Hercules started to open and the big airplane slowed down.

A loud clattering noise started under the hood and the car lost even more power. The transport's ramp was fully down now just inches off the runway, and several crewmen were frantically waving him on.

The front tires bumped up on the ramp and he nearly lost control of the car as it swerved sharply to the right. But then he inched the rest of the way up onto the ramp. The crewmen leaped to the side as the Rover's rear wheels hit the ramp and suddenly the car accelerated like it had been shot from a cannon into the belly of the airplane.

McGarvey slammed on the brakes and the car slewed to the left, finally coming to a halt against cargo restraining straps that had just been raised.

McGarvey slammed the transmission into park, and as the rear cargo deck closed, and the big airplane gathered speed, he laid his head back, his hands still gripping the steering wheel as his heart began to decelerate.

He closed his eyes, and thinking about the Russian jeeps heading toward them, willed the airplane off its front landing gear, and then into the sky.

One of the crewmen came to the driver's side. The window had been smashed out. "Mr. McGarvey?" he shouted over the roar of the engines.

McGarvey opened his eyes and grinned with such intense relief that his mood boardered on the manic. "Actually I'm Evel Kneivel. McGarvey's a better driver than that."

EIGHTEEN

Washington, D.C.

What is the purpose of your visit to the United States, Mr. Guthrie?" the Dulles International Airport passport official asked.

"Business," Ali Bahmad replied. "And maybe a day of sailing on the Chesapeake." He smiled pleasantly. "I'm told that it's quite nice this time of year."

"Fishing isn't what it used to be," the officer said, stamping the British passport. He looked up. "But you're right, it's real nice down there. Have a pleasant stay."

Bahmad pocketed his passport and, carrying the slim attaché case that had been handed to him in London, sauntered down the dingy corridor and out into the customs arrivals hall, a small man without a care in the world. He wore a loose-fitting natural linen suit by Gucci, a collarless white cotton shirt, and a soft yellow ascot tied loosely around his neck. His two bags were Louis Vuitton. He was a dapper, seasoned international traveler.

"Do you have anything to declare, sir?" the uniformed customs officer asked. The man looked like a bulldog, and Bahmad had to wonder if he came from Queens or Brooklyn in a questionable neighborhood. It would be difficult, he decided, to be pleasant day after day under such circumstances.

"Nothing," Bahmad said, handing the man the declaration form he'd filled out on the 747 coming in from London.

Another customs agent came over with a drug-sniffing German shepard that circled Bahmad's two bags on the low counter, and then sniffed the attaché case. The dog looked up at his handler as if to say, no.

"Would you like me to open my suitcases?" Bahmad asked. "Just dirty laundry, I'm afraid."

"That won't be necessary, sir," the officer said. He made chalk marks on all three pieces, then turned away indifferently as the other agent with his dog went off to another passenger's luggage.

Bahmad summoned a porter for his things, and heading out into the terminal, and across to the taxi stands outside, it amused him to think what he could do to the customs officer with little or no effort. When he finished it would be enough to give the man's family nightmares for the rest of their lives.

He'd changed some pounds into dollars at Heathrow and he gave the redcap a nice tip, and ordered the cabbie to take him to the Corinthian Yacht Club in southwest Washington on the Anacostia River, then sat back to enjoy the ride.

"We can take the Beltway. It's longer, but much faster," the driver, an east Indian, suggested.

"Go through town, I haven't been here in a long time and I'd like to see some of the sights."

"Yes, sir," the driver said. He noticed in the rearview mirror that his passenger was looking out the window obviously not wanting to talk. Which was fine with him. Brits gave him a headache.

Bahmad smiled his secret smile, his face a bland mask of indifference. It was 4:30 in the afternoon local time, and he was amazed, as he was every time he traveled in the west, at the number of big, shiny cars on the road. After living for so long in the mountains of Afghanistan and in desert training camps in Libya and Iran, you tended to forget the quotidian face of the enemy. Rapers of the soil, despoilers of the earth's resources and peoples, conspicuous consumers indifferent to the plight of the other eighty or ninety percent of the world, Americans should have been miserable. But the sky over the Virginia countryside was clear of all but a few puffy clouds, there were no burned-out cars or trucks along the side of the highway, no tanks on the overpasses, no helicopter gunships swooping low. Despite his mission, Bahmad was able to relax and thoroughly enjoy himself as he hadn't for entirely too long a time.

Two days out of Afghanistan and already he was beginning to realize how much he despised the life of a terrorist in hiding in the Middle East. The lack of simple amenities got to him. The dirt, the abysmal ignorance and the fanatic adherence to Islam—to any religion for that matter—was depressing. His mother and father, before they had been killed by the Israelis, had lived an oftentimes very good and even elegant life in Beirut. And he had enjoyed his time spent in London and here in Washington, even though he hated the Americans who in their blindness supported the Israelis against every other people. That was what his fight was all about. Not religion, not any ideology or idealistic notions about the destiny of the Arab peoples. His motivation was simple revenge.

That, and the fact he enjoyed what he did for a living.

Coming back like this though brought another memory to mind, and he was somewhat disturbed by it. During the six months he had worked at the CIA's Langley headquarters he had met a woman. She worked as an analyst in the Directorate of Intelligence, and had little or no intelligence value for him, but she was nice. Her name was Anne Larson, she was divorced and was raising two children on her own. Weekends they were off with their father, and Bahmad spent time with her. She was a kind and patient lover, and although she was a little odd because of the work she did, she was always pleasant to be with. For months after he had left Washington he thought about her everyday. But then he dropped out, and ran back to Lebanon. Since then he seldom gave her a thought, though when he did it was with regret. He wondered what a life with her would have been like. Certainly it would not have been as lonely as the life he had led in the Afghan mountains. He wondered where she was now.

"Men like you are Imans of your profession," bin Laden told him. "Religious leaders. Dedicated and lonely by necessity."

The early rush hour was in full force by the time they crossed the Roosevelt Bridge onto Constitution Avenue, and the cabbie was content to let the meter run as they crawled past the Ellipse and the White House on the left, the Washington Monument on the right. He dropped down to Independence Avenue past the Smithsonian and then took South Capitol Street, turning off before it crossed the Douglass Bridge over the Anacostia River. Finally the taxi passed through the yacht club gates and Bahmad ordered the driver to the slips where they pulled up at a very large motor yacht, all her flags flying in the pleasant breeze, the boarding ramp down.

Bahmad paid off the driver and, when the cab was gone, stood looking at the boat. She was the *Papa's Fancy*, a 175-foot Feadship out of Newport, owned by a wealthy New Jersey banker with considerable though secret financial ties to the bin Laden worldwide empire. He'd agreed to lend the yacht to Bahmad for as long as he needed her, no questions asked. As it turned out, the boat had been docked at a shipyard farther down the Potomac where her annual inspection and refit had just been completed, and had been moved up here yesterday on a moment's notice. She was the biggest boat in the club and had garnered a lot of attention already.

A slightly built man in his early forties with a ponytail and earring, but dressed impeccably in crisp white trousers and a yacht club polo shirt, trotted up from the dockmaster's office.

"Mr. Guthrie, welcome to CYC, sir. I'm Terry the dockmaster. If there's anything I can do to make your stay more pleasant just ask me, sir."

"Thanks," Bahmad said with a pleasant smile. "We're all hooked up and provisioned?"

"Yes, sir. Your crew took care of that first thing when they got here yesterday," Terry assured him. "May I help you with your bags?"

"That won't be necessary," a pretty, athletically built young woman with a deep tan called out coming down the ramp. She was dressed in white shorts and a dark blue shirt, CHERYL—PAPA'S FANCY stitched above the left pocket.

Terry gave her an appreciative look, then nodded pleasantly and walked off.

"Welcome to Washington, Mr. Guthrie," Cheryl said, picking up the bags. "If you'll come with me, I'll show you to your quarters and afterwards Captain Walker would like to have a word with you."

"Where is he at the moment?"

"I believe he's checking something in the engine room."

"Ask him and the rest of the crew—all the crew—to join me in the main saloon immediately."

Cheryl gave him a worried glance. "Yes, sir."

At the top of the ramp they stepped onto a broad, gently sloping deck, the gleaming superstructure rising above them, the bridge forward and the main saloon aft. She showed him the way, then disappeared with his bags.

The yacht was in immaculate condition. The furnishings and appointments were out of *Yachting* magazine or *Architectural Digest*. Thick carpeting covered the floors, rich, thickly cushioned furniture was arranged tastefully and the large windows admitted the late-afternoon sun through thin venetian blinds. Some very good artwork hung on the richly paneled walls, and the second movement of Vivaldi's *Four Seasons* played softly from built-in speakers.

Bahmad set his attaché case down, and was pouring a glass of white wine from the extensive bar, when a tall, distinguished man with white hair came in with a much shorter, heavier, younger man. Both were dressed in whites. The older man's epaulets were adorned with four gold stripes, the young man's with three.

"Mr. Guthrie," the older man said, extending his hand. "Welcome aboard, sir. I'm Captain Web Walker."

Bahmad shook his hand. "I'm happy to be aboard, Captain."

"May I introduce my first officer Stuart Russell."

Bahmad shook hands, and moments later the rest of the crew showed up; the engineer, Blake Walsh, two aides, two chefs and four young deckhands, including the young woman who had helped with his bags. They were short-handed because Bahmad was the only guest, and he'd wanted to keep the numbers low.

"A package was to be delivered for me," he said.

"Yes, sir. It arrived this morning, and I had it put in your quarters."

"Very well," Bahmad said. The crew was looking at him somewhat apprehensively. They didn't know what to expect. He put down his wine. "I don't know what you were instructed about the nature of this cruise."

"Just that the ship was to be put completely at your disposal for as long as you required her, sir," the captain said.

"I'm here on business," Bahmad said. "Somewhat stressful business, I'm afraid."

The captain's lips compressed.

"Which means that when I am not conducting my business, there will be no long faces around here. I want smiles, music, good food and drink, and that's an order. Do I make myself clear?"

The captain grinned. "Yes, sir. Perfectly clear."

Bahmad laughed. It was so ridiculously easy, he thought. "I'm going to freshen up now. When I get back I want something very good to eat, and I'll want some champagne. Cristal, I should think. Can we manage that?"

"With pleasure," the head chef said.

"Afterwards I'll want a tour of the ship, and then I'll be going into the city for a few hours, so I'll need a car."

"Whenever you're ready," Captain Walker said. "In the meantime should we be preparing to sail?"

"Not for a while. It's time for a little R and R." He gave Cheryl a smile. "Pass the word to Terry that we're having a party tomorrow evening. He should know who to invite."

"I'll talk to him right away."

"Lighten up, okay?" Bahmad told them, getting his attaché case. "You'd think that this was a bloody funeral." He gave them another warm, reassuring look. "Now, if someone could show me where I'm bunking I'll take a shower."

Cheryl took him up to the owner's suite, which was just aft of the bridge. Like the rest of the yacht, the three rooms were spacious and extremely well appointed. Large windows looked out across the yacht basin toward the National War College with its pretty grounds on Greenleaf Point.

"This is just lovely," Bahmad said.

"Yes, sir. She's a nice ship," Cheryl said earnestly. "Would you like some help unpacking?"

"Thanks, but I can manage."

"Yes, sir. And welcome aboard. If there's anything you need just ask."

When she was gone Bahmad took off his jacket and hung it in one of the closets, then splashed some cold water on his face in the bathroom.

He'd had a lot of time to contemplate exactly how he was going to accomplish the two tasks bin Laden had sent him here for. Killing Elizabeth McGarvey would have to be done in such a way that it would have the minimum affect on the second phase—that of providing a diversion so that the nuclear weapon could be moved into position beneath the Golden Gate Bridge at the moment the Special Olympics runners were there, and then exploding it. If the authorities suspected that McGarvey's daughter had been killed as an act of revenge by bin Laden then the mission would be made all the more difficult as he had tried to explain to Osama. Her death would have to look like a random act of violence.

A drive-by shooting, a botched robbery while she was stopped at a 7-Eleven, a burglar caught in the act in her apartment. But that would take surveillance. Being at the right place at the right time, with a plan to get away when it was done. He had to know her movements, her habits. McGarvey's daughter was not much older than Sarah had been, but she was a trained CIA field officer who already had experienced some difficult situations. The worst thing he could do would be to underestimate her.

He dried his hands and face, checked to make sure that the door was locked, then opened his attaché case and went through the material he'd been given in London. There were a dozen photographs of McGarvey's daughter, some of them straight head shots, others in settings ranging from the CIA's main gate, to her in spandex running shorts and a sweatshirt in some park. Also contained in the intelligence briefing files were the locations of her usual hangouts, starting with her apartment in Georgetown, to her mother's house in Chevy Chase, and several restaurants she frequented in and around Washington. She was an active young woman, with a circle of friends from the Company. From time to time she made the drive down to the CIA's training facility in Williamsburg, and until very recently she had been posted to Paris. All that had come from bin Laden's contacts.

Bahmad looked out the window for a moment. She'd obviously been recalled because of the murders of Trumble and his family, and because her father was going to Afghanistan. It meant that McGarvey already had some concern for his daughter's safety. And presumably the safety of his ex-wife as well.

The file also contained photographs of her, some with her daughter, and some on the country club golf course where she belonged. She was a striking woman, self-assured, even haughty looking. Nothing at all like Bin Laden's wives, or most other Muslim women for that matter. She epitomized, in Bahmad's mind, the arrogant American woman. Too bad, he thought, that she wasn't a target as well.

The equipment he had requested had been sent down from New Jersey packed in a large aluminum case of the sort often used by professional photographers. Included in his package from London were the keys.

He hefted the case onto the bed and opened it. It was heavy, about sixty pounds, and contained what appeared to be a camera, lenses, light meters and canisters of film all fitted into shapes cut into the foam rubber tray. Lifting the tray out and setting it aside revealed a lower compartment that held the things he had requested, secured in bubble wrap. One by one he unwrapped each item and inspected it. Included were a Glock 17 pistol, two spare magazines of 10mm ammunition and a silencer. The weapon was in perfect working order. Next he took the other items out of the case. A thin, nine-inch stiletto, a case-hardened steel lock pick set, a small but powerful penlight, an electronic hotel lock card decoder, a thick envelope containing ten thousand dollars in cash, a half-dozen valid but untraceable credit cards, three complete sets of identification and a satellite phone complete with an extra battery pack. Finally he withdrew a small leather case that contained what looked like the remote control for a television set.

Bahmad handled the controller with great care. At the proper time and place, a dozen keystrokes would arm and fire the nuclear weapon. So much power, he thought with a sensuous pleasure.

Killing McGarvey's daughter had never been a part of his preliminary planning. But the rest was, and it had taken all of three months to have the equipment gathered and waiting for him should bin Laden give the order.

He put everything back in the aluminum case, locked it and set it down. Then he got undressed and went to take a shower. A bullet in the head during an interrupted burglary, he thought. It would be the simplest and easiest method. But first dinner and drinks. He began to sing a song that he'd learned in London about a young woman who sold shellfish in Dublin's fair city.

Chevy Chase

It had been a very stressful few days for Kathleen Mc-Garvey. Kirk's leaving so suddenly on what even Rencke thought could turn out to be a dangerous fool's mission had obliged her to think long and hard about their upcoming marriage, and how she was going to hold up under what could never be a normal relationship. Having a daughter in the business didn't help much either. There were times when she wasn't sure of anything, especially her own resolve. Looking objectively at herself she knew that there were other times when she was incredibly self-centered, even selfish to the point she didn't want to hear what anyone else had to say. But she loved Kirk, she had never stopped loving him, and that was one constant embedded so deeply in her heart that nothing could ever tear it loose.

The problem was within herself. In the old days, when she was threatened, she became a bitch. It was a defense mechanism that she used to shield herself from getting hurt. But that was just as stupid, she had come to feel, as Kirk's penchant for running off to be alone when he was hurt. She insulated herself emotionally; he did so with distance. They both would have to change if they were going to make their marriage work this time. And that was something, Kathleen decided, that she wanted more than anything.

She looked out the window of the front bedroom. A dark blue van was parked down the block. One of Dick Yemm's people. The Company was keeping a watch on her twenty-four hours a day. Instead of comforting her, however, she felt a dull, gnawing fear in her stomach. People who needed bodyguards were people in harm's way, and she didn't know if that was the part of Kirk's job that she hated the most, or if it was his frequent absences. But already it was beginning to get to her; everything about the CIA and what it stood for, what its mission was, and the people who worked over there and around the world, gave her the willys whenever she thought about it.

No place was safe for any of them. Allen Trumble and his family had learned that terrible lesson at Disney World, for God's sake.

The telephone rang. She crossed the hall to her bedroom and picked it up. "Yes," she said sharply.

"He's out," Rencke said.

Kathleen closed her eyes, and released the pent up breath. "Thank God," she said. "Is he all right, Otto?"

"He was pretty banged up, Mrs. M. Dehydrated, fatigued, some cuts and bruises, but nothing life-threatening. He'll be okay."

"When does he get home?"

"He's at the military hospital in Riyadh for now, but they're planning on moving him to Ramstein sometime in the next twelve to twenty-four hours."

Kathleen gripped the phone tightly. "You said he was okay. Just cuts and bruises. What's going on, Otto? I want the truth, goddammit."

"Bin Laden's people found out that he was carrying the GPS chip, and they operated on him to remove it. The stitches came out somehow and he lost a lot of blood."

Kathleen closed her eyes again and mentally counted to ten. "The dirty bastards," she said softly. She opened her eyes. "What else is wrong with him?"

"Nothing serious, Mrs. M, I swear to you. He's been sedated and they're pumping fluids into him. He wanted to get on the first plane for home, but they wouldn't let him. Right now he's getting exactly what he needs—sleep."

"I'll fly to Frankfurt tonight. I can drive down to Ramstein and be there by noon."

"Bzzz. Wrong answer, Mrs. M."

"Then the Company can arrange to fly me over there direct."

"You wouldn't do him any good by being there," Rencke said miserably. "You'd only be compounding the security problems." Rencke sounded frightened. "I'd do anything for you. Lie down in front of a train, fight a pack of alligators, but not this. Please just stay there. As soon as we can get Mac out of there we will. I promise you. Please Mrs. M. Please."

"I'm frightened," she said softly.

"So am I," Rencke replied. "But you gotta stick it out here and let us do our jobs."

She nodded. "Okay," she said. "Just keep me informed, will you?"

"Count on it."

When Kathleen put down the phone it struck her as ominous that Otto had admitted that he was frightened too. According to him Kirk was going to be all right. So what else was coming their way?

Georgetown

It was after 11:00 P.M. by the time the pleasant neighborhood of three-story brownstone apartment buildings finally began to settle down. Bahmad had a slight headache from the wine, and from the effects of jet lag. He turned the block at Dumbarton and Thirtieth Street, and passed Elizabeth McGarvey's building for the fourth time in as many hours. The windows of her third-floor apartment were still dark, and her car, a bright yellow Volkswagen Beetle, was still nowhere to be seen.

He drove a dark blue Mercedes that the boat crew had

arranged for his use. This quality of car was nearly invisible in this neighborhood. It blended with the other Mercedes and Jaguars. His entry into the United States had been without incident, and he couldn't imagine that anyone was looking for him, let alone knew his face. Here and now he was completely anonymous, exactly as he wanted it, and exactly as he meant to keep it. If anyone took notice of him he would kill them.

At the end of the block he turned the corner and found a parking spot. Switching off the headlights and engine, he checked the rearview mirror. No one was following him. Just ordinary traffic.

He waited for a bus to lumber by then got out, locked the car and headed back to the corner and then down Thirtieth Street to Elizabeth's building. He let himself in, finding himself in a tiny alcove, stairs to the right, apartment 1 to the left. Three mailboxes were set in the wall straight ahead. Elizabeth McGarvey's was apartment 3 on the top floor. Unlike similar buildings in New York City there was no security here except for the apartment doors themselves. He had a feeling that after tonight that would change.

There was no elevator, so he took the stairs two at a time, moving quickly and silently on the balls of his feet. He wore light brown slacks, a striped button-down shirt and a light jacket against the evening damp. Like everything else about him, the clothes were unremarkable.

The door to the second-floor apartment opened and he heard a woman say something, her words indistinct. A man answered angrily. Bahmad held up on the stairs, contemplating turning around and leaving the building, or remaining here and killing the couple should they discover him. The voices were cut off when the door was slammed. He slipped out his knife and listened for footsteps in the corridor, but the building was silent. Whoever it was had gone back into their apartment.

He moved cautiously up the last few stairs and peered around the corner. The landing was empty, the apartment door closed. He sheathed his knife and went the rest of the way to the top floor.

At the door to Elizabeth's apartment he knocked softly, and waited. But after a minute when no one came, he took out his lock pick set and had the door open in under thirty seconds. He took out his pistol, screwed the silencer on the end of the barrel, then after checking the stairs behind him, slipped inside, sweeping the gun left to right, looking for a target. But Elizabeth was not at home.

He closed and locked the door, and silently went back to the bedroom to make sure that the woman wasn't here, asleep in her bed after all. But the apartment was empty. It was pleasant if inexpensively furnished, with a lot of books, a stereo system and a lot of CDs. But something was wrong.

Stuffing the gun in his belt he went into the bathroom, closed the door and turned on the light. It was reasonably clean, but something nagged at the back of his head. Something was out of place. Or, rather, something was *not* in its place. Something was missing.

There were towels on the racks, but no pantyhose or bras hanging over the shower rod. On the sink counter were several bottles of perfume and lotions, but there were water marks where two bottles were missing. There was no toothbrush or toothpaste in the medicine cabinet, and a quick search of the shelves and other cabinets revealed no birth control pills or diaphragm, no douches or feminine deodorant sprays. He knew enough about Western women to understand that these were all common items in most bathrooms. But they were missing.

Elizabeth McGarvey had moved out. The questions were how long would she be gone, and where had she gotten herself to.

He switched off the bathroom light, waited for a minute for his eyes to adjust, then went back into the bedroom. The bed had been hastily made, which meant she wasn't a neat housekeeper or she'd been in a hurry to get out of here. But most of the clothes were still in her closet, only a few empty spaces indicated that she had taken something, but not everything. It was the same in the chest of drawers. Some undergarments and tee shirts were obviously missing, but most had been left behind.

Bahmad retraced his steps through the apartment, wiping down the few spots where he might have left fingerprints despite his care not to do so. He checked the street from the living room window. There were several empty parking spots out front, as before, but no yellow VW.

He let himself out of the apartment, relocked the door, crept silently downstairs and left the building. Now he needed to find out where she had gone. If it was back to Paris, this mission would become complicated. But the Special Olympics weren't for another two and a half months, so he had time to spare, though each time he crossed an international border there was the risk of discovery.

But then another thought struck him all at once. When he got back to the car he took out his satellite phone and placed a call to a special number in the Taliban Military Intelligence Headquarters in Kabul.

Colonel Hisham bin Idris answered on the second ring. "Hello."

"Is the situation resolved?" Bahmad asked.

"I had sincerely hoped so," the colonel replied cautiously. "You are not telephoning from nearby, are you?"

"No, but I wanted to thank you on behalf of . . . everybody."

"You cannot return here."

"I understand that," Bahmad said, reassuringly. "We have every intention of respecting your wishes. You have done so much for us—"

"Yes, yes, but what do you want?" Colonel bin Idris demanded impatiently.

"There is that other matter I asked you to help me with."

The colonel hesitated for just a second, as if he'd been distracted. "He's dead."

"Are you certain? Did you see the body?"

"What was left of it. He got caught in the mob and they tore him apart. There wasn't much left."

"How sure are you that it was him?"

"Very sure," Colonel bin Idris said.

"Then thank you again. It is a debt we shall never be able to repay—" Bahmad said, but he was talking to an open line. The colonel had broken the connection.

Bahmad switched off the phone. When a young woman's father was brutally murdered in a faraway land there was only one logical place for her to go. Sooner or later Elizabeth McGarvey would show up at her mother's home, if she wasn't already there, to grieve. He smiled. He would get to kill McGarvey's wife after all.

Falls Church, Virginia

At that moment Elizabeth McGarvey was taking her overnight case and hanging bag from her car parked beside Todd Van Buren's old Porsche. His apartment had once been the carriage house for the family estate. His parents lived in the mansion a quarter-mile up the curving driveway through some woods. They didn't approve of the fact that he worked for the CIA, but he had been raised to be independent, and they tried not to interfere too much in his life. His independence was one of the things she most admired about him. In some ways he reminded her of her father.

The night was still, the air sweet this far out of the city. Elizabeth hesitated, frightened, at his door. She had thought long and hard about making this move. They'd been lovers for three months. But she valued her own independence, and she didn't know how she would tell her father, let alone face her mother. But she wanted Todd on more than an occasional basis. She wanted to wake up in the morning beside him, she wanted to show him what kind of a cook she was—her father had taught her a number of French bistro recipes—and she wanted to find out what kind of a

cook Todd was. She wanted to be with him when he was
sad as well as happy; angry as well as content; confused as
well as assured. She thought that she was falling in love
with him, but before she made a commitment she wanted
to be sure. Tonight, especially, she wanted to be held, to
be comforted.

The light over the stoop came on before she could ring
the bell and Van Buren opened the door. His eyes lit up,
and he started to say something, but then did a double take
when he noticed her bags. The expression on his face was
comical, and Elizabeth laughed, even though she was in a
brittle mood.

"Am I going to have to stand here all night?" she asked.
"Or should I drive around the block a couple of times while
you get rid of your girlfriend?"

"Your dad's going to kill me." He took her hanging bag,
and stepped aside so that she could come in. She gave him
a peck on the cheek.

Only the light over the leather easy chair was on, a beer
on the table beside it, and a book opened on the ottoman.
The Sade CD she'd bought him was playing softly. Like
her, Van Buren was dressed in jeans and a tee shirt.

She followed him into the bedroom where he hung her
bag on the closet door. "I'm glad you're here, Liz." He was
bigger than her, but he had the compact build and fluid
movements of a soccer player. He was an exotic weapons
and hand-to-hand combat instructor at the CIA's training
facility, and he sometimes worked special assignments for
the Directorate of Operations. She loved his butt, the angles
and planes of his masculine face, and especially his hands
on her body. He was strong yet very gentle.

When he turned back to her, she was suddenly overcome
with an overwhelming sadness, and her eyes began to fill.
She felt like a complete fool, anything but a McGarvey. "Is
it okay that I'm here? Are you mad at me?"

"What's the matter, Liz." Van Buren was alarmed.

"Can I stay here at least tonight?" She hated this weakness in herself. Her father despised weaknesses in people.

"You can stay forever, if you want," he said seriously. He took the overnight case from her and set in on a chair, then took her in his arms.

"Don't say that yet," she warned. But then she couldn't talk. She clung to him, her body wracked with sobs. She felt worse than a fool, like a sniveling idiot, but she'd been frightened about her father's safety for so long that she couldn't help herself. It was enough for now that she had someone to hold her. Someone other than her mother who had taken the news that her husband had gotten out with more panache than even Elizabeth thought she was capable of. This time her mother had been too strong.

"I love you," Van Buren said.

She parted and looked into his face, wanting to make sure that he wasn't making fun of her. She didn't think she could take that right now. She felt so vulnerable, and yet she knew that she could take him apart. But he was sincere. He honestly cared, and she could see it in his eyes.

"You called me a spoiled brat," she said stupidly, because she couldn't think of anything else to say.

"Yeah, and you've got a chip on your shoulder," he said. "But you can be *my* spoiled brat if you'll ease up a little and let me take the lead every once in a while."

She couldn't help herself from laughing. She nodded. "Just don't get any macho attitudes like ownership."

"Works both ways, Liz," he said. He got out a handkerchief and wiped her cheek. She took it from him and did it herself.

"Now, will you tell me what the hell is going on? Is it your dad? Is he okay?"

"They're taking him to Ramstein. He's pretty banged up, but the docs say he'll be fine."

"Christ. How's your mother holding up?"

"She's dealing with it," Elizabeth said. "I just came from there. Dick Yemm is with her, so I told her that I had to get back to work. I couldn't stay there tonight."

Van Buren gave her a sympathetic look. "Are you sure about this?" he asked sincerely. "I mean if you just want to stay the night so you won't have to be alone right now, I'd understand. I can take the couch."

She touched his handsome face. "It was going to happen sooner or later. The reasons are all wrong right now, at least they are for me, but I'm glad it's sooner."

"So am I," he said. He took her in his arms again, and now she was done crying. His body felt warm and strong and familiar. Comforting. Like coming home to a place you never knew how much you missed until you were there, she thought warmly.

They kissed deeply, their hands all over each other; exploring, feeling. He picked her up and brought her to the bed. They undressed each other, and then made love, softly and passionately, even though she wanted to rush. She let him take the lead, and when they were finished she was glad she had.

Chevy Chase

The dark blue van obviously didn't belong parked on the street across from Kathleen McGarvey's country club home.

Driving past, careful to keep his speed normal, his eyes straight ahead, Bahmad spotted a dark figure waiting behind the wheel. He had to consider the possibility that the CIA had placed a guard on the woman, which meant that they might be expecting an act of retaliation by bin Laden. It complicated his plans, but not impossibly so. Not yet. He still had time.

At the end of the block he turned right and headed back to Constitution Avenue. The logical thing to do was return to the yacht for a few days, then sail out to Bermuda, or up to Maine and Canada, waste time conspicuously, as planned. Be seen and yet not be seen for what he really was. Get his name in the society columns, make friends, spend money. Become the wealthy international playboy, not bin Laden's paid assassin.

But he had promised that McGarvey's daughter would die. The thought of killing her had a certain symmetry to it, considering Sarah's death, and he had to admit that it excited him too. McGarvey had been an arrogant bastard. Killing his daughter and his wife would be interesting to say the least.

Bahmad smiled his secret smile, and for a moment or two he wondered in one part of his brain if, like bin Laden, he too wasn't losing his mind. There was a time as a child playing in the park near his house in Beirut when he'd led a life that could be considered normal. Although his memories of that time were hazy and imperfect now, he did remember that he had been a happy child.

Elizabeth's VW was not parked in the driveway of her mother's house. Of course it could have been locked away out of sight in the garage, but that didn't matter tonight. She would come to her mother to grieve and they would both die, as would the CIA officer on guard duty.

But the timing would have to be right. For that he would need some additional help and equipment. Turning over a number of scenarios in his mind he drove by the entrance to the Chevy Chase Country Club, and as usual a plan came to him all in one piece; the moves and countermoves arranged in precise battle order like the pieces on a chessboard.

Be seen, and yet not be seen. That was the technique that had allowed him to survive so long in this business. Driving back to the yacht he was actually looking forward to the party aboard tomorrow night. In a few days he would have the people he needed in place, and Captain Walker would have arranged a summer membership for him in the Chevy Chase Country Club, the fifteenth fairway of which abutted Kathleen McGarvey's backyard.

NINETEEN

Afghanistan-Pakistan Border

The four men and five horses carrying the bomb had drifted through the mountains seemingly on the wind. Traveling day and night, their leader, Mustafa Binzagar, had allowed them to stop only briefly to eat and rest. They had worked their way a hundred sixty miles down the Panjshir Valley in less than four days, and Mustafa knew that when they delivered the package their journey would be ended in more than one sense of the word. The task that bin Laden had set them to do would be over, but so would their lives in Al Qaeda be finished. There were other training camps scattered around Afghanistan, but with bin Laden gone, and no new leader to replace him, their very existence would be meaningless. During the trek they had not seen another living soul, which gave Mustafa plenty of time to think about his predicament. But he had not come up with a solution. He was nothing but a mujahed, a lowly foot soldier with nowhere to go. No family who would accept him, no friends, and now no base or purpose.

He stood at the edge of the last glacier before the border and looked down the sweeping valley into Pakistan. There was nothing to be seen in the pitch-black of the night except for an airport beacon, which because of the clear, thin mountain air reflected green and white off the glacial ice even at a distance of thirty kilometers. They had been instructed not to cross the border because they did not know the schedule of the Pakistani patrols. But he'd been given no orders beyond this point, except that they were to be met by two men who would use the words, *Sarah lives in Allah's mansion.* He felt a sense of bitterness and even betrayal that in the excitement he'd forgotten to ask what came next.

Hussein al-Rajhi came up the hill from where they'd tethered the horses and made a rough camp. "There's enough wood for a small fire if you want some tea. Or should we save it until morning? It would help if we knew when they were coming."

"I don't know," Mustafa said dreamily. He had become mesmerized by the airport beacon on the horizon, and what the light represented.

"Are you sure that we have come to the correct place?"

Mustafa turned to him. "This is the tongue of the glacier, and that's the airport at Chitral." He took out one of his last cigarettes and lit it, cupping it in his hand so that the glowing tip would be invisible to anyone who might be watching from the valley. "Start the fire. I'm cold and I could use some tea." He passed the cigarette to Hussein. "It won't be long now, and we'll be starting back."

"Where will we go—"

"I don't know, maybe Khost!" Mustafa said angrily.

Hussein took a couple of drags and handed the cigarette back. He shot a glance toward the horses. "She was a woman beyond understanding."

Mustafa had to smile despite his morose mood. "That she was. Even her father had no control over her."

"But she was strong."

Mustafa shook his head thinking about her. "She might have eventually changed except for the American. He poisoned her. Mohammed told me everything."

Hussein nodded. He'd heard the stories too, about how the American had tried to rape her, and how Mohammed had gotten shot in the hand saving her. Infidels were beyond understanding. And in the end nothing any of them did could have saved her from the missiles. "Maybe we should stay with her. The rest of the way to Mecca."

Mustafa looked at him shrewdly. The idea was brilliant,

and although it had never occured to him, he felt now that it was a thought, like a word on the tip of the tongue, that would have come to him at any moment. "There might not be room for all of us on the airplane."

"The package is very heavy. It would take two men to handle it."

"Us?"

Hussein nodded.

Mustafa took out his pistol, checked the action and switched the safety off. Hussein did the same, and without another word they went down the hill where Ismail and Suleiman were tending to the horses. They looked up.

"Are they coming?" Ismail asked.

Mustafa raised his pistol and shot him in the face from a distance of less than two meters. Hussein, who had come up behind Suleiman, shot him in the back of the head at point-blank range. Both shots were muffled by the hillside.

Suleiman was just eighteen and very strong. His legs were still twitching when Mustafa walked over. "Finish him."

Hussein bent over the mujahed and fired a shot directly into his temple. At that moment Mustafa fired one shot into the back of Hussein's head, driving him forward, his body flopping down on Suleiman's.

Such a waste, he thought. But when there was only enough food on the table for one, it naturally belonged to the strongest man. There might not be room aboard the airplane for two men, but there certainly would be for one. And the package wasn't that heavy after all.

They were right on time for the rendezvous, but he'd not seen anyone coming up the hill from the east, so he figured he had at least a couple of hours to get his story straight about how the other three had turned around and gone, and do what was needed here.

He loaded the bodies on three horses, and led them a couple of hundred meters back the way they had come, then dumped the bodies on the ground near a large pile of rocks. He tied the horses' reins loosely over their necks, and slapped each on the rump, sending them racing into the night. They might go for several miles before circling back, but Mustafa figured by then he'd be long gone from here.

He laid the three bodies on top of each other and then started piling rocks on them. It was a difficult job and after a few minutes he was sweating heavily, but he worked without stopping until the bodies were completely covered and the arrangement of rocks looked reasonably natural. Unless someone looked close they would miss the grave.

He headed back to the camp, lighting a cigarette, his next to the last, and let himself come down. The tough part was over. Now, no matter what happened, he had no one to worry about except himself. There was still time, he decided to make a small fire and brew some tea.

He came over the last rise above the camp and stopped short. A man dressed in a Pakistani army uniform was reloading the package on one of the horses.

Mustafa stepped back, his hand going to the pistol inside his vest, when someone came up from behind.

"We wondered where you had gotten yourself to," a man said in Dari.

Mustafa swung around. This one wore a Pakistani army uniform with captain's pips on his shoulder boards. He carried a pistol in a holster but made no move to draw it.

"What are you doing on this side of the border?" Mustafa foolishly asked. "This is Afghanistan."

"We're here on a mission of mercy."

Mustafa pulled out his gun. "I don't know what you're talking about."

"We're here for Sarah," the Pakistani captain said gently. "She lives in Allah's mansion, and we've come to take her the rest of the way home."

Mustafa let the relief wash the tension from his body. He put his pistol away. "Good," he said. "I sent the others back, I'm coming with you."

"There's no room," the captain said. "Besides, you have no papers." He took out his pistol and shot Mustafa in the forehead, just above the bridge of his nose. "Foolish man," he muttered half under his breath. By sending his three companions away the stupid mujahed had made a difficult task easy. Allah be praised. In three hours they would have the holy package aboard an airplane on its way to Karachi, their part of the mission completed in time for a couple hours of sleep before morning prayers.

"Insha'Allah."

The White House

It wasn't until after four in the afternoon before Roland Murphy finally got over to the White House to brief the President. He had held off to give the NRO time to recheck their analysis, and to get some new photos from the next series of satellite passes, and for Rencke to make sure that they all understood exactly what they meant.

The President was waiting for him in the Oval Office with his national security adviser Dennis Berndt, but no one else.

"Bin Laden has survived," Murphy told them without beating around the bush. He took a dozen enhanced photos out of his briefcase and spread them on the coffee table in front of them. Attached to the images were the computer-generated identification probabilities which were nearly at one hundred percent.

The news did not come as a complete surprise to them. Murphy had called two days ago to alert the President to the possibility. But now that it was confirmed Berndt was his usual disdainful self.

"What the hell took so long, General?" he demanded.

"I wanted to make absolutely sure first. I didn't want to go off half-cocked. We have enough problems as it is."

"Are you finally sure now?" Berndt smirked. "No possibility that the CIA could be wrong . . . again?"

"There's always that possibility, Dennis," Murphy said. "But being an ass won't help the situation."

Berndt started to say something, but the President held

him off. "So we missed again, and now he's going to strike back, and I think we all know what that means." The President gave Murphy a bleak look. "At least we got Mc-Garvey out of there. Is he going to be okay?"

"They're releasing him from Ramstein sometime tonight. He should be back here in the morning," Murphy said. "But he might not have the answers either."

"Is he fit to return to work?"

"I haven't talked to him yet, Mr. President, but I can't imagine how I could stop him from coming back. He's going to have plenty to say."

"It was just plain bad luck this time," Berndt said.

"No, Dennis, it was poor planning," Murphy shot back. "If we had given Mac a little more time he would have come back with the deal we sent him over there to make. As it is now there'll be no more talking. Bin Laden has got the bomb and he's going to use it against us."

"You don't know that for sure, General," Berndt said, still trying to slip out of any responsibility. "Could be we did the right thing. Maybe this time we put the fear of God into bin Laden and he's going to back off. Have your people taken the time to at least give that possibility a consideration. Let's not close any doors here."

"That was discussed," Murphy said. "But we discarded the idea as wishful thinking."

"I don't see why," Berndt said, turning to the President. "Maybe we should put out feelers through the Taliban government. Offer some sort of a reparation payment in exchange for getting word to bin Laden."

Murphy took several more photos out of his briefcase and spread them on top of those already on the coffee table. "That won't work, Dennis, and this is why." He was still having trouble accepting the young woman's death. It was the worst thing that could have happened.

"What's this now?" Berndt asked. He'd lost a lot of his usual bluster. When he calmed down he was quite bright. The trouble was he was easily excited.

"These are shots of bin Laden carrying a body across his

camp minutes after the missile raid was over."

The President picked up one of the photographs and studied it for a long time. His shoulders seemed to sag. "Who is it?"

"His daughter," Murphy said softly. "Her name was Sarah. She was just nineteen years old."

The President closed his eyes for a moment. "You wouldn't have brought these over if you weren't sure about this too." He looked up. "How did it happen?"

"It looks as if she helped escort McGarvey out of the camp. She was coming back when the attack began, and she was caught out in the open."

The President's eyes were drawn to the photograph of his daughter on the desk. "I never meant for that to happen," he said softly.

Murphy nodded. "It was a tragic accident, Mr. President, that none of us anticipated. But bin Laden will almost certainly strike back. Maybe even against you."

"He has the motivation now, if he never had it before," the President agreed.

"She was a terrorist who—" Berndt said, but the President cut him off with a withering glance.

"She was just a baby girl, Dennis. Nineteen."

"I'm sorry, Mr. President, but accident or not, we cannot back down now. We're going to have to go after the bastard with everything we have. The bounty hasn't worked, and we'll never know if McGarvey's attempt to negotiate a solution would have worked—all that is too late now. We have to kill him. I don't think there can be any argument about that now, can there be?"

"How difficult would it be for us to arrest him?" the President asked. He was grasping at straws and Murphy could sympathize with him.

"First we'd have to find him, and that in itself might present a big problem. The Taliban may have finally kicked him out of Afghanistan, and if that's the case he could be almost anywhere."

"Khartoum," Berndt suggested.

"That would be my first guess," Murphy conceded. "But even if we did find him, arresting him would be problematic. There would be casulaties, possibly heavy casualties."

"Kill him," Berndt said.

Murphy eyed the national security adviser with all the more distaste because this time he had to go along with him, even though he didn't agree. "That might be the only viable option."

The President got up and went to the bowed windows where he stretched his back. This was the first real test of his administration, and he was learning, as every other President had, that there were never any easy answers, and that even the power of the United States was very limited.

"Maybe the bomb is already here," he said.

"Mac didn't think so."

"Would killing bin Laden stop someone else from using it against us? Does he have an heir apparent?"

"We don't think he is training anyone to take over, but of course we can't be sure about that. What we do know is that he's the one holding the organization together. Personal loyalty. He's a hero to the Islamic peoples. They respect and trust him. When he's gone the money will certainly dry up, and so will the contacts."

The President turned back. "Can we do it?"

On the way over here Murphy had known that his briefing would probably come to this. But he no more had the answer now than he did an hour ago. "I don't know, Mr. President."

"McGarvey got to him once, maybe he can figure out how to get to him again," Berndt suggested.

"It's not that easy. Bin Laden *wanted* to be found. He wanted the meeting. This time it'll be different. He'll be expecting someone to come after him, so if we do something like this—assuming that we can find him in the first place—we'll have to hit him very hard, but not with missiles—with ground troops. And most likely without the knowledge or consent of the local authorities." Murphy shook his leonine head. "There's a lot of room for disaster there, Mr. President."

"We're not going to be held hostage by that sonofabitch like Carter was with the Iranians," the President said forcefully. "I'm deeply sorry about his daughter, but he chose to keep her with him on the battlefield. And he chose to acquire a goddamn nuclear weapon and threaten us with it. His choices, General, every one of them. What does the CIA suggest we do about it?"

"I'd very much like to see bin Laden dead, and the CIA will use all of its resources to that end even though it's against the law and against national policy, if that's what you want."

"There's no other choice."

"Very well, Mr. President. But before we get started I would like that in writing."

Berndt started to object, but once again the President held him off. This was one administration that did not leave its people hanging in the wind. "It'll be on your desk first thing in the morning, Roland." The President gave him a penetrating look. "But I want you to keep in mind what we were faced with here before you think about making any public or historical announcement."

"Of course." Murphy closed his briefcase and got to his feet. "Bad business, all of this," he said. He thought the President had made a poor decision. But then any other decision would have been just as wrong. He knew what McGarvey was going to say about all of this, and for once he had to completely agree with his deputy director of Operations. The politicians had truly screwed up what could have been a successful operation. And now they were faced with a much worse problem; an angry, highly motivated madman with the capability and the willingness to explode a nuclear weapon on U.S. soil.

"We didn't create the situation, Roland," the President said. "He did."

"Yes, sir. But we might be looking at an even bigger problem."

"What's that?"

"If he should somehow pull this off—get the bomb here and detonate it—it won't be the end. It'll just be the beginning."

CIA Headquarters

Murphy had served four Presidents, his tenure as DCI by far the longest in the history of the CIA, and during that time he had been a part of every crisis to hit the United States in nearly twenty years. He'd seen it all; from the fallout precipitated by the breakup of the Soviet Union, to the embassy crisis in Iran, the wars in Kuwait, Grenada, Panama, Bosnia and Kosovo, the terrorist attacks against Americans in Africa, Italy, Germany, the Middle East and even here at home against our airline industry; spies from the Walker family to the Bureau's Robert Hanssen and the CIA's own Aldrich Ames and a dozen others whose cases never hit the media; downsizings and budget restrictions and congressional witch hunts. But there was one thing that never changed, and that was the need for the CIA or some intelligence-gathering organization like it. President Truman's Secretary of War Henry Stimson's famous quote that gentlemen do not read other gentlemen's mail didn't apply then, and it certainly didn't apply now.

Riding in his limousine across the river he thought again about his retirement, something he'd been doing a lot of lately. It wasn't enough to know how many missiles and tanks and submarines the other country had, you needed to know if they intended to use them, and when and where. That was a job for a much younger, much less cynical man than himself. He'd seen it all, he had the experience, but he was burning. He was finding that there were times when he simply didn't give a damn.

He didn't believe that, of course. In twenty years every problem the CIA had solved was immediately followed by ten new ones. For every ten successful operations that never hit the media, there was one failure that was splashed all over the front pages of every newspaper in the country. The CIA screws up again! And they howled for blood, oh, how they howled for blood up on the Hill. Their cries were driven by their constituents and the next election. He was starting to ask himself what kind of howls of protest their constituents would be making if there wasn't a CIA, and if we were constantly being blindsided because we were too shortsighted to open other gentlemen's mail?

One segment of the media was sharply critical of the administration for talking to bin Laden. No negotiations with terrorists, they said. Another segment of the media criticized the missile attack on his camp. The U.S. was being a bully again, moving carriers into an intimidating position and attacking a sovereign nation. The administration would weather these storms, previous administrations had, but the real problem was that no one suggested any solutions.

Okay, don't negotiate with terrorists. What then, Murphy asked himself. The critics didn't say.

Okay, don't attack the terrorist's base camp, don't destroy his weapons, or his will to continue to slaughter innocent civilians. What then? No one was making any real suggestions other than to stop doing whatever it was that pissed off the terrorists in the first place.

Dismantle all of our godless institutions, like IBM and General Motors and Microsoft. Take all the money from the billionaires and give it to the poor people. Make it a law that families could not live in big houses and drive fancy cars unless everyone else on the planet could live in a big house and drive a fancy car. Let's take away all incentives. Don't use pesticides, or cut trees, or use animal antibiotics, or irradiate food, but make sure that everyone on the planet is fed as well as everyone else on the planet. Get out of Saudi Arabia, get out of Bosnia and Kosovo, give the American Indians back all of their land including Manhattan, spend the entire GNP on welfare programs for the rest of the world. If we have too much because we're

clever enough to have earned it, give it away. Dismantle
our army and air force and especially our navy. Give in to
every special interest group here and in every other country
in the world, because they have rights too. Take the flag
down and toss it in the trash.

Murphy's limousine took the CIA exit off the George
Washington Parkway and followed the road up to the main
gates. They were passed through without stopping and
parked in the back at the DCI's private entrance. His bodyguard, John Chapin, opened the door for him and escorted
him up to the seventh floor.

"You can stand down, John. It's going to be another late
night," Murphy said at the door to his office.

"Yes, sir," Chapin said, not surprised. He'd seen the look
on the general's face when he came out of the Oval Office.

Murphy went through the outer office into his own office,
his secretary jumping up and trailing behind him. "You've
had a dozen calls, nothing urgent, the memos are on your
desk. Mr. Adkins wanted to speak to you when you returned. And Mrs. Murphy would like to know when to expect you home."

"Late," Murphy said, putting his briefcase down and
loosening his tie as he went around his desk. He lifted the
phone and hit Adkins's number. "Come on over, Dick, we
need to talk."

His secretary brought him a mug of coffee, black, no
sugar, and the briefing book with the afternoon summaries
of the news stories from the top fourteen foreign newspapers. "Would you like me to stay for a while?" she asked.

Murphy shook his head. "It's going to be one of those
nights. You might as well go home."

"I'll call Mrs. Murphy first."

"Thanks."

When she was gone, Murphy turned and looked out the
windows at the rolling Virginia countryside. Everything
was green and new and fresh. His forty-two-foot Westsail
ketch was docked at Annapolis, and he wished that he and
Peggy were aboard her now. Cocktails this early evening

with a few friends. Maybe find a reasonably quiet spot to anchor a few miles downriver. Something on the grill, then to bed with the setting sun and up with the rising sun in the morning. He closed his eyes for a moment, and he could almost smell the sea smells, feel the gentle rocking of the boat.

Dick Adkins, McGarvey's chief of staff and acting DDO, knocked once and came in. "How'd it go, General?" he asked.

Murphy turned around. "They want us to kill him."

Adkins stopped in midstride. "Just like that?"

"With bin Laden dead they feel that his organization will fall apart, and they'll no longer be a threat."

"That's assuming we could get to him in time—if at all."

"Well, we're going to try to find him as well as the bomb, and hope to God we're not too late."

Adkins smiled wryly. "Hell, General, I don't know what's going to be worse—tracking down bin Laden again, or telling McGarvey what they want us to do."

"He'll have plenty to say about it," Murphy said.

"Indeed he will."

Karachi, Pakistan

The three-wheel Fiat delivery truck with PRANDESH DELIVERIES, LTD. stenciled on its doors rattled to a stop in line at the west wharf of the International Terminal Customs Center. When it was his turn, the driver, a small man with wide dark eyes, handed a copy of the bill of lading, repair order and temporary customs release form to the uniformed inspector.

As the inspector took the forms back into the customs shed, Kamal Azzabi lit a clove cigarette and nervously drew the sharp smoke deep into his lungs. He had picked up the package and paperwork at a repair shop near the airport. He didn't know what was in the container, nor did he want to know. His only job was to deliver it to dock 24 west.

No problem, except that he had been paid too much cash, which made him suspicious, and he had been warned not to deviate from the route laid out for him or else someone would come for him and his family.

He'd almost turned down the job, but he needed the money and his mullah had asked him to do it as a personal favor. It was nearly time for afternoon prayers and then supper. That and the monetary windfall was all he could think about. Even the terrific heat didn't bother him today.

A couple of minutes later the inspector came back with another uniformed officer and a large black dog on a leash. Azzabi tossed his cigarette away, and it was all he could do to keep from pissing in his pants. It was drugs back there. He was suddenly convinced of it, and he was going to jail for the rest of his life. Why else would they have brought out the dog?

He started to get out of the truck to come clean, tell them about the money, when the customs inspector came over.

"Did you pick this up for repairs yourself?" the inspector asked.

Azzabi had no idea what the man was talking about. But he bobbed his head. "I don't remember."

"Well, it says on the order that it was you."

Azzabi stole a glance in the rearview mirror. The dog's forepaws were on the back of the truck bed and he was sniffing the fiberglass container.

"Is this the same cargo that you picked up from dock 24 yesterday or isn't it?"

Azzabi bobbed his head again. "Yes, of course it is," he said. His bladder was very loose.

The customs inspector signed the forms and handed them back. "Okay, you're clear."

Azzabi just stared at him for several seconds. Out of the corner of his eye he saw the other officer heading back to the customs shed with his dog.

"Is there something wrong with your hearing?" the inspector shouted.

"No, sir," Azzabi said, and he drove out onto the

crowded docks busy with the activities of loading and unloading ships of all sizes, shapes and descriptions, his truck
just another delivery van among literally hundreds.

The 694-foot container ship *M/V Margo* was in the final
stages of loading the last of more than two hundred containers on its wide cargo deck when Azzabi went up the
boarding ladder and found the loadmaster.

The huge man glared at him. "What do you want?"

Azzabi handed him the papers. The loadmaster glanced
at them, then looked down at the truck. He said something
into a walkie-talkie, then signed the receipt, handed it back
and walked off, shouting something at two men perched
atop the stack of containers towering six high.

By the time Azzabi got back to his truck the package
was gone. "Good riddance," he muttered with relief and
drove off, wondering if he should tell his wife the full ex-
tent of his windfall or keep a little for himself.

TWENTY

Chevy Chase

Bahmad sat forward as Kathleen McGarvey's gun-
metal gray Mercedes 560SL convertible came off
Laurel Parkway and headed south on Connecticut
Avenue toward the city. He got a good look at her as she
passed and he was mildly vexed that she did not seem distraught.

The dark blue windowless van with government plates
came right behind her. The driver's eyes slid casually past
Bahmad behind the wheel of the Capital City Cleaning van

at the stop sign on Kirke Street, and then he was gone in traffic.

"Was that her?" Misha bin Ibrahim asked from the back. He and the other one, Ahmad Aggad, who had come down from Jersey City, were idiots, but they would do as they were told and they were expendable.

"Yes, we're going in now," Bahmad said. He waited for a break in traffic then crossed Connecticut Avenue and headed up Laurel Parkway.

Her house was at the end of a cul-de-sac. In the two days it had taken Bahmad to arrange for the help, the van and the other equipment they would need, he'd spot-checked the neighborhood and done some phone calling.

On both days Kathleen McGarvey left her house around eleven in the morning and returned between two and three. Presumably she'd gone out to lunch. It was only slightly bothersome that she'd apparently not yet learned about her husband's death, but things like that often took time, and it might not be something the CIA wanted to make public so soon.

Both days she'd been followed by the same van. None of the databases he'd run the tag numbers through were more specific than to list them as General Accounting Office, which could be anyone. Most likely the CIA for special domestic operations, or even the FBI's counter-espionage division.

He got lucky with his phone calls. The problem was watching her house until the daughter showed up without alerting the woman or her watchdogs. But the house two doors down from Kathleen McGarvey's would be unoc-cupied for another two weeks. It was a break. He'd phoned each of the houses on the block and when he'd called the one at 15 Laurel Parkway a recorded announcement was kind enough to inform him that the Wheelers would be out of the country on vacation until July third.

"I don't understand if we're going after the daughter, why not watch her apartment?" bin Ibrahim said.

Bahmad glanced at him in the rearview mirror, cowering

in the back with the white coveralls. "Because she has moved out and we can't be certain when she'll return."

"How do you know she will come to her mother?"

"She'll show up here, leave that part to me. Your only responsibility for now is to keep watch for her yellow Volkswagen and call me the instant it shows up."

"Then we will kill her?"

Bahmad nodded.

"We have no problem with that, brother, but what about afterwards? I do not want to spend the rest of my life rotting in some jail cell."

"Nothing will go wrong," Bahmad said. "If you follow my orders no one in the neighborhood will even know that anything has happened until we're long gone the same way we came in. By the time they find this van you'll be on a plane for London, and once you get there you'll be in the pipeline on the way home."

"If I see a clear shot I'm taking it," Aggad said contentiously. He'd been in the States for five years and he was used to being his own boss.

"You'll get yourself caught and shot down."

"No way, man. I'd be long gone before the cops even got the call."

Bahmad looked at him in the mirror, his expression completely bland. "I'm not talking about the police, Ahmad," he said softly. "I'm talking about me."

The two in the back fell silent.

"You will do exactly as you are told if you want to get paid, and if you want to live to spend your money. Do you understand?"

They nodded resentfully. They knew nothing about Bahmad except that he came highly placed in bin Laden's organization. But in the few hours they'd been with him since he'd picked them up at the Greyhound bus station in Baltimore they'd come to respect if not fear him. He exuded extreme self-confidence and competence. In this business that almost always meant extreme danger to anyone who might cross him.

The neighborhood was quiet when they backed into the driveway of the two-story Tudor. Bahmad keyed the variable frequency garage door opener, and the door came open. He backed the van inside, and while bin Ibrahim and Aggad were unloading their weapons, surveillance equipment and supplies, he defeated the house alarm system and let himself in through the kitchen.

The house was quiet, the curtains drawn. A quick check of all the rooms revealed that the family was truly gone.

"No lights, and stay well back from all the windows," Bahmad instructed them.

"We've done this sort of thing before," bin Ibrahim said.

"See that you do it well this time," Bahmad replied. "Use the cell phone to call me as soon as the yellow Volkswagen shows up. The phone is encrypted, so it is safe."

"How far away will you be?" Aggad asked.

It was a reasonable question. "Twenty minutes, twenty-five at the most."

"Okay, let's hope it's soon," Aggad said glancing toward the living room. "I don't want to have to deal with snoopy neighbors."

"No one in this neighborhood has taken any notice that we're here," Bahmad assured them. "It's why we waited until the woman and her bodyguard were gone. Just keep your heads down and your eyes open."

"Consider it done," Ibrahim said.

Aboard Gulfstream VC111
En Route to the U.S.

"It'll be good to be home, even if it's only for a little while," Thomas Arnette said, returning from the head and dropping into his seat.

"I hear you," McGarvey forced a smile. He felt detached, as if he wasn't connected to his body, but he had to pull himself together because they weren't out of the woods yet. Not by a long shot.

Arnette, who worked as a case officer for Allen Trumble and now Jeff Cook in Riyadh, had been assigned to stick with McGarvey. He was short, slender and dark with an easy, ingratiating smile that belied his sharp intelligence. He was one of Trumble's handpicked Arab experts. Each time McGarvey had come awake in the hospital, Arnette had been there. And it was Arnette who had arranged McGarvey's early release and this flight.

"When do you go back?"

Arnette smiled tightly. "I'll check with the Middle East desk tonight, and then fly back tomorrow. Jeff is going to have his hands full, because it's going to start getting pretty dicey. There's anti-American riots just about everywhere, and there's no telling when they'll escalate to some real violence."

"It's spreading from Kabul?"

"Like wildfire," Arnette said, giving McGarvey a critical look. "Mr. Adkins ordered us to keep you out of the loop until you got back to Langley. It was the doctors' suggestion, actually. They wanted to give you a little time to mend."

"I don't know what's worse, imagination or the truth."

They were the only passengers aboard the air force VIP jet. The attendant was doing something in the galley, and the door to the flight deck was closed. "It's a bitch, Mr. McGarvey, but whoever ordered the missile attack ought to be hung. It flat-out didn't work." Arnette was Georgia country, and very pragmatic. His type was rare in the CIA, or anywhere else in the government for that matter.

"It didn't work last time either."

"But we keep trying. Just like the Energizer Bunny."

McGarvey laughed, and a sharp stitch of pain grabbed his side. It felt as if his ribs were going to pop out of his body right through his skin. And his head was ready to explode. He winced.

"Are you okay?" Arnette asked, concerned.

Sweat popped out on McGarvey's brow, but he nodded. "I'll live, but I have to go to the head."

"You gonna make it on your own?"

"Unless we hit an air pocket." McGarvey hauled himself to his feet, spots jumping in front of his eyes. "Trouble is that I've spent the last few days flat on my back and I've stiffened up a little."

"That's not what the docs said."

McGarvey glanced out the windows. They were finally over the Atlantic, and there was nothing to see. But they'd be in Washington in a few more hours. "Get me another brandy would you, Tom?"

"How about something to eat?"

"Sure. But another drink first." McGarvey made it back to the head, and when he was inside and had the door locked, his legs began to buckle and he sat down on the toilet lid. He could see the reflection of his face in the mirror above the tiny sink, but the edges were blurry as if something was wrong with the glass. The compartment was getting dark too, but when he looked up at the light fixture he could tell that it was on.

He tried to stand but couldn't, and he slumped back, his head against the bulkhead. The plane was spinning around and around making him sick to his stomach. The wound in his side ached with a dull throb, and his entire body was drenched in sweat. But the worst was his head, which pounded as if someone had stuck a high-pressure air hose in his ear and was filling up his skull.

The compartment was almost completely dark now, he couldn't even see his own reflection, but there were flashes of lights behind his eyeballs; lightning streaks across his brain in time with sharp, piercing stabs of deep pain inside his head.

For several seconds it was all he could do just to sit there and hold on, his arm draped over the edge of the sink. But then the episode passed almost as quickly as it had begun. The lights came back on, the plane stopped spinning and the shooting pains inside his head faded. He released the deep breath he'd been holding and let his body sag.

After a minute or so he got up, splashed some cold water

on his face, dried off with some paper towels and went out to the main cabin and back to his seat.

"Are you really okay, Mr. McGarvey?" Arnette asked, looking up.

"I've felt better, but I don't have much of a choice here. I'll have a ton of shit to deal with when I get back."

"That you will."

The attendant came back with their drinks. "Dinner will be ready in about a half-hour. Steak and lobster, and I have a nice Nouveau Beaujolais that oughta go down pretty smooth."

"Sounds good," Arnette said,

When the attendant was gone, McGarvey started to raise his drink, but something Arnette had said suddenly struck him, and he put the glass down.

"You said that Dick wanted me kept out of the loop while I was in the hospital. What'd you mean? Exactly."

"They didn't want you getting upset. Besides, you were mostly out of it on pain killers."

"You said that our missile strike didn't work?"

Arnette nodded uncertainly.

"Did bin Laden survive?"

"Yeah," Arnette said morosely. "There's not a doubt in anyone's mind that he's going to hit back. But when, where and with what is anybody's guess."

"Shit," McGarvey said under his breath. It couldn't have been worse news. He thought about calling Adkins, but they'd have their hands full over there, and there was nothing he could say or do now that would make any difference. He needed more information, and he needed to be there.

He closed his eyes and willed the airplane to fly faster.

Andrews Air Force Base

McGarvey awoke around 6:30 A.M. with the morning sun blasting in the windows as they turned on final approach to Andrews Air Force Base outside Washington. For the first few moments he was disoriented, wondering where the hell he was, but then he remembered and his hand went to the tender spot on the side of his head.

Dinner had been fine, but the drinks, especially the wine, had left him with a dull headache and a gummy mouth on top of his other ills.

He sat up and peered out the window. The countryside looked neat and clean, organized and modern compared to Afghanistan. For a little while he allowed himself the luxury of enjoying the moment, something he was rarely able to do. He was always working out scenarios for himself and everyone around him. Very often they were of the worst possible kind. At the fringes of his thoughts now was the question about bin Laden and men of his ilk—the terrorists of the world. Why did they hate us so badly that they wanted to tear all this down while at the same time beating at the gates to get in? It made no sense. But he was being naive, which was especially odd for a man of his experience, and even dangerous for a man in his position. He'd never found an answer to what he considered was a very basic question. Jealousy, he'd always thought, was too easy an answer. It was possibly something that he would never know.

"Good morning," Arnette said, and McGarvey turned to him.

"Hi."

"Are you feeling any better?"

McGarvey managed to smile. "I'll live, but I don't know if that's such a great idea. How about you?"

Arnette shook his head. "Oh, I never sleep on airplanes," he said. "But I usually get a lot of reading done." He held up a paperback novel.

The flight attendant came back with a glass of orange juice and a couple of pills. "Tylenol Extra Strength," he said, handing them to McGarvey. "You had a rough night, I figured these might help."

"Thanks," McGarvey said. He took the pills and drank

the juice. He'd spent a lot of bad nights, but just lately they had piled up.

"Check your belt please, sir, we'll be on the ground in a couple of minutes."

"Yeah." McGarvey thought about the work he was facing, and the probability that they would fail. "Tell the pilot good flight."

"Yes, sir," the attendant said, and he went forward to his jump seat.

McGarvey turned back to Arnette. "You might as well ride out to Langley with me."

"Thanks, but Dave Whittaker said he'd be sending somebody for me, and they're taking you out to Bethesda, the docs want to check you out."

"I've had enough hospital for this week," McGarvey grumbled and he looked outside as they came in for a landing. There would be plenty of time for hospitals later. For the moment he had a war to fight, a war that he wasn't at all sure they could win given the rules they had to fight by.

The Gulfstream taxied past the terminal and parked in an empty hangar. McGarvey got up as the door was opened and the stairs lowered. Several armed air force cops surrounded the airplane even before the engines had spooled completely down. Dick Yemm was waiting with McGarvey's limousine. It was a beautiful warm morning but muggy after the Afghani desert and mountains. McGarvey shook hands with Arnette while Yemm opened the limo's rear passenger door.

"Are you sure I can't give you a lift?" McGarvey asked.

"No, sir, my ride'll be along shortly," Arnette said. "You know, maybe you should consider leaving the field work to the kids next time."

"That's a thought," McGarvey said. "Thanks for your help."

"Hey, no sweat. It's why they pay me the big bucks."

McGarvey walked over to the limo and shook hands with his driver/bodyguard.

"Welcome home, boss," Yemm said.

"It's good to be back, Dick. Let's see how fast you can get me over to Langley."

Yemm hesitated for a moment. "We're supposed to take you over to Bethesda ASAP."

"Later," McGarvey said tersely. He ducked down to climb in the back seat and saw Elizabeth sitting in the corner, a big smile on her face.

"Hi, Daddy," she said in a small voice, her excitement and concern for him barely suppressed.

He was stopped for just a moment. "Hi, Liz," he said. He got the rest of the way in and grunted with pain. Elizabeth reached out a hand to help him.

"Daddy, what's the matter?"

"I'm still a little stiff from climbing mountains," McGarvey said, masking his pain and sudden dizziness. "Thanks for coming out to pick me up. How's your mother?"

"Happy that you were coming back in one piece," Elizabeth said looking at him critically to make sure that he was really all right. "I told her to stay home this morning because you'd have to be debriefed. She understood, but she'd like you to call her as soon as you get a chance."

Yemm got behind the wheel. "How about it, boss, Bethesda or Langley?"

"My office, Dick."

"They wanted to check you out first," Elizabeth said.

"The office," McGarvey repeated to his driver, and as they headed out, he turned his attention back to his daughter. "Okay, sweetheart, what's the story? We have a problem, it's written all over your face."

"Bin Laden survived," Elizabeth said, girding herself. She'd always hated being the bearer of bad news. Her father's major fault, in her estimation, was wanting to protect everybody around him no matter what the cost was to his relationship with them, even leaving them. Her biggest problem, by contrast, was wanting to make everybody around her happy while still trying to somehow juggle her fierce independence into the mix. It couldn't always work that way, and as a child she lied a lot; varnished the truth, as her father would say. But now in the real world in which people could and did get hurt without the absolute truth, that was no longer possible.

"Tom Arnette told me on the way over. He must have left the camp by now. Do we have any idea where he went?"

"He's probably gone to ground in Khartoum, but we're not sure yet. Otto's working with Louise Horn over at NRO." She smiled a little. "They're quite a team."

"Bin Laden's going to come after us and we're going to have to be ready for him."

They passed through the main gate, the air force policeman snapping them a crisp salute, and then got on the Capital Beltway, the morning rush hour traffic horrendous.

"Was it bad over there?" Elizabeth asked.

"We could have had a deal," McGarvey said heavily. "I think that he's dying of cancer, and he wanted to make sure that his family would be taken care of." He shrugged. "But he does know how to run a war, and his people are behind him one hundred percent."

"I went to school in Switzerland with his daughter, Sarah. What did you think of her?"

"She's a bright girl—" McGarvey stopped suddenly, realizing that she was trying to tell him something. "What?"

"The NRO got some really good high-angle frames of the camp during the raid and a few minutes on either side of it. We figured that Sarah left the camp about the same time as you did, and maybe she helped escort you part of the way back."

"Did she get caught in the attack?"

Elizabeth's lips compressed, and she nodded. "She was killed." She reached for her father's hand and squeezed it. "I saw the file photo we have of her and remembered her from that school outside of Bern. She's younger than me, and she was only there for a year, but I still remember her because of the bodyguards." Liz looked away. "Now she's dead."

"What's our confidence level on this?"

"Very high," Elizabeth said. "We got some very good enhanced images of bin Laden with his daughter's body in his arms."

"Christ," McGarvey said shaking his head. "There'll be no reasoning with him now."

"It wasn't your fault," Elizabeth said. "Maybe he'd still listen to you if you could reach him."

McGarvey looked at his daughter with a sudden over-whelming love and fear. He'd gotten inside bin Laden's skin for a few minutes up there in his mountain cave. Or at least he thought he had. But just now, just at this moment, looking at his daughter, he was sure that he *really* understood bin Laden. Understood a father's anguish.

"If his people had killed you I wouldn't listen to him," McGarvey said softly. "He's coming after us now with everything he has. And it's going to hurt."

Fanaticism is a monster that could tear a society apart, Voltaire wrote two hundred fifty years ago, and it was just as true now as it had been then. "The fanatic is under the influence of a madness which is constantly goading him on."

A daughter's death at the hands of the infidels was the ultimate goad.

CIA Headquarters

McGarvey walked into his office a few minutes before eight. His daughter accompanied him. Now that he was back and he had found out about Sarah's death, he had an unreasoning fear for Elizabeth's safety even here in the building. His secretary wasn't here yet, and he had a full plate so he could justify keeping her by his side, even though her job was in Rencke's section.

He took off the blue jacket the air force had loaned him, tossed it on the couch and went to his desk, which was loaded with memos, telephone messages and mail.

"Get your mother on the phone, would you?" McGarvey asked his daughter. "And then have Otto come up."

"Do you want some coffee, Dad?" Elizabeth asked, a secret smile on her lips.

"When you get a chance." McGarvey turned on his computer, and as it was coming on-line he called Adkins's office next door. "I'm back."

"You're supposed to be in the hospital."

"Thanks, I'm glad to be back too," McGarvey said with a chuckle. An outside line on his phone console began to blink, and Elizabeth motioned to him that it was her mother. "I want a meeting at eleven in the main auditorium with all our DO and DI department heads, the FBI's counterterrorism people, INS, State, the DoD, Defense Intelligence, the bomb people over at the ATF, Doug Brand—the new chief of Interpol—and anyone else you can think of."

"He's coming after us."

"No doubt about it, Dick," McGarvey said. "As soon as you set that up come on over, we have some work to do."

"Will do," Adkins said. "It *is* good to have you here, Mac, as long as you don't push yourself."

"Yeah, right," McGarvey said. He broke the connection, and before he picked up the outside line he asked Elizabeth to call Dave Whittaker up. Whittaker was the DO's Area Divisions chief in charge of all the foreign desks at Langley as well as all the Agency's bases and stations worldwide. He punched the button for the outside line. "Hi, Katy."

"Welcome home, darling," Kathleen said. "How are you?" Her voice was soft and wonderful. McGarvey couldn't help but smile.

"I'm a little battered and bruised, but it's nothing life-threatening, so you can stop worrying about me."

"I worry about you even when you're in my arms," Kathleen said. "Are you going to be able to get out of there sometime in the near future?"

"Tonight. And that's a promise."

"Shall I wait supper?"

"I might be late."

Now Kathleen laughed. "What's new," she said. "I'll start something around eight."

Rencke walked in, his red hair flying all over the place, his eyes red and puffy. It looked as if he hadn't slept in a week, but he was excited.

"Gotta go, Katy," McGarvey said. "Love ya."

"I know," Kathleen said, and McGarvey broke the connection. He'd never understood that response before, but now he did, and it felt great.

"Oh, wow, Mac, am I ever glad to see you," Rencke gushed. "Big time." He hopped from one foot to the other, as he did whenever he was happy.

"I'm glad to see you too, pal," McGarvey said. "But you look worse than I do. When's the last time you got any sleep?"

Rencke completely ignored the question. "We've wiped out bin Laden's daughter, and guess what? That makes him one motivated dude."

"He's also very well informed," McGarvey said. He told Rencke about the meeting with bin Laden in the cave, including the fact they knew all about the GPS chip. "He could have an informer somewhere inside the NRO."

"Hackers," Rencke said dreamily. He was making connections. His eyes went to the computer on McGarvey's side desk. "The Taliban phoned Riyadh Ops and told them to send the C-130 an hour early or not at all," he said softly. "And when it was taxiing away from the terminal they came after it." Rencke focused on McGarvey. "Don't you see, Mac, they were expecting you, and they'd been asked to stop you. By bin Laden. He's into everything. He has connections everywhere because he's rich, ya know?"

"We have to stop them from getting into our system," McGarvey said.

"I'll work on it," Rencke replied absently. He came around behind McGarvey's desk and studied the menu displayed on the computer. "Have you logged in yet?"

"No."

"Well, if they're in the system there's no use letting them know that you've survived and that you're back to work." Rencke shut off the computer and went back to the front of desk where he stood like a schoolboy who has just done a tough problem on the blackboard. "It might give us a small advantage," he said.

"Good point," McGarvey agreed. "Has there been any word from bin Laden or his people about the raid?"

"Not so much as a peep," Elizabeth said. "I have a half-dozen search engines going on the Net, but we've come up empty-handed so far." Elizabeth looked perplexed. "But I don't get it, Dad. You'd think he would want to get the maximum mileage from his daughter's death. I mean guys like that usually take advantage of *anything* that comes their way. Something like the evil empire killing innocent women and children. Something. Anything."

"Would bin Laden know for certain that we knew his daughter had been killed?" McGarvey asked.

"He could know our satellite schedule," Rencke said. "But if we don't issue an apology, something he might expect us to do, there's no way for him to know for sure."

McGarvey turned back to his daughter. "Do you mention her death in your search engines?"

Elizabeth shook her head uncertainly. "No."

"Okay, that's one piece of information we won't put out," McGarvey said.

Understanding dawned on Elizabeth's face. "He figures that if we know that we killed his daughter, we'll also know that he's going to come after us."

"Something like that," McGarvey said tiredly.

"But, Dad, that makes us the same as him," Elizabeth protested. "He's going to use his daughter's death to give himself an advantage over us. And now we're going to do the same thing."

"That's right, Liz," McGarvey said, liking it even less than she did. But he had traveled with Sarah, eaten with her, talked to her, had even saved her from rape. "Have we come up with anything new on the Russian weapon?"

"No, and we probably won't," Rencke said. "The Bolshies are running scared and they're covering up now, 'cause they know the score."

"Did you get into the old Lubyanka mainframe?"

"It was easy green," Rencke said. "But there wasn't much. They're not even talking about it amongst themselves." He got a wistful look on his face that was almost comical in its intensity. Someone who didn't know him would believe that he had lost his mind or had zoned out. But then he smiled shyly. "I figured there had to be something, ya know. So I snooped around their out-station files, and you'll never guess what I came up with." Rencke looked around for someone to guess, but then shrugged. "There was a military trial yesterday. A captain and a colonel were found guilty of theft and dereliction of duty. Pretty common these days. But they were executed. Lined up in front of a wall and shot dead, big time. And guess where all this took place."

"Tajikistan," McGarvey said.

"Yeah," Rencke replied. "Yavan Depot, right where the weapon came from. Which means we're not going to get diddly from the Russkies. They're going to deny everything. We are definitely on our own, kimo sabe."

"The bomb is on its way," McGarvey said.

"You can bet the farm on it."

TWENTY-ONE

M/V *Margo*

I told you that we should have waited a few days," First Officer Joseph Green said.

Captain George Panagiotopolous glanced over at the pissant little man standing in front of the radar. The storm was going to be a good one, he could not deny that, but it wasn't a typhoon. He'd sailed through those by whatever name they were called—hurricane, anticyclone, extratropical storm—in four different oceans. Rough, dangerous, uncomfortable, but not impossible for a ship like the *Margo*.

He walked over to the bank of ship's phones and called his deck officer/loadmaster Lazlo Schumatz in his quarters. "This is Panagiotopolous, it looks like we're going to get that weather sooner than expected. Are you ready?"

"The deck cargo is secure, and Heiddi's section should be finished in the holds in about an hour. Do you want me to go down there?"

"It might not hurt," the captain said.

"What are we in for?"

Panagiotopolous glanced again at Green, who was staring intently out the windows across the cluttered cargo deck toward the bows, which were already beginning to rise and fall with the action of the increasing waves. "We're in for a force eight, maybe a nine."

Schumatz laughed. "Thirty-five to forty-five knot winds, and you call me? What, is Green quaking in his boots again?"

The captain was a great respecter of rank. He didn't hold

with disrespect. "Maybe you should double check the deck cargo as well, especially before it gets any rougher," he said.

"As you wish."

"Thank you." The captain hung up the phone and followed Green's gaze out the bridge windows. The *Margo* was a tight ship. With an overall length of 654 feet and a beam of ninety-six, she could transport nearly one thousand containers in her seven holds and lashed to her cargo deck. A pair of Sulzer diesels could push her through the seas at sixteen knots, and since her 1978 launch from the Cockerill Yards in Hoboken, New Jersey, she had never been in a collision or any serious accident at sea. She'd been retrofitted with new hatches and bow thrusters at Tampa Marine Yards in Florida in 1985, and had undergone a complete rebuild in 1996. But now they wanted her back for a second overhaul even though it was too soon, and there was not enough wrong with her to pull her out of service for the two months it would take. But it was the owners' decision and there was no arguing with them.

They would sail up the Red Sea, transit the Suez Canal, cross the Med, and then head out across the Atlantic to the Port of New York where they would unload their cargo. From there it would be Tampa, and after that it was up to the owners. Everything was up to the owners, always. Panagiotopolous had been at sea for most of his life, and he understood the score. His job was to sail the boats, and leave the business and the politics to others. Not his reponsibility.

Green turned and gave the captain a bleak look. He was just a kid and he was frightened. But he was also the principal stock holder's son, so he had to be treated with respect. And he did have his first officer's papers.

"These kinds of storms are confidence-builders," the captain said, not unkindly. "Once you've gone through forty-five knots, and you see that you and your ship have done just fine, why then forty-five knots will never present a problem again."

"But fifty knots will," Green said, relaxing a little. "What's the biggest storm you've been in?"

"I'll tell you about it sometime over a beer," Panagiotopolous said. He had his own upper limit like all men did.

"How big?"

The helmsman was studying the binnacle compass even though they were on autopilot. But he was listening.

"A hundred sixty knots," the captain said quietly. He grinned. "And I was pissing in my pants."

Green looked nervously out the window. "In other words this is no problem."

"Something like that."

CIA Headquarters

General Roland Murphy appeared as if he hadn't slept in a week, but unlike Rencke who looked like a wild man, Murphy looked ill. The skin hung on his jowls and neck, and his complexion was pasty. McGarvey was shocked by his appearance. He'd never seen him this way. The rumor was that Murphy was going to retire in six months, but McGarvey had to genuinely wonder if the man was going to make it that long. The general had worked for the CIA almost as long as McGarvey had been involved with the Company. During that time they had never been friends, but they'd maintained a mutual respect. They each were the best at what they did, which was one of the reasons why Murphy had gotten behind McGarvey's appointment as DDO last year, a move that stunned some people and angered others, and why it had gone through without a hitch. But he seemed to have greatly diminished in the week or so that McGarvey had been gone. Both of them had been beaten up by the mission.

He got up from behind his desk and extended his hand. "Welcome home, Kirk. I'm glad to see you in one piece."

McGarvey took his hand and was happy that the general's grip had not weakened. "Thanks, but I would rather have come home to a better set of circumstances."

"Partly my fault, I'm afraid," Murphy's face fell. "When you went off the air we thought you were dead and bin Laden was playing games with us."

"Dennis Berndt's idea?"

Murphy nodded. "Everyone's except Otto's." He motioned for McGarvey to take a seat, and then he slumped back down in his chair. "I assume that you've already been briefed about bin Laden's daughter."

"I got the high points on the way in from Andrews."

"A terrible business."

McGarvey nodded, there was nothing else to say about it. "I've called a National Threat Assessment meeting for eleven."

"That's cutting everyone a little short, isn't it?" Murphy said, glancing at the desk clock. It was a little before 10:00 A.M. "The President wants to see you."

"He'll have to wait until this afternoon," McGarvey said, and before Murphy could object he went on. "The bomb is on its way here, General. We don't know how it's coming, where it's coming or even when it's coming, but we have to deal with the problem. The sooner we get to it the greater our chances for success are going to be."

"Which are?"

"I don't know," McGarvey said tiredly. "But the advantage is definitely his."

Murphy took a memo out of a file folder and passed it across the desk. It was on White House stationery and was signed by Haynes. "You're going to be asked to assassinate bin Laden."

McGarvey read the note and passed it back. "At least this is one President who's not afraid to take responsibility," he said. "But he's too late by at least six months, which is about how long it would take to pull off something like that—if it could be done at all." McGarvey's headache was coming back, and he passed a hand over his eyes. "Those days are gone, thank God." He shook his head. "But even if we could push a little red button right this instant, and bin Laden would suddenly cease to exist, the bomb would still come here."

"Not without his orders."

"He's gone to ground now. He set the machinery in motion, and even he might not be able to stop it even if he wanted to."

Some of Murphy's spark came back. He'd personally seen just about everything that could happen in the shadow world, and he still controlled the largest and most powerful intelligence agency in the world. "Okay, how do we proceed?"

"We're going to tighten our border controls to start with. We're putting tracers on all of bin Laden's known associates and business connections here in the States and everywhere else. We've got the word out to be on the lookout for a special package. Something that'll be getting more attention than whatever it's disguised to look like should be getting. And we're watching the possible routes. It started out in Tajikistan and had to have been transported overland through the mountains into Afghanistan. Assuming it's on the move again it either has to be taken east to Pakistan or west to Iran. We have people on the ground who will be moved into positions to watch the roads, the trains, the planes and the ships."

"What's your best guess?"

"Best guess or worst fear?" McGarvey asked. "Because the worstcase scenario would be the simplest. They load the bomb on a commercial airliner, and as it approaches either New York City or Washington it goes off."

"Security at every international airport around the world will have to be tightened. Just like after Lockerbie."

"Maybe it'll go by ship to Hamburg, then by truck to Frankfurt and from there by air to Washington," McGarvey said. "Or any other combination you'd like to dream up."

"I see your point."

"Maybe it'll stay in Tehran for a month, or maybe in Paris or London or Marseilles or Tripoli, and then when our security measures start to loosen up, which they will, it'll be moved again. Leapfrogged here."

"Does he have a timetable?"

"That's a possibility we're going to have to consider. Could be he's going to hit us on the Fourth of July, or maybe Labor Day; maybe Thanksgiving or Christmas." McGarvey shook his head again. "Do you want to try for Lincoln's birthday?"

Murphy sighed deeply. "If we had held back on the missile attack we could have avoided all of this."

"Maybe," McGarvey said. "He might have been stalling for time after all. Kept us talking while he moved the bomb into place."

Murphy gave McGarvey a sharp look. "But you don't believe that."

"Doesn't matter. We have a situation in front of us now, and we have to deal with it. Nothing else is important." The recriminations and finger-pointing would come later, McGarvey thought. Right now it was a question of motivation, dedication. "How are you feeling, Roland?"

Murphy smiled wanly. "That's supposed to be my question to you."

"I've felt worse. But when this is over I'm going to take a long vacation. Someplace *without* a mountain view."

"Next time send someone else out into the field, okay? I want my DDO running the show, not becoming the star attraction."

"No one likes the thought of getting old," McGarvey said.

"No," Murphy agreed. When McGarvey was gone a snatch of something started running around in the back of his head. He couldn't quite put his finger on it, but the line had something to do with dancing on a grave. It was disturbing, all the more so because his memory was imperfect, and because he wondered if it was a portent.

• • •

McGarvey entered the CIA's main auditorium at 11:00 A.M. sharp and went directly to the podium on the small stage. A table was set next to it. He felt like hell, but he did not let it show. There were nearly a hundred people hastily assembled, all of them law enforcement or intelligence-gathering officials, and most of them experts in counterterrorism. Adkins and his own staff took up the back rows, along with Tommy Doyle and some of his people from the Directorate of Intelligence. Rencke was held up downstairs with Jared Kraus in Technical Services, and Elizabeth was with him.

"Thank you for coming out on such short notice this morning. My name is Kirk McGarvey and for those of you who don't know me, I'm the deputy director of Operations. I've called this meeting because the CIA believes that the United States is facing the worst threat of terrorism in its history. And we're going to have to work together to try to stop it." He dimmed the lights and clicked on the projection unit.

The slide showed the engineering diagram of the Russian nuclear bomb. "This information comes to us from Department of Defense and Department of Energy files," McGarvey said. "The device on the screen is a Russian nuclear demolitions weapon which they call *atvartka*, or screwdriver. It has a nominal yield of one kiloton, it fits into a package about the size of a large suitcase, and detonation-ready it weighs between eighty and ninety pounds.

"It does not leak radiation, so Geiger counters cannot detect it and our conventional NEST forces will not work. Its conventional explosives are so well sealed that bomb-sniffing dogs are of no use. It's shockproof, heatproof, waterproof and so extremely simple to operate that it does not require a trained technician to fire it. In short, ladies and gentlemen, the perfect terrorist's weapon."

McGarvey had their attention. He switched to the next slide, which showed a photograph of the actual device with a serial number next to it. "The nuclear weapon with this serial number was stored, until recently, at the Yavan Depot outside of Dushanbe, Tajikistan. Because of the decaying political situation in many of the former Soviet Union's breakaway republics, security for and accountability of such equipment is lax at the very best."

He clicked to the next slide, showing two Russian officers. "Colonel Vladislav Drankov and Captain Vadim Perminov, who were in charge of security at the depot, were found guilty of dereliction of duty and theft by a military court. They were executed yesterday."

The next slide came up. It showed a map of the region between Tajikistan and northern Afghanistan. Several routes through the mountains were marked in red. "We believe that these two Russian officers sold the nuclear weapon for thirty million U.S. dollars in cash to Osama bin Laden, who brought it by horseback through rebel-held territory to his base outside of Charikar as early as three months ago."

"How the hell long has the CIA known about this?" the FBI's Fred Rudolph demanded. He and McGarvey had worked together before. They had a great deal of respect for each other. But now Rudolph was mad. And he was clearly shook up, everyone in the audience was.

"About eight weeks, Fred," McGarvey replied. "But we were not sitting on our hands. We had an operation in progress."

"Evidently it wasn't a success, or you wouldn't have called us here," Rudolph said. "The missile raid was an exercise in futility. Are you going to tell us that bin Laden survived?"

"It's worse than that," McGarvey said. He brought up the next image on the screen which showed the satellite shot of bin Laden carrying his daughter's body. "This was taken from one of our Keyhole satellites within minutes after the missile attack on bin Laden's mountain camp was completed. The figure at the lower left of the photograph is Osama bin Laden. As you can see, he survived. Subsequent photographs show that he was apparently not hurt."

McGarvey looked up at the screen. "He's carrying someone who did not survive the attack, however."

He clicked to the next picture, this one the file photograph of Sarah. "This is Osama bin Laden's nineteen-year-old daughter, Sarah. It is her body he is carrying. It was she, along with at least eighteen of his mujahedeen, who was killed in the attack."

"Oh, shit," someone in the audience said.

"As you may expect, bin Laden is now well motivated, and he will attempt to bring the nuclear weapon into the United States sometime in the very near future—although we don't know when—to hit a target that will inflict the maximum damage on us in retaliation for the death of his child. It's up to us to stop him."

"This is what the President meant in his speech," Rudolph said softly, but McGarvey heard him. "It would have been helpful to our investigation if we had known all the facts."

"National security concerns—" McGarvey said.

"Come on, Mac, we can't do this in the dark," Rudolph pressed. He was stunned, he was angry and he was frightened. They all were. "If we had known the score *before* Allen Trumble and his family were gunned down we might have been able to do something to prevent it. To prevent all of this. And then afterwards we were kept in the dark again about the raid. Why?"

"It was to protect my life," McGarvey said. He paused a moment to let that sink in. "We thought that Allen Trumble and his family were killed by a faction who did not agree with bin Laden. Someone who wanted to use the bomb against us, even though bin Laden himself was apparently getting cold feet and wanted to talk to us."

"Are you saying that you went over there and met with him?"

"Yes, I did."

"Then why the missile attack?" Rudolph asked.

"It was a mistake."

The auditorium was suddenly very quiet. McGarvey

could see that they were evaluating the situation through the various perspectives of their own positions and experience. It was exactly what he wanted them to do. They were all coming more or less to the same conclusions: Either someone had made a colossal blunder bordering on the criminal, or McGarvey was lying to them to protect his own job. There wasn't a person in the group who believed the latter.

"It's on the way here," Rudolph said.

"We're going to have to assume that it is," McGarvey said. "All of you have extensive files on bin Laden so I'm not going over his background except that before you leave you'll each be given a diskette containing the CIA's entire file. Nothing will be held back. We can't afford the luxury. But I will tell you something that you most likely don't know, and that's not yet in the files. Bin Laden is probably dying of cancer and very possibly he doesn't have much time left. It's one of the reasons he agreed to meet with me, and now it's all the more reason for him to hurry this last attack."

"Maybe he'll make a mistake," someone said.

"Let's hope he does, but don't count on it," McGarvey said. "He spent thirty million to get the bomb, and he means to use it. Which means he has a carefully worked out plan and a timetable. Neither of which we know."

"We'll have to keep this from the public to avoid a panic," the State Department representative said.

"I agree," Rudolph said. "But if we're going to have any chance of heading this off before it gets here we're going to have to pool our resources. *All* our resources."

"Agreed," McGarvey said.

The door at the rear of the auditorium opened and Rencke came in. He was pushing an aluminum case loaded onto a handcart. Elizabeth came in right behind him and took a seat in the back row as he started to the front.

McGarvey turned up the lights. "Dick Adkins will coordinate the operation from our crisis center. Besides the usual computer links we'll maintain a twenty-four-per-day hotline, and I would like each of your departments to do the same."

"This has to be a two-way street in more than name only," Rudolph said.

"You have my word on it," McGarvey promised. "Are there any questions?"

Rencke had reached the stage. He lifted the aluminum case off the cart with some difficulty, and brought it up on the stage where he set it down on the table to the left of the podium.

"I have a question," Rudolph said. "Is that what I think it is?"

"Yes, it is," McGarvey said.

Rencke keyed the five-digit combinations on the two locks, released the latches and opened the lid of the case, which was about the size of a large suitcase. Next he activated the keypad and entered an eleven-digit code. Immediately an LED counter across the top of the keypad began to count down by the hundredth of a second from ten minutes.

"This is one of our nuclear demolition weapons," McGarvey said. "But it's almost identical in design and operation with the Russian version. Before you leave this morning I'd like you to come up and take a look at what you're going to be dealing with."

Rudolph was the first on the stage, and he looked up nervously from the keypad. "This thing is running," he said.

"The physics package in this one is a dummy," McGarvey said.

"What does it do when it hits zero?" Don Marsden, from the State Department's special unit on counterterrorism asked.

"I don't know," McGarvey admitted. He turned to Rencke.

"I don't have a clue either," Rencke said. "But it might be interesting to stick around and find out."

Marsden grinned nervously. "I'd like to, but I have to get back to my office."

"Me too," Rudolph said.

• • •

McGarvey stayed to answer a few more questions, but everyone went with Adkins to get their briefing diskettes by the time the counter on the dummy bomb hit zero. McGarvey was staring at it, but nothing happened. It hit zero and the keypad went blank.

Rencke relocked the case and loaded it on the handcart. "The army wasn't happy about admitting they had this, let alone letting us use it," he said. "But it impressed the hell out of everybody."

"I hope so," McGarvey said tiredly. He just couldn't seem to get his act together. It was as if he was a couple of paces behind himself, and couldn't catch up, and he found himself being distracted by stray, disconnected thoughts that had nothing to do with the present moment.

Elizabeth came from the back of the auditorium and gave her father a critical look. "Are you okay, Daddy?" she asked. "Maybe you should go over to Bethesda after all and let the doctors look at you. Then go home, at least until morning."

"I'm making an early night of it, I promised your mother. But I still have work to do, and the general and I are briefing the President this afternoon."

"My search engines are all in gear. If there's anything out there we'll find it," Rencke said. "In the meantime if you're up to it I want to run some eyes and voices past you. I might be able to come up with an IdentiKit portrait of bin Laden's chief of staff from what Allen was able to tell me, and what you can come up with. At least it might narrow down the search."

"Run a parallel search with my background plugged in," McGarvey said.

"Do you think that you've met this guy before?" Rencke asked excitedly.

"Maybe, but I just can't put my finger on where, or in what context. He sounded English, but I don't think he was."

"What makes you think that?" Elizabeth asked.

"I don't know, sweetheart, just something in my gut." He was feeling disconnected again, and he looked up to make sure that the room lights hadn't gone out because his vision was starting to get dark. He followed Rencke and Elizabeth up the aisle and out of the auditorium, his left hand trailing on the seatbacks for balance. Bits and pieces of Voltaire were running around in a jumble in his head, but they made no sense. For the first time since he could remember he truly felt afraid.

TWENTY-TWO

Arabian Sea

The M/V *Margo* smashed directly into the increasing waves. By the time the crew had finished checking the cargo integrity in the seven holds the storm had fully developed. The weather report from Karachi was wrong. By now the winds had passed the predicted maximum of forty-five knots and were gusting at times to more than seventy knots. Almost a category-one typhoon. Captain Panagiotopolous was confident that his ship could handle the storm, but he wasn't so sure about some of his crew, many of whom were inexperienced, or about the two hundred-plus containers chained to the cargo deck, some of which had already started to come loose.

He stood on the bridge looking down at the floodlit deck. Rain swept horizontally, and each time the bows came crashing down, seawater inundated the ship back to the superstructure, carrying away anything that wasn't tied down. Schumatz and three of his deck crew were down there now rerigging the chains holding a stack of forty-foot containers, six high and four wide. The captain had thought about turning the *Margo* downwind to give the crewmen a dry deck, but the roll would be worse and the chances for an accident sharply increased. If one of the truck-sized containers came loose it could start a chain reaction that could sweep every container off the deck and possibly even cause enough damage to the ship to disable or sink her.

The irony would be superb, he kept telling himself. One third of the deck cargo consisted of Chinese-made life rafts packed into fiberglass containers bound for San Francisco. His walkie-talkie squawked.

He keyed it. "This is the captain."

"We got the bastard," Schumatz shouted over the shrieking wind.

"This blow is likely to last another twenty-four hours."

"A link in one of the chains shattered. I'm telling you that it was a one-in-a-million chance. There must have been a void or a crack in the sonofabitch bar stock."

"Check all the others."

"That'll take half the goddamn night."

"All the chain came from the same chandler. You know what it means if a container comes loose."

A white-faced First Officer Green was looking at him. Panagiotopolous gave him a reassuring nod.

He keyed the walkie-talkie. "Do you copy that?"

"I hear you," Schumatz shouted.

"Do you want some more help?"

"No, goddammit. Just keep this bastard as steady as you can."

"The conditions will probably get worse so check the inner stacks first."

"Run the bridge, Panagiotopolous, and let me do my job," Schumatz shouted.

The captain bit back an angry retort because his deck officer was correct. He looked out the window as Schumatz appeared from behind one of the stacks. Schumatz had to brace himself against one of the containers to keep his footing as he looked up at the bridge. He stood like that for a moment to make the point that the decks were his territory, and then disappeared again.

The crew's comfort and happiness were always second to the safety of the ship. Always. And Captain Panagiotopolous was damned if he was going to lose either in a bullshit little blow like this one.

Arlington, Virginia

McGarvey was sitting on a table in an examining room at Urgent Care West, a medical clinic just off the parkway in Arlington. He came here whenever he wanted to see a doctor without the CIA knowing about it. The trauma medicine specialist, Mike Mattice, who'd just finished examining him was writing something in McGarvey's file.

"Am I going to live?" McGarvey asked.

Mattice, a large man with very broad shoulders and a pleasant, almost gentle smile, looked up seriously. "If what's going on inside your skull is what I think it is, you could be in some serious trouble." They'd developed a friendship over the past ten years, and Mattice had treated him for everything from the flu to gunshot wounds. He told it like it was, never pulling any punches.

"What's wrong with me?"

"Hairline skull fracture, probably a subdural hematoma. It means that you have a little arterial bleeder in there under the left temple. Unequal pupils, occasional blurring of your vision." Mattice was sitting on a stool next to a table. He was all business. "I'm sending you up to see a friend of mine at University Hospital in Georgetown. You're going to have a CAT scan and he's going to read it."

McGarvey started to object, he didn't have the time, but Mattice held him off.

"He'll keep his mouth shut, if that's what you still want. But this time it's serious, nothing to fool around with. There could be a lot of bad stuff going on inside of your head, could end up making you permanently blind, maybe paralyzed, probably scramble your brains." He gave McGarvey a critical look. "Have you had any dizziness?"

"No," McGarvey lied.

"Darkening of your vision?"

"No, a little blurring, but that's all."

"Disconnected thoughts, mood swings, memory loss?"

McGarvey shook his head, and Mattice shrugged skeptically.

"Maybe we're lucky and I'm wrong. But I want to see the CAT scan."

"What if you're not wrong?"

"Your condition will get worse, like I told you."

"How soon?"

"What the hell aren't you telling me?" Mattice demanded.

"How long, Mike?"

"From the onset of the first serious symptoms maybe a few days, a week. There's no way of telling until we get some pictures."

"Assuming the worse, what then?" McGarvey asked. He'd known that something was seriously wrong with him, but there was too much at stake now for him to simply walk away from his job unless his own situation was desperate.

"We go in, fix the bleeder, drain the blood and put you back together."

"How long would I be out of commission?"

"Six weeks," Mattice said evenly. He glanced at the wall clock. "I want you up there by three. Do you have someone who can go with you?"

McGarvey hopped off the table. "Not this afternoon, maybe later in the week."

"Not good enough—"

"I'm briefing the President on something at three, and there's no way in hell I can miss it. We're facing too much shit right now."

"I could call your boss."

"And violate doctor-patient confidentiality?"

"Hell, I'm a good Catholic but I'd lie to the Pope to save a patient," Mattice said with a rueful smile.

"It's going to have to wait for a couple of days, Mike."

"Dammit."

"That's the way it has to be."

Mattice got up and helped McGarvey with his jacket. "The first sign of dizziness or darkening of vision, I want you back here. And I want your word on it."

"I'll do the best I can."

Mattice started to object, but McGarvey held him off again.

"If you're right, it's my life on the line, and I won't screw around by taking unnecessary risks. But something bigger than you want to know about is going on right now and I can't back away from it."

A mask of professional indifference suddenly dropped over Mattice's eyes. "It's your choice," he said, brusquely. "Do you want something for the headaches?"

"They're not that bad."

Mattice picked up McGarvey's chart. "When you're ready for the CAT scan, call the desk and they'll set it up for you. In the meantime take care of yourself." He shook his head and walked out.

The White House

McGarvey managed to get back to CIA headquarters in time to ride with Murphy in the DCI's limousine to the White House. He'd driven himself over to the clinic and unless he'd been followed no one knew where he'd gone.

"It's going to be no use pointing fingers or jumping down Dennis Berndt's throat," Murphy said tiredly. "The situation is what we have and it's up to us to deal with it as best we can."

"I agree," McGarvey said distantly. In the morning he would sit down with Adkins and Rencke and go over the entire mission to find out how the bomb was getting here and how to stop it. Even if he did have the operation immediately, and was put out of commission for six weeks, he would at least be able to make some decisions during that time, unless his brain was permanently scrambled.

"I was informed that your briefing this morning was a good one."

"I told them what was coming their way, and what we needed to do to stop it."

"The President will want nothing less."

McGarvey looked over at Murphy. "He's going to get more than that, General, because bin Laden may be going after him specifically. Maybe his family too."

"The man's not that crazy," Murphy said, clearly disturbed.

"We were," McGarvey said.

"That was different."

McGarvey held back a sharp reply, the words almost immediately escaping him. The day had gotten dark, and his stomach was turning over. He laid his head back and closed his eyes, a bad feeling under his tongue, and his body suddenly in a cold sweat. He was seeing the dreamy, distant expression on bin Laden's face in the high mountain cave. The man was ill, and McGarvey could feel the sickness in his own body; the pain, the fear and the frustration that life was even more fragile and fleeting than you ever imagined it was.

"I said, what we did was different," Murphy repeated, but then he trailed off.

McGarvey was hearing the words through the noise of a waterfall, but for thirty or forty seconds he was unable to respond. He couldn't even think of what to say, nor could he move. Gradually the noise faded, however, and it seemed as if his thoughts came back into focus by degrees until he could open his eyes and sit up.

They had come to the west gate of the White House and the security people passed them through.

"Are you feeling up to this, Mac?" Murphy asked.

"I'm going to make it short, and then I'm going over to Katy's house for a stiff drink, some dinner and ten or twelve hours of sleep. I just can't seem to catch up."

"I know the feeling," Murphy said. "And if you want my advice, turn off the phones."

"I will."

By the time they pulled up to the west portico, and Murphy's bodyguard opened the limo door for them, McGarvey had recovered sufficiently to get out of the car and follow the DCI inside. His legs felt like rubber and he was still queasy, but he figured that he would get through this okay.

They were ushered into the Oval Office at three o'clock on the dot. The President was seated at his desk. With him, besides Dennis Berndt, were the Director of the U.S. Secret Service Arthur Ridgeway and the Director of Protective Forces Henry Kolesnik. Kolesnik had been at this morning's threat assessment briefing. His was the Secret Service division that watched over the President and his family.

"Welcome home, Mr. McGarvey," President Haynes said, rising and extending his hand.

McGarvey shook hands. "It's good to be back, Mr. President, but we have a bigger problem now than when we started."

"Kill bin Laden and our problem is solved," Berndt said.

"Not this time," McGarvey disagreed.

"Why not?"

"Because bin Laden has already left Afghanistan and has gone to ground somewhere. Finding him would take too much time, the bomb is already on its way here."

"You don't have any proof of that," Berndt objected angrily.

"Sit down, Dennis," the President said, somewhat irritated, and he motioned the others to chairs.

"I've already briefed the President and Mr. Berndt on the substance of your briefing this morning," Kolesnik said. He looked like a linebacker for the Minnesota Vikings, with broad shoulders, a thick neck and a very short haircut. His eyes were penetrating, and seemed to take in everything and everyone in the room all at once. He was not smiling.

"Good, it'll save us some time," McGarvey said.

"You'll get whatever resources you need," the President assured him. "The military, if you want them. Maybe Dennis is right. If the CIA can find out where bin Laden is hiding we can send the marines in after him. Whatever it takes."

"The bomb is already on its way here, and he might not even know where it is himself."

The President looked at McGarvey for a long moment. "I didn't have much of a choice. As far as we knew you were dead."

"I understand. But the point is we have a new situation now and we have to deal with it."

"Well, it certainly would help if we knew the intended target," Berndt interjected prissily. "Maybe if we kidnapped him we could get some useful information, whether he knows where the thing is or not."

"We know what he's going to try to hit," McGarvey said. "Or at least we've got a pretty good idea."

"What?" the President asked.

"You, Mr. President. And your family."

"How do you know this?"

"You ordered the cruise missiles to his camp and killed his daughter. Now he's going to try the same thing in retaliation; to kill you and your daughter."

Berndt started to bluster again, but this time he thought better of it. Everyone's eyes were drawn to the photograph of Deborah Haynes on the desk. She was pretty, with a Siberian cast to her features, but with long, streaming blond hair and innocent eyes.

"That's about what we figured," Kolesnik said. "But protecting the President and his family will be next to impossible unless they go to a secret location and stay there until we can find and secure the device."

"It's something to be considered."

"No," the President stated flatly, and before Kolesnik or Ridgeway could object, he went on. "Every President since

Kennedy has been faced with the same decision. And they all made the same choice; they stuck it out. If I took your suggestion and headed for the hills there'd be a brand-new cottage industry springing up overnight. If you want a President out of Dodge City, just threaten to kill him and he'll run. How about congressmen, governors, mayors, hell your next-door neighbors?" The President looked again at his daughter's picture. "It's up to us to stop men like bin Laden, and every other lunatic out there who wants to pull us down to their level." He sat forward. "I made a promise to the American people that if they hired me for this job I would do whatever was necessary to take back the fear, and I'll be damned if I'll run."

"But you can minimize your risks," Murphy said.

"I appreciate the suggestion, General. But if the device comes in by air and is detonated over the city, say somewhere fairly close to where we're sitting at this moment, I wouldn't have much of a chance. Isn't that correct?"

"If we had five minutes' warning we could get you and your family downstairs," Kolesnik countered.

"What about the rest of Washington?" the President asked rhetorically, his voice soft. He shook his head. "This isn't an assassin's bullet we're talking about. Something aimed directly at me alone. We're talking about an act of terrorism. Something that could kill thousands."

"That's right, Mr. President," Murphy agreed.

"Then it's up to us to stop them before the bomb gets here."

"We'll try. In the meantime you'll have to curtail your schedule. At least try to make it easier for your people to protect you."

"No."

"Goddammit, Mr. President, we'll do whatever we can to protect your life, but you're going to have to help us," Murphy said sharply. He was the only man in the office who could talk to the President of the United States like that and get away with it.

McGarvey shook his head. "Sorry, General, but the President is right. Cutting back his public appearances won't make a bit of difference unless he goes all the way and hunkers down in a bomb shelter. It's up to us to figure out exactly how they mean to hit him and get there first."

"Is there anyone else in this room who thinks this is crazy except for me?" Berndt asked.

No one answered him.

"The ball is back in your court, McGarvey," the President said. "What do you suggest?"

"Go on television tonight and tell the country what you've told us here."

"That would get bin Laden's attention," Kolesnik said. Obviously he was the only one who understood where McGarvey was coming from.

"It'd be like thumbing our noses at them," Berndt objected.

"That's right. It would make bin Laden and his people look like fools. They would *have* to make the attack, and the sooner the better."

"You're looking for them to make a mistake, is that it?" the President asked. "Drive them out into the open, make them take chances that they would not have taken otherwise?"

"Yes, sir."

"Wait a minute," Berndt broke in. "What are you talking about? What chances?"

McGarvey wanted to smack some sense into the silly bastard. Yet Berndt was very good at his job of advising the President on national security concerns. At least he was unless he was backed into a corner and was in danger of being made to look like a fool. Like now. Then he became an impossible ass.

"If they want to change plans in midstream because of what the President has to say on television tonight, they'll have to communicate with each other," Kolesnik explained patiently. "Probably by telephone, which the National Security Agency will be looking for."

"That's a little thin, isn't it?"

"It'd be a start, Mr. Berndt."

"Like poking around in the dark hoping for a lucky break."

"That's right. But there'd be a bunch of very good people out there doing the poking around."

"I'll go on television at nine o'clock," the President said.

"I'll call Tom Roswell with the heads-up," Murphy promised. Roswell was head of the NSA headquartered at Fort Meade. "We might know something as early as tomorrow."

"Good," the President said. "McGarvey, we'll try to work *with* you this time instead of against you."

"Thank you, Mr. President." Too little too late? McGarvey wondered. He and Murphy rose and they shook hands with the President. At the door he turned back. "You might want to consider something else, sir. Explain what happened in the cruise missile attack and apologize for killing his daughter. It'll probably cause a storm of protest, but you would have taken the high ground."

"That was my plan. I'm truly sorry that it turned out the way it did, and I'll say so. But it will have nothing to do with taking the high ground, as you put it."

It was about what McGarvey hoped the President would say. He and Murphy left the Oval Office and headed back to the west portico.

"He's a good man," Murphy said. "Maybe we'll come out of this in one piece after all."

"As long as Berndt stays out of the mix we might just have a chance."

Murphy shook his head. "Not much chance of that, Mac. The man wants to be President."

Chevy Chase

McGarvey got out to his ex-wife's house a few minutes before seven. He drove himself in his Nissan Pathfinder despite the risk of his vision going haywire. He figured that he could pull off the side of the road if it happened again, but he wanted to be away from the CIA, if only for this one evening. It was something that was becoming more and more important to him.

A gray Chevy van was parked across the street from Katy's house. As McGarvey turned the corner he phoned the special operations number that rolled directly over to the van. "This is McGarvey, I'm coming up the block."

"Gotya, sir," the security officer said.

"Any activity tonight?"

"It's been real quiet so far, just a little local traffic is all," the officer said. "Sir, where's your driver?"

"I gave him the night off," McGarvey said, pulling into Kathleen's driveway. "And I'm putting out the Do Not Disturb sign, so the phones will be off. If you come knocking on my door it better be real important."

"Yes, sir," the officer said. McGarvey broke the connection, then switched the cell phone off and laid it on the passenger seat.

The day had been warm, and when Kathleen came to the door she was wearing shorts and a tee shirt, nothing on her feet. Her hair was up in a wrap. A momentary flash of irritation crossed her face, changing immediately to one of relief and concern. She never liked being caught unprepared, especially when it came to her appearance.

"Hi, Katy," he said, coming in. He kissed her on the cheek, closed the door with his foot, and then took her in his arms and held her very close. She was shivering.

"I was worried about you," she whispered urgently.

"I know. But I'm back now."

"Elizabeth let the cat out of the bag. She told me where you'd gone and what you were trying to do. Then we heard that something had gone wrong with your chip and I didn't know what to think." She studied his face. "You look pale, Kirk. Are you in pain?"

"Some bumps and bruises, but no bullet holes this time," he said. Kathleen looked worn out. "Can I stay the night?" he asked. "No phones. I even switched off my cell phone, and I told the mounty outside to mind his own business."

Kathleen smiled. "The boss give you the night off?"

"Something like that," McGarvey said. "Do you have anything in mind? Or do you want to hold off for a little while to figure out if you really want to get back to being a CIA wife?"

She touched his cheek. "I love your face," she said. "Fact of the matter is that I never stopped being a CIA wife. But this time I'll try to be a little less demanding." She was wearing his mother's ring, the one he'd given her at Jake's.

"How about if I fix myself a drink while you go up and take a shower?" McGarvey said. "I'll shower when you're done. The President's going to be on TV at nine, and we want to see him."

"Is he going to talk about bin Laden and the attack on his camp?"

"He's going to tell everybody that we missed bin Laden and killed his daughter by mistake. The President's going to apologize for it."

Kathleen's hand went to her mouth. "My God. He's going to come after us now."

"The President knows the danger to him and his daughter, and they're not going to take any chances."

"I meant us," Kathleen said. "You and Elizabeth."

"We'll get to him first," McGarvey promised her with more assurance than he felt. "We know what's coming and we know all about his contacts and networks. Our people are on a worldwide alert, and every law enforcement agency in the country has started an all out manhunt."

"It didn't help Allen Trumble and his family, and those other people."

"This time we know that it's coming, so he can't take us by surprise again."

She reached past him and turned both locks on the door, and then activated the alarm system. "Where's Elizabeth?"

"She's still at work. She and Otto are running search programs."

"Does she know what's coming our way?"

"Yes."

Kathleen thought about it for a moment, then nodded. "I'll shut off the upstairs phones, and you can catch the ones down here." She gave him a wistful look, as if she knew that he wasn't being completely honest with her, yet wanting to believe that he was. "Why don't you cut up some onions. We're having stroganoff, so if you want mushrooms, cut those too." She smiled. "Unless a DDO is above such mundane household chores."

"As long as you don't let it out," McGarvey said. He patted her on the butt, and headed into the kitchen reasonably at peace for the first time in weeks. The mood wouldn't last, he knew, but for now the problem of bin Laden would hold.

In the quiet darkness of the night McGarvey went downstairs, got a Coke from the refrigerator and stepped outside to smoke a cigarette by the pool. The sprinklers on the golf course were running, and combined with the clean smell of fresh-mown grass, the evening was perfect.

McGarvey was content. He and Kathleen had always been good together in bed, but tonight their lovemaking had been particularly warm, tender and satisfying. Afterward he had held her in his arms and watched her go to sleep.

The sky to the south was aglow with the lights from Washington, but in the opposite direction, over the golf course, the sky was filled with stars. The night sky was something that he'd not paid much attention to until Afghanistan. They were the same stars, yet here the sky was familiar and friendly, while over there the constellations themselves looked foreign, cold, indifferent, dangerous.

He had to wonder how they could possibly understand each other if even the same sky overhead looked different. Talking with bin Laden in his high mountain cave they had spoken English, and although he understood the meaning of the words that the Saudi terrorist was using, he did not understand what they meant to bin Laden. A common language, but without a common understanding.

There wasn't even a common understanding about their daughters. It was the one point that McGavery thought he and bin Laden could connect with. But they might as well have been from different planets, the incident with Mohammed and Sarah on the way up proved that. Yet McGarvey was still certain that if the missile attack had never happened he and bin Laden could have come to some sort of an agreement.

He couldn't help but think about Sarah and Elizabeth, and compare them. They were both naive in their own way; Sarah about life in the West, and Liz about life with a man. They were both filled with energy. They were stubborn, willful, yet they had warm, giving and loving natures. Had the circumstances of their births been reversed, McGarvey had little doubt that both women would have fit well in their reversed roles.

They were daughters of driven men.

The President had said something about bin Laden's daughter on television tonight, but for the life of him McGarvey couldn't quite put his finger on what it was. Something about terrorism.

He laid his cigarette in the ashtray and glanced to the south, but the lights of Washington had been turned off, or at least lowered. He had to squint to make out the end of the pool. He was sick to his stomach, and suddenly extremely dizzy and weak. He managed to hold onto the edge of the patio table and slump down in a chair, his head spinning so fast to the left that he had to look up to the right in order to stop himself from pitching to the patio bricks.

The night was black, and had become silent except for the sound of his own rapidly beating heart in his ears. Something smelled bad, like the open sewer he'd crossed somewhere—he couldn't remember where, though he knew that he should be able to.

He lowered his head and gripped the edge of the table so hard that the muscles corded in his right forearm. His breathing was shallow, and for a minute or two he wasn't even aware of where he was.

Gradually, however, the dizziness and nausea began to subside, his mind began to clear, he began to smell the grass and water smells, and see the night sky again. But he was left weak and shaken, his heart still pounding.

"Kirk?" Kathleen called from the patio door.

He turned as she came outside, her body clearly outlined beneath the thin material of her nightgown. "Here," he said, and she came across to him.

"What's the matter, darling, can't sleep?" she asked.

"I was thirsty."

She sat down beside him and laid her hand on his arm. "I was dreaming about Elizabeth, but I don't remember what it was about except that I woke up." She looked at his eyes. "You weren't there and I got scared all over again."

McGarvey managed a reassuring smile, though he still wasn't a hundred percent. "I'm here, Katy."

"Well you sound like you're half-asleep sitting there," she said. She took his hand. "Come on back to bed. Nobody's going to call, and I've not set the alarm. In the morning I'm going to make bacon and eggs, grits and my mother's biscuits and gravy. Damn the cholesterol, full speed ahead."

McGarvey smiled at her. "I love you, Kathleen."

She returned his smile. "Katy," she corrected.

TWENTY-THREE

Chevy Chase Country Club

Nothing new had happened until the President's speech to the nation last night. Elizabeth McGarvey had not come to her mother yet, and the only reason Bahmad could think of was that there had been a delay in releasing the news of her father's death. The Taliban were often like that. By 8:00 A.M. the sun was already warm, and sitting on the country club's veranda drinking a cup of coffee before his tee time, Bahmad idly gazed up the eighteenth fairway in the general direction of Kathleen McGarvey's house, outwardly in perfect control, but inwardly seething. There could be little doubt that bin Laden had seen the President's broadcast, nor was there any doubt in Bahmad's mind how the man was reacting. Bin Laden would be filled with an insane rage. He would be beside himself that the President had not only mentioned Sarah by name, but that the United States had killed her. It would be viewed as an act of massive arrogance on the part of a White House that was completely indifferent to the plight of more than sixty percent of the world's population who lived in poverty. If, as a nation, you had the money to be an active trading partner, or if you had the oil or other natural resources necessary to feed a voracious economy that placed no restrictions on the conspicuous consumption of its citizens, then you could belong to Washington's elite club. If not, you were nothing but pond scum; interesting under a microscope, but of no consequence in the real world. Bin Laden would want to strike back and do it now rather than stick with their schedule. If he did something foolish it could jeopardize everything, especially their element of surprise.

It was midafternoon in Khartoum, the heat of the day. In bin Laden's condition he should be resting now, but Bahmad knew better. Bin Laden would be fuming, pacing back and forth in the compound's second-floor greeting chamber. He would stop from time to time to stride over to one of the windows, pull back the heavy drapes and look outside, half expecting to see . . . what? Enemy tanks coming up the street for him? Guided missiles falling out of the sky to kill the rest of his family? The guards who were constantly at his side would be nervously fingering the safety catches on their rifles wondering where the enemy that their leader was so nervous about would be striking from. Would they be strong enough to give their lives for him without hesitation? Enter the gates of Paradise with clean souls?

In another part of the house, bin Laden's wives, especially Sarah's mother, would be dealing with their grief in their own way. Bahmad wondered if bin Laden had talked to them, tried to console them, or if he left them on their own? It was one part of bin Laden's life that he wasn't sure of. They had seldom talked about family matters except that Sarah had been his pride; his light; in many respects the *reason* for his existence.

The President's announcement last night meant nothing. Elizabeth McGarvey would come to her mother's house in due course, and she would die. Then, in the early fall as planned, Deborah Haynes would die. Bahmad could see every step in perfect detail. It was like a well-crafted machine, a thing of simple beauty. But its delicate mechanisms could be easily fouled with the wrong move now.

The men he'd been talking with when he'd first arrived at the club were out on the first tee and the foursome he'd signed up with hadn't arrived yet, leaving Bahmad temporarily alone and out of earshot of any of the other members.

He took out his cell phone and hit the speed dial button for the number of their relay provider in Rome. After one ring the call was automatically rolled over to a secret number in Khartoum. This was answered after three rings by one of bin Laden's young assistants.

"Ahlan, wa sahlan." Hello, he said, somewhat formally, which meant he wasn't alone.

"This is Bahmad, I wish to speak with Osama." Bahmad spoke in Egyptian Arabic, the universal tongue.

" 'Aywa."

There was a chance that this call was being monitored by the National Security Agency. But Bahmad doubted that even the NSA had the ability to screen every single call made everyday around the entire world. The job would overwhelm even the most powerful computers. U.S. technology was fantastic, but not that good.

"You would not be calling unless there was trouble," bin Laden said, coming on the line.

"On the contrary, everything goes well. It is trouble that I wish to avoid." The Arabic sounded formal in Bahmad's ears after speaking English for several days. "Didst thou see the President's broadcast last night?"

"Yes."

Bahmad could hear the strain in bin Laden's voice. "You can accept the apology and I can withdraw. No harm will have been done."

"The harm has already been done. Irreparable harm to this family. Dost thou not understand?" Bin Laden switched to a slang Arabic used in a part of northern Afghanistan. *"The daughters of the infidels will die like the pigs they are!"*

"Then I shall proceed as planned."

Bin Laden hesitated, and Bahmad could hear his indecision in his silence.

"Thou must accomplish every aspect of the mission."

"I understand," Bahmad said. "According to the timetable."

"There can be no mistakes."

"There will be no mistakes if we act in unison."

"There is very little time—"

"In Paradise there will be all the time of the universe."

Again bin Laden hesitated. He had never been a rash man. He thought out his every move, as he was doing now, for which Bahmad was grateful. "Do not disappoint me," he finally said.

"I will not," Bahmad replied.

"There will be no changes. The package is on its way. Do you understand?"

" *'Aywa.* " Yes.

"Allah be with you."

National Security Agency

Navy Lieutenant Johanna Ritter, chief of European Surveillance Services, sat at her desk at the head of a row of a dozen computer consoles in a long, narrow, dimly lit room. Along one entire wall a floor-to-ceiling status board showed the major telecommunications hot spots serving Europe; places where telephone, radio and television signals tended to be concentrated. Satellites, telephone exchanges, radio and television network headquarters, cable television hubs. Ninety-five percent of all civilian traffic was funneled through these systems. Though thirty percent of all military traffic was handled by civilian facilities, the other seventy percent was monitored in another section of the NSA.

Lieutenant Ritter's specific assignment was monitoring European hubs. The main telephone exchange in Rome suddenly lit up in purple on the board, which designated a hit in a special search program that had been designed for them by the CIA's Otto Rencke.

She brought up the console on her monitor that was intercepting the signal. It was Chief Petty Officer Mark Morgan. "Mark, what's so interesting in Rome?"

"The vorep is chewing on it, Lieutenant, but it sounded

like bin Laden to me." VoReP was the Cray computer Voice Recognition Program.

"Do we have a translation yet?"

"Just a partial, ma'am. But we have an area trace on the originating signal. It looks like it came from right here in the D.C. area. But it was masked, so that's about the best we can do."

"I want to hear this myself. I'm on my way." Ritter unplugged her headset and went back to Morgan's console. At thirty-two Ritter was the single mother of twin eight-year-old girls. She'd joined the navy right out of college, and because she was overweight, and in her own estimation not all that pretty, she had decided to make the navy a career. It was a good choice because she was very intelligent, yet good with detail, and she was very dedicated, in part because she figured she'd never get married and she needed to support her girls and her mother, who was their nanny. The world was tough, but as she imagined her movie star hero Kathy Bates would say: A woman's gotta do what she's gotta do.

Morgan's console was the third from the end. He was temporarily off-line, his monitor showing the signal and content processing programs at work chewing on it.

"What do we have, Mark?" Ritter plugged her headset in. Morgan looked up and gave her a smile. Although he was eight years younger than her, she thought that he was devastatingly handsome. The problem was he knew it.

"Vorep gives it a ninety-seven percent bin Laden." Morgan hit the replay button. "What we have so far from the machine translation will come up in the box."

There was silence at first, then a series of tones as the signal made its way through the telephone exchange in Rome. "Ahlan, wa sahlan," a young man's voice came over her headset. "Hello," the single word came up in the box on the monitor.

Ritter pressed her headset a little tighter, and listened to the rest of the conversation, which lasted just one minute and three seconds. Both men sounded as if they were under extreme stress, she read that part easily.

"Okay, it looks as if we've bagged bin Laden, but who is Bahmad? And what happened to the translation program near the end?"

"Vorep has nothing on Bahmad, and it'd be my guess that they switched to a local dialect that we don't have." Besides being good looking, Morgan was brilliant. His father was a special agent with the FBI, and with less than six months to go on his enlistment a number of companies were beginning to make him offers. As his release date got closer the NSA would offer him a deal as well. Like a lot of civilians working for the agency, he would be doing the same job only making four or five times as much money as the navy paid him. Ritter was afraid, however, that if she quit the navy hoping for better pay, which she needed, no one would make the offer.

"Replay the second half," she said.

Morgan ran the last part of the telephone conversation again, and this time Ritter could hear the change in dialects, though the translation program was still running a blank.

"Try Russian," she said.

Morgan switched languages with a couple of keystrokes. This time the computer came up with a number of words; some like *water buffalo* and *barn animals* that didn't seem to make any sense in the context, but others, like *daughter, package, en route* and *timetable*, that did.

"Okay, this looks like what the CIA wanted," Ritter announced, straightening up. "I'll take it from here and get it over to Langley. In the meantime I want you to clear your board and stick with the Rome exchange." She gave him a warm smile. "Good job, Mark, but keep your eyes open, I have a feeling that this is just the beginning."

"Yes, ma'am," Morgan replied. He said it like Ritter had told him something so obvious it was stupid.

Ritter caught the inflection. He was a little shit, and one of these days someone was going to bring him down a notch for his own good. But that didn't change the fact he was cute.

Chevy Chase

"Do you think that bin Laden will accept the President's apology?" Kathleen asked after breakfast.

"He might," McGarvey said, putting on his jacket. He came over and kissed her on the cheek. "What would you think about getting out of Washington for a while?"

"Would you come with me?" She looked up at him, knowing full well what his answer would be. He shook his head. "Do you think that he'll send someone to harm Elizabeth because of what we did to his daughter?"

"It's possible."

"Fine." Her old attitude of disgust showed on her face, but then she softened. She was working at it. "In that case she's right where she belongs, by her father's side. And me leaving town wouldn't do a thing to help."

"It won't always be like this—"

Kathleen laughed softly. "You've said that before. Tell me something new."

"I love you."

"That's better." She reached up and kissed him. "Maybe we can do something this weekend."

"Check the movies, see what's playing," McGarvey said. He got his car keys and left the house. It was a few minutes after eight and the morning was warm and muggy, it was going to be a hot day. He waved at the security officer in the van across the street and was about to get into his car when Elizabeth pulled up in her bright yellow VW, a big smile on her round, pretty face.

She jumped out of her car, came over and gave her father a kiss. "Morning, daddy. How's Mother?"

"Fine. Are you just getting off work?"

She nodded. "But I got Otto to promise to get a couple

of hours of rest, and I came over to pick up a few of my things."

"Anything new?"

Her face darkened. "Nothing yet, but Otto won't give up. I think he'd work himself to death if somebody wasn't there to watch out for him."

"I'll make sure he gets some sleep this morning. Why don't you go home and do the same yourself, you look as though you could use it. If something comes up I'll give you a call."

She suddenly look embarrassed. "I won't be there," she said.

"Are you staying here?"

"I've moved in with Todd." She girded herself for a storm, but McGarvey just gave his daughter a smile.

"He's a good man. Don't give him a hard time, he doesn't deserve it."

Elizabeth's jaw dropped open. "Dad?"

McGarvey laughed. "Good luck breaking the news to your mother though."

CIA Headquarters

Rencke was lying on top of his conference table, which was strewn with notes, computer printouts, files and photographs. He'd managed to catch only a half-hour of rest when the call to his office number rolled over to the cell phone in his pocket. He had his computer tied to his phone as well. If one of his search engines came up with something it would automatically notify him. But this was a human call, the ring was different.

He answered it without sitting up or opening his eyes. "Yes?" He hadn't slept in four days, and he felt gritty.

"Otto, this is Johanna at Fort Meade. I have something for you. A call from a man named Bahmad to Osama bin Laden through what looks like a relay service provider in Rome."

Rencke sat straight up as if his tailbone had been plugged into a light socket. "When?"

"Just a few minutes ago. We don't know where bin Laden is located, but the originating call came from somewhere in the D.C. area."

Rencke held the phone in the crook of his neck, pulled his laptop over and brought up the NSA's mainframe. "What were they speaking, Johanna? Arabic, English, Russian? What?"

"Egyptian Arabic at first, but then they switched to another dialect, probably northern Afghani. The Russian translator program picked out a few words. But when I tried using a blend—Russian and Arabic—the program just locked up."

"I've got your console, do you have a password?"

"Just a sec, I'll download the file."

The screen split in three. On the left the Arabic text came up. In the middle the same text came up in the Western alphabet. And on the right the incomplete translation came up.

Rencke was having trouble focusing, having a hard time accepting what he was seeing on the screen. Almost never did the thing they were looking for drop out of the sky into their laps. Most of the time it was a guessing game. But not this time. *Daughter, en route, package, timetable.* The message could not have been plainer.

"What's vorep's confidence on bin Laden's voice?"

"Ninety-seven percent and change."

"Anything on the other man?"

"He's not in our files, but he sounded a lot calmer to me than bin Laden."

Another fact dropped into place for Rencke. He was Trumble's quiet man in the corner; bin Laden's chief of staff, Ali Bahmad, the one who had discovered McGarvey's GPS chip. Now they had a complete name and a voice, they would be able to find something in the CIA's files somewhere, he was sure of it. He blinked. "Wait," he said. "Bahmad is here, in Washington? Did you say that?"

"Somewhere in the area. We can't be any more precise than that."

Rencke broke the connection and started to call McGarvey, but then he shook his head and called Johanna Ritter back. "Sorry about that," he told her when she came on.

"No problem," she said.

"Anyway, thanks." Rencke broke the connection again and hit the speed dial for McGarvey's locator number. After several seconds a warbling tone indicated that he was offline. Next he tried Kathleen's house, but evidently the phones had been switched off there too, he called the security officer in the van in front of her house.

"Yes."

"This is Rencke in the DO. The phones are off in the house. Is Mr. McGarvey there?"

"He just left. Problem?"

"Could be. Keep your head up."

"Yes, sir. But his daughter just got here. Do you want me to talk to her?"

"I'll take care of it," Rencke said. "Keep your eyes open."

Rencke's nerves were jumping all over the place. He didn't want to alarm Mrs. M., but the bomb was en route as they figured it was, and Bahmad was already here. What *was* their timetable?

He tried McGarvey's locator number again with the same result as before. He jumped off the table and started pacing and snapping his fingers. Bahmad was here. The bomb was enroute. So what was going to happen in the meantime? What *could* happen in the meantime? Why was bin Laden's right hand man here himself?

Rencke dialed *MHP, and the number was answered on the first ring.

"Maryland Highway Patrol, what is your emergency please?"

"My name is Otto Rencke. I'm calling from the Central

Intelligence Agency and we need your help right now to get a message to one of our people."

"Sir, it is a criminal act to knowingly falsify an emergency—"

"He is en route here from an address on Laurel Parkway in Chevy Chase. He's driving a gray, Nissan Pathfinder, D.C. tags, baker-david-mike-five-six-eight. He needs to contact his office immediately. I'll alert our security service as well as D.C. Metro, but time is of the essence." Rencke kept his voice calm and deliberate even though he wanted to shout. The man was just doing his job the best way he knew how.

"Like I said—"

"Your caller ID is coming up blank," Rencke said patiently. "I'll release my phone and you can verify the number I'm calling from." He entered a four-digit code. Five seconds later the 911 dispatcher was back.

"Sorry about that, sir. I have a unit rolling. What's his name?"

"Kirk McGarvey," Rencke said. "And tell your people to step on it, would ya?"

Chevy Chase Country Club

The country club was starting to fill up with the morning weekday crowd. Bahmad thought of all the contingencies he had considered in his plan to kill the two women. The capture of bin Laden, the defection of one or more of the men who were carrying the bomb or who knew about it, or who were working on any of a dozen other vital elements of the mission. But he had not considered the possibility that McGarvey was alive.

He was scarcely able to believe what the fools watching Kathleen McGarvey's house were telling him. McGarvey had been there all night, and they had not called. Their job was to wait for his daughter to show up, so that's *exactly* what they had done.

They had not used their heads. They had no real idea what they were doing. They were ignorant, uneducated simpletons. Worse than that, they were stupid.

"Do you want us to make the hit now?" Aggad asked eagerly.

"Is the CIA van still parked in front of the house?"

"Yes, it's been there all night."

McGarvey was alive and had come to his wife's side and yet the CIA still watched her. Bahmad wondered what that could mean. Obviously they thought that his wife was still in danger. From whom?

"Was the daughter alone, or did someone come with her?"

"She was alone. What do you want us to do?"

Bob Hutton, one of Bahmad's foursome came out to the patio from inside the club, spotted him and started over. With McGarvey back it changed everything. Or did it, he asked himself. Rightfully the decision to continue should be Osama's. But making the one overseas call had been dangerous enough, making a second would be pushing the envelope.

There was no time. McGarvey could return at any moment, or the daughter could leave. Bahmad looked up as if he had just spotted Hutton, waved and then shook his head in disgust.

"Do nothing, I'll be there in a few minutes. Ready your weapons. Do you understand?"

"Yes."

Bahmad broke the connection, pocketed the phone and got to his feet as Hutton reached him. "Bad news from one of my business associates," Bahmad apologized. "I have to make a meeting, so you'll have to start without me."

Hutton glanced uncertainly at the jamup at the starter's hut. "I don't think that we can get a delay."

"I'll only be a half-hour. I shouldn't miss more than one or two holes, the way you gentlemen play."

Hutton laughed. "Low blow. You'll have to take a penalty."

"A stroke a hole, and I'll still spot you five."

"Loaded for bear this morning, are we?"

Bahmad clapped him on the shoulder, though he wanted to rip the bastard's heart out, and smiled. "I'll meet you out on the course. Take my clubs with you, would you please?"

Cabin John, Maryland

The solid night's sleep, only interrupted once, had done him some good, McGarvey had to admit. But seeing Elizabeth this morning all bright and happy, her entire future ahead of her, made him think about Sarah bin Laden, her life cut short before it had even begun, and it made him a little morose.

Traffic on I-495 heading south toward the river was heavy as usual at this time of the morning and it would get even worse once he reached the GW Parkway to Langley.

It was the United States government going to work, and that's what got him about bin Laden. The man had taught his daughter that the United States was evil. That they were all a bunch of monsters bent on destroying the world. They were murderers, rapists, despoilers of the earth. They were out to defile Dar-Islam, the only true religion. Except that the "they" were out here on the Washington ring road with McGarvey this morning; some of them drinking coffee from McDonald's Styrofoam cups, most of them still half asleep, a lot of them thinking about their own children, their mortgages, the upcoming weekend—soccer, swimming, Little League. Monsters, every one of them.

McGarvey picked his cell phone off the passenger seat, switched it on and pocketed it.

Now that the President had gone public with the accidental killing of Sarah bin Laden there would be an almost intolerable pressure on bin Laden not only by Iran, Iraq and the Sudan, but by himself to do something right now. The State Department had issued warnings to all embassies, especially in Islamic countries. Every CIA base, station and special interest section had been alerted to what was probably coming their way. Later today the State Department would also make an announcement to the media warning the American traveling public, and especially those Americans living and working overseas, to take special precautions.

The U.S. had been blindsided at the Khobar Barracks in Saudi Arabia, at the Trade Towers in New York City, and by the tribal problems in Somalia, but this time everyone was about as ready as could be. Every law enforcement organization and intelligence agency in the country was on full alert.

McGarvey's cell phone chirped. He got it on the second ring. "This is McGarvey."

"Oh, wow, Mac, where are you?" Rencke said in a rush.

"On 495 outside Cabin John coming up on the river. Has there been a response already?"

"It looks like it. This morning, about forty minutes ago, NSA picked up a telephone conversation between bin Laden and Ali Bahmad. He's the guy from bin Laden's cave who knew about your GPS chip, and the same one Trumble said sat in a corner without saying a word during the meeting in Khartoum." Rencke was all out of breath, even more so than he usually was when he was excited and had the bit in his teeth. "We couldn't get a fix on bin Laden, the call went through a service provider in Rome, but Bahmad is here in the area somewhere. We didn't get a fix, but he's here."

"Who initiated the call?"

"Bahmad."

"Do we have a translation?"

"Just a partial. They were probably using a northern Afghani dialect, and we're trying to find someone to help out, but we got enough to know that you were right all along. The bomb is already on its way here."

"Did they say where or how?"

"If they did, we haven't gotten to that part yet. But

NSA's translator program got another word out of it. *Daughter*."

McGarvey's stomach did a flop. He checked the rearview mirror, then shot over to the far left lane and jammed on his brakes. He eased onto the grassy median, the Pathfinder's rear end fishtailing in the grass and soft ground.

"Hold on a second, Otto, I'm turning around," he shouted. He dropped the cell phone in his lap, and stomped on the gas as he careened across the broad median, judged the oncoming traffic and bumped up onto the interstate heading back to Chevy Chase.

"We know why Bahmad is here, you were right about that too," Rencke was saying when McGarvey picked up the phone. "I shot this over to the Secret Service so they know what might be coming their way, but I can't get ahold of Mrs. M. or Liz. The phones at the house are shut off and Liz turned off her cell phone just like you did."

"I'm on my way back there now. Who's pulling surveillance duty this morning?"

"Mike Larsen. I've already given him the heads-up."

"Tell him that I'm on my way, and if Liz tries to leave, keep her there. Call Dick Yemm and tell him what's happening. And then have the Chevy Chase cops head over there."

"I've already done that. And I called the Maryland Highway Patrol to be on the lookout for you, and to give you the message to call here."

A highway patrol cruiser suddenly swerved off the opposite side of the interstate and shot across the median, its lights flashing.

"They found me," McGarvey said. "Call them now, tell them that I got the message, give them Katy's address and tell them to go straight out there. I'll try to keep up."

"Standby," Rencke said.

McGarvey was doing one hundred miles per hour, trying to be careful not to cause an accident, but his nerves were jumping all over the place, and he was afraid that his vision would go haywire at any moment. He wanted to fly. He kept seeing bin Laden's face when they were talking about their daughters. By his own words no one was an innocent, and he would want revenge now.

Rencke came back. "They're getting word to every unit in the vicinity, but the daughter that bin Laden talked about was probably the President's."

"I think you're right, but I'm not going to take the chance."

"Oh, shit, I didn't mean it that way, you gotta believe me. I'm doing everything I can to protect Liz."

"Take it easy, Otto, I know that you're doing your best. Call State and the Bureau right away and give them whatever you can dig up on Bahmad. I think that he's bin Laden's chief of staff."

"He is, and not only that—he worked for British Intelligence about eight years ago. And he even came over here on a six-month study exchange program."

The voice suddenly clicked into place for McGarvey. He'd been back to headquarters for a couple of weeks about that time. "Christ, I think I met him once, just for a minute. Where'd you get this information?"

"Out of our own records. He was in the system all the time."

"How about deep background, or anything else that might be useful?"

"It's in archives. I have a runner on the way down there now to dig up what she can for us."

The highway patrol cruiser, its lights still flashing, pulled up beside McGarvey, and the officer motioned that he was going on ahead. The Crown Victoria was a lot faster than the Nissan and it pulled away.

"As soon as you come up with something, anything at all, Otto, get it to me," McGarvey instructed.

"If he makes another telephone call through Rome we'll nail the bastard, guaranteed."

Chevy Chase

Bahmad drove his Mercedes directly to a parking ramp off Connecticut Avenue where he switched with the Capital City Cleaning van. He put on a pair of white coveralls over his golfing clothes, buttoning the top button. As he pulled out of the ramp and headed back to Laurel Parkway he took out his Glock 17, switched the safety off and laid it on the seat beside him.

He took care to keep a couple of miles over the speed limit to minimize attention. Traffic was heavy streaming into the city, but light in the opposite direction. When he rounded the corner onto Laurel Parkway he called the house.

"Are you ready?" he asked, when Aggad answered.

"We're in the garage now."

"Is the girl still there?"

"Her car is still in the driveway," Aggad said.

Bahmad turned left toward the end of the cul-de-sac and he saw the yellow VW in Kathleen McGarvey's driveway, the same dark blue van as before parked across the street. "Keep out of sight now, I'm going to open the garage door."

"Okay."

Bahmad put the phone down, hit the garage door opener then stopped across from the driveway and backed up to the garage, keeping an eye peeled for anyone getting out of the blue van. He pulled halfway into the garage, then climbed into the back and opened the rear door.

"You took your time," Aggad grumbled. He and Ibrahim were wearing white coveralls too. They quickly loaded their weapons into the back of the van and climbed in.

"Did you leave anything behind?" Bahmad demanded.

"Nothing," Aggad replied sullenly. "Let's get this over with."

"Fingerprints?"

"I said nothing."

"Very well," Bahmad shrugged. He climbed back into the driver's seat as they shut the rear door, and headed down the driveway, pressing the garage door opener switch.

He rolled down his window, then picked up his pistol as he pulled up beside the CIA surveillance van. A young man inside leaned over the back of the passenger seat and then powered down the window.

"Can I help you?" he asked.

Bahmad smiled, raised his pistol and fired one shot at point blank range into the man's forehead, shoving him backward, then pulled across the street into Kathleen McGarvey's driveway.

"Stay with the van," he told Ibrahim. "If anyone shows up, kill them."

Elizabeth came racing down the stairs. She'd been in the front bedroom packing her things and had happened to look out the window when Mike Larsen went down. For a split instant she was frozen, unable to believe what she was witnessing. But then her training and instincts kicked in, she dropped the overnight bag and headed out.

Her mother was just coming from the back with some socks and underwear. "These were in the dryer—"

Elizabeth waved her back, and crossed the stairhall to the door. She turned the lock and deadbolt and checked out the side window as two armed men climbed out of a van and started up the driveway.

"What is it?" Kathleen asked calmly.

"Trouble," Elizabeth said, cursing herself for leaving her pistol and cell phone with her purse in the car.

Kathleen dropped the laundry. "Is there time to go upstairs to get my phone?"

"No."

"Then we'll go out the back door and across the golf course. If we can reach the clubhouse we should be safe."

She turned on her heel and went back into the kitchen, Elizabeth right behind her as the doorbell rang.

Bahmad looked through the tall narrow window beside the front door in time to see Elizabeth disappear down a corridor to the back of the house.

He stepped back and shot the lock out of the door. It would not open. It took him a second to realize that there was a second lock, which took three shots to destroy before he could get inside.

He rolled left, keeping his pistol up. Elizabeth McGarvey was a trained CIA agent, and she was probably armed. It would be stupid of him to get shot to death now by a girl.

Aggad slipped into the hallway and rolled right, keeping his AK-47 high on his shoulder, just like the American marines were taught to do with their M-16s. Bin Laden's soldiers were selected not necessarily because of their intelligence, but because they were professionals. Aggad was acting like one now. Not like a hothead, Bahmad thought gratefully.

They leapfrogged down the corridor, and through the kitchen into the enclosed patio room that looked out onto the pool and across the golf course.

Elizabeth McGarvey and her mother were running as fast as they could go up the fifteenth fairway toward the clubhouse: A foursome on the green was so intent on their game that they hadn't noticed them yet.

"We'll never catch them on foot," Aggad observed.

Bahmad calculated the distances, but he knew that Aggad was correct. The realistic thing for them now was to get the hell out of here, ditch the van and get back to the boat. Survive to strike another day. It had been one of the techniques that had allowed him, and in fact the entire Islamic movement, to survive this long: Hit and run. Swift like the wind, and just as invisible. A method, he'd told bin Laden, that had been used by the American revolutionaries to kick the British out of the Colonies.

But not this time.

"What do you want to do, man?" Aggad demanded.

"They're heading to the clubhouse. We'll take the van. I know a short cut."

Bahmad raced back through the house, and pulled up short in the driveway for just an instant. In the not-so-far distance he could hear a police siren, and then perhaps others farther away. Many others.

Run away to fight another day, the thought crossed his mind. But he shook it off because he knew exactly what he was doing. He could see the entire operation unfolding as he wanted it to, despite the unforseen variations this morning. He had never failed before. He wasn't going to fail this time.

Elizabeth wished she had her gun. She could hear sirens in the distance, but she knew that it wouldn't take long for whoever it was after them to figure out where they'd gone and come after them. One of them in the driveway had been carrying an AK-47. A one-wood out of someone's golf bag was going to be no defense. She thought about heading directly into the woods across the fifteenth and sixteenth fairways where they could hide while her mother caught her breath. But her mother seemed to be having no trouble keeping up. It was her tennis playing, Elizabeth supposed. And she thought that her mother was right; if they could reach the club there would be people and they might be safe. At least long enough for the cops to catch up with them.

Maryland Highway Patrol Trooper Tom Leitner was a good quarter-mile ahead of McGarvey as he turned onto Laurel Parkway. His siren was going and traffic had parted for him, but this street was deserted except for a light-colored commercial van coming toward him.

"All units, all units in the vicinity of fifteen Laurel Parkway, Chevy Chase, shots have been reported," the dispatcher said over the radio.

Leitner grabbed the microphone. "Bethesda, unit 27, I'm there now. But there's no activity. What do you have?"

"Unit 27, Bethesda, neighbors reported several shots fired at the front of the house. Two men, possibly Caucasian, both slightly built, driving a white Capital City Cleaning van, tag number unknown, possibly involved. Use extreme caution."

Leitner passed the van and his gut tightened. It was *the* van. He jammed on his brakes and did a U-turn, his tires smoking as he spun around. The van suddenly accelerated, swerved off the road and careened across the lawn between two houses. He knew what the driver was trying to do, and he followed the van.

"Bethesda, unit 27, I'm in pursuit of the white van, D.C. tag number tango-niner-seven-eight-eight. He's heading north off Laurel Parkway onto the golf course. Officer requests immediate assistance." He shot out between the two houses, raced through an opening in the trees at the back and spotted the white van heading directly up the broad, undulating fairway, golfers scattering in every direction.

McGarvey's phone chirped as he rounded the corner onto Laurel Parkway from Connecticut Avenue in time to see the highway patrol cruiser take off between the houses.

"They're heading across the golf course," Rencke said breathlessly.

"Who is?" McGarvey shouted.

"Mrs. M. and Liz. The neighbors saw them. There's a white van after them, two men. The highway patrol is right behind them."

"I'm right there," McGarvey said. He hauled the Nissan over the curb and raced between the houses. "There's a lot of trees and thick brush on the course, a million places for them to hide. I want you to get some helicopters in the air."

"MHP is already on it."

McGarvey tossed the phone aside. Everything that could be done was being done. But it was his wife and daughter out there running for their lives. He shot out through a gap in the trees and found himself on the fifteenth fairway. The van had almost reached the woods near the women's tee about two hundred yards away, and the Maryland Highway Patrol cruiser was closing with it fast.

Katy and Liz would be trying to make it to the clubhouse where there would be people this morning, and possibly safety. It was the only logical choice for them. He could see that the driver of the van had figured out the same thing and was heading directly toward the first fairway. But he was making a mistake. The way he was going led to a small cart path bridge over a creek that the van could not cross. They would have to double back and cross the seventeenth fairway before they could head to the clubhouse.

He would be able to cut them off by heading directly across the fifteenth and sixteenth fairways right now.

A long streak of flame shot out from the side door of the van, and a second later the police car exploded in a ball of flame, its roof flying fifty feet into the sky.

Elizabeth emerged from the line of trees separating the fifteenth and sixteenth fairways, her mother right behind her, when there was an explosion behind them. RPG or LAWs rocket, something came to her from her training. She turned as a fireball rose into the pale blue sky.

"My God," Kathleen said.

"That wasn't meant for us," Elizabeth told her mother. "Maybe the bastards had an accident." They ran for the broad, sloping green. About seventy-five yards ahead the fairway narrowed to a cart path that crossed a small wooden bridge over a narrow creek. On the other side they could angle over to the seventeenth fairway, which folded back on the eighteenth and first, and directly to the clubhouse. Once they crossed the creek they would be home free because she didn't think that the van could make it across on the bridge.

She didn't like running away though. If she had her gun she could send her mother on ahead, and wait here to ambush them. They were screwing with the McGarveys now. Of course if her father and Todd were also here nothing would get past them. At the moment, however, running was their *only* option.

They were nearly at the bridge when the van crashed out of the woods, skidded sideways out of control, almost tipping over on the fairway, then straightened out and headed directly toward them.

Elizabeth could see that there was no time now to make the bridge. Their only hope was the creek itself, whose banks were five feet high. If they could make it that far they might be able to reach the safety of the woods on the opposite side of the fairway.

"Mother, the creek," she shouted.

"Right behind you, dear," Kathleen said.

Bahmad saw what they were trying to do, and he knew with satisfaction that they would not make it that far by the time he ran them down. A supercalmness came over him. He could see everything that had to be done, and the order in which it had to be accomplished. Once the daughter and her mother were taken care of, he would drive the van to a service road on the far side of the eighteenth fairway. Aggad and Ibrahim would take it back to their rendezvous point and he would meet them tonight when he would kill them. There would be no loose ends.

A gray SUV of some kind burst out of the woods on his right, and headed directly toward them. Bahmad could do nothing except swerve to the left, directly across the fairway and into the dense trees and underbrush.

It was McGarvey. He got just a brief glimpse, but it was enough to recognize the man behind the wheel, and suddenly Bahmad wasn't so sure about anything. The tide might have turned. Now it was he who was running for his life.

McGarvey saw Katy and Liz off to his right by the edge of the creek. He had only an instant to see that they were okay, and no time to be relieved, before he had to turn his attention back to the van. He was right on top of it. As it plunged into the woods he crashed into its rear left quarter, sending it skidding out of control to the right through some thick underbrush, finally slamming to a halt against a large tree.

He hauled the Nissan left, as he jammed on the brakes sliding to a halt finally twenty yards behind the van. He whipped off his seat belt and pulled out his pistol. But there was something wrong with his fingers, he couldn't quite seem to switch the safety catch lever to the off position.

A man climbed out of the van, and although the day had somehow gotten very dark, McGarvey could see that he was raising what looked like a LAWs rocket tube to his shoulder.

It was hard to keep on track, hard to think straight. It was all he could do to relate what the man beside the van was trying to accomplish with the simple concept of *danger*.

McGarvey fumbled with the door latch, his fingers like sausages at the end of his impossibly long arm. When the door swung open suddenly, he half-slipped, half-fell out of the Nissan, banging his head on the door frame as he went down.

He was on all fours, the world spinning around him, but he still had his pistol. He had to get away. He didn't know why, just that he had to get away from here right now! He started to crawl on all fours directly away from the Nissan and into some deeper underbrush.

The day lit up with a tremendous flash and bang, followed by a searing hot blast of wind that picked McGarvey up and sent him crashing into the brush.

There were shots, he could understand that, but his world was reduced to a series of brightly colored lights and images from a kaleidoscope, sliding and moving all over the place.

"Daddy?"

Someone was holding him up, brushing dirt and debris from his face. He thought it was Elizabeth, but then Kathleen was there too, holding him in her arms, her eyes wide and frightened.

He heard shooting, and he understood that Liz had picked up his gun, but it didn't matter so much this time because he was with Katy. He managed to smile up at her, before he slipped away into a dark, swirling haze.

Bahmad walked into the clubhouse, went directly to the bar and ordered a Bombay martini, up, very dry and very cold. Most of the other members were out by the first tee trying to figure out what all the commotion was about. Explosions, gunfire, sirens; it sounded as if someone was making a movie.

"What's happening out there, sir?" the bartender asked as he fixed the drink.

"I'm sure I don't know," Bahmad said. His nerves were jumping all over the place, but by dint of an iron will he gave the appearance of bored indifference. "I was late for my tee time, I was supposed to catch up with my foursome on the second hole, and now this." He shook his head. "But then we're too close to D.C., what can you expect?"

His martini came, full to the rim, and even though he was boiling over with an almost out-of-control blinding anger, he lifted his glass, took a delicate sip and replaced the glass on the bar napkin without spilling a drop.

The first phase of the operation, attempting for absolutely no valid reason to assassinate McGarvey's daughter, was bin Laden's idea. Because of unforseen circumstances and because the Taliban had provided him with misinformation about McGarvey, the mission had failed. Bahmad considered himself lucky to have been able to shed his coveralls and simply walk away in the confusion, just another man dressed for golf out on the course. Aggad and Ibrahim shot dead by the young woman.

The second phase of the operation, however, was his and his alone. He would not fail. He smiled, the first glimmers of contement and anticipation for a project coming to him.

"Is the drink to your liking, Mr. Guthrie?" the barman asked.

Yes, indeed," Bahmad replied. "It couldn't be better."

DEBORAH HAYNES
TWO MONTHS LATER

Babylon is fallen, is fallen;
and all the graven images of her
gods he hath broken into the ground.

ISAIAH 21:9

TWENTY-FOUR

Khartoum, Sudan

Riding in the back of a battered Mercedes sedan from the airport, Bahmad willed himself to remain calm. This soon before an operation there was only one reason for his sudden recall; for some reason bin Laden wanted to call it off.

In ninety-six hours Deborah Haynes and more than one thousand other handicapped runners would cross the Golden Gate Bridge at the same moment the cargo ship *Margo* sailed beneath the bridge with Joshua's Hammer. The two events were coming together as surely as the sun rose and set. But if no one was there to detonate the bomb at the correct time all would be lost.

He looked out the windows at the passing scenery as he battled his impatience. He was still nearly overwhelmed with anger and bitterness from his failure in Chevy Chase. Yet he could see with a critical eye the wild disrepair everywhere in the city; sandbagged street corners, armed patrols, some of the boys wearing uniforms others wearing the ragtag clothing of the rebel factions, and overall the atmosphere of mad confusion and extreme danger.

It was nothing at all like what he had left in Bermuda where he'd taken *Papa's Fancy* after the debacle. And certainly nothing like New York where he'd dismissed the crew ten days ago and left the yacht.

He'd had a lot of time to think about the war he'd been waging for most of his life, and he had come to the conclusion that when this project was finished he was getting out for good.

Bin Laden's compound was off Sharia al-Barlaman a few blocks from the People's Palace and about the same distance from the Blue Nile. The afternoon was very hot. A reddish-yellow haze swirled through the city, whipping around the corners of buildings and up narrow alleys, causing flags and banners to stream and snap. This was the time of year for fierce desert sandstorms. If they were big enough they even encroached into the cities themselves, like now.

In fact little if anything of any significance had changed here in nearly one thousand years, Bahmad thought morosely. Bin Laden and the others in the various organizations in the jihad such as the Armed Islamic Movement (AIM), the Islamic Arab People's Conference (IAPC), the Sunni's Popular International Organization (PIO), the Islamic Action Front (IAF), the Hisb'Allah, the Islamic Liberation Party and dozens more were fighting mostly with words and the occasional terrorist bomb. Even Joshua's Hammer, though it was a nuclear weapon and would cause a convulsive wave of fear across the United States, was only a gnat's bite on a giant.

The real education that every terrorist should be required to have was a complete tour of America's industrial cities, the electronics assembly plants, the military bases, the nuclear processing facilities, assembly plants and storage depots, the electrical generating stations, the ports, the highways, the sprawling medical centers and pharmaceutical research and manufacturing conglomerates, rather than the slums and storefront mosques of a few cities in New York, New Jersey and California. Even bin Laden had no real idea what he was up against. None of them did.

Time to get out, Bahmad told himself. Especially after Chevy Chase. That had been too close a call for him. At the end something had happened to McGarvey. He had been wounded or he had hit his head, but he was out of it, and Bahmad had started to turn back until the daughter had come to her father's side. She had picked up his pistol and killed Aggad and Ibrahim. Against two-to-one odds she had prevailed.

The car arrived in the anonymous neighborhood of tall stuccoed walls with red-tiled roofs behind them a few minutes after 4:00 P.M. Two solid wooden gates sprung open, and they were admitted into bin Laden's compound just as a sleeker, newer black Mercedes S500 pulled out. Bahmad caught a brief glimpse of the lone passenger in the back seat. It was Dr. Hassan Abdullah al-Turabi, head of the National Islamic Front party, and Sudan's attorney general. He was also bin Laden's longtime friend and mentor, and possibly the most powerful and important man in the entire armed Islamic movement.

The fact that he had come to bin Laden and not the other way around was significant. Something definitely big was in the wind, which was probably the reason Bahmad had been contacted through intermediaries to drop everything and come here to bin Laden's side. It would also explain why bin Laden had not telephoned him directly by encrypted satellite phone; he hadn't wanted to take the risk that somehow the call would be intercepted.

Four armed guards immediately surrounded the car as the wooden gates were closed and barred by another two men. Bahmad got his leather bags and got out of the car. Nafir Osman Nafeh, the NIF party's chief of intelligence, came across the compound, his robes flowing behind him, and gave Bahmad a warm embrace.

"Did you have a safe trip?" he asked.

"A confused trip. I don't know what I'm doing here."

One of the guards took Bahmad's luggage, and his driver got out and frisked him. He wasn't armed, but if he had been he would not have allowed such an affront to the dignity of bin Laden's chief of staff.

Nafeh watched with a tolerant smile, and when the driver stepped back and gave him a nod, he took Bahmad's arm and together they walked across the central courtyard which was crowded with a half-dozen cars and three American Humvees.

"It is good to have you back my old friend," Nafeh said in hushed tones. "There is much work to be done before we can begin the next phase of our struggle."

The man was an ass, Bahmad thought. He talked like a mujahedeen recruiter trying to drum up enthusiasm among young boys. But the real reason for the recall suddenly became clear to Bahmad. Dr. Turabi and the NIF had somehow found out about the bomb, and for some reason they were pressuring bin Laden into calling off the attack.

"There is always much work to be done, because the struggle is ongoing," Bahmad said, using Nafeh's own words on him.

The intelligence chief beamed. "I was saying the very same thing to Osama at our meeting with Dr. Turabi this morning. And he agreed wholeheartedly." Nafeh rubbed his nose.

Quitting was a thing that bin Laden would resist with everything in his soul because of the death of his daughter at the hands of the Americans. It was why Turabi had come here in person to give the order, and why Nafeh had stayed behind to act as Bahmad's personal escort.

They entered the main building and took the stairs up to the second floor. There were armed guards in the corridor. But overall there was an aura of a hospital or a mosque. The atmosphere was heavy, the silence deep.

The meeting had been held in the receiving chamber and bin Laden was still there, looking out the windows. He turned when Bahmad and Nafeh came in, smiled and walked across the room to embrace Bahmad as a long-lost brother. He looked well, as if he had somehow regained his health, and the worry lines in his face, his downcast eyes, were gone.

"I am sorry to have pulled you away from your vacation in the lap of luxury," bin Laden said.

"I am sorry that I failed you in the first phase of our mission."

Bin Laden inclined his head slightly. "He is quite a remarkable man. But I was wrong to send you to kill his daughter. I can see that now." He motioned for them to have a seat on the cushions. When they were settled he poured them tea.

"Now perhaps we can resolve our differences so that we can get on with our legitimate business," Nafeh said pompously.

There were no armed guards in here, and the significance was not lost on Bahmad. Here, at this time and place, bin Laden was nothing more than an ordinary soldier in the jihad. He was being punished.

Bahmad spread his hands. "I'm sorry, but I am at a loss."

"Don't play the fool with me, it's not convincing," Nafeh said sharply. "We're searching for a spectacular operation in the United States, but killing innocent Muslim children—handicapped children—will not be sanctioned."

Bahmad let his voice go cold. "What are you talking about?"

"The Tajikistan bomb. We know all about it. We know that it's already in the United States, and we know that you plan on blowing up the Golden Gate Bridge at the moment President Haynes' daughter is crossing it in a footrace. But two thousand other crippled children from two dozen countries will also be on that bridge. Many of them Muslims. Such an action against our own people could never be condoned. It is forbidden."

"I agree," bin Laden said. "I can now see the error in my thinking."

He was lying, Bahmad was sure of it. "What do you want me to do, Osama? Everything is in place."

"The bomb is in storage at the shipyard in New Jersey and it will remain there until the NIF comes up with another plan," bin Laden said. He looked to Nafeh for confirmation, and the intelligence chief nodded sagely.

"It will not be wasted," he said. "When the correct moment comes it will be used."

"Then the plan to get the bomb to California is to be

abandoned?" Bahmad asked, testing. Perhaps the plans had changed. Perhaps the bomb wasn't aboard the *Margo* already en route up the American West Coast.

"Yes, it is to be abandoned. Our contract with the trucking firm that was to drive it across country will be canceled. Do you understand what you have to do?"

Bahmad smiled inwardly. The bomb had never been in New Jersey and there had never been any kind of a contract with a trucking firm. So the plans were not changed after all. "Perfectly."

"Then you know what your orders are," Nafeh said.

Bahmad turned to him and arched an eyebrow. "From you, never," he spat. "I take my orders only from Osama."

"It will be as the party wishes," bin Laden assured the intelligence chief. "But Ali will have to return to the United States immediately to make sure that everything is dismantled properly. If we mean to make use of the bomb at some future date it will have to be protected. The people already in place, secured."

"Perhaps it is a job too difficult for him. I can arrange for several of my Afghans to accompany him."

Bahmad's eyes flashed. "I know the men you're talking about. They're idiots."

"They follow their orders, and get the job done," Nafeh shot back. "Even simple tasks such as killing young women." Bahmad could have killed him, but he willed an outward calmness and even smiled. "I was given faulty intelligence from the Taliban that Kirk McGarvey was dead when in fact he was not. And at the moment of our attack we were surrounded by the police. Something went wrong, and there wasn't much we could do."

"You left your Afghanis behind." The term was now being used all over the Islamic militant movement to mean soldiers of courage.

"They were expendable."

Nafeh glared at him. "See that you do a better job dismantling the operation. We won't accept another excuse. Perhaps you will find that you're expendable too."

"As you wish."

"Now leave us. Your business here is finished, and I have other matters to discuss with Osama."

Bahmad got to his feet, his eyes locking with bin Laden's.

"Do you understand everything that you must do?" bin Laden asked.

"Completely."

Bin Laden nodded. "My faith goes with you. *Insha'Allah.*"

New York City

Bahmad's flight from Paris touched down at Kennedy about 11:00 P.M., and by the time he had retrieved his bags, cleared customs and caught a cab to the Hudson River boatyard it was midnight. There were lights on in the forward cabins and in the main saloon of *Papa's Fancy*, and he saw a shadow pass a window. He stood in the darkness just beyond the end of the dock to watch.

There was no one around this late, and had there been he would have avoided them. He'd come back only to pick up the things he'd left aboard before heading out to California.

Now this.

He hadn't spent enough time at this boatyard to recognize the few cars that were parked in the lot, but none of them was obviously a government vehicle. Nor did he think that whoever was aboard the yacht was a burglar. No, it was probably one of the crew who'd returned to check on the yacht, or to pick up something that they might have left behind.

On the surface of it, that was just fine, except for one detail. If whoever was aboard at this moment had returned because they were suspicious of Bahmad and were going through his things it could mean trouble.

He had portrayed himself as an independently wealthy

international businessman and playboy. But the aluminum case in his stateroom contained weapons and other devices; not things that an ordinary businessman would carry.

He considered turning around and leaving without his things. There was very little in his stateroom, except for the remote control detonating device, that he could not easily replace. Yet most of it was illegal under American law. And the nature of the equipment would raise some red flags with the FBI and CIA, because much of it could be traced to similar sources of the equipment in the van.

He had to weigh that possibility against the fact that the yacht's owner had secret business dealings with bin Laden and with the Islamic jihad. He had given up the boat for Bahmad's use without hesitation and without so much as a single question. Perhaps the crew had been briefed to ask no questions either, and to do nothing except what they were told to do. Even if they found the case and opened it they might do nothing.

Bahmad decided that he could not afford to take that risk. For all practical purposes he was now working on his own, independent not only of the movement, but of bin Laden, whose hands were completely tied. If Bahmad ran into trouble he would have to deal with the problem himself. Whatever resources he needed would have to come from his own connections, as would the extra manpower if and when he needed it.

Which meant he could not make any more mistakes like he had in Chevy Chase, nor could he leave any clues. Or witnesses.

For a moment he was back in Beirut as a child with his parents; happy and safe, feelings that he'd not experienced since their deaths at the hands of the Israelis. From that moment he had, in effect, become a loner. He believed in no one, trusted in no one, and most importantly, depended on no one for help.

This was nothing new to him.

Hefting his bags he walked out onto the dock, making no effort at stealth. The gate at the head of the yacht's boarding ladder was open, and when he stood on the deck he stopped to listen. There were no sounds from within the boat. They were connected to shore power, so the generators to power the lights weren't running, but neither was the air conditioner. The night was warm. Whoever was aboard was not planning on staying for long, yet they weren't afraid of showing lights.

Bahmad went aft and entered the warm, stuffy saloon from the party deck as Captain Web Walker came from the forward part of the yacht. He wore civilian clothes; deck shoes, khaki trousers and a short-sleeved white Polo shirt with *Papa's Fancy* embroidered on the pocket. He seemed nervous about something.

"You're back," he said. "I thought I heard someone come aboard."

"I didn't expect to see you here," Bahmad said pleasantly.

"I came down for the week, so I thought that I'd check on things. Are you going to need the yacht? Shall I recall the crew?"

"Not for ten days, maybe a little longer," Bahmad told him. He put down his bags and went behind the bar where he poured a cognac. "Care for a drink?"

"No, thanks," Walker said. "Everything's fine here, so I'll be going."

"A moment, if you would, Captain," Bahmad said mildly. It was obvious that Walker was lying. "Did the owner tell you why he wanted you to check on the yacht tonight?"

The captain was a distinguished man, but he looked like a deer caught in headlights. He wanted to bolt, but he was rooted to the spot. "As I said, I happened to be in the city."

"Yes, yes, I know all of that, but the owner did ask you to check on things, didn't he?" Bahmad kept his tone friendly. A couple of yachtsmen discussing a simple fact.

"He gets nervous when no one is aboard to watch over things."

"I don't blame him." Bahmad put his glass down and

came around the bar. "Did he tell you what you were supposed to be looking for?"

The captain tried to smile. "Primarily that the vessel hadn't sunk at the dock," he said. "It's happened to other boats."

"For which the captain would take the blame."

"Naturally."

"As he would take the blame if there was contraband aboard." Bahmad laid a hand on Walker's shoulder. "Drugs, maybe booze. Something that we might have picked up in Bermuda and didn't declare when we came back."

"No one is worried about anything like that."

"Weapons then. Guns with silencers and hollowpoint bullets."

The captain swallowed.

"So, you came back on the owner's orders to search my stateroom. You found the case and you opened it. The question is who did you call? The FBI?"

The captain backed up. "I just got here, I haven't called anyone—" He realized his mistake and clamped his mouth shut.

Bahmad smiled again. "What did you take?"

"Nothing, I swear to God."

Bahmad turned him around and roughly shoved him up against the bulkhead. "Hands on the wall, feet spread."

"What the hell is this all about?"

"Do it." Bahmad gave him a shot in the ribs, and the captain grunted as if he'd been struck by a sledgehammer, but he did as he was told.

Bahmad quickly frisked him, but came up with nothing except the captain's wallet, some money, keys, handkerchief, comb, glasses and penknife."

"What did you take?" he asked again.

"Nothing—"

Bahmad drove his fist into the same spot in Walker's side. The man cried out in pain and his knees started to buckle. "What did you take?"

"I tossed the case over the side. I swear to God it's at the bottom of the slip."

Bahmad was surprised. It wasn't what he had expected. "Why?"

"I was told to do it before you got back."

There it was—the answer. Someone from Nafeh's staff had called the yacht's owner and asked that Bahmad's weapons be found and destroyed. They were fools. He didn't need the equipment. Not even the remote detonator because the weapon could be manually set to fire from the keypad with as long as a twenty-four-hour delay.

"Then what?" Bahmad asked, though he didn't care what the answer would be, he was merely distracting the captain for one necessary moment.

He shoved Walker flat against the bulkhead with his left hip, then grabbed the man's head with both hands and twisted it sharply backward and to the right. The captain's neck broke with an audible pop.

Bahmad let go and stepped back, allowing Walker to slump to the floor. The captain's legs twitched, and his eyes blinked furiously as his face turned purple. Bahmad thought it was funny and he smiled. Killing a man this way was silent, but it took a good bit of time. Not only was his spinal cord severed, but his windpipe was crushed so that his airway was cut off at the same time his heart stopped.

After a while the captain stopped twitching and Bahmad set about wiping down everything he had touched with his bare hands and searching the yacht for anything incriminating. He thought about finding the yacht's diving gear and retrieving his equipment, but that would take too much time, not only to find it and bring it up, but to clean it and dry it all off. He decided to leave it at the bottom of the harbor. The captain's body would be found sooner or later, but he didn't think that anyone would go diving beneath the boat until it was too late to make a difference. He would get new weapons.

He would get a hotel room tonight and in the morning he would fetch his things from storage and catch the early flight to Los Angeles. Just a few more days now and he would be free.

He found that he was looking forward to his retirement with a great deal of relish.

Aboard *Air Force One*

"How are you doing, sweetheart?" President Haynes asked his daughter.

She looked up, a sweet smile on her face. "Hi, Daddy," she said. "The clouds look like castles this morning."

Haynes looked out the window. They were over Iowa en route to San Diego at about 30,000 feet, and the cloud formations did indeed look like castles. Like the one at Disneyland where they were going tomorrow. The International Special Olympics' opening ceremony was three days from now, and Haynes was making a sweep through California in support of Governor S. Howard Thomas who was up for reelection in November. It was going to be a hot contest with a lot of major issues, not the least of which was abortion, which Haynes was against, but had to support publicly because of his party's position; a ban on smoking in all public places including beaches, parks and even streets, something he thought made some sort of sense but was a ridiculous infringement of people's freedoms by a heavy-handed government; and the elimination of the state income tax, even while Florida was grappling with the creation of a state income tax and Haynes himself was proposing the end of federal income taxes in favor of a flat-rate sales tax.

Whatever position he took, there would be a hundred different voices opposing it, five dozen powerful lobbyist groups clamoring to get the attention of Congress and at least twenty talking heads on weekend morning television analyzing and dissecting every single move he and every other politician made. And it brought a smile to his face. This was what American politics was all about. The almost constant bickering, the dissentions, the name-calling and sometimes even mudslinging, the attempts at bribery and influence-peddling, the investigations and sometimes even impeachment proceedings; the give and take of compromise. All of it was working *exactly* the way the designers of the system had meant it to work. There was no dissolving of Congress or of the government, no tanks coming up Pennsylvania Avenue in another military coup, no President and his cabinet fleeing the country, no armed revolution pitting one people against another, leastways not since the Civil War.

"The clouds do look like castles," Haynes said. He looked into his daughter's eyes. She seemed very happy. "Are you looking forward to the Olympics this weekend, sweetheart?" She was always so open and straightforward that he could tell what she was thinking and how she was feeling.

"I'm nervous, but I was thinking about something," she replied.

"What's that?"

"Just about everybody else is going to be just as nervous as me. Mom says all I can do is my best and don't worry about anyone else, 'cause they'll be trying to do their best. I hope. But I'm still nervous. Is it okay?"

Haynes glanced up as his chief of staff Tony Lang came around the corner. He looked nervous. Everybody aboard did. Haynes gave his daughter a peck on the cheek. "It's okay to be nervous, but not scared."

She thought about it for a moment, then nodded, her pretty blue eyes lighting up and a smile brightening an already impossibly bright face. "Gotcha." She looked like a cross between a blond, blue-eyed Scandinavian beauty and a mysterious, almond-eyed Siberian.

Haynes studied his daughter's round face for a moment, and his heart suddenly hardened. God help the sorry sonofabitch who ever tried to harm so much as a hair on her head. He felt a genuine sorrow and guilt for what had happened to bin Laden's daughter. He wished that he could somehow make it right, or at least explain to bin Laden how it had happened. But he could not. What he could do was protect his own child, while at the same time protect the freedom of the United States.

"Gotta go," he said, but his daughter was already looking out the window again. She could grasp some fairly complex ideas, but usually not more than one of them at a time. She was in some ways lucky, he thought.

He joined Lang and they went forward into the corridor separating the family's space with the President's private study and conference room.

"Henry would like to go over a few things with you, Mr. President, and Sterling wants to know if you'll agree to an off-the-record chat with the media sometime this afternoon before we touch down."

"Tell Henry to come up, and I want you to sit in on it too, because I have a few ideas—assuming he's talking about security for the games in San Francisco."

Lang nodded. "He's running into some brick walls, and he's probably going to ask you to pull your daughter out of the ISO."

Haynes's jaw tightened. "Not a chance. And you can tell Sterling that I'll talk to the media, but the issues will be limited."

"Anything but the games?" Lang asked.

"That's right," Haynes said angrily. He went forward, pausing at the open curtain to his wife's office. She was in conference with her press secretary and they looked up and smiled.

"Did you talk to Deb?" his wife asked.

"Just now. She's a little nervous, but she'll be okay."

"Would you like me to come back later, Mrs. Haynes?" the First Lady's secretary asked, starting to rise.

The President waved her back. "No. Henry wants to go over the arrangements for San Francisco, so I've just got a minute."

"Are we going to be okay up there?" The President's wife asked.

"We're going to make it okay, Linda, by covering all the bases, not by hiding," the President told her firmly. He held her eye for a moment, and a silent message of reassurance passed from him to her. She visibly relaxed. "I wouldn't take the games away from her for anything."

"It's been two months and nothing has happened," she said. "Do you want me to touch on it in my talks?"

Haynes thought about it and nodded. "It might not be a bad idea. But use a light touch, and maybe you'd better run it past Marty." Martin Schoenberg was the President's chief speech writer.

"Sure."

The President went to his conference room. He pressed the button for his steward, who appeared instantly. "How about some coffee, Alex?"

"Coming right up, sir."

Haynes was in shirtsleeves; not as informal as Clinton had been, but a lot less tense than Nixon. He set a hard-working but relaxed tone in his administration, and the people he'd gathered around him thrived in the atmosphere.

His coffee came in a large mug bearing the presidential seal, and a moment later Lang showed up with Kolesnik.

"Good morning, Mr. President," the chief of the Secret Service Protective Division said.

"'Morning, Henry. Tony said you had something for me."

"Yes, sir, but I'm afraid that it's not very good news. San Francisco is a mess. There's just no way that we can guarantee your safety or that of your daughter in the games. It's as simple as that. We'd like you to pull your daughter out and cancel your part in the opening ceremonies."

"We've gone over this a hundred times."

"Sir, a lot of those athletes are coming from Muslim countries. Their families are coming with them; moms, dads, brothers, uncles. At least men who claim to be brothers and uncles. And there's just no way we can check all of them. If bin Laden wanted to send an army to San Francisco, he could do it easily."

"But he's not going to do that."

"I'm sorry, Mr. President, but we can't be sure," Kolesnik countered. He handed the President a list of all the Special Olympians expected for the games. "There're nearly three thousand of them, plus relatives or guardians and coaches. At least four hundred are Muslims. But that's not the worst of it. Bin Laden has supporters just about everywhere, which means that the assassin or assassins could be German or Italian, or Japanese, even American."

The President flipped through the lengthy list, knowing exactly who these people were. Down syndrome runners, paraplegic swimmers, blind discus throwers, palsied high jumpers; athletes with dozens of afflictions doing the best they could. "That's exactly why bin Laden won't make his strike in San Francisco. He'd be killing Muslims. His own people. He'd never survive such an attack."

"In a strange way, Mr. President, you may be wrong for all the right reasons," Kolesnik said. "By killing his own people he would be sending a very clear message that absolutely no one is safe from him. It could dramatically increase his stature and that of the NIF, if anyone can follow such logic."

"Well, I for one cannot."

"The psychologists on our staff brought it up as a possibility, sir." Kolesnik was frustrated, but it was clear that he'd expected to run into a brick wall. "If it came to that, Mr. President, the Secret Service could supersede your orders." Under certain circumstances in which the President's life was clearly in danger, the Secret Service did have the power to override a President's wishes, even by gentle force if necessary, and take him out of harm's way.

"Don't even try to go there, Henry," Haynes warned.

Kolesnik straightened up. "Until you fire me, Mr. President, I'll do my job the best way I know how even if it means disagreeing with you."

The President handed the list back. "Is there any evidence that bin Laden is planning to hit us in San Francisco?"

"No, sir." Kolesnik replaced the list in his file folder. "But the bomb is already here in the States."

"Anything on that from the FBI or CIA that I haven't seen?"

"No, sir."

"They tried to get McGarvey's wife and daughter and they failed. Maybe that's it," the President said. "Bring me some hard information and I'll cancel the entire ISO. Until then do what you can." Haynes softened. "I want you to know, Henry, that I'm not trying to be a bastard here. I appreciate the extraordinary efforts that your people take every day to keep me and my family safe. But you have to understand what I'm faced with. Whoever sits in this chair still has to go out and press the flesh on occasion, even if it means putting his life on the line. And that's just the way it is."

"Yes, Mr. President, we do understand," Kolesnik replied. "We'll do the best we can."

"That's all I can ask from anybody."

TWENTY-FIVE

M/V Margo
Off Cabo San Lazaro, Baja California

There's something damned funny going on, if you ask me," Captain Panagiotopolous told his deck officer. It was after breakfast and they were steaming north at seventeen knots about two hundred miles off the Baja California peninsula. They were slightly ahead of schedule and if the weather held they'd be in San Francisco at least eight hours early.

The entire trip starting in Karachi three months ago had been a cocked-up affair, in the captain's estimation, although nothing terribly untoward had happened to them other than the brief but intense storm in the Arabian Sea. But there'd been an odd flavor to the home office communiques from Paris, a vagueness that the captain had never noticed before in his twenty-five years at sea. It was the new executives probably; kids who'd never been to sea themselves and yet felt competent to run a shipping company with a fleet of thirty-eight vessels that stopped at just about every port in the world. But the snotnoses did know computers.

For two months while the *Margo* was in dry dock at the Tampa Marine Yards in Florida, Panagiotopolous had gone home to visit his family in Athens. But after just a few days he remembered why he had left in the first place. He took a small boat out to Delos where he worked up a sweat helping prune olive trees. Honest labor. Appreciated labor. When he got back to his ship he was refreshed, ready to go. But after a brief inspection he saw that none of the repairs done to the ship had been necessary. Some painting, a new reefer in the galley, a few new pieces of navigation equipment on the bridge; nothing essential.

He got to wondering what the hell was really going on. For instance, why had the *Margo* been yanked from service at that particular moment for unnecessary repairs. Instead of earning money, the company had lost a bundle. And, why had the deck cargo bound for San Francisco been unloaded and stored at the shipyard instead of being transferred to another ship?

Or what the hell were they doing with a helicopter tied down on the rear deck?

Panagiotopolous wasn't surprised by taking on last-minute cargo. It happened all the time. But it was the way in which it had been handled in Colon at the eastern terminus of the Panama Canal that was odd. They were ordered to drop anchor in the holding basin, and within the hour the self-loading cargo vessel *Antilles Trader* out of

Havana came alongside. A company representative came aboard with a bill of lading. The helicopter was to be loaded on the *Margo*'s afterdeck for delivery to M. L. Murty, Ltd., in San Francisco. The documents were in order, but since it was Cuban equipment bound for a U.S. port a special clearance was needed, something the representative didn't have. When the captain called the company on SSB he was told in no uncertain terms that the *Margo* was his ship and his responsibility. He would either have to sail without the papers, or a new captain would be found to replace him. The clearance papers, he was promised, would be delivered to the ship with the harbor pilot in San Francisco Bay. If he was stopped in U.S. waters by the Coast Guard he would have to talk his way out of his problem.

"It makes no sense," he said.

"I agree," Schumatz replied. They stood on the port wing looking aft. "I could fray the cables and let the sonofabitch fall overboard. Nobody would be any the wiser. The insurance company would bitch, that's if the company even made a claim. Without the proper papers we shouldn't be carrying it, so if it simply disappeared they might say nothing."

"Why are they taking the risk? That's what I don't get. The ship and our cargo could be impounded."

"Obviously the company thinks it's worth it. Hell, even if we deliver the chopper the new owners will never get it registered with the FAA. Not without the proper documents. Does that make any sense to you?"

"I hadn't thought of that," Panagiotopolous said. He stared at the machine. It was a small helicopter, capable of carrying only the pilot and three passengers. But it was apparently in serviceable condition. According to Schumatz, who had supervised its loading, there was even fuel in the tank. Another thought struck him. "There's plenty of clearance for the rotors. Someone could pull the lines free and take off, couldn't they?"

Schumatz's eyes narrowed. "What are you getting at?"

"Does anybody aboard know how to fly one of those things?"

"I don't. Do you?"

Panagiotopolous shook his head thoughtfully. Something wasn't right. It wasn't adding up. There was some element that he was missing.

First Officer Green came from the bridge with a message flimsy. "We just received this," he said, handing it to the captain.

"Thank you," Panagiotopolous said. "Do you know how to fly a helicopter, by any chance, Mr. Green?"

Green's face brightened. "As a matter of fact I do, sir. The company has a couple of Bell Rangers, which I've used."

"Could you fly that one?" the captain asked, indicating the Cuban helicopter on the aft deck.

"They all fly pretty much the same, so I suppose so. But I took a look at it when it came aboard, and it's a piece of junk. Doesn't have much of a range, either, so I wouldn't get very far."

"Anyone else aboard know how to fly one of those things?"

Green shook his head. "I don't think so, Captain. They cost a ton of money to maintain, let alone fly, and I don't think we have any millionaires in disguise on our crew list. Why did you ask?"

"We were just wondering why the company ordered us to take it to San Francisco at the last minute."

"I haven't a clue. I could call my dad and ask him, I suppose. But like I said, it's a piece of junk. I don't know anybody who'd want it except as a museum piece."

"That's probably it," Pangiotopolous said. "Thank you."

"Yes, sir." Green started to leave, but then turned back. "Oh, that's a U.S. Coast Guard traffic advisory that we just got. There's going to be a shipping restriction under the Golden Gate Bridge Saturday morning from ten hundred hours until fourteen hundred. I've already done the navigation. If we can keep our present SOG we'll be under the bridge at least six hours early." SOG was the actual speed over the ground that the ship made good, which included the effects of ship's speed through the water, the ocean currents, the wave action and the effect of the wind on the bulk of the vessel.

"Thank you, good work," the captain said, and Green went back inside.

"What's that all about?" Schumatz asked.

Panagiotopolous quickly read the brief U.S.C.G. advisory. "Something's going on, probably bridge repairs, so they're closing down all shipping traffic inbound as well as outbound." He pocketed the message. "It won't effect us though." He glanced again at the helicopter. "Ask around, would you Lazlo? Find out if anyone else can fly one of those things."

Schumatz nodded. "What about Green?"

"I'll keep an eye on him."

CIA Headquarters

It was coming up on noon at the headquarters gym. McGarvey had had a particularly bad bout of depression this morning, so intense that he'd had difficulty concentrating on getting through the morning, let alone doing any real work. He'd fought depression most of his adult life and extreme physical exercise not only kept him in shape for field work, but it somehow combated his dark moods. If he could get through one or two hours of hard work, anything for him was possible afterward.

Murphy had ordered him to take an extra week off, but that was impossible. He'd had the operation to fix the bleeder in his head and relieve the pressure on his brain, and he'd recovered fully. But bin Laden and Ali Bahmad were still at large, and the bomb was still out there somewhere. His wife and daughter had almost been assassinated. The President, who steadfastly refused to back down, was putting his own daughter in harm's way. And the Arabic languages expert Otto had found had translated the rest of the one and only phone conversation between bin Laden and Bahmad that they'd managed to record.

The daughters of the infidels will die like the pigs they are.

Bin Laden had used the plural—daughters—not the singular. It meant that McGarvey's *and* the President's daughters were targets.

According to the timetable, Bahmad had told his master. *The package is on its way.*

But that was two months ago, and since then the only piece of information they knew with reasonable certainty was that bin Laden was holed up in his compound in Khartoum. Possibly even under a loose house arrest by Sudan's National Islamic Front.

It was this last bit of information that was so puzzling. The analysts in the Directorate of Intelligence were telling him that if bin Laden were under house arrest it could mean that the bomb project was being delayed or canceled. McGarvey wasn't so sure. Bin Laden was an independent man, and he was dying. He certainly wouldn't delay the project, because he might not live long enough to see it done. Nor would he cancel it. No, Bahmad was still here in the U.S., with the bomb, and he meant to use it. The question was where and when.

If you get close enough to bin Laden, kill him, Dennis Berndt had suggested. It wasn't that easy, McGarvey thought. It never was. But he was finally beginning to realize that killing bin Laden might just be their only way out. But it was hard, when he was depressed, to keep his mind on track. Hard not to just walk away from the problem, something that he'd never done in his life.

He wiped his face with his sweat towel at the side of the fencing strip and took a drink of Gatorade as he tried to figure out a strategy. Todd Van Buren, his opponent, was not only twenty-five years younger, his reflexes were supersharp because he worked as a hand-to-hand combat instructor at the Farm. The fact that he was sleeping with the boss's daughter didn't seem to have any effect on his enthusiasm for the touch. But he did have one weakness. He was primarily a foilest, and that's how he was trying to fight épée this morning.

McGarvey walked back to the en garde line, his mask under his left arm. "One more touch?"

Van Buren nodded. "Getting a little tired, Mr. McGarvey?" he asked, grinning.

"We'll see," McGarvey said. Strong physical exercise had always helped him focus on the moment instead of his past, yet it was still hard to concentrate. As soon as he allowed his mind to drift, even a little, bin Laden's face and that of his daughter's swam into view.

He came to attention and brought the hilt of his weapon momentarily to his lips in a salute. Van Buren did the same. They donned their masks, brought their left arms up in a graceful arch over their rear shoulders, and raised their weapons to the en garde position.

On a silent signal between themselves they began. Van Buren came out first, testing for McGarvey's response and speed of response. First a feint in four. McGarvey stepped back easily out of range and took Van Buren's blade in a counter six, trying for the easy displacement and quick thrust for the touch. But Van Buren rode the pressure of McGarvey's blade downward, aiming his own lightning-quick thrust to McGarvey's leading knee, barely missing before McGarvey nimbly retreated out of range.

They were at la Belle, a tie score, and neither of them wanted the double touch. They both wanted to win.

McGarvey momently lowered his blade in what might have been taken as an unintended *invito*.

Van Buren declined, retreating out of range himself. "It's not going to be that easy this morning, Mr. M.," he said.

Before Van Buren got the entire sentence out, McGarvey made an explosive ballestra and lunge feint to Van Buren's sword arm just above the bell guard. Surprised, Van Buren retreated again, making what he thought would be the easy parry. But McGarvey disengaged, dropping his blade beneath Van Buren's and coming up on the outside of his opponent's bell guard.

Van Buren, quick as McGarvey knew he would be, parried the thrust as he retreated, but instead of coming on guard, Van Buren raised his arm slightly to start a flick.

There it was, the foilest's mistake in épée.

A flick was nothing more than a deft snap of the wrist that caused the more flexible foil blade to snap like a bullwhip, the point arching gracefully over the opponent's bell guard for the touch. An épée blade, however, was too thick and too stiff for a flick to be very effective unless the swordsman had an exceedingly strong wrist. Even so, in order to make it work the attacker sometimes cocked his swordhand slightly, leaving the under part of his wrist behind the bell guard open for just a split instant.

McGarvey brought his point in line, angulated at a deceptively slight upward angle and held his ground. Van Buren's arm snapped forward in a powerful flick, but before his point could make the arc, his wrist made contact with McGarvey's waiting épée tip.

Even as the green light came on, indicating McGarvey's valid hit, and locking out the flick, Van Buren realized his mistake. He skipped backward, and immediately raised his left hand, acknowledging the hit.

McGarvey took off his mask and saluted Van Buren, who did the same. They switched their masks to the crooks of their weapon arms and shook with their bare left hands.

"You knew it was coming, didn't you," Van Buren said, grinning.

McGarvey nodded. "Yeah. You were concentrating so hard on the flick that you forgot about defense for just an instant."

"I'll remember that for the next time."

They parted and walked to the ends of the strip where they unplugged themselves from the scoring reels, and it struck McGarvey all at once that bin Laden's attention would be taken up with his own troubles right now. Not only his illness, but the apparent trouble he was having with the NIF. If the DI analysts were correct, bin Laden would be meeting on a daily basis with his Islamic fundamentalist pals. There would be a great deal of activity at his compound. He would be traveling again, trying to explain his position, consolidate his support, trying to get the green light to proceed.

Either that or he was busy stalling them. If that were the case he'd never leave the compound. He would stay put, letting the Islamic liberation fighters come to him. If he was stalling for time the traffic to his compound would be one-way.

"I said that I have to drive back to the Farm this afternoon," Van Buren said next to him.

McGarvey turned around. "Sorry, I guess I was wool-gathering. What's happening down there?"

"Summer session. Liz is going with me for a few days, if you can spare her. She has some field experience that I'd like her to share with the class." Van Buren grinned. "The screwups along with the good stuff."

"If she thinks that she can spare the time, then go ahead," McGarvey said. "She's a handful, isn't she?"

"That she is."

"Don't underestimate her, Todd." McGarvey gave him a hard stare, playing his role as father now. "She's my daughter, don't forget it."

Van Buren suddenly got very serious. "No, sir," he said.

McGarvey clapped him on the shoulder. "Save the flick for foil, unless you want to use the preparation as an *invito*."

"You would have found another weakness, wouldn't you, sir?"

"I would have looked for one," McGarvey agreed. He gathered up his equipment and went into the locker room to take a shower and change clothes while Van Buren put away the scoring machine. He was finished in ten minutes and on his way up to Rencke's office on the third floor, no longer depressed. He had the bit in his teeth now.

"I want to see everything we've come up with on bin

Laden's Khartoum compound over the past two months," he said, coming down the narrow aisle between computer equipment.

Rencke looked up from his monitor and broke out into a big smile. "Just what the docs ordered, beating the kids at something they do good. It's that thing he does with the flick, isn't it?"

"How the hell did you know about that?"

Rencke scooted his chair to an adjacent monitor and brought up a series of stop action frames on a split screen; one side showing the bout that McGarvey and Van Buren had just finished, and the other showing stick figures fighting the same bout, their every action and reaction analyzed and tagged with vector diagrams. "When the boss is in the dumper everybody wants to know what to do. So I got elected."

"Don't ever take up fencing, Otto."

"Have someone coming at me with sharp, pointy objects? Not a chance, Mac." Rencke scooted back to his primary monitor, cleared the screen and brought up a satellite view of bin Laden's Khartoum compound. There were several Mercedes and three Humvees parked inside the gates, but there was no sign of people. "Take a look at this. We just got our satellite back."

"Is he still there?"

"There's activity, so I suspect he's there." Rencke looked up. "Are we thinking about another cruise missile strike? There's a children's hospital right behind it, and a Catholic school next door. Great propaganda stuff."

"No missiles. I want to know about the traffic patterns over the past couple of months. Has bin Laden or anyone else from the compound been going visiting, or has all the traffic been incoming?"

"Are you talking about the DI report this morning?"

"It got me thinking that bin Laden might be stalling for time."

"It would help explain why there's been only the one phone call between bin Laden and Bahmad. If they were sticking to their original timetable, bin Laden wouldn't have to do anything except lie around biding his time until it happened."

"Something like that," McGarvey said.

"But Bahmad might have already left," Rencke suggested. "Maybe he was here just long enough to set everything into motion. There were only two guys in the van at Chevy Chase that day. Both of them were bin Laden's people, we know at least that much. If Bahmad had wanted to come after Liz he would have been there himself. Instead he just sends the two goons. He could be gone."

"We never found the gun that killed Mike Larsen," McGarvey said. "It could mean that there was a third person in the van. Somebody that nobody saw."

Rencke stared at the computer screen for a long time. "There's probably a couple of thousand satellite photographs of the compound over the past sixty days, I'll check them all. But we need their timetable. And we need it right now." Rencke looked up again, his eyes round, his face serious. "This weekend the President's daughter is going to take part in the International Special Olympics in San Francisco. If the bomb went off there it'd sure as hell make a big statement."

"It's crazy," McGarvey said.

"You could say that, but this President's not gonna back down for anything. You gotta admire him just a little."

"But he's putting his own daughter at risk."

"And himself too," Rencke said. "He's doing the opening ceremonies."

"Okay, I want everything you've got on the games ASAP. We'll take another look at them."

"All right. But we've got one thing going for us though. A bunch of those people are Muslims. He might not want to kill his own people."

"That didn't stop him in Riyadh or Africa," McGarvey shot back sharply. "If San Francisco is their target the bomb is already there, and so is Bahmad." He couldn't believe he had missed it. Where was his head? "I'll get our people started, and then send the heads-up to the Bureau. In the meantime I'll try to convince the general to talk some sense into the President."

."What about Liz?"

"She's supposed to go down to the Farm with Van Buren this afternoon, but I'm going to keep her here. I'm calling a staff meeting at two and I want everything you can come up with on bin Laden by then. I want to know if he's still there, I want to know if he's done any traveling over the past two months, and I want to know who's come to see him."

"Are you going after him?"

"Let's take care of this weekend first. If we can get to Monday in one piece we'll take the next step." McGarvey's eyes narrowed. "I'm tired of screwing around, Otto. One way or the other we *will* deal with bin Laden once and for all. He's fucked with us for the last time."

San Francisco

"This could be a nightmare," the FBI's San Francisco Special Agent in Charge Charles Fellman said. It was very windy on the Golden Gate Bridge, and some of his words were blown away, but everyone knew what he was saying, and everybody agreed.

"It's our job to see that it doesn't get that far," Jay Villiard replied. He was a short, intense man who had been a gold shield detective in Manhattan's Midtown precinct until going to work for the U.S. Secret Service. He was an advance man for major presidential trips. His job was to convince the local law enforcement agencies to do things his way. "Tried and tested, ladies and gentlemen, tried and tested," he liked to say in response to objections.

"The Coast Guard has sent the Notice to Mariners on the five-mile bridge restrictions. But what about ferry traffic?" Beth Oreck asked. She headed the San Francisco Harbor Authority.

"All traffic."

Beth was a large-boned woman with a broad face. She looked at him over the glasses perched on the end of her nose. "In that case we have a problem."

Villiard focused on her. "Yes?"

"Pilot boats. They take the harbor pilots out to incoming ships. If they're held in port we won't be able to start getting shipping back to normal for three or four hours after the restriction is lifted."

"Send the pilots out before the restriction takes effect. They can wait aboard their assigned ships until the bridge is cleared." Villiard waited only a moment for any further objections from her before he looked up at the bridge towers that soared 746 feet above the water. "I want people up there watching the roadway from both directions."

"We're already on it," David Rogan assured Villiard. He was chief of the San Francisco Police Antiterrorism Unit. "I'm putting pairs of my SWAT teams guys on each side of the roadway, on both sides of the bridge."

"I agree," Villiard said. "The bridge will be searched Friday night twelve hours before the event, and again Saturday morning two hours before the start."

No one offered any objections.

Villiard walked over to the rail and looked out over the harbor back toward Alcatraz Island. After a moment Charles Fellman joined him. The others stayed at the two vans that had taken them from Candlestick Park over the route that the presidential motorcade and Special Olympians would take.

"This is about bin Laden, isn't it?"

Villiard looked at him, his lips compressed, and he nodded. "Nothing in two months. The CIA says he's holed up in Khartoum, and they haven't come up with a single shred of evidence that he'll strike here and now." Villiard shook his head. "There'll be runners from Sudan, Saudi Arabia, Yemen, even Iran. He'd be a fool to try anything. But I've got a terrible feeling about this weekend."

Fellman, who'd worked with him before, nodded. "I

know what you mean. But you have the same feeling before *every* event."

"You're right."

"So we redouble our efforts. Push the exclusion zone back to ten miles; hell, fifteen."

Villiard shook his head. "The goddamned bomb is the size of a suitcase, Chuck. How the hell do you find something like that hidden in something like this?" He swept his arm to include the entire bridge, and perhaps the entire bay area.

"You don't," Fellman admitted after a few seconds.

"But you keep trying," Villiard said. "There's no other choice this time. We keep doing the same things; tried and tested."

CIA Headquarters

"Nothing is going to happen this weekend, Mac, and you know it as well as I do," Murphy said.

McGarvey had to agree intellectually. He knew all the reasons bin Laden would not strike the President's daughter in the midst of hundreds of his own people. Yet he could not shake the feeling that had come to him downstairs in the gym. Bin Laden was so desperate to win before he died that he was going to make a foolish move; like Van Buren had with his inappropriate flick. It would be an all-out thrust that he knew could have the consequences of causing his own destruction, but he was willing to take the risk. He had seen it in the man's eyes and in his voice at the Afghanistan meeting, as well as on the phone call.

The effective blast radius of the bomb was more than a mile. Parked in the middle of the Olympic Village it would wipe out all the athletes plus a lot of the surrounding neighborhoods. Hidden somewhere in Candlestick Park stadium, so long as it wasn't shielded by too much concrete and steel, the nuclear explosion would kill everyone in attendance including the President's daughter who would be down on the field, and the President and First Lady on the speakers' platform during the opening ceremonies. Hidden somewhere on the Golden Gate Bridge, anywhere between the two towers, the bomb would serve the exact purpose it was designed for, taking out large bridges. The center span would drop into the bay and no one would survive. That included the President and his wife who would be in the convoy of cars leading the half-marathon from Candlestick Park to Sausalito—Deborah Haynes somewhere in the pack.

"I hope you're right," he told Murphy. They were in the DCI's office, the sun streaming through the tall windows.

"I'm not trying to say that we're out of the woods. But I don't think San Francisco is his target."

McGarvey thought again about bin Laden's voice on the phone call that NSA intercepted; he was a changed man from the one who had negotiated a bomb for his family's freedom. Even harder and more desperate than he had been in the cave. "I want you to try to get to the President again. One more time, General, try to convince him to pull his daughter out of the games and come home."

Murphy shook his head. It was obvious that he had tried more than once and failed. "Not a chance," he said, and before McGarvey could object he held up his hand. "He's read all the transcripts and listened to the phone conversation. He knows the risk he's taking, but he also knows the risk he'd be taking if he packed it up and hid in a bomb shelter until we found it. He told me to tell you that he knows you must be faced with a similar problem allowing your daughter to remain working for the CIA, and not sending her away somewhere out of harm's way until the monster is caught."

McGarvey wanted a cigarette, but he felt like hell as it was. He'd known the answer that Murphy would give him. He'd merely been trying to delay the inevitable decision that he was going to have to make.

"I've called a staff meeting for two," he said looking up. "We have a lot of work to do."

"Here we go again," Murphy replied heavily. He turned away momentarily unable to meet McGarvey's eyes.

"Nothing's changed, has it?" McGarvey thought about his past, about everything that he'd done in his twenty-five years with the Company. Had he made a difference? He sometimes doubted it. Leastways nothing had changed because of him in the long run. "We don't have the luxury of time, so it could end up being messy. I want everybody to know that from the beginning. Another missile strike is out, for humanitarian as well as political reasons. Nor do I think it would be a good idea to send in the marines, and Khartoum is too far inland for any kind of an effective SEAL operation. It's going to have to be one-on-one."

"Do we have anybody on the ground out there?"

"Not the kind of an operative that we need," McGarvey said. "I'll set up a forward headquarters in Riyadh. It's just possible that we can flush bin Laden out of his compound by setting up a meeting somewhere. Something he could not afford to miss. Maybe just across the border in Yemen."

"But you're not going out on the mission, Mac," Murphy said firmly. "You're not going to try to kill bin Laden yourself."

"It doesn't matter who kills him, General, he has to die."

La Jolla

Chenna Serafini's view was a much narrower one. Killing bin Laden would solve only one of her problems. He was just one of dozens, perhaps hundreds or even thousands of crazies out there who would like to do harm to the President and his family. Her job, one that she was proud of and took very seriously, was to stop them, with her own life if necessary. More specifically she was the lead officer on the detail to protect Raindrop, the code name for the President's daughter.

She was thirty-four, divorced, no children, parents dead, no brothers or sisters. Her entire life revolved around her job. So much so, in fact, that she was already beginning to have bad dreams about the day a new President and First Family replaced the Hayneses. She expected that everyone else on her detail should share the same enthusiasm. They did not, of course, and it was a never-ending source of vexation for her.

The best deal today was that Deborah was staying put. The President and First Lady had left early this morning for a breakfast fundraiser, and were at this moment attending a thousand-dollar-a-plate luncheon at the San Diego Hilton. They had left Deborah here at the La Jolla estate of their old friend and campaign contributor, the real estate multimillionaire Gordon Wedell and his wife Evelyn. The Wedells, currently in Europe, had loaned the house to the President and his family, as they had on several other occasions. Wedell liked the arrangement because when it came time to sell the place its value would be greatly enhanced by its famous guests. The Secret Service liked it because the house was perched on a cliff overlooking the Pacific and was easy to secure. The President and Mrs. Haynes liked it because it was comfortable, and Deborah loved it because they had horses, an Olympic-size swimming pool, tennis and racketball courts, and a place for her to run, all in perfect safety.

Chenna got out of the jeep across from the horse barn and raised her binoculars. Deborah Haynes, dressed in gray sweats, her long blond hair streaming behind her, was coming around the far turn of the one-mile oval horse track. Terri Lundgren, her coach, astride an ATV, paced her on the outside just a few feet away. Even from here Chenna could see the pure, unadulterated joy on Deborah's face as she loped, rather than ran flat-out. She was turning in respectable eight-minute miles at the start, and from what Chenna had seen over the past couple of years since Terri Lundgren had come aboard, the girl could continue at that pace all day.

Directly behind her, and a few yards back, agent Bruce Hansen took up the rear astride his own souped-up version of an ATV. If anything started to go bad he could get to Deborah within seconds, and if need be he could get her out of there at speeds ranging up to eighty miles per hour.

Chenna turned her chin slightly so that her lapel mike would pick up her voice and activate the VOX. "Hey, you're lookin' good out there, Romeo One. But I thought that you were going to start running with her instead of riding."

"I'm out of breath just watching her. She's getting too good for me. Do you want to try?"

Hansen, who was one of Chenna's favorites, had been an Olympic sprinter eight years ago. He'd not won any medals, but he'd come close. And the main thing was that he had made the U.S. Olympic team. Everyone on the detail was proud of him.

"I wouldn't make it one lap," Chenna radioed. "Bring her in, cook's got lunch ready to go."

"Roger that," Hansen said. He sped up alongside Lundgren, who broke off and angled over to Deborah.

The President's daughter slowed down, and seemed to stumble as if she had trouble concentrating on talking and running at the same time. But then she looked over to where Chenna was standing, gave a wave, and bounded across the track, this time running flat-out.

Chenna was used to the girl's athletic abilities; she'd watched them develop. But someone seeing the President's daughter for the first time would have reason to be nervous. Deborah had Down syndrome, and like many people with that handicap she was double-jointed. Watching her run was like watching a Raggedy-Anne doll; her arms and legs flew in every direction as if she was going to crash and land in a jumbled heap. But she never did. She was as surefooted as a young gazelle, and under Lundgren's tutelage she had become a world-class athlete. She was expected to win Saturday's half-marathon, or at least place in the top three or four out of a field of fifteen hundred runners.

Charlie McGivern, the horse master, came out of the barn

and lit his pipe. Chenna caught the movement out of the corner of her eye and turned slightly to see who it was as her right hand headed automatically toward her pistol in a shoulder holster.

He was used to Secret Service agents around the place. He waved.

Chenna grinned and waved back. Charlie was one of the good ones. His wife had died a few years ago and he had nobody, so he doted on the President's daughter whenever she came to visit. He'd even made a special saddle for her with her initials carved into the left and right fenders.

He watched Deborah run for a moment or two, Lundgren and Hansen following her, shook his head and went back into the barn. Chenna knew what he was thinking, and sometimes she had to agree with him. Being a sitting President's daughter had to be tough. It was no life for a kid, and yet Deborah thrived. She had friends who loved her and she was protected every single moment of every single day.

"Chenna," she cried with total joy, her arms wide open. She grabbed Chenna, who was short but solidly built, on the run with a tremendous hug and easily lifted her off the ground. Everything the girl did was with overflowing enthusiasm. It was one of the reasons that Chenna loved her assignment.

"You're getting strong," Chenna said, laughing.

"I eat my Wheaties," Deborah bubbled. "Did you see me running?"

"I did, and I can't get over the improvement. You're really getting fast."

"I can't keep up with her," Hansen admitted. "And that's a fact."

"I'm very proud of her," Lundgren agreed. "But the best part is that she's got even more potential. Look out, Ferrari!"

Deborah giggled in pure joy and clapped her hands. It was a daily ritual they went through, but none of them minded because of the utter happiness it gave her.

"Okay, gotta run some more now," she said, jumping up and down to keep loose. Sweat covered her face, but she didn't seem to notice.

"Lunch first," Lundgren said, handing Deborah a towel. "Then we're going to do a little resistance training in the gym, and afterwards laps in the pool."

"Can I run later?"

Lundgren looked to Chenna for approval.

"Maybe for an hour," Chenna said. "But then you'll have to get ready for dinner. You're going to be with your parents tonight in town."

Deborah immediately calmed down. "I think I'll wear the blue dress tonight. And the black heels and pearls."

Chenna, who was a tomboy, shook her head. "That's going to be up to your mom."

Deborah smiled knowingly and nodded. "I think it'll be the blue dress," she said with confidence. "And right now lunch sounds good."

CIA Headquarters

McGarvey walked across the hall to the DO's conference room at two in the afternoon. He had managed to pull together what information they had so far on bin Laden's compound and his probable movements in the past two months since he'd left Afghanistan. But if they were going to mount an operation to take him out they would have to know a lot more. For instance: They knew that he was never without guards, but almost nothing was known about them; how they were selected, where they came from. If they were going to find a way to get to bin Laden it might have to be through one of his guards. They also had to know more about his communications; who he talked with and how. They needed to know who was coming to see him on a regular basis, and what they were probably talking about. It was possible that he and the NIF had had a falling out, and maybe he could be gotten to through the Sudanese government. They needed to know where his wives and children were staying; who shopped for his groceries and who prepared his meals; where his water came from, and if there was a possibility of poisoning it. Assassinations were not always accomplished with a bullet to the brain.

It was a far cry from teaching at Milford, he told himself. Voltaire would probably have understood what he was trying to do, though the philosopher would have wondered what might become of a man who tried to stamp out evil by doing evil deeds himself. McGarvey had been asking that question all of his life.

"Good afternoon, Dick," McGarvey said. Surprisingly Adkins was the only one here so far.

"I told everybody else two-fifteen. I wanted to talk to you first," Adkins explained.

"I should have brought you in this earlier, sorry about that, but I had a lot of thinking to do. The general's not real happy, but he can't see any other way out either."

"Well, you've got everybody's attention. Considering the information you've been asking for, the word is already out. But nobody is disagreeing with you—at least not in principle," Adkins assured him. "The problem is going to be the trigger man."

"I'm going to set up shop in Riyadh," McGarvey said.

"Right," Adkins said. "I can't imagine that the general went along with that."

"I'm just going out there to make sure that Jeff Cook gets the word. He knows what resources he has on the ground."

Adkins gave him a wan smile and shook his head. "Somehow I find that hard to believe. So will everyone else. Beating Van Buren on the fencing strip is one thing, but going back out in the field banged up the way you are is another."

"We might not have to send any of our own people," McGarvey said. He knew that this was the kind of reaction he would get. "If we can lure him to a meeting somewhere in Yemen, just across the border, Saudi intelligence can put up an operation to grab him."

"That might work," Adkins said after a moment's thought. "But he's survived for too long to fall for anything easy. Whatever the meeting is about, and especially whoever it's with, will have to be damned convincing."

"I agree," McGarvey said. "Assuming that Turabi and the NIF are having some sort of a dispute with bin Laden it could be about the bomb. I mean that's not such a leap of imagination. Maybe they think it's over the top. Too extreme right now, especially with the moderates in Iran."

"Okay," Adkins agreed with some uncertainty.

"We're guessing that the bomb went through Pakistan, possibly out of Karachi, maybe by ship or by plane."

"That's a possibility we've looked at, Mac. But we haven't come up with a thing. Hell, we don't really have anything here except speculation."

"But it's possible," McGarvey pressed the point.

Adkins nodded.

"Okay, so Pakistan has its own troubles with us right now over the nuclear question and over their new military government, so they can't afford to upset us. If the ISI asks for the meeting on neutral ground in Yemen to promise bin Laden that they'll give him anything he wants providing he turns over the bomb to them, he'll come." ISI, or Interservice Intelligence, was the Pakistani intelligence agency.

"What's to stop him from picking up the telephone and calling them, besides his paranoia?"

"We do, from Riyadh. We'll leak the word that we've redirected our southern India Jupiter satellite into position over the Sudan." Jupiter was the program to closely monitor Indian and Pakistani communications because they had gone nuclear.

"Do you think that if he's in custody or dead, that it'll stop Bahmad from going ahead with whatever plan they hatched?"

"I don't know, Dick," McGarvey said. He sat down. "We've had no luck finding him or the bomb, and assuming we can get through this weekend in one piece, maybe an end run will be the only practical thing to do."

"That's assuming the Saudis will want to announce that they've finally caught bin Laden," Adkins pointed out. "There'd be a lot of repercussions against them and us. Most of the Islamic world would be up in arms."

"They are anyway, Dick." McGarvey shook his head. "No matter how this thing turns out we're going to end up being the bad guys. And that's just the way it is."

TWENTY-SIX

Los Angeles

It was a few minutes past 10:30 A.M. when Bahmad entered the Frémont Building just off Pershing Square. He was dressed conservatively in a blazer, gray slacks and club tie, and carried a thin attaché case. He'd recolored his hair salt-and-pepper gray.

He took the elevator to the eighteenth floor offices of Omni Resource Financing, Ltd. "Gordon Guthrie to see Mr. Sanchez," he told the pretty receptionist. He handed her his card.

"Do you have an appointment this morning, sir?" the young woman asked cooly. "Mr. Sanchez is in conference at the moment."

"No appointment, luv," Bahmad said. "But if you'll just give him my card, he'll see me."

The receptionist picked up the telephone and pressed a button. "Luis," she said and she hung up. A moment later a young Hispanic man, very sharply dressed, came out, took the card, glanced at Bahmad and went back inside.

Bahmad smiled. "Have you worked for Mr. Sanchez very long?"

"Yes, sir. Would you care for a cup of coffee?"

"No thank you. I won't need more than a minute or two of his time."

She gave him a smirk and turned back to a pile of mail that she had been sorting. Bahmad drifted over to a very nice Picasso print on the textured wall, but when he got closer he saw that it wasn't a print after all, it was an original. He looked around the large, very well furnished reception area. Six other paintings ranging from a Gainsborough to a Warhol, all originals, hung on the walls with absolutely no sense of coordination or theme. But then he supposed it was to be expected. Emilio Sanchez had no class but he headed the largest Mexican heroin/cocaine cartel in history so he had plenty of money. Unlike the Colombian drug lords who operated out of jungle fortresses and seldom took the chance to travel far from their safe havens because they were afraid of being captured, Sanchez conducted his affairs out in the open here in Los Angeles as a respected, if flashy, businessman. He had his financial fingers into everything from real estate to offshore oil exploration, and from Silicon Valley high-tech companies to portfolios of blue chip stocks.

All of it was a front for a highly sophisticated money laundering operation that no government in the world had uncovered yet. Sanchez himself had been nothing more than a small-time gangster in Mexico City until eight years ago when bin Laden's people had sniffed him out, and set him up in business here.

Since then he'd become a godless, arrogant bastard filled with self-importance, but he was getting the job done. In the last three years alone more than two and a half billion dollars had passed through Omni Resource Financing, and the next three years had promised to bring more of the same. Until now, Bahmad thought. In a few days everything would change, and there would be no going back for any of them.

"Mr. Guthrie," the receptionist called.

Bahmad turned and gave her another smile. "Yes?" Luis stood respectfully at the open door, and the receptionist's demeanor had changed from one of dismissal to one of respect.

"Mr. Sanchez will see you now, sir."

"Thank you," Bahmad said. He followed the young man down a broad, thickly carpeted hall, more originals on the walls, past several large offices in which a lot of people were very busy at work, to a palatial corner suite of beautifully furnished offices with floor-to-ceiling windows that afforded a magnificent view looking east across the city toward the San Gabriel Mountains.

Emilio Sanchez, dark and dangerous looking, sat scowling on a leather couch by the windows, two men seated in chairs across a broad coffee table from him. One of them got up and came across the room, smiling.

"Welcome to Los Angeles, Mr. Guthrie," he said. "I'm Francisco Galvez, chief of corporate security." He looked like a cop, with dark eyes that seemed to miss nothing, square shoulders and a firm grip. The other man was very thin, almost emaciated, with a heavily pockmarked face. He wore thick glasses. He was smoking a cigarette and the ashtray in front of him was nearly half full. He seemed very nervous. Sanchez, on the other hand, was short, going bald, somewhat paunchy and seemed surpremely confident.

"You might be just the man I came to see," Bahmad said pleasantly.

Galvez who only knew that Bahmad worked for bin Laden, gave him a searching look, then brought him across the room where he introduced the thin man as their CFO Juan Zumarraga, and then Sanchez. Neither of them rose to shake Bahmad's hand, nor was he offered a seat.

"What can we do for you?" Galvez asked directly.

Good, Bahmad thought, there was to be no time for pleasantries. "I'll take just a moment of your time," he said, smiling politely. "Since this has nothing to do with your financial operations, Mr. Zumarraga can get the fuck out of here, and somebody can get me a beer." He glared at them. "Now."

He sat down in Galvez's chair, opened his attaché case and took out a map of the west coast of Baja California.

After a moment Sanchez nodded. Galvez went off to get the beer and Zumarraga got up and left. Bahmad marked the approximate position of the *Margo* on the map and handed it across the table to Sanchez. They had been told to expect him, but that had been a couple of months ago, before the missile raid on bin Laden's camp. A lot of attitudes had changed since then.

"She's a cargo ship northbound. I have to get aboard her sometime within the next twenty-four hours. Preferably tonight."

Sanchez glanced at the map, then handed it to Galvez who'd come back with the beer. "What's in it for us?" he asked.

Bahmad considered the question for a moment. "Your continued employment," he said. "You're doing an acceptable job, and we would like to keep it that way."

Sanchez was amused. "Things have changed. Maybe I will simply continue on my own. I have connections."

Bahmad considered that for a moment too, and then shrugged. He put the beer aside, took the map from Galvez and put it back in his attaché case. "Someone will be sent to assassinate you and your family. That will include your wife and children, as well as your mother and your young sister, Juanita."

Sanchez sat forward. "You fucking come here and threaten me?"

Bahmad spread his hands. "I'm merely the messenger from our friend," he said. "I have no part in his plans, Mr. Sanchez. Believe me, I am nothing more than what you might call a bagman. But it is important that I get aboard that ship very soon."

Sanchez was shaken, though he tried to hide it. He knew very well what bin Laden and his people were capable of. "How is Osama now?"

"I wouldn't know," Bahmad replied coldly.

Sanchez bit his tongue. He gave his security chief a questioning look.

"We could chopper Mr. Guthrie to Long Beach and fly him down to Rosario in the Gulfstream by three," Galvez said. "How far off shore is your ship?" he asked Bahmad.

"A hundred miles by now, I should think."

"Miguel could have him out there by dark in the Cigarette."

"Do it," Sanchez ordered. "Anything else?" he asked Bahmad.

"Forget that I was ever here," Bahmad said, rising.

CIA Headquarters

McGarvey tired easily, though he was getting better. His staff was putting together the mission parameters, and Dick Adkins would make sure that they stayed on track. McGarvey had his own agenda to work on this afternoon, and at the moment he didn't want any interference.

Killing bin Laden and getting away safely would be difficult but not impossible if the plans stayed dead simple. Put a committee on it and the first thing that would come up was proof that the mission could not succeed. One man could not do it on his own. The job would take a small army. But the logistics for such a strike would be impossible to keep simple. Look what had happened when Jimmy Carter tried to mount a rescue operation in Tehran. The project should be scrubbed.

And maybe we were already too late, Adkins had suggested after the staff meeting. Killing or arresting bin Laden could very well be a moot point if the bomb were to be detonated in the middle of the planning stage. *Then you'd better make it quick*, McGarvey had shot back sharply. Adkins was used to him by now, but McGarvey had seen that his remark had been over the top. It was too bad, but they had work to do to avert a disaster. He would apologize later.

Bin Laden was holed up in Khartoum, the troubled and complicated capital of a troubled and complicated country torn apart by almost continuous fighting. Its oil reserves were thought to be as vast as Saudi Arabia's. Religious factions were fighting each other. And the Iranian military was in Sudan in a very big way because of the strategic importance of the country. It had leases on military bases in Port Sudan and Suakin that ran until 2019, thousands of Iranian soldiers were in training on Sudanese soil and there was a powerful Iranian-funded radio station in Port Sudan that beamed Islamic propaganda to the entire region.

But the CIA also had a hand in Sudanese politics, something that McGarvey had only come to realize after he'd become deputy director of Operations. He was trying to extricate the Company from the morass, but it had become a Dennis Berndt pet project, and getting out was impossible for the moment. Money and arms were being funneled to the Sudan's People's Liberation Army of Christian Nilotes. They weren't doing much to change the nature of the politics over there, but they were a source of potential embarrassment to the U.S. It was something he'd tried to explain to the White House, but his arguments fell on deaf ears. Leave politics to the politicians, he'd been told.

There were any number of the SPLA's soldiers who could be pursuaded to try for a hit on bin Laden. McGarvey had seriously considered the possibility. But there wasn't one chance in a million that any of them would be successful, let alone survive the attempt. They were farmers turned amateur soldiers. They did not have the discipline, the equipment, the training or the dedication to carry out such an operation. They might be able to supply the shooter with a relatively safe haven after the kill, and possibly the means of getting him out of the country, but nothing else.

A detailed street map of downtown Khartoum was displayed on his computer monitor. The map was keyed to the National Reconnaissance Office's digital file of satellite photographs. He clicked on the vertical borders and brought them inward until they encompassed the block in which bin Laden's compound was located. He did the same with the horizontal borders, then clicked on the photoreconnaissance record. A menu came up showing more than a hundred shots, some of them infrared, of the area within the box, each marked with a date and time. He pulled up a series that had been taken over a five-day period starting two months ago, just after the missle raid.

It was too much to hope that one of the satellites might have caught bin Laden himself showing up, but he was looking for the same kinds of patterns he'd asked Rencke to look for. Was the traffic to the compund mostly from the outside, or were bin Laden or his people traveling out of the compound to attend meetings elsewhere in the city, or the region?

A big problem was that bin Laden had an inside track on the satellites' orbits. It could be someone on the inside of the NRO, or possibily even computer hackers who'd gotten into the system, found out what they wanted to know and then got back out, all without being detected by one of the new antihacker programs. Rencke thought that was a slim possibility at best. Actually figuring out what satellite would be overhead at any given time was fairly simple for someone who knew some mathematics and some rudimentary orbital mechanics. If you plotted a satellite's movements across the sky at night when it could be seen, a mathematician could predict where it would be at any given time. Thus whenever a photorecon satellite was overhead there seemed to be a sharp drop in traffic in the area around the compound.

Finding nothing in the first series of photographs, McGarvey narrowed the horizontal and vertical borders to box in nothing but bin Laden's compound. As before a menu came up showing a series of photographs that were taken in the past seven years since the compound was first identified as a possible bin Laden stronghold. The number of photographs was well over one thousand, practically speaking, a dead end for him, McGarvey thought.

Rencke came from Adkins's office unannounced. "You're not going to get anywhere like that."

McGarvey looked up, vexed that he was being interrupted. "Try knocking next time."

"I only meant that I've been over all those pictures. You already know what I came up with." It suddenly dawned on Rencke what McGarvey was really up to and his eyes widened. "Oh, wow, Mac, you can't be serious. Not after what you already went through."

"It has to be done."

"If you say so," Rencke said. He started hopping from one foot to the other. "But use somebody else."

"There isn't anybody."

"You mean that there's nobody you'd be willing to send on such a mission," Rencke countered.

McGarvey shook his head. "You might be beating a dead horse no matter what we do," he said. "Unless he comes out of his compound, or unless we can lure him out of it, he's going to stay pretty safe for the duration."

"That's about what I came up with, ya know. And it's different this time, not like the others."

He had McGarvey's attention. "What do you mean?"

"You don't have my search engines so it'd take you a long time to figure out what's happening. The last three times that bin Laden was in residence he didn't stay put. He traveled all over the place. He even flew over to London once. Tehran, Beirut, Tripoli, everywhere."

McGarvey turned to stare at his computer screen.

"He's hunkered down," Rencke said. "It means that he doesn't want to take any risks."

"Either that or he's too sick to travel now."

"In that case guys like Turabi and General al-Bashir wouldn't be showing up on his doorstep on such a regular basis." Lieutenant General Omar Hassan Ahmad al-Bashir was the president of Sudan and the leader of the National Salvation Revolutionary Council. "That's what I came to tell you. He's staying put for a reason. And the heavy hitters are coming to see him for the same reason."

"He's waiting for the bomb to go off, and they're trying to talk him out of it."

"Bingo," Rencke said without his usual enthusiasm. "It's just like you figured."

"Find the bomb, find Bahmad and keep the President and his family out of harm's way. We have the best people in the country working on it, but so far we've struck out." McGarvey looked up. "All we can do is keep trying. Starting this weekend in San Francisco."

"Don't forget Liz," Rencke said with feeling. "They tried to hurt her once, they might try again."

Rosario de Arriba, Mexico

At ten thousand feet the Baja California coast was little more than a hazy, pale brown slash against the deep, electric blue of the Pacific Ocean, but as they came in for a landing Bahmad could see the Rosario Marina where he would pick up his ride. It was very large and modern, but there were only a few boats tied up at the more than five hundred slips. The parking lot behind the restaurant-condominium complex was nearly empty too. A lot of the boats had to be out of fishing charters now, and the handful left were powerboats, all of them large and expensive.

"We've gotten some of the heavy hitters to sign up, but the flood hasn't started yet," the Gulfstream pilot Wayne Hansen observed. "The word'll get out."

Bahmad sat in the copilot's seat because he thought it might be possible to catch a glimpse of the *Margo* on the horizon. But they never flew that far off shore, and he did not direct the pilot to do so. He wanted to keep the need to know at an absolute minimum.

"Is this place new?" he asked.

"Opened last year. Sanchez built it. The man's a genius. He figured the marina would keep the *federales* busy watching his nighttime activities, and they'd be too distracted to pay attention to what he was doing during the day." Hansen clenched a small cigar still in its plastic wrapper in the corner of his mouth. "Smart."

"I couldn't agree more," Bahmad said.

They lined up for their landing, the afternoon very bright now, and Hansen lowered the flaps and came in slightly crabbed because of a crosswind. He was a very good pilot. "Should I wait for you?"

Bahmad shook his head. "You might as well go back to California."

"I hope you like fishing and drinking, 'cause there's not a hell of a lot more to do here yet."

Customs was perfunctory; they didn't even check his bags. Ten minutes after touching down he rode in an air conditioned shuttle over to the marina, where he was directed to *Aphrodite* near the end of B dock.

The boat was a black-hulled Cigarette of about fifty feet on the waterline. Long and low she looked very sleek. Bahmad knew something about this type of boat. He'd attended a meeting aboard one in Monaco about five years ago. Its low profile made it very difficult to detect by radar, its powerful engines could push it to speeds up to eighty knots if the sea conditions were correct, and if the engine compartment was properly insulated and the exhausts baffled and led below the waterline she could be extremely hard to detect even by infrared sensors. She could outrun just about anything that the Mexican or U.S. Coast Guards could put to sea.

According to the pilot *Aphrodite* was used almost exclusively for overnight and long weekend cruises that were arranged by Loves Unlimited, a swingers club from Los Angeles. In reality she was used to head off shore during the day and meet with another ship where she would take on several tons of heroin or cocaine. From there she would race north to the U.S. border, where she would drop the weighted containers about a mile or two off a deserted beach at a precise GPS location for later pickup.

A slender man wearing a baseball cap, brightly flowered

Hawaiian shirt and white shorts stood on the foredeck coiling up a thick power cord. He looked up as Bahmad approached. His eyes were dark, and there was a five- or six-day growth of whiskers on his angular face.

"Captain Fernandez?" Bahmad asked.

"Who wants to know?"

"I'm Gordon Guthrie. I believe that you are expecting me."

"Come aboard," the man said. He stowed the power cord in a locker, and directed Bahmad to the aft sun deck, then below through a smoked Lexan door.

Everything that Bahmad could see about the boat was first class, very expensively and professionally done. The hatches, the fittings, the ports, all of it was extremely heavy duty. If the entire boat had been custom built and outfitted this way, Bahmad thought, it would withstand a typhoon.

"He's here," the crewman said.

A huge, shirtless man with long black hair and a thick black beard, seated at the saloon table studying a chart, looked up. Thick black hair covered his chest, and lay in great patches on his shoulders and flanks. Even the backs of his hands were covered. He smiled, his teeth perfectly white.

"Señor Guthrie, here you are." He extended a hand, but Bahmad ignored it, cocking his head to listen. He thought he heard someone pounding on something below decks.

"Who else is aboard?"

"Besides Antonio here, no one else except for Hernando, who takes care of the engines." Fernandez's eyes narrowed. "What were you expecting?"

"A larger crew."

"We manage."

Bahmad laid his bag down, opened his attaché case, took out a Bank of Mexico, S.A. envelope and handed it to the captain. "I would like to hire you, your crew and this boat."

"We are already yours," Fernandez said. He opened the envelope and took out the bank draft. It took a moment for it to register and when it did he looked up surprised and very interested. "This is a lot of money."

"There will be a second draft for a further half million U.S. dollars when we're finished." Bahmad gave the captain a significant look. "Of course the exact nature of this transaction is strictly between us. It need never leave this boat."

"What do you want us to do?"

"Hijack a cargo ship."

"What about the crew?"

"There are seventeen officers and men, but two of the officers are mine. Most of the remainder of the crew won't know what's happening."

"Those that do?"

"We'll kill them."

Fernandez sat back. "What then?"

"You'll get your second check and you can come back here or go wherever you would like to go."

Fernandez looked at the bank draft again. "How do I know that this is legitimate?"

"Telephone the bank."

Fernandez nodded. "I think I'll do just that."

"Good. In the meantime I want to meet your other crew member, I want to see your radio equipment and I want something to eat. We have a busy night ahead of us."

M/V *Margo*
West of Isla San Martin

"This is unit two standing by on schedule. This is unit two standing by on schedule, over." Green was on the radio telephone, obviously waiting for a reply. The crewman normally on the bridge with him had gone below to fetch more coffee. Green had spilled his on the deck. Captain Panagiotopolous had been on deck checking the helicopter. When he came back inside he spotted the crewman and asked why he wasn't on the bridge. He stood now in the shadows of the chartroom just aft of the bridge, watching and listening.

"Unit one, this is unit two standing by on schedule, over."

Green was not getting the reply he wanted, and he was becoming frustrated. Something made him turn around and he spotted the captain, his face falling almost comically.

"How long have you been standing there, sir?"

Panagiotopolous came out into the light. "Long enough to want to know what the hell you're up to. What's this unit one and unit two stuff?"

"It's a company code. I was trying to contact my father."

Panagiotopolous glanced at the SSB radio attached to the overhead. It wasn't set to any of the company's frequencies. "You're lying, Green. Now I want to know what's going on here!"

"It's your off-watch," Green snarled. "You should have stayed in your quarters instead of coming here." He reached inside his jacket and pulled out a pistol.

Panagiotopolous, surprisingly light on his feet, was across the bridge in two steps and he batted the gun out of Green's hand. "You little shit. Pulling a gun on me."

Green stepped back and tried to hit Panagiotopolous in the head with the radio telephone handset. But the captain had been in his share of barroom brawls during his long service as a merchant mariner, and he knew all the tricks. He ducked like a boxer, slipped the blow and shoved Green hard enough against the radar console that the breath was knocked out of the first officer. Nevertheless Green tried to fight back, but he was outweighed by at least seventy-five pounds. Panagiotopolous slammed him against the console again, this time knocking the flight out of him.

The portside door swung open and Schumatz came in. He looked from Green to the captain in surprise. "Do you need some help, Captain?"

"Green pulled a gun on me."

Green tried to say something, but Schumatz was across the bridge in a few strides and he knocked the first officer to the floor. "I told you that I didn't trust the sonofabitch." He looked up. "What was the little pissant trying to do, sabotage the helicopter?"

"No. He was up here trying to call someone on the SSB."

"My father," Green croaked from where he was crouched on the floor still clutching the phone.

"That'll be easy enough to check," the captain said. "I'll call the company."

"It's the middle of the night over there," Schumatz pointed out. "Maybe we should wait until morning."

Panagiotopolous turned back to Green. "Why did you pull a gun on me?"

Green looked away defiantly. The captain snatched the telephone from him.

"Unit one, this is unit two, go ahead." There was nothing but the soft hiss of a dead frequency. He hung up the phone. "Put him somewhere secure. I don't want him sneaking up on me tonight and slitting my throat."

"I'll put him in the dry storage locker in the galley," Schumatz said. "He won't be bothering anyone. I'll get his gun."

"Just get him out of here, I'll take care of the gun," Panagiotopolous said.

"Do you want me to send Rudi up?" Rudi Gunn was the second officer.

"He's scheduled to come on at midnight. I'll stay until then," Panagiotopolous said. He looked at Green. "See if you can get anything out of him, Lazlo. Something is going on around here that I can't quite put my finger on."

CIA Headquarters

"I don't think so, Liz," McGarvey said.

"I'm sorry, Dad, but I'm not leaving until you see my point," his daughter said. It was seven and they were alone in his office. He'd known that she was bringing trouble by the look in her eyes and the set of her shoulders. Girding herself for a battle.

Yet what she wanted to do went way beyond the pale of her duties as a CIA case officer, even in this instance in which she had so much personally at stake. Elizabeth had almost lost her life on the golf course. It was just luck that McGarvey had gotten there in time to spot the van heading out onto the fairway and recognize it for what it was. Just blind luck that he was there to break up what would have been a good hit. Both shooters had been heavily armed and both were well motivated. Since Elizabeth had been cut off from her weapon, she'd done the only thing left open to her, and that was to run. But it was exactly the wrong thing to do. The terrorists had herded her and her mother into a killing ground and would have finished the job if Liz hadn't gotten to her father's gun.

Now she wanted to step up to the plate again; deliberately put herself into harm's way. He was proud of her and angry with her at the same time. And vexed too. *Goddammit, nothing was ever simple.* But she had a point and he knew it.

"I'm going to your mother's," he told her. "I need something to eat and a few hours' sleep. You can ride down with me to my car."

"Good, maybe Dick can talk to you—"

"This has nothing to do with my driver," McGarvey said. "You're an intelligence officer, not a Secret Service bodyguard."

"But I know her, Dad," Elizabeth said.

McGarvey stopped. He tried to work out where she could possibly have met the President's daughter. It was impossible, he told himself. They came from two different worlds.

"What are you talking about, Liz?" he asked her.

"I've been doing my homework on her and Sarah bin Laden," she replied. She looked away for a moment and shook her head. "We're all cut out of the same cloth, you know."

"That doesn't make any sense."

"It does! We're about the same age, our fathers are, for better or worse, important men and we all have handicaps. Sarah couldn't have any kind of a normal life because there was a price on her father's head and they were stuck in the mountains. Deborah has Down syndrome. And I—" Her lower lip quivered.

"And you what, Liz?"

She looked up into his face, searching, as if she was looking for an answer. "I want to be just like you, Dad. I want to follow in your footsteps, but I can't. I can't."

"There's nothing wrong with that, sweetheart."

"But I wanted it all my life," she said. "And now I'm falling in love with Todd, and he wants me to get out of the Company. My mother and father want me to quit. Somebody is trying to kill me. And I'm scared." She was appealing to her father for help that he could not give her. "But Sarah was scared too, and so would the President's daughter be if she knew what was going on. It's why I have to be with her until we stop the bastard."

"I can't."

"You have to, Dad. It's what we do for a living."

"The Secret Service is watching her. Twenty-four hours a day. She can't make a move without them seeing it."

"That's the difference. They're *watching* her. I want to go out there and be *with* her. She deserves at least that much from us, don't you think?"

McGarvey nodded after a long time, and he never suspected how much pain such a simple gesture could bring him. "Take Todd with you, okay?"

"Okay."

New York City

"His name is Gordon Guthrie," Cheryl Cook said in the main saloon of *Papa's Fancy*. She was distraught. "But I don't know where he came from. England, maybe."

Jim Lane, NYPD gold shield detective, looked up from his notebook with interest. "Why do you think that it was this guy and not one of the crew, or maybe a burglar caught in the act?"

Cheryl had come down to New York to be with Captain Walker for a few days. They had been having an affair over the past six months, and although she knew that it would never come to anything, she did love him in a way. They were supposed to meet at the Plaza, but when he didn't show up she came over to see what was going on. She still couldn't believe what she had walked into. She looked over to where she had found his body. She could still smell the foul odor of his death lingering on the air.

"The captain got along real well with the crew, but Mr. Guthrie showing up all of a sudden was creepy."

"Creepy how?"

"We were in the middle of our annual haul-out when Mr. Richter, the owner, ordered us to drop everything and get up to Washington to meet him."

"What's so creepy about that?" Lane's partner, Nicole Nickles, asked.

Cheryl shivered. "Just the way he came aboard, smiling all the time. But there was something wrong with his eyes. Like he had X-ray vision, or something. Whenever he was around I felt like I wasn't wearing any clothes."

"Where'd he go?" Lane asked. The young woman had made the initial 911 call, and until the ME had taken a look at the body and found the probable cause of death, she'd been a chief suspect.

"The day after we got back from Bermuda he told us that he was done with the yacht for a couple of weeks. He packed up everything except the aluminum case and left."

"You already told us about that. But the case isn't on the boat now. Could he have come back and got it?"

"Anything's possible," she admitted. "But if you find him, you'll have the captain's murderer. I'd bet anything on it." She lowered her head and began to cry. "Damn."

Nicole put a hand on the girl's shoulder. "We'll find him.

Guaranteed," she said. "But we're going to need your help. Is that okay?"

Cheryl looked up and nodded.

"We're going to need a better description of him. You can work with a police artist to come up with a drawing of his face. And then you can look at some photographs. Are you up for that tonight?"

"Whatever it takes to catch him."

"Okay, just hang in there. We have a few things to take care of here, and then we'll drive you downtown."

The yacht was filled with evidence technicians who were going over everything with a fine-toothed comb. So far they hadn't come up with much except that the man identified as Guthrie had fine, light brown hair, which they found on the pillows in his cabin.

Lane turned back to the girl. "By the way, why did Captain Walker pick last night to check on the yacht?"

"I think Mr. Richter asked him to do it."

"Any idea why? I mean was this something that normally happened when the crew was away for a while?"

"Not often, but sometimes. Especially if there was a storm, or something like that."

Lane pocketed his notebook. This case wasn't going to be as open and shut as some of the ones they got. In fact he had a gut feeling that it wouldn't even be theirs for very long. He'd shared his feeling with Nicole and she agreed with him. A federally documented yacht just returned from a long trip outside the U.S. A suspect who might not be an American. An absentee owner. No apparent motive. And worst of all the lack of fingerprints. Ed Bowser, their chief evidence technician, said that they were finding only one set of fingerprints throughout the boat, plus a second set that was probably the young woman's confined to a few spots in the main saloon.

"If you want my best guess, I'd say that someone who knew what they were doing wiped down the entire boat. The prints we're finding will turn out to be the captain's."

"He came back to check on the empty boat, so what exactly did he check?" Lane asked.

"That's the best part. Besides here in the saloon and up on the bridge, the only other area that we're finding prints are in the guest stateroom. And they're all over the place in there. Looks like the good captain came in, checked something on the bridge and then tossed the one cabin."

Looking for an aluminum case, Lane thought. He took Nicole aside. "Let's get a dog over here to sniff out what we might be missing."

"Drugs?"

"Could be," Lane said. "In the meantime I'm going to put what we have so far on the wire, see if Guthrie's name turns up anyplace else. And we'll get it over to the feds. Who knows, we might even catch a break."

Nicole chuckled. "Yeah, right."

CIA Headquarters

Rencke left his office a little before midnight and walked down the corridor to the bathroom surprised that everything was so quiet. When he was working he sometimes forgot about time. All that mattered was the job at hand. And so far he was coming up empty-handed and it puzzled him.

He had a half-dozen computer search programs going simultaneously, searching the Net and every database he could think of for a number of basic bits of information: bin Laden's whereabouts and movements, Ali Bahmad's whereabouts and movements and the bomb's whereabouts and movements, plus anomalies in the entire investigation. The bits and pieces that didn't seem to fit into any pattern; the stray telephone conversation, the odd satellite shot, the interrogation of a prisoner somewhere that turned up something that seemed out of place.

Anything. Anything at all.

Back in his office he telephoned Lieutenant Ritter at NSA. "Hiya, kiddo, anything new?"

"Nothing from the Rome exchange," she answered. "We're checking across the board with the vorep upgrades. If bin Laden talks to anybody by phone or radio we'll know about it."

"He's still holed up in Khartoum, or at least we think he is, so you can concentrate there," Rencke said, dismally. "What about the programs I gave you to use?"

"Otto, if I'd gotten them from anybody but you, I'd have to say that they're worthless." She sounded just as frustrated as he did. "Whoever knows anything about the bomb, they're keeping quiet about it."

"Nothing out of Afghanistan, maybe Iran or Yemen, or even Saudi Arabia?"

"Zippo."

Rencke ran a hand across his eyes. "Anyway, thanks, Johanna. Keep on truckin'."

"One of them is bound to make a mistake somewhere. We'll catch up with them."

"Yeah," Rencke said, and he hung up. He sat back and closed his eyes, not even interested in having a Twinkie at the moment. Maybe he was losing his touch. Maybe he could no longer see the colors. Maybe he'd used up his edge. It happened to everybody sooner or later, even to McGarvey, or so the DO's gossip mill was saying.

Fifteen years ago when he was trying to work out an exceedingly complex CIA computer program system that involved multidimensional bubble memories and intricate mathematics, he hit on the notion of thinking of systems as colors. A shade of lavender, for example, brought into his head the LaPlace transformations. Red was for curl, blue for spin, and more involved melding of colors were for tensor calculus matricies, quantum mechanical statements, chaos equations and a couple of new fields that an Indian mother of three had come up with that only a handful of people in the world understood or had even heard about.

The color this time was orange. He opened his eyes and looked at his monitors, all of them presenting steady streams of data, diagrams and pictures. The information was useless, less than useless without the one piece that would start tying the bits together. Even the universe had been created one pair of particles at a time after the Big Bang. For a minute or two he thought about going home to get some sleep. But he didn't want to leave because he would have to admit that he had failed. He picked up the phone and called Louise Horn next door in the NRO.

"Tell me yes, and make me the happiest man on the planet," Rencke said, trying to keep it light.

"I'd love to, Otto," she said. "But nothing's changed. They're all bedded down over there."

A faint spark stirred in Rencke's gut. "It's only seven in the evening in Khartoum. Nothing's stirring right now? Not even a mouse? All day, maybe?"

"What are you getting at?" Louise said, but then she stopped herself. "Oh, I see," she said. "No one has been in or out of the compound in the past twenty-four hours."

"Not so much as a delivery van?"

"Nothing," Louise said. "What's going on?"

"They're bunkering. Means the battle is going to start any second," Rencke explained excitedly. "If anything moves in or around the place, and I do mean *anything*, I want to know about it right then."

"Will do—"

"Gotta go," Rencke told her. He broke the connection and called Johanna Ritter again. "I think whatever's going to happen is going down any minute. Within a few hours maybe, but certainly before the end of the weekend. Have there been any calls whatsoever to the compound?"

"I don't know. We've just been looking out for bin Laden or Bahmad."

"I want you to start monitoring every single call, in or out of there, and get them over to me immediately."

"Okay, I'm sending the heads-up right now," Johanna said.

One of his computer programs began to chirp. The screen went pale orange. Rencke broke the connection and slid over to the monitor. The screen was split. On the left was a FBI advisory and APB from its New York office. Gordon Guthrie, a Caucasian male, early to mid-forties, five-eight, a hundred fifty pounds, thining light brown hair, brown eyes, no distinguishing marks, possibly a British citizen, was wanted for questioning in a homicide aboard the yacht *Papa's Fancy* docked at the Hudson River boatyard, New York City. No fingerprints. Police artist drawing to follow.

On the right was the reason his search engine had picked out the bulletin and went orange. *Papa's Fancy* had been docked at the Corinthian Yacht Club here in Washington, and had cleared customs for departure to Bermuda the *day after* the Chevy Chase attack.

Rencke pulled up the artist's sketch and grinned like a kid at Christmas. "Oh, boy," he said. "Ali Bahmad. Gotcha!"

TWENTY-SEVEN

Aphrodite
Southwest of Ensenada, Mexico

"There she is," Captain Fernandez shouted over the terrific noise.

A very strong radar return was showing up on the twenty-mile ring. "How do you know that it's the right ship?" Bahmad demanded. It was getting too late to make stupid mistakes.

"She's heading in the right direction, she's going at the right speed, she's the right size and she's the only fucking ship out here, amigo," the captain replied tightly. He wasn't used to being questioned.

They were alone on the *Aprhodite*'s open bridge; the

captain at the wheel, Bahmad seated next to him and the radar screen between them. It was midnight, and the other two crewmen, Antonio Morales and Hernando Mendoza, were below. They'd been drinking beer for the past four hours since they'd left Rosario, but the captain assured Bahmad that when the time came they would function with their *cojones* intact. The seas were fairly calm, but the motion and noise aboard the speedboat slamming through the water in excess of sixty miles per hour was tremendous.

Before they'd left the dock, Bahmad had finally made SSB radio contact with the *Margo*. Green had foolishly allowed himself to be discovered by the captain and locked up. It might necessitate eliminating the entire crew immediately rather than later.

"Can the three of us operate the ship?" he'd asked his other contact aboard.

"With all the automatic systems it'll be no sweat. We can set the autopilot to work with the GPS navigators and thread a needle ten thousand miles away without touching a control."

"Very well."

"The port quarter ladder will be down starting at midnight, and I'll block the radar sets aft."

"What if one of the crew spots us?" Bahmad asked.

"I'm on top of it. Can you bring some extra muscle to do the job tonight? Someone we can trust?"

"Yes."

"See you soon, then. *Insha'Allah*."

"*Insha'Allah*," Bahmad muttered. He switched off the SSB and smiled.

"Is there trouble?" Captain Fernandez asked. He'd heard only half the conversation. He and the other two were seated at the saloon table while Bahmad made the call from the nav station.

"Nothing that we can't handle, providing you're willing to carry out your orders."

"For a million dollars I'd screw the Pope."

"Nothing quite that drastic," Bahmad assured him. He

glanced over at the other two men. Morales, the man he'd first met on deck, was staring at him and Bahmad made a mental note to keep an eye on him. He'd done nothing out of the ordinary, however, since they had left the dock and slipped out of the harbor. But there was something about the man that didn't sit right with Bahmad.

They were one hundred miles off shore now, and not even the strong lights of Ensenada were visible on the horizon. The stars were out, but there was no moon. The night was so dark that Bahmad could not tell where the sky ended and the sea began.

"We're to make our approach from the port quarter," he shouted to the captain. "Their radars will be blinded from the rear, and a boarding ladder will be lowered for us."

"I don't want to run into a hornet's nest. Are you sure that everything aboard that sonofabitch is secure?"

"I'll go up the ladder first. If something goes wrong you can take off."

Captain Fernandez eyed Bahmad with suspicion. "I'll leave Antonio with my boat."

"As you wish, but we'll need to arm ourselves with the MAC 10s."

"What kind of trouble are you expecting?"

"None, if you do as you're told. But we need to take care of the crew. *All* of them, except for my two officers. There'll be an extra two hundred fifty thousand in it for you. *Just* for you, and not your crew."

"Fifteen men," the captain shouted.

"That's right," Bahmad replied. "Do you have a problem with it?"

The captain looked away for a minute, obviously wrestling with his conscience. Bahmad found it amusing, especially considering the business Fernandez was in.

"I have no problem," the captain finally said.

M/V *Margo*

Lazlo Schumatz slipped into the silent galley and waited a full minute in the darkness. The cook and his assistants were not usually down here at this hour of the night, though at sea some men got restless and wanted something to eat. But not tonight. He made his way across the dining area and through the kitchen to the pantry. He unlocked and opened dry storage locker A.

"I was starting to wonder how long you were going to leave me in here," Green said angrily. He stormed out of the locker.

"If you hadn't been so stupid you wouldn't have been caught." Schumatz handed him a 9mm Glock pistol. "It's just about time."

"Did you make contact?" Green demanded. He followed Schumatz out of the galley and aft.

"A few hours ago." Schumatz opened the steel outer door to the port rail and checked the after deck. Sometimes crewmen came back here to smoke. But the deck was deserted now. "I think that we're going to do the entire crew tonight."

"The captain's mine," Green shot back. He had been nursing an anger against Panagiotopolous ever since the storm in the Arabian Sea.

Schumatz nodded. They were going to be using the new navigational equipment installed during the layover sooner than he'd expected. But killing the crew now would simplify matters. They wouldn't have to try to hide Guthrie for two days.

They went out on deck. Green opened the rail gate and secured it as Schumatz unlashed the boarding ladder, opened the control box and activated the small motor that lowered it.

Aphrodite

The *Aphrodite* pulled alongside the *Margo*'s port quarter. Captain Fernandez matched speeds and timed the approach so perfectly that Mendoza, waiting on the bow had no trouble grabbing the boarding ladder skimming just off the surface of the water. He tied them off.

Morales took over the controls.

"Keep it steady, we won't be long," the captain shouted to him.

"What if there's trouble?"

"There won't be. Sonofabitch, don't take off with my boat and leave me behind."

"Don't worry, I haven't been paid yet," Morales said.

Fernandez grinned and slapped him on the shoulder. "There'll be plenty for all of us, amigo. Even enough for you to buy your Ferrari."

M/V Margo

Bahmad, his MAC 10 drawn and at the ready, was first up the ladder. Schumatz and Green were waiting for him. They'd never met each other, but Bahmad recognized them from their dossiers. At first they were uncertain, but then Bahmad lowered his weapon. "So good of you to invite me aboard, gentlemen."

Schumatz guffawed and Green chuckled.

"May I presume that there have been no further problems?" Bahmad asked.

"Everything's quiet now," Schumatz assured him. "I just released Joseph from the lockup five minutes ago. The captain is in his cabin, and I convinced him not to call the company until later this morning, so we still have a few hours."

"Very good." Bahmad waved Fernandez and Mendoza

waiting below to come up. "Who is presently on the bridge?"

"Second Officer Gunn and an AB," Green said.

"That leaves twelve other crew."

"There's two in the engine room. Everybody else is in their rooms asleep or watching television. The next watch isn't scheduled until six."

Fernandez and Mendoza appeared at the head of the ladder and came aboard. Bahmad introduced them by first names only. They didn't shake hands, but they all looked at each other nervously.

"What's the plan?" Schumatz asked.

Bahmad had worked out this operation in precise detail, as he did all his operations. Leave nothing for chance, he'd always maintained, yet be ready for any contingency.

"If the captain were to call a meeting in the galley would everybody show up? Even the on-duty crew?"

"Of course," Schumatz replied.

"Take our two friends to the galley, turn on the lights and then hide yourselves," he told Green. "Stay out of sight unless the situation falls apart. I don't want the crew getting spooked seeing the three of you charging in with guns drawn."

"What about the captain?" Green asked.

"Lazlo and I will fetch him."

"Let's do it," Fernandez said. He wanted to get this business over with and be gone.

They all went inside. Green and the two drug runners went forward to the galley, while Bahmad and Schumatz took the stairs up eight decks to the captain's quarters aft of the chart room and bridge. Except for the throbbing noise of the engines the ship was as still as a tomb compared to the speed boat. But it was nothing as quiet as it would be an hour from now, Bahmad thought.

So far the only real glitch had been in New York aboard *Papa's Fancy*, but he had a hunch that even that was going to work out to his benefit in the end. Chevy Chase had already been forgotten, relegated to another section of his brain that was able to deal with failures by forgetting about them while at the same time learning from his mistakes. There would be no mistakes this time. He was sure of it.

Schumatz listened at the captain's door for a couple of moments. He looked up and shook his head.

"If he cries out will they hear it on the bridge?" Bahmad whispered.

"No."

Bahmad motioned for him to do it, and Schumatz knocked on the door.

"Captain, I have to talk to you. We have a problem." Schumatz tried the door but it was locked. "Captain?"

"Just a minute," Panagiotopolous said impatiently.

Bahmad stepped to the side. Schumatz held the pistol out of sight behind his right leg. The door came open and the captain was there, fully dressed, Green's pistol in his hand.

"What's this?" Schumatz stepped back in surprise, almost stumbling over his own feet.

Sensing that something was wrong, Panagiotopolous started to turn, but he was too late. Bahmad diverted the captain's gun with his left hand and jammed the barrel of the MAC 10 into the man's face.

"Your death at this moment would be pointless, Captain," Bahmad warned in a reasonable tone.

The captain tried to raise his pistol, but Bahmad tightened his grip and jammed the submachine gun harder against the man's cheek.

"I *will* kill you."

Panagiotopolous held himself in check for another second or two, but then came down. Bahmad took the pistol from his hand, thumbed the safety catch on and stuffed it in the belt of his slacks at the small of his back.

"What the hell, Lazlo. I trusted you."

Schumatz shook his head. "This has nothing to do with you."

"Who the hell is this bastard then, and what is he doing aboard my ship?"

"All in good time," Bahmad said. "First we're going to

assemble the crew and I'll make everything clear. But I want to assure you that we mean you absolutely no harm. If you cooperate this will all be over with by morning."

"Is Green one of yours too?"

"Yes. He's a little hotheaded, I'm afraid. But he will be reprimanded." Bahmad stepped aside and motioned for the captain to precede him. "I think the galley will do nicely for our meeting."

"I knew that something was wrong," the captain muttered. He led them to the end of the corridor and downstairs.

The lights were on in the galley dining room, otherwise it was deserted. Green and the others had to be hiding in the kitchen. There were four metal picnic-style tables attached to the deck, plus the head table for the officers. Bahmad sat down next to the captain at the head table and concealed his gun between them. The ship's interphone was on the bulkhead behind them.

"I would like you to call the crew now. That includes Mr. Gunn and the second man on the the bridge, the two in the engine room and the other ten who are off duty. I don't care what you tell them, but if you try to issue any kind of a warning I will kill you instantly, then we will hunt the rest of them down and kill them, after which we will sink this ship. On the other hand if you follow my instructions to the letter we'll simply lock you and your crew up, take what we have come for, which is only one very small package, and then leave."

"How will we free ourselves?"

"I've brought plastic explosives. We'll place a small charge on the door lock with a timer set for eight this morning. It will give us plenty of time to make our escape." Bahmad smiled sincerely. "Believe me, Captain, I don't want to kill anybody. There'd be no advantage in it for me."

Something dawned in the captain's eyes. "The helicopter is yours?"

"That's right," Bahmad said, "Mr. Green will be our pilot. All very neat, all very simple if you will cooperate."

The captain turned to Schumatz who had stuffed his pistol in his pants pocket and stood by the door. "Lazlo?"

"It's just like he says, Captain. Nobody's going to get hurt."

Panagiotopolous shook his head again as if he couldn't believe what was happening, but then reached back for the telephone and entered a three-digit number. "Attention all hands," his voice boomed throughout the ship. "Attention all hands, this is the captain. I want to see everybody in the galley on the double. That includes the bridge and engineering duty crews." He looked at Bahmad, and repeated the announcement. When he was finished he released the talk switch and hung up the phone. "Where's Green?"

"He'll be here in a minute," Schumatz said.

The phone buzzed and Panagiotopolous picked it up before Bahmad could stop him. "This is the captain."

Bahmad prodded him in the side with the gun.

"If there's no traffic within our twenty-five kilometer ring leave us on autopilot, make sure the alarm is set and the both of you get down here. Now."

The captain replaced the phone.

"Your bridge officer?"

"Yes. He's a conscientious man. He'll be along shortly."

"Then we'll wait."

Panagiotopolous gave Schumatz another baleful look. "You had this planned from the start, didn't you? Was it in Karachi, or was it even earlier than that?"

"That doesn't matter—"

"Goddammit, I want to know. If it started in Karachi then the company is involved."

"The company is not involved," Bahmad said. "But even if it was, it would make no difference."

"Yes it would," Panagiotopolous said. He suddenly looked old and tired. "It would to me."

The first of the crewmen showed up a minute later. "What's up, Mr. Schumatz?" he asked. He eyed Bahmad seated with the captain.

"Sit down, the captain wants to tell us something," Schumatz told him, and the crewman took a seat as others drifted in. Some of them were in bathrobes and had obviously been sleeping, while others were fully dressed and looked wide awake. The two from the engine room, their white coveralls dirty, came in, followed by Gunn and the able bodied seaman from the bridge.

"That's the lot," Schumatz said, closing the door.

The fourteen men assembled were curious, but none of them seemed alarmed or in the least bit suspicious until Bahmad prodded the captain to his feet with the MAC 10.

Several of them jumped up.

"Sit down or I shall kill your captain," Bahmad warned. The first few seconds of these kinds of situations were always the most dicey. Anything could happen if the crew acted in concert.

Some of the men turned in desperation to Schumatz who had pulled out his pistol. But he pointed his gun at them.

"Do as he says, gentlemen," Schumatz shouted. "Sit down! Now!"

Now they were confused, some of them frightened, others sullen, obviously looking for a way out. But they had lost the moment when they could have done something, and Bahmad smiled inwardly at this little triumph. In general people were like cattle.

"My name is not important," Bahmad said. "But with the help of Mr. Green and Mr. Schumatz I am taking over this ship for the next eight hours. We're going to lock you in the pantry dry storage area while we conduct our business. When we are finished you will be released unharmed. I give you my word. The last thing we want or need is a bunch of injured men. It's not why I'm here." Bahmad looked at them. There were a couple of men who were obviously potential troublemakers, but it was too late for them to put up any effective resistance, and he could see in their eyes that they were just realizing that fact now.

"At least stop the ship before you leave," the captain told Bahmad. "I don't want to run into anything."

"As you wish," Bahmad said. "You'll be a little cramped, I'm afraid, but it shouldn't be too bad for a few hours."

"Who the fuck are you trying to bullshit?" one of the crewmen demanded angrily. "You're going to kill us all."

"Why would we do such a thing?"

"You don't want any witnesses."

Bahmad smiled faintly. "If that were the case we would have killed those of you who were sleeping in your beds and taken the bridge and engine room first. It certainly would be a lot less messy than calling you all down here and shooting you dead."

The crewman had no answer for that and he said no more, but he was suspicious.

"On your feet, please," Bahmad instructed. They did as they were told with a lot of hesitation. But there was no leader among them and they didn't know where to turn or what to do. "I would like you to follow Mr. Schumatz, in single file please, to the dry storage locker. If anyone decides to try something, I will shoot the captain first and then turn my gun on you."

No one said a thing.

"Very well," Bahmad said. He nodded to Schumatz who walked into the kitchen and through to the pantry where he opened the heavy door into the large walk-in locker, then stepped aside, his pistol at the ready.

"What's this all about, Mr. Schumatz?" one of the younger crewmen asked. "Is it drugs?"

"You'll read all about it in the newspapers in a few days, Rudi," Schumatz said. "Now inside with you so nobody has to get their ass shot off."

"Well, I hope you rot in hell, you dirty prick," Rudi Gunn said, and he walked into the storage locker.

The captain was the last in and he turned to face Bahmad. "Eight hours?"

"Or less," Bahmad assured him. He motioned to Schumatz who swung the door shut, the lock dropping into place with a loud snap.

Bahmad turned around. "Joseph," he called.

Green, Fernandez and Mendoza came around the corner from the other side of the kitchen. Green's face was animated with excitement. "That was goddammed smooth," he said. He held his pistol in both hands, and he kept looking at the locker door. "Are we going to kill them now?"

"First things first. I want you to go up to the bridge and stay there for the time being. I'm going to have Lazlo stop the ship, but I want you to make sure that the autopilot is set and that we're on course, and make sure that no one has been trying to reach us by radio. From this point on we have to be on the watch for the U.S. Coast Guard."

"But I want—"

"I know, Joseph, but for now I need you on the bridge," Bahmad said soothingly. "Your time will come."

Green backed up and looked at the others, but then his head bobbed. "Okay, but when the time comes I want Panagiotopolous." He turned and left.

"I'll tend to the engines," Schumatz said.

"Give us an hour and then come up to the bridge, please."

Schumatz glanced at the locker door then left.

"Why are you stopping the ship?" Fernandez asked suspiciously. He was jumpy.

"We're going to set some explosives and sink her here."

Fernandez's eyes strayed to the locker door. "You're going to let them drown, huh?"

Bahmad shook his head. "Either finish the job, or walk away right now and we'll call it even."

Fernandez and Mendoza exchanged a look and Mendoza nodded. "I say kill them now."

"Sí," Fernandez said with some hestitation. He pulled the MAC 10's top-mounted bolt and he and Mendoza stepped apart directly in front of the locker door. When they were ready he nodded.

Bahmad unlatched the door, pulled it open and quickly got out of the way. Someone inside shouted something in desperation, but Fernandez and Mendoza opened fire, unloading their thirty-round magazines in a couple of seconds, immediately reloading and firing again.

The noise hammered off the steel bulkheads. Spent shells skittered hollowly like metal popcorn across the deck. And finally the screams and cries of the *Margo*'s crew subsided until Fernandez stopped shooting and stepped back.

"*Madre de Dios*," he said softly, and he crossed himself.

Everyone in the storage locker was down. Blood was splashed everywhere; on the overhead, the walls and boxes on the shelves, and lay in thick pools on the floor.

"Make sure that they're all dead," Bahmad said.

"You do it," Fernandez answered in disgust.

"Finish the job, Captain. It's what you were hired for."

Mendoza was excited. He reloaded and went to the locker door. He fired a couple of shots into the bodies, then a couple more. Fernandez joined him, reloading his gun, and he too fired into the bodies.

Bahmad raised his MAC 10 and fired a short burst, at least a half-dozen rounds catching the two drug runners in the backs of their heads. They were driven forward into the locker on top of the pile of bodies, none of which was moving any longer.

Bahmad stood for a long time listening to the relative silence, and waiting. The storage locker doorway had a raised lip so very little blood had gotten out into the pantry, only a few splashes here and there on the deck.

Finally the distant vibration of the engines died and he could feel the change in motion as the ship began to slow down.

He laid the MAC 10 aside for a moment to push Fernandez's and Mendoza's legs all the way inside the locker and close the door, then went back through the galley to the main athwartship corridor. A radio played music from somewhere, barely audible. It sounded Latin. A woman was singing. Other than that, the ship was very quiet.

Outside, he looked over the rail. The *Aphrodite*'s bridge was deserted, and the boat wallowed at the end of her tether, her engines idling with pops and throaty rumbles in neutral. Everything had gone smoothly to this point, but he smelled trouble now.

He scrambled down the ladder to the speedboat and hopped nimbly aboard the foredeck. He nearly lost his footing on the slowly pitching deck, but then regained his balance and sprinted aft to the open bridge. When the *Margo*'s engines had been shut down, Morales had dropped the *Aphrodite*'s engines into neutral and since he was no longer needed to tend the helm he'd gone below. But why? To do what? Get a beer?

Bahmad dropped down on the deck between the curving windscreen and the sleek radar bridge just as Morales, a pistol in his hand, came from below.

"What the fuck—" he said, rearing back.

Bahmad calmly raised his MAC 10 and fired a burst into the man's chest, driving him backward down into the main saloon with enough force that he broke his spine on the edge of a cabinet before landing dead in a bloody heap.

One step at a time. It was all coming together. He could see with perfect clarity each step he had taken from the mountains in Afghanistan months ago when he had first devised his operation, here and now to this point. There wasn't much left to do except deliver the package at the correct time and place, and history would be his.

Careful not to step in the gore, Bahmad went below and let his eyes sweep the cabin. There were several empty beer cans on the table, an empty speed-draw holster on the cushioned setee and a bullet-resistant vest lying next to it. It was curious that the man hadn't taken the time to put it on if he thought there was going to be trouble, unless he'd been interrupted. The SSB radio was on and still tuned to the frequency that he'd used to contact the *Margo*. Nothing was different, and yet he sensed something; something just outside of his awareness, something he couldn't quite put his finger on. He was missing something that was possibly important and it irritated him.

He glanced at Morales's body, then went forward to the head where he shot out the seacocks for the toilet and sink.

Water immediately began gushing into the boat in two-inch streams.

He did the same for the seacock serving the galley sink, and the seacocks for the aft stateroom toilet, sink and shower sump.

Already the water was a couple of inches above the floor boards, the bilge pumps unable to keep up. Bahmad opened several portholes so that the boat would sink easier without trapped air, then went up to the open deck, closing and latching the door.

Aft on the sundeck, he pulled up the two large teak floor-boards exposing the slowly idling engines nestled in their spotless, silver insulated compartments. They were huge ten-cylinder supercharged diesels and needed a lot of water for cooling. Two hoses, each of them five inches in diameter, sucked raw water from the sea through strainers and directed the flow to the massive heat exchangers. Bahmad reloaded and shot both hoses completely apart. Instantly two streams of seawater with the strength of firehoses began rushing into the engine compartment, flooding the air intakes. Within seconds the diesels sputtered and died.

Bahmad calmly climbed back up onto the foredeck and made his way to the bow. The boat was already down six inches on her lines. He jumped across to the *Margo*'s boarding ladder, then took out his stiletto and cut the tether holding the powerboat.

The *Aphrodite* slowly began to drift away, her bow much higher now than her sinking stern. She would be completely gone in minutes.

Topsides Bahmad found the control for the boarding ladder and brought it up, secured it in its cradle and closed the rail gate.

The last he saw of the *Aphrodite* before he went inside, she was fifty yards away, her aft deck awash, her bow rising up at a sixty-degree angle.

U.S. Coast Guard Station
San Diego, California

"Coast Guard Station San Diego, Petty Officer Wickum." the young man answered. It was 2:00 A.M. and he'd just started on his fifth cup of coffee this shift to keep awake. Absolutely nothing worth a shit was on television tonight.

"This is Special Agent Susan Ziegler with the Drug Enforcement Agency, let me talk to your OD," she said urgently.

"Yes, ma'am, stand by." Wickum slid over to the duty officer's door. The young ensign, his feet propped up was reading a copy of *Playboy*. "Got a woman from the DEA on one for you, sir. Sounds stressed."

The OD put the magazine down and picked up the phone. "Ensign Rowley, may I help you, ma'am?"

"I'm Special Agent Susan Ziegler, DEA. I'm about a hundred miles south of you, just outside Ensenada. Is your MECODIR program up and running?"

"Ma'am—"

"I'm on your list, Ensign, look me up. Star-seventeen-bright. Do it quick because you might have a problem coming your way."

"Stand by," Ensign Rowley said, he put her on hold. "We've got a possible MECODIR request," he told Wickum. "Pull it up while I make sure she's who she says she is." MECODIR was a Message Content and Direction program that was new to the Coast Guard. Receivers scanning millions of frequencies automatically monitored radio transmissions from seaward around the clock, recording their content and the direction they came from for review by the Coast Guard itself along with a host of other law enforcement and intelligence-gathering agencies. It was a NASA-designed program that had gone operational six months ago. Messages were stored digitally for up to one month. If they were not retrieved by then they were automatically erased. Maydays, or other standard distress calls, kicked off alarms so that human operators could intervene.

Susan Ziegler's name and the proper identifier code were listed in the authorized users manual and he reconnected with her.

"Yes, ma'am, we're up and running."

"We received a partial message that we think came from one of our deep cover agents about twenty minutes ago. Since then there's been nothing. We think that he's aboard a fifty-foot speedboat called *Aphrodite* somewhere off shore. We're not sure how far out he was, but we picked him up on fourteen three-ten at oh-one-forty hours on a relative bearing of two-five-four degrees. Puts him a little south of west from us."

Wickum slid back to his console and brought the ME-CODIR program up on his monitor.

Ensign Rowley could see him on the other side of the glass partition. A couple of the other night-duty operators drifted over to see what was going on. "Okay, ma'am, we're pulling that up now. Be just a couple of secs."

"I want a cross bearing so we can tell exactly where he is, and a filter wash on the message. It was broken up. Sounded like heavy interference of some kind."

Wickum raised his hand. He'd found it.

"I'm transfering to a headset," Ensign Rowley said. He put the call on hold, grabbed a headset, went out to Wickum's console and plugged in. "Ma'am?"

"I'm here." She sounded strung out.

The message came up on Wickum's screen. "We have it," Ensign Rowley said. "It's weak. Relative bearing two-one-five. Stand by." Wickum entered the bearing Susan Ziegler had given them and the computer instantly crossed the two and came up with a map position. "That's ninety-seven nautical miles southwest of your position, ma'am. We're bringing up the audio now."

Wickum played the very garbled message through once. It lasted only five seconds and was extremely broken up, as if the antenna were bad or blocked. He put the message on a loop so that it would repeat itself over and over again, and began dialing in circuits that would filter out some of the interference and allow the computer to help reconstruct some of the words. It was like fine-tuning a radio to get the best reception. The machine could do it on its own, but human operators still did a better job.

Very slowly a few recongizable words began to emerge from the mush. "... home plate ... we've ... trouble." There were three seconds of nothing useable. "... going down, but ... Stand by! Stand by!" The message ended after that.

They played the message several more times, but nothing else became recognizable.

"Okay, that's our agent and it sounds like he's in trouble."

"We'll start the precoms and excoms tonight, but we can't send a chopper up until morning. If you're declaring an emergency we can get a cutter headed that way within the hour though." Precoms, short for preliminary communications, was a quick search by radio for any and all ships in the vicinity of the last known position of the vessel in distress. Excoms, or extended communications, expanded the search pattern to a much broader area including marinas, lighthouses and other facilities on shore. A lot of the time vessels calling Mayday were found hours later safe in some harbor, not bothering to call anybody to say they were safe.

"I'm declaring a Mayday, Ensign. But if he's aboard the *Aphrodite* and he's in trouble you can expect armed resistance. Pass that along to your people."

"We're on it, ma'am," Ensign Rowley said. "If you come up with anything new shoot it up to us, would you?"

"Right," Susan Ziegler said, and she rang off. Ensign Rowley went back into his office to start calling in people. It was going to be an interesting night after all.

M/V *Margo*

The wind whipped around the corner and Bahmad had to brace himself against a piece of angled steel in order to accomplish his task without making a mistake.

They were heading directly west at their best speed of nineteen knots in order to put the most distance between them and where *Aphrodite* sunk before dawn. Something about Morales and the setup aboard the drug boat had continued to bother him until they had gotten underway, and it finally came to him.

The SSB radio in the *Aphrodite*'s main saloon was set to the *Margo*'s frequency. The one Bahmad had used to make contact. But he finally remembered that before they had left Rosario the captain had switched the set to a different frequency. Morales had been up on deck at the time and had not seen it.

It was a small discrepancy. But paying attention to such seemingly minor details had saved Bahmad's life before. It was possible that Morales had radioed somebody and when he heard Bahmad coming back aboard he had switched frequencies.

When it got light they would turn north again, on a parallel course to their previous one, but more than seventy nautical miles to the west of the *Aphrodite*.

The last of the inner latches clicked up, and Bahmad raised the lid of the bogus life raft cannister to expose the control panel.

Green was in the chart room replotting their course to San Francisco, and Schumatz was below tending to the engines. There was no one to see him. He was alone and he could feel the power emanating from the device. The Americans had invented nuclear weapons, the other nuclear powers simply stole the secrets from them. And now that might was coming home to roost. Live by the sword, die by the sword. That was the adage Westerners foolishly liked to bandy about. But none of them really understood what they were saying.

That would change in less than thirty-six hours.

Shining the narrow beam of a penlight on the keypad Bahmad entered the ten-digit activation code, and the panel suddenly came to life.

He hesitated for several seconds, his fingers poised above the buttons. Even now he could walk away from this insanity. He could kill the other two, rig the ship to sink and fly the helicopter to a deserted stretch of beach and make his way to Mexico City from where he could disappear. He had learned to fly helicopters courtesy of the British SIS, a fact he'd concealed from the others.

But he would go ahead with this for the same reason he had come up with the plan in the first place. The infidels had killed his parents. It was a fact that no act on earth or in heaven could erase. His parents would never return from their graves. What he had done in the name of Islam, and what he was doing now, was not his fault. He'd been made to do this thing by the one senseless act the American-backed Israelis had carried out on innocent civilians. Now they would pay.

He sat back on his heels in the darkness for a few moments longer, contemplating exactly how long it would take him to get to the helicopter, start the engine, lift off and fly to a safe distance before the weapon exploded.

The hills would help. He could duck down behind one of them on the Sausalito side of the bridge.

He entered sixty minutes and five seconds on the keypad, and entered the start code. The panel beeped softly and the LED counter switched from 00:60:05 to 00:60:04, then 00:60:03, 00:60:02, 00:60:01.

Bahmad pressed the interrupt button and the counter stopped at 00:60:00. He entered another series of codes that removed the nuclear weapon's failsafes and entered in their places a series of counter-measures that would make it next to impossible to shut the bomb down.

Now simply pressing the start button would begin the countdown at sixty minutes, and nothing could stop it from happening.

TWENTY-EIGHT

Chevy Chase

The headaches were back. McGarvey got out of bed at six, quietly so as not to awaken Kathleen, and went into the bathroom. He softly closed the door, switched on the light and looked at his haggard image in the mirror. The hair on the side of his head where the surgeon had gone in with a tiny laser cauterizing tool had grown back. There was a ninety percent cure rate. But if the headaches returned it meant they'd missed a bleeder and would have to go back in. It'd mean another six weeks of convalesence.

He hadn't had any choice in the matter the last time, but he was going to have to hang on now. Whatever was going down was going to happen very soon. All the evidence pointed to it, and his gut bunched up in knots as it did before every major mission. The biggest problem they still faced was not knowing where the attack would come. So far they hadn't come up with a single clue.

Bin Laden and his staff were bunkered in Khartoum. There had been no definitive word on where his wives and children had gotten to, but since none of the CIA's assets in the region had made any positive sightings, they were guessing that bin Laden's family was with him in the compound. In some way that had been the most ominous bit of news all afternoon. Bin Laden had lost one daughter, he didn't want to lose another child. He had brought them to his side, to the one place that he considered was safe, unassailable. They couldn't stay there forever, of course. The situation in Khartoum was far too unstable. But for now it was where they were staying; waiting.

Bin Laden would have made plans though. He knew that he could be dead before the year was out, so he would have worked out what would happen to his family afterward. After not only his death, but after the nuclear attack on the United States. Maybe the CIA could guarantee the safety of his family in exchange for the bomb. They could try.

"Yeah, right," he told his image in the mirror. It'd be the same kind of a deal that we'd offered him just before we'd killed his daughter.

He took a couple of Extra Strength Tylenols with a glass of water, then rinsed his face, switched off the light and went back into the bedroom. Kathleen was up and she was putting on a robe.

"Sorry, Katy, I didn't mean to wake you," he said, coming around the bed to her.

"It's time to get up anyway," she said. They kissed, and she looked at him critically. "Did you sleep all right?"

"I've had better nights, how about you?"

She touched his face. "Fine," she said. "But you look tired."

"When we get past this one, you and I are going to take a vacation. A cruise."

She smiled warmly. "I'd like that. Why don't you take the bathroom first, and I'll get breakfast started."

"Nothing heavy, Katy, this is going to be a tough one." Kathleen gave him another smile, as if he'd just stated the obvious. He grinned sheepishly. "If I knew how to golf, I'd retire right now."

"You could learn," she said, and she went downstairs.

McGarvey lit a cigarette and went to the window that overlooked the golf course. The sprinklers were still on, but the first golfers would be on the course within a half hour. The windows in the house were bulletproof Lexan plastic. Eight weeks ago the doors and locks had been seriously beefed up and the CIA had installed a state-of-the-art security system around the entire property. But somebody on the fifteenth fairway could pull an RPG out of his bag and punch a hole in here like a knife through Swiss cheese.

A cheery thought to start off the day, he told himself. But he was back for the duration this time. He wasn't going to run out in a stupid attempt to draw off the bad guys. This time when they came looking for someone to hurt, they were going to find him. His jaw tightened. One-on-one. That's what he really wanted. Sorry that your daughter was killed, but you put her in harm's way. Killing hundreds, probably thousands of innocent people would not bring her back.

His anger, which had percolated all night, spiked and he savagely ground out his cigarette in the ash tray. One-on-one, he told himself again, going into the bathroom. Him and Ali Bahmad on any field of play with any weapons he wanted. Soldier against soldier. Not soldier against women and children; especially not handicapped women and children.

When he came out of the bathroom Kathleen had laid out gray slacks, a white shirt, club tie and the blue blazer for him. Rencke had made the comment a few weeks ago that since Mrs. M. had taken over, McGarvey was starting to look pretty sharp. "Watch it," he'd warned Rencke. "She'd love to get her hands on you."

Rencke hopped from one foot to the other. It was a tiny moment of lightness in an otherwise bleak few months, and it made him smile now, but just for a moment because he had another big hurdle to get over this morning. Something he had put off last night. He had to finally tell Kathleen exactly what Liz was facing. He had a pretty good idea how she was going to take it because this wasn't the first time Liz had been put in harm's way, but at least he was no longer afraid that Katy would turn her back on him like she had done before. "We're in this together, darling," she was telling him now. "You and me, no matter what."

He stopped in the middle of getting dressed. For the first time since Paris he couldn't say that he missed working on his book about Voltaire. He'd worked on it for a long time. But at this stage of his writing he needed to be in the libraries of Europe pouring over the philosopher's letters, reading his notes and manuscripts in their original drafts; talking with scholars. Work, he decided, that was just as real as what he was doing now; in fact possibly even more genuine than what he was doing for the CIA, and in some ways more satisfying because it was like playing detective; but work that was not as necessary as controlling evil. In that, at least, Voltaire would have agreed wholeheartedly.

Kathleen had used the spare bathroom and she looked fresh and bright, but she was troubled. She poured McGarvey a cup of coffee at the kitchen counter. "You look nice," she said distantly.

"What's the matter?"

"Otto called. He wants you to call him right back. And your car is here."

"Sorry, Katy," McGarvey said. He phoned Rencke's direct line. "What have you got?"

"There was a murder aboard a yacht in New York City less than forty-eight hours ago," Rencke said excitedly. "It looks like the work of Bahmad."

"Call Fred Rudolph, and then let the President's Secret Service detail know about it. I'll be there in twenty minutes."

"The FBI is already on it. I'll talk to Villiard. We're close, Mac."

McGarvey went back to the counter and got his coffee. "Gotta go, Katy. This could be the break we've been waiting for."

Kathleen was on the other side of the counter, a funny look on her face. "I figured as much, that's why I didn't make breakfast. Where's Elizabeth?"

It was the hurdle. McGarvey girded himself. "She's working."

"There's no answer at Todd's and the locator wouldn't even take a message."

"I sent them to San Francisco."

She assimilated that information for a moment. "The President's daughter is running in the Special Olympics. Do you think that bin Laden will try to harm her?"

"We thought so, Katy, but we might have been wrong."

"But you sent our daughter there."

"To be with the President's daughter."

She held herself very still, very erect, until finally she nodded. "Okay," she said. She came around to him and straightened his tie. "I'm having a hard time with this, Kirk. But I swear to God that I'm trying."

"It's never easy, Katy."

"Whose idea was it to send Todd with her?"

"Mine."

"Good," Kathleen said. She patted his lapels. "Be careful, Kirk."

"Will do," he promised and kissed her. Dick Yemm was waiting in the driveway with his car, the morning absolutely beautiful.

CIA Headquarters

"Could somebody else have come aboard the yacht and killed the captain?" McGarvey asked Rencke.

Adkins came over and he looked almost as strung out as Rencke. They'd both been pulling a lot of overnighters.

"Not likely, if you're thinking robbery," Rencke said. "The only thing missing is an aluminum case that the girl said had been delivered to the yacht here in Washington two months ago."

"Looks as if the captain came to the yacht searching for it when he was interrupted," Adkins said. "That's what the police are saying. It could have been the bomb."

"That doesn't make any sense," McGarvey said. "They took a big risk by just bringing it into the States. Why would they take it out to Bermuda and then back again? Why triple their risk?"

"There are lots of hiding places on a yacht that size," Adkins pointed out. "Fred Rudolph has sent a Bureau counterespionage team up there. If there's anything to be found they'll find it. But for now it looks as if Bahmad came back to the yacht to pick up the case, walked in on the captain who was searching his cabin and killed the man. He's somewhere in New York. Wall Street maybe. Or maybe the top of the Empire State Building right in the middle of midtown. If it were to blow at noon, let's say on a Monday, it'd kill a lot of people."

McGarvey turned away and walked to the end of the row of computer racks. Rencke had all but taken over the DO's main computer center as his personal domain. It was large, the equivalent of a half-dozen supercomputers, fanning out from a central area that contained a dozen monitor consoles. The morning shift computer operators were starting to drift in, but they stayed respectfully out of the way.

After Washington, *Papa's Fancy* had sailed off to Bermuda where Bahmad and the crew partied. To kill time. Not just to wait for the dust from the Chevy Chase attack to settle, but to wait for a specific date. Back to New York Bahmad dismisses the crew and disappears for ten days. To wait a little longer? Why not in Bermuda? Because the plans may have changed and he needed new instructions. Then he shows up at the yacht at the very same moment the captain is there. Perhaps the captain searched the yacht on the owner's instructions. But there were way too many coincidences for McGarvey, all of them starting with the failed attack in Chevy Chase, and ending presumably at any moment with the detonation of the nuclear weapon.

He walked back. "How do we know it was Bahmad?"

"All the descriptions the Bureau has gotten so far are a match," Rencke said. "They've talked to three of the crew from the yacht and the staff here in Washington at the Corinithian Yacht Club. Everything adds up, and it'll be the same in Bermuda."

"What about the owner?"

"Alois Richter, Jersey City. Until a couple of years ago he was involved with a company called Tele/Resources, which—surprise, surprise—is an agent for the bin Laden family. He left the day before yesterday on business in Europe. No one knows where he is at the moment."

"How about the marina in New York?"

"No one noticed him," Rencke said. "But all the better hotels in the city are being checked. No one thinks they'll come up with anything, but they're trying."

"Airlines?"

"Those are being checked too. But the hairs that were found in Bahmad's bathroom had been died gray. He's changed his appearance."

Rencke was an absolute mess; his clothing was filthy, his long red hair totally out of control, and his complexion sallow from spending almost no time out of doors. But his eyes were bright and an electric current seemed to surround him. He had the bit in his teeth.

"It's very soon, isn't it, Mac?" he said reverently.

"It looks like it."

"So what do we do next?" Adkins asked.

"Keep looking for him and the bomb on the assumption we're wrong about New York, and the bomb was never aboard the yacht. I'm going up there. It's probably a waste of time, but I want to see the yacht."

Los Angeles

Tony Lang came in with Henry Kolesnik a couple of minutes before 6:00 A.M. The President looked up from his breakfast alone in the living room of the Century City Plaza Hotel's presidential suite, his nerves giving a start. Something had happened.

"Good morning, Mr. President," his chief of staff said

brightly. "We have some good news, I think."

Whenever possible, especially if they were on the road, the President liked to have his breakfast in private with his wife and daughter. But it had been a late night and the girls were leaving for San Francisco later this morning, so they were sleeping in.

"What is it?" the President asked, quelling his irritation.

"The CIA called two hours ago," Kolesnik said. "Ali Bahmad, the guy we think bin Laden sent over with the bomb, has been placed in New York City, and he's apparently been there for a while. The FBI is looking for him, but now we've got a decent description."

The President's eyes narrowed. "Am I missing something, Tony?"

"We just might be off the hook in San Francisco," Lang said. "The Bureau thinks that the bomb may have been aboard a private yacht in a New York marina two days ago."

The President understood what they were getting at, but he didn't think they did. "San Francisco has been under a microscope for the past seventy-two hours. If the bomb isn't already in place, it's not coming. It wouldn't get through. Is that about right, Henry?"

"Yes, sir. You were right all along, Mr. President. San Francisco never was his target."

"Well, I am relieved to hear that," the President said sharply. He got up, nearly knocking his chair over.

"Yes, sir," Kolesnik said uncertainly.

"We don't have to worry about a nuclear device being detonated in San Francisco killing me, my wife and my daughter, and maybe tens of thousands of other people."

Lang saw it, and he backpedaled. "We didn't mean it that way, sir."

"If I were president of California that indeed would be good news. But of course that's not the case. I'm President of the entire United States, which includes New York City, which is, I think you're telling me, the target for the largest terrorist attack ever planned in all of recorded history."

"I see your point, Mr. President," Kolesnik said. He was a professional, not a politician, so he didn't back off. "The Bureau and the CIA are handling the investigation on the East Coast. In the meantime my job is to protect you and your family. From my standpoint learning that New York City may be the target rather than the Special Olympics *is* good news."

The President's stomach was sour. Breakfast was over, and his day was about to begin. In situations like these he sometimes asked himself that if he knew then what he knew now, would he have quit campaigning for the White House and gone home. The answer was of course no. Most of the time the job was interesting; not much different than being the CEO of a very large and complicated corporation. But at other times, like now, he felt like a father driving a car, his family asleep, trusting him to do a good job in a blizzard at night on a very dangerous road. His decisions could mean life or death. And he was completely alone to make them.

New York City

McGarvey and Dick Yemm took the CIA's Gulfstream bizjet to LaGuardia. From there they choppered across to the West Thirtieth Street Heliport near the Penn Central Yards. A car was waiting for them, and Yemm drove him to the marina. He had to show his credentials to a cop at the *Papa's Fancy* boarding ladder before he was allowed to go aboard. Yemm waited on the dock.

The yacht was a mess. The main saloon had been all but dismantled; the furniture had been cut apart; the bar and cabinets reduced to pieces; ceiling tiles removed, wall panels taken off and set aside and the carpeting and padding pulled up to show the bare metal of the deck.

"We didn't find a thing," a man in shirtsleeves said coming from the forward passageway. He looked like a ward politician, or a Teamsters boss. Tough and gnarly. "You McGarvey?"

"Yeah," McGarvey said. They shook hands.

"I'm Kevin O'Brien, FBI Counter-espionage. Mr. Rudolph said you wanted to come up and take a look." He glanced around the saloon and shrugged. "We took it down to bare metal and didn't find a thing other than what's on the amended police report, so I sent everybody home."

"No radiation?"

O'Brien shook his head. "Nada. That would have been a bad sign anyway. Would have meant that the device was leaking, which would have given us a whole host of other problems."

McGarvey pegged O'Brien as a former street cop. Probably from right here in New York. He'd be a good man to have at your back in a crisis. "There was supposed to be an aluminum case here. Any sign of it?"

"We found some indentations on the carpet beside the bed in the master suite. Traces of aluminum oxide. It could have contained the device. The package was just about large enough, and our forensics people estimated it weighed between fifty and eighty pounds, from the depth of the indentations." O'Brien shrugged again. "Makes you wonder though, just how cool and collected the sonofabitch would have to be in order to lie down and go to sleep next to a nuclear weapon."

"If he's who we think he is, he's cool enough to push the button," McGarvey said. This had been a waste of time after all. He was picking up no sense whatsoever that Bahmad was ever here, let alone why he chose a yacht as his base of operations. Nor was he any further ahead in trying to work out the man's tradecraft.

"Well, he's had a two-day head start and he left nothing behind. He could be just about anywhere."

McGarvey started to turn away when what the FBI Counterespionage agent just said struck him. Bahmad didn't have a two-day head start. He had an eight-week head start. The bomb was never aboard the yacht. There was no reason for it to be here. The aluminum case contained Bahmad's equipment for the strike: weapons, explosives, maybe lock picking sets and surveillance devices. Things that he might need in order to set up the attack and then get away afterward. Maybe a remote detonator for the bomb.

"Did you find any weapons?"

"A Ruger Mini-14 in stainless and a couple of Beretta 9mm pistols in the captain's quarters. A couple of boxes of ammunition. About what you'd expect to find on a boat like this."

"No explosives?"

"You mean like Semtex?" O'Brien shook his head. "Nada."

"Was the captain armed?"

"He had nothing on him when the gold shields showed up."

"Was he carrying any keys?"

"He had a key to get in, and the key locker in his cabin was open."

"The bulk of his fingerprints were found in the master stateroom?"

"That's right," O'Brien said. "What are you getting at, Mr. McGarvey?"

"I think that the captain was ordered to search the master stateroom. Probably for the aluminum case."

"Right. And this guy kills him because of it."

"Maybe," McGarvey said. "Or maybe the captain had already gotten rid of it and was killed to keep his mouth shut. Get a diver over here, I want to find out what's at the bottom of this slip."

M/V *Margo*
Southwest of San Diego

They had turned north around dawn and were making fifteen knots on their new course of 340 degrees which would close slowly with the U.S. mainland when the Coast Guard helicopter came at them out of the sun.

Bahmad was in the chartroom going through the ship's documents and memorizing the captain's papers and company orders when Green came to the doorway.

"It's the goddamned Coast Guard," he said, out of breath. Bahmad looked up calmly. Green was pale.

"Have they attempted to make contact with us? Is it a ship?"

"It's a helicopter, a Sea King, and it's heading right at us."

Bahmad put down the dividers and followed Green onto the bridge. The helicopter was at about eye level just off to the starboard and pacing them. Bahmad found that he wasn't surprised by its presence, nor was he going to allow himself to become distressed. If the Coast Guard was on a drug interdiction mission they would have sent a cutter with a boarding party, but there were no ships on the radar. He was going to play it cool for now because he had no other choice. If the Coast Guard actually put someone aboard the mission would be over.

Bahmad picked up the VHF radio handset and keyed it. "Good morning, Coast Guard, this is the *Margo*. Would you care to come aboard for some fresh coffee and doughnuts?"

"Thanks for the invite *Margo*, but it'd be a little tough setting down. Switch to twenty-two and identify yourself please, sir."

Bahmad switched from channel 16 to the Coast Guard frequency. "I'm George Panagiotopolous, the master."

"What is your cargo and destination, sir?"

"We're carrying twenty-seven containers of Italian tile, fifteen containers of teak furniture, three hundred seventeen containers of Nike shoes, and the remainder, four hundred eighteen containers of marine life rafts, plus one helicopter on the afterdeck bound for San Francisco."

"Looks like a Russian chopper."

"Sorry, I don't know a thing about such machines, except

that this one is inoperable and it's heading for a museum."

"How many POBs, skipper?"

Bahmad held his hand over the mouthpiece and gave Green a questioning look.

"Persons-on-board," Green whispered.

Bahmad turned back to the radio. "In addition to myself, we are sixteen men and officers, no passengers."

"When was your last course or speed change?"

"About thirty-six hours ago," Bahmad said. "What brings you gentlemen all the way out here this fine morning?" If they were looking for drugs they would have already asked the *Margo* to heave to.

"We received a possible distress call last night about seventy miles southwest of here. Did you pick up anything, skipper?"

"There was nothing in the log."

"Did you see any traffic last night?"

"Nothing, Coast Guard. Like I said, the log is blank except for positions, weather and sea states."

"Okay, skipper, sorry to have bothered you," the Coast Guard said. "Have a good one." The helicopter peeled off to the right, seemed to hesitate for a moment, and then headed east back into the sun.

"What the fuck was that all about?" a greatly relieved Green demanded.

"Whatever it was, it's no longer any concern of ours," Bahmad said, smiling faintly. "The Coast Guard has looked us over and has given us a clean bill of health. We won't be bothered again."

New York City

It took less than an hour to summon a New York City Police Department search and rescue dive team to *Papa's Fancy*. McGarvey told the two men exactly what they were to look for, but to pick up anything that looked suspicious. A half-dozen uniformed cops showed up and expanded the area cordoned off by police tape to include the entire dock. A small crowd of people, some of them marina employees, others yacht crew or owners, gathered in the parking lot and adjacent docks to watch. The divers, police sergeants Benito Juarez and Tom Haskill, suited up and slipped into the water at the bow of the yacht.

"What if they find the aluminum case down there?" O'Brien asked.

"Depends on what's inside it," McGarvey said absently. Yemm had gotten out of the car and came over. He was watching the crowd with suspicion.

"The bomb?"

"I don't think it was ever aboard," McGarvey said. "This will be his weapons, and maybe the remote detonator."

O'Brien looked at the black water roiled up by the bubbles rising from the divers' scuba equipment. They were slowly working their way aft. "I don't get it. Why would the captain dump the stuff overboard?"

"Because he was ordered to do it. Bin Laden might be getting cold feet, so the captain was told to get down here and grab whatever he could. It was just bad luck that Bahmad showed up at the same time. I'm betting that the captain spotted Bahmad coming aboard and tossed the case overboard. About the only thing he could have done." McGarvey was working all that out in his head as he spoke.

"So Bahmad killed him because of it, and then he took off. Means we're out of the woods, doesn't it? No detonator, no explosion?"

"The bomb can be set off manually."

O'Brien looked at the water again. "Then if the detonator is still down there, it means he was in too big a hurry to bring it up. He had to get somewhere. Could mean that the bomb isn't here in New York after all."

"Something like that," McGarvey said, still working it out. Bahmad had come back for his things, which meant that the attack was going to happen very soon. Yet he didn't bother trying to recover any of it. That's if the case was actually at the bottom of the slip.

The divers surfaced just aft of the flare of the bows and passed up a line. "It's down there, just like you said," Haskill called up to McGarvey.

Two uniformed cops hauled the muddy aluminum case to the surface and then pulled it up onto the dock. McGarvey walked over and hunched down in front of it.

"Maybe we should get the bomb squad over here first, boss," Yemm suggested.

"No need," McGarvey told him. "It's already been opened. The locks have been forced." He popped the latches and opened the lid. Some water came out. In addition to some cameras and photographic equipment the case contained a gun, a silencer, some ammunition, a lock pick set and an assortment of other things.

He pulled out a small leather case and from it withdrew an electronic device that looked very much like a television remote control.

"The detonator?" O'Brien asked in a hushed tone. Even Yemm was impressed. The police officers were impressed.

McGarvey nodded. "No telling the range," he said. He carefully eased the battery cover open on the back of it and pried the nicad battery out. Only then did he allow himself to relax, and release the pent-up breath.

"This guy isn't going to give up, is he?" O'Brien said.

"I don't think so," McGarvey said. He put the detonator and battery in separate pockets and got up. "Get the rest of this stuff down to Washington and see what your people can come up with."

"What about the yacht?"

"The owner won't be coming back," McGarvey said, but his mind was elsewhere. He was sure now what bin Laden's target had been all along. And he had done exactly what bin Laden would have wanted him to do by sending his daughter to California to be with the President's daughter. Now he was going to have to figure out how to save both of their lives.

Los Angeles

At ten of twelve President Haynes was racing through downtown Los Angeles in the back of his limousine with his chief of staff Tony Lang and his press secretary Sterling Mott. They were going over some last-minute changes to the lunch speech he was giving to the Association of California Mayors at the Convention Center. Normal traffic was backed up at every intersection to allow the motorcade, sirens blaring, lights flashing, to pass. Since it was the lunchtime rush hour he didn't think that a poll of stalled motorists would elect him to any office, not even that of dog catcher. It was one of the downsides that any city hosting a presidential visit was faced with. But L.A. cops were used to just about everything, and within a minute after the eight car, four motorcycle motorcade had passed, traffic was back to normal.

A telephone in the console beside Lang chirped softly and he picked it up. "This is Tony Lang."

The President looked up.

"Just a moment," Lang said, and he touched the hold button. "It's Kirk McGarvey, Mr. President. He'd like to talk to you."

The President's jaw tightened. McGarvey had sent his own daughter out to help look after Deborah. If it had been anyone else doing it, he would have taken it as grandstanding. But that wasn't McGarvey's style. But what the hell did he want now? "Where's he calling from?"

Lang glanced at the display. "New York City. It's a cell phone."

"Maybe it's good news," Mott suggested.

"Right," the President said dryly. He held out his hand for the phone. "Good morning, Mac. What do you have for me?"

"The bomb is not in New York, Mr. President. It was

never here. I think it's already in San Francisco. You have to cancel the games."

The President closed his eyes for a moment. He could count on the fingers of one hand how many people he could trust implicitly. McGarvey was one of them. "One hundred percent sure?"

"Ninety percent. It's your call, sir, but the bomb could be just about anywhere in the city."

"What's your best guess?"

"Candlestick Park."

The President felt a cold knot of frozen lead in his gut. "Our daughters are there right now. Mine to practice and yours to keep an eye on her."

"Yes, sir."

The President could hear a note of resignation in McGarvey's voice, and he understood exactly what the man was going through. What both of them were going through. "If you're so certain why don't you pull your daughter out of there?" It was a low blow, but he had to know what McGarvey's reaction would be.

"Because she has a job to do."

The President nodded. It was the answer he had expected. "We all do, Mac," he said gently. "I'll have the Secret Service tear the place apart again, but I won't cancel the games because I still don't believe that bin Laden will kill his own people."

"I understand, Mr. President," McGarvey said. "I'll be in San Francisco this afternoon then."

San Francisco
Candlestick Park

"Ms. McGarvey, I'll take you down to meet her now," Chenna Serafini said. "We're identifying you as one of her personal trainers."

"Sounds good," Elizabeth said. "But my friends usually call me Liz."

Chenna allowed herself to relax just a little. She had no idea how the CIA was going to act out here, and especially not in the person of the daughter of the deputy director of Operations. "Okay, Liz. It's just that we're all pretty protective of Deb. And not just because it's our job. She's a good kid."

"That's what I've heard," Elizabeth said. She was dressed in a dark blue jogging outfit with the ISO linked rings logo on the back. She carried a Walther PPK in a quick-draw holster under her left armpit, and a comms unit that fit nearly out of sight in her ear like a hearing aid. The unit was voice-operated, and the tiny microphone picked up her words through the bones in the side of her head. They walked out of the skybox high above the field where hundreds of athletes and their coaches were working out, and took an elevator to the ground level. There were Secret Service and FBI agents everywhere. Orders had come down to tear the stadium apart for the third time in an effort to find the bomb, and the cops were doing so with discretion but with a lot of enthusiasm. There were hundreds of other people in the stadium as well; family members, journalists, technicians, ISO officials and a handful of park staff. Everyone had been vetted, and no one got near the stadium without the proper pass.

Todd Van Buren had gone off with Bruce Hansen to review the security procedures for the start of tomorrow's half-marathon. He shared Elizabeth's feeling that protecting the President's daughter in this crowd would be next to impossible, but they had no other option than to try.

Down in the field the day was absolutely gorgeous; a lot cooler and windier than Washington, but just perfect for most of the track and field events. They got into an electric golf cart and Chenna drove them to the opposite side of the field where Deborah Haynes was going through her stretching and warmup routines with Terri Lundgren. Elizabeth was struck all at once by how beautiful the President's daughter was. She could have been a runway model from somewhere in eastern Russia; Siberia maybe, except that when she looked up, her eyes were somewhat blank. Her face was animated, but something was missing; something that was hard for Elizabeth to put her finger on even knowing that the girl suffered from Down syndrome.

When she saw them pull up, her face lit up like a million-watt lightbulb and she bounded over. "Chenna," she cried. They hugged.

"I brought someone over to meet you," Chenna said. "Her name is Liz and she's going to be working out with you during the games."

Deborah gave Elizabeth an oddly appraising glance as they shook hands. "Do you work for the CIA?"

Elizabeth was somewhat taken aback, but she smiled. "What makes you think that?"

"Ah, I heard my mom and dad talking about it this morning. Are you a spy?"

"I guess you could call me a spy," Elizabeth said, exchanging glances with Chenna and the other Secret Service officers standing nearby. "They sent me over to help keep an eye on you."

"Oh, cool," Deborah said with genuine enthusiasm. "Can you work out with me? Can you run?"

"I can give it a try, Deb, but I don't know if I can keep up with you. I heard that you were awfully good."

Deborah's face went blank for just a moment. "That's an oxymoron . . . awful and good."

Elizabeth had to laugh. "That it is."

"Let's go," Deborah suddenly shouted. She looked to her coach for approval and Terri Lundgren gave her a nod.

"Just take it a little easy, we don't want to kill the new girl on the first day."

Deborah laughed from the bottom of her toes, then turned and practically leaped onto the track as if she had been shot out of a cannon. Elizabeth scrambled to catch up, and after forty or fifty yards they settled into a very fast loping run. Dozens of flags from all the participating nations fluttered and snapped at the top of the stadium, while in the stands more than a thousand spectators watched the athletes work out on the field—pole vaults and high jumps, shot puts and discus throws. A couple of dozen runners shared the track with them, and when Elizabeth looked over her shoulder she saw Chenna and Terri Lundgren in a golf cart pacing them on the outside line. For a second or two she seriously wondered if she was up for this, but then she turned back and began to enjoy the moment that for the President's daughter was one of absolute and total joy.

San Francisco
FEMA Operations Center

"We have orders to do it all over again," Secret Service unit leader Jay Villiard announced.

There were only a few groans from the dozen people assembled because each of them knew what they were facing, and none of them had any illusions that stopping bin Laden was a hundred percent certainty no matter how many people and resources they threw at the problem.

Setting up the mission nerve center in the Federal Emergency Management Agency's ops center seemed appropriate under the circumstances. Besides, it was located downtown in a hardened concrete shelter in the basement of the federal building. Earthquakeproof, flood- and fireproof, they all sincerely hoped that it would be nuclear bomb proof if it came to that.

"We're scheduled to make our final sweep of the bridge at midnight. I have assets already in place," the San Francisco PD's chief of antiterrorism David Rogan said. "Does it make any sense to start one now?"

"We do the same for every presidential visit if we think there'll be trouble, David," Villiard said from the podium. "By the numbers; a hundred times if need be. We do it this way, people, because the method is tried and true. It works."

There were two tiers of consoles facing a big projection

screen on the wall behind the podium. Rogan picked up the phone at his console and looked up at the screen as he began issuing orders to start the search of the Golden Gate Bridge and its approaches.

A giant map of the Bay Area from Pacifica and San Bruno in the south, to Sausalito and Tiburon in the north and to Oakland, Berkeley and Richmond in the east was projected on the big screen. Candlestick Park was highlighted in red as was the route that the half-marathon runners would take tomorrow at noon: West Park Road to Third Street; south to the Bayshore Freeway, one lane of which would be barricaded; north to U.S. 101; from there north to Van Ness Avenue where the road made a jog, and onto the bridge. On the Marin County side the runners would head east, off U.S. 101, past Fort Baker and then the last mile and a half to the finish line at the Sausalito houseboat docks. Buses would be waiting to return the runners to the Special Olympics village at Candlestick Park.

Tens of thousands of spectators from all around the world were expected to line the route. More than one thousand city, county, state and federal cops would be there to keep them away from the runners so far as that was humanly possible. But nobody would get close to the presidential motorcade leading the race, or to Deborah Haynes who was expected to be among the first fifty runners by that point.

Two dozen helicopters would pace the runners from behind, directly above and at the head of the pack. A pair of Coast Guard cutters would be stationed, one on the bay side of the bridge and the other on the ocean side, to make sure that the only vessels moving during the race were the pilot boats. The biggest concentration of manpower would be at the start and finish of the race as well as on the bridge. All traffic on the bridge itself would be halted a half-hour before the first runner hit Van Ness Avenue and would not be allowed to resume until the last runner had safely made the Fort Baker turn on the Marin County side.

All air traffic in and out of San Francisco International

Airport would be rerouted around Daly City to the south and San Quentin to the north. Everything in between would be a no-fly, exclusion zone for the duration of the race.

Every known or suspected member of any hate group, anarchist society or even mildly left wing organization had been interviewed. Any person or organization that had even the slightest hint of being Arabic, having Arabic ties or having so much as checked out a copy of the Koran in the last two months from the public library system was screened; their driver's license numbers, car tags and Social Security numbers or passport numbers were computer searched. All of it was done as quietly and as discreetly as possible.

The FBI's San Francisco SAC Charles Fellman checked his 401k retirement fund the day before yesterday and gave a realtor friend the heads-up on their Russian Hill home. With all the civil rights they were trampling on he figured that he might be looking for another line of work sooner than he'd counted on.

"If we're sweeping the bridge we might just as well go over the park again, Jay," he suggested. "But it's going to be tough with everybody out there. Have you seen the place since last night? It's a madhouse."

"Our people started a half-hour ago," Villiard told him.

"How about us?" Toni Piper, the San Francisco FEMA director, asked. "I can field a hundred volunteers to canvas the neighborhoods along the route." She was the one who had come to Villiard with the offer of the FEMA ops center. She was a dynamic woman with flaming red hair. "Might not turn up a thing, but it can't hurt."

"If something actually develops they could be placing themselves in the middle of it," Villiard said.

Toni shrugged. "They're used to dealing with earthquakes, you know. Buildings falling on their heads."

"Do it," Villiard said, making his decision. "But make sure that they carry proper IDs. I don't want to turn this into a three-ring circus, my people arresting yours."

"I'll have them on the street within the hour," she said.

Villiard gave her a smile. She was on the ball. She'd had her people organized and standing by even before she'd been given the green light. Maybe she belonged in Washington. He'd have to see.

The phones on the various consoles were starting to ring now, and the noise level was rising as people began gearing up for the first crucial thirty-six hours. The Olympics would be here for ten days. Just because something didn't happen tomorrow didn't mean that they were home safe. But by this time tomorrow night, Villiard thought, the biggest period of danger would be past, the machinery for dealing with the threat would be firmly in place and running and he would be able to breathe his first sigh of relief in two months.

Thirty-six hours. Please God, he told himself, just get us through the first hurdle and I promise a double novena, all eighteen days of it.

Candlestick Park

"Just this way, Mr. President," Marty Grant, one of his Secret Service agents, said, holding the door. "The skybox has been cleared for you."

The team owner's private elevator took them directly up to the glass enclosure used by the media during sporting events. The cameras and equipment were in place, but the technicians were gone, replaced by four additional Secret Service agents. They'd gone through a lot of hassle to pull this off.

"This is great," the President said. "Tell Dick Evers thanks for me. I didn't want to cause a fuss, but I wanted to see my daughter."

"She's on the track, Mr. President," one of the agents said, handing him a pair of binoculars. "Out by the right field foul line."

The President adjusted the focus and found Deborah right away, her long blond hair streaming behind her unmistakable. A young woman in blue sweats was running with her. At first he thought she was the chief of Deborah's Secret Service detail, but then he spotted Chenna riding shotgun in a golf cart with Terri Lundgren.

"Who's the girl running with Deb?"

One of the agents also watching through binoculars said something into his lapel mike. "Elizabeth McGarvey, sir."

Watching them running together it was clear that Deborah was the superior athlete, though not by much. But it was also clear in his mind the great difference that existed between the two young women. Elizabeth had her entire future ahead of her; varied, interesting, maybe with a husband and children, maybe alone. There would be challenges in her life, problems to overcome, situations to be faced and dealt with. Deborah's life on the other hand was already determined for the most part. She would be protected, loved and cared for around the clock. She would never marry or have children. The dangers she would face were only because of who and what her father was. And the major challenges she would have to overcome were her mental limitations. Every morning when he got up, President Haynes prayed to God that Deborah would never fully understand her handicap. It was a rotten, selfish attitude, he knew that. But he wanted to protect his only child from all harm, not only to her physical self, but to her self-esteem.

He lowered his binoculars, and he couldn't help but think about Sarah bin Laden. Her death was something that he would regret for the remainder of his life. He could clearly understand bin Laden's rage, and he didn't even want to think about what he would do in the same circumstances. God help the sorry bastard who ever harmed a hair on his daughter's head.

"Too bad the First Lady isn't up here to see this," Tony Lang said, watching through binoculars. "Deb's a heck of a runner." The First Lady was meeting with three separate women's groups this afternoon and wouldn't be coming up from Los Angeles until later this evening.

"That she is," the President said. "Marty, would you tell

Chenna to bring her up here, and ask Ms. McGarvey if she would join us."

"Yes, sir," the chief agent on his detail said. He spoke into his lapel mike, listened, then spoke softly again. "Be just a couple of minutes, Mr. President."

"Thanks." The President raised his binoculars and watched as Chenna caught up with them. The two daughters climbed into the back of the golf cart for the trip across the field. It was a madhouse down there; handicapped athletes from all around the world were doing their best, the same as everybody else. Deborah was having the time of her life, and he would not have taken this away from her or from the others, for all the bin Ladens in the world.

They disappeared down one of the tunnels below, and a minute later the elevator came up. When the door opened Deborah spotted her father, bounded across to him and threw herself into his arms.

"Daddy," she cried. She was very strong, and her entire body hummed with an electric joy. He was never more proud of her than he'd ever been in his life. "Did you see me down there?" she bubbled. "Did you see me running?"

"I sure did, sweetheart. You looked wonderful."

"Not awfully good?" she asked, crinkling her nose.

"That too," the President said. Deborah laughed, and he wondered what he had said that was so amusing to her.

"I'm afraid that it's a little joke between us, Mr. President," Elizabeth said.

"An oxymoron," Deborah explained.

"I see," the President said. "You're Elizabeth McGarvey?"

"Yes, sir," Elizabeth said, and she shook hands with the President. It was clear that she was respectful, but she wasn't the least bit nervous. She was a lot like her father, the President decided; a heads-up person. McGarvey was stamped all over her. When she matured she was going to be one hell of a woman.

"Thanks for coming out here and helping out."

"Yes, sir."

The President picked up a discordant note. "You don't think that this is such a hot idea?"

"No, sir. The games should be canceled immediately, or at least postponed until we bag the bad guy."

Deborah watched the interplay as did everyone else.

The President suppressed a slight smile, though he was a little irritated. "You *are* your father's daughter."

Elizabeth's shoulders squared up a little. "Yes, sir," she said with a barely concealed pleasure.

"Do you understand why I can't do that?"

Elizabeth started to say something, but then she smiled. "Yes, sir, I believe that I can." She glanced at the President's daughter. "My father'll be here tonight."

"Yes. What about tomorrow?"

"For me, Mr. President?" she asked. "I've already got permission from the ISO to run in the half-marathon, if you have no objections."

The President was deeply touched. "I can't ask you to do that, under the circumstances."

Elizabeth grinned and looked at Deborah again. "I know what you mean, Mr. President. I'm probably going to run my legs off trying to keep up with her."

CIA Headquarters

"Start all over again," McGarvey said in the computer center. Rencke was still at his console and he looked like death warmed over, but his eyes were alive. McGarvey had to wonder if Otto was on something, a stimulant of some sort, but now was not the time to ask. "We'll start from the assumption that the bomb is already in San Francisco. Probably Candlestick Park. The Secret Service and Bureau are doing everything they can to find it, so we'll leave that end to them. But if we can get a clue as to how it got here, maybe it'd give us an idea where to look for it."

"Liz is there," Rencke said. "Right in the middle of it."

"I couldn't stop her," McGarvey said. He felt as miserable as Rencke looked. "Maybe she'll see something that everyone else is missing."

"Van Buren is with her. He'll move heaven and earth to make sure that nothing happens to her. Pretty good motivation, don't you think?"

McGarvey laid a hand on his old friend's shoulder. "I'm sorry, Otto—"

Rencke smiled a little. "Don't be, Mac. I'm the uncle, remember? Not the love interest." His smile broadened. "Besides, Mrs. M. made me an honorary family member. It'd be incest, ya know."

"Then I'd have to kill you."

"Yeah," Rencke said glumly. He looked at his computer screen. "It got across the Atlantic either by air or by ship. And from there it got to California by air, by road or by rail."

McGarvey's headache was bad now, making it hard for him to focus. They were missing something, he felt it, and he had felt it all along.

"So we cover all the possibilities," Rencke was saying. "It's like a double-ended funnel with the small ends in Afghanistan and California." He looked up, but it was obvious that his mind was already elsewhere, chewing on the problem, setting up parameters and methodologies. "Violet," he mumbled.

"As soon as you come up with something call me," McGarvey said.

While Adkins was setting up his transportation, McGarvey went home to grab a quick shower and a change of clothes. He called his wife on his cell phone on the way out to Andrews Air Force Base.

"I'm leaving for San Francisco now."

"It's going to happen tomorrow or Sunday, isn't it?" she said after a slight hesitation.

"I think so, Katy. I can't stay here."

"I know you can't. But listen to me."

"I'm listening."

"Come back to me, Kirk. Bring Elizabeth with you. Just come back."

"Promise," he said.

M/V *Margo*
West of Los Angeles

Green came onto the bridge out of breath as if he had run up the stairs from the engine room two at a time. He was a mess, Bahmad saw, his eyes were bloodshot, he had a serious five o'clock shadow, his uniform was dirty with blood or oil stains and his complexion was sallow. But the navigation he'd worked out that would take them north to the Farallon Islands where they would turn east into the Golden Gate was already entered into the autopilot. If they did not touch the controls the *Margo* would sail on her own into San Francisco Bay.

"Something's happening with one of the engines," Green said.

Bahmad had been dozing in a chair he'd brought from the captain's cabin. The afternoon sun slanted at a low angle through the bridge windows. For as far as the eye could see the electric-blue ocean and pale blue sky were clear of all traffic. Only a high contrail marked the passage of a Hawaii-bound jet.

"What's the problem?" Bahmad asked languidly.

"There's some kind of a vibration in the shaft bearings. They're starting to heat up. Lazlo traced it to the port engine. The gearbox may be frying itself. He wants to shut down the engine and take the cover off the heat exchanger."

"What will that do to our speed?"

"It'll cut it in half unless we push the starboard engine. But if we do that we could end up a shit creek. Both engines could go down."

"Is Schumatz an engineer?"

"You don't have to be a fucking engineer to read a temperature gauge."

"For all he knows the temperature of the gearbox could be well within normal operating limits—"

"The dial is marked red."

"And the mechanism could run for a week, perhaps cross an ocean before it had to be tended to. But we need less than twenty-four hours."

"I'm not going to get stuck out here with a locker full of dead men. I say we take the helicopter and the three of us fly to Los Angeles."

"We need to get to San Francisco."

"The ship will make it on its own. It's even programmed to make the turn at the Farallon buoy."

"But you said the port engine might not make it."

"So we won't be on schedule. I don't give a shit, do you understand, you fucking wog?"

Bahmad suppressed an evil grin. People were so easy. "Why didn't Schumatz come up here and tell me himself? Or pick up the ship's phone and call me?"

"How the hell should I know? Why don't you go down there and ask him yourself?"

"I think I'll do just that," Bahmad said. He got up, turned slightly as if he was heading for the door, pulled his pistol, thumbed the safety catch off and turned and shot Green in the forehead at a range of less than five feet.

The first officer's head snapped back, his arms shot out and he was flung to the deck, killed instantly.

Bahmad cocked an ear to listen to the sounds of the ship now that Green had stopped complaining. They were still making fifteen knots, which would put them in the Golden Gate around ten in the morning, two hours before the runners were expected to be on the bridge. Everything was going as planned.

He stuck the Glock 17 in his belt and headed down to the engine room. From what he personally knew about the Sulzer diesel engines there was nothing to worry about. As long as they had sufficient fuel and air they would run practically forever. It would take a catastrophe to stop them. Such as something a motivated man might do.

His step lightened. First he would take care of Schumatz, then he would get something to eat and finally get a few hours' sleep. The radar's proximity alarm would warn him of any impending obstacles in their path. He needed to be alert. Tomorrow promised to be a long, interesting day.

Golden Gate Bridge

It was ten o'clock already and the lights of the city were on. Traffic on the bridge was heavy, made more difficult for the motorists because a half-dozen highway patrol cars blocked one lane for fifty yards at the crown of the span. McGarvey stood at the rail. He'd had a hell of a time convincing Dick Yemm to stay behind, but he had more freedom of movement without a bodyguard. He'd already managed to check out the security arrangements at the park and on the bridge, though he'd missed Liz who'd gone with the President's daughter to a welcoming ceremony in the Olympic Village.

More than three hundred city, state and federal law enforcement officers aided by Golden Gate Transit people were searching the bridge as unobtrusively as possible. But passing drivers couldn't help but notice so they slowed down to gawk, which further snarled traffic.

An unmarked Chevy van with federal government plates came up and stopped in the far right-hand lane behind a GGT maintenance truck. Jay Villiard got out and came over.

"How does it look?"

"Hello, Jay." McGarvey said. They shook hands. "If you can't search the city you might as well search the bridge."

"That's what we figured." He bummed a cigarette from McGarvey. "Lousy habit. Maybe I'll give them up again next week."

"How'd you do it last time?" McGarvey asked. He was ready to pull the pin himself, mostly because Kathleen had taken up smoking because of him, and he hated to see her with a cigarette in her hand.

"Cold turkey. It's the only way. Tried and true," Villiard answered. "Why is it that I don't think you brought good news with you. God only knows we need some, because we haven't turned up a thing."

"We thought we had a pretty good lead in New York," McGarvey said, and he briefly explained what had happened. "We're back to square one, right here."

"The President won't quit."

"I know, I've tried, and so has Murphy."

"Bin Laden won't quit either," Villiard said glumly. They leaned against the rail watching the night deepen. "I met your daughter; pretty sharp kid. My people are already in love with her."

"That's nice to hear."

"Are you pulling her out?" Villiard asked.

A genuine pain stabbed at McGarvey's heart. "No," he said. "She wouldn't go if I ordered her out anyway." He turned to face Villiard. "You have kids, Jay. Do they always listen to you?"

Villiard laughed. "I have a fourteen-year-old daughter who hasn't listened to me since she was ten. I was trying to tell her something, you know, something to help. Anyway, when I was all done she put a hand on her hip, raised an eyebrow, and said: 'Obviously.'" Villiard laughed again. "I told my wife that maybe we should just kill her and make a new one."

McGarvey had to smile. He knew the feeling. He flipped his cigarette over the rail, then looked up at the towers soaring high overhead, the cable bundles tracing perfect arches. "If I were going to do it, this would be the place."

Villiard followed his gaze. "It'd be a triple play if he could take out the President, the President's daughter, and the bridge. Not to mention your daughter and a couple of thousand runners and spectators." He paused. "There won't be a nonsecure aircraft of any type within five miles, or a boat we don't know about within three miles. No cars, trucks or buses. Nobody on foot with any kind of a package bigger than a purse. Every television van will be assigned a cop. We've searched the bridge and everything around it three times and we'll do it twice more before the race tomorrow. We'll have sharpshooters in the towers, Coast Guard helicopters overhead, Coast Guard cutters in the water on both sides of the bridge, and even though you're not supposed to be able to launch this thing on a missile, we'll have men watching every place from where a missile could be launched." He shook his head. "Goddammit, we've got it covered. Just like in the textbooks. Just like every time before. Tried and true. It works. But I'm real scared."

"It'd have to be pretty close to take the bridge out," McGarvey said.

"A plane right overhead or a boat under the span, we've got them covered."

"Someplace on the bridge."

"We've searched every square inch of it from both ends and top to bottom."

"How about inside the concrete?" McGarvey asked. "Have there been any repairs in the past six or eight weeks? New concrete poured on the roadways, maybe in the piers? Someplace the bomb could be buried?"

A startled expression crossed Villiard's face. "I never thought of that," he said softly. He was the expert and he'd been caught flatfooted. It showed in his eyes. "I'll get on it right now." He started to go, but McGarvey stopped him.

"Better put some divers in the water around the base of the towers too. Bin Laden's chief of staff is an inventive bastard."

Villiard nodded tightly. "Anything else?"

"Not for now."

"I'm going to get my people together. We're going to rethink this thing from the get-go."

"It's not the stuff that *we* think of that gets me worried," McGarvey said.

"Yeah," Villiard replied. "It's the shit that we *don't* think about." He studied McGarvey's face. "Where you going to be?"

"Around."

"Sleep?"

"Later."

"I know what you mean," the Secret Service agent said, and he left.

It was going to be a long night, McGarvey thought, pulling out another cigarette. He felt battered. He was still on eastern time, so for him it was after two in the morning. Time to sleep. Perchance to dream? It was exactly what he was afraid of, because lately in his dreams he was seeing Sarah bin Laden's bloody body lying in a field of flowers like in the *Wizard of Oz*. His daughter and the President's daughter were running up the hill toward her when there was a bright flash over the Emerald City and they were torn apart just when they thought that they were home safe.

TWENTY-NINE

M/V *Margo*
Southwest of the Farallon Islands

On the bridge the radar proximity alarm sounded. Bahmad who had been listening to the police, harbor control and Coast Guard frequencies in the chart room came out to see what was ahead of them. The sky to the east was getting light with the dawn. They were still far enough off shore that he could not pick up the coast line, though he could see the smudge of the distant mountains inland. The radar was painting a very large object within the thirty-five mile ring directly ahead. It was the high rock face of one of the Farallon Islands. He checked his watch. They were right on time.

According to the ship's SOP manuals, a Notice to Mariners they'd received yesterday and the radio chatter he'd listened to most of the night, he'd been presented with an apparently insoluble problem. No shipping was to be allowed anywhere near the bridge while the runners were crossing. The separation zone was a minimum of three miles. Ships coming in early were to drop anchor in the holding basin to the west of the center span and wait for the all clear. But then, about an hour ago, the solution presented itself all at once in a neat and tidy package, as these things usually did.

As soon as the *Margo* cleared the Farallons and made the pre-programmed turn to starboard that would bring them to the holding basin in the Golden Gate, he was supposed to call for a harbor pilot who would be brought out on a pilot boat. It could not have been better. In effect the stupid bastards were going to do his job for him.

His step was light and he whistled a little tune as he went to prepare Joshua's Hammer for the final countdown.

Candlestick Park

McGarvey sat in the stadium a third of the way up at the fifty-yard line sipping a cup of coffee trying to get rid of a blinding headache. He'd accomplished nothing of any value overnight, and he was frustrated with himself. He was missing something, they all were. But he couldn't put his finger on it. He'd called Rencke twice during the night, but both he and Adkins were coming up empty handed.

"We've still got time, ya know," Rencke said. "It's turning purple."

"What's that mean?"

"I don't know yet," Rencke cried in anguish. "Maybe you should get Liz outta there, ya know. Something."

"Take it easy. We're doing this one step at a time. We've

got it covered at this end. All we need now is one thing, how the bomb got here."

"I'm on it, Mac. Holy shit, I swear to God, I'm on it—" Rencke broke the connection, leaving McGarvey very worried about him. He thought about having Adkins pull him out, but that would be even harder on Rencke than leaving him where he was.

The stadium was coming alive with the dawn. A portable stage had been set up in midfield for the opening ceremonies set to start at 11:30 A.M. President Haynes, California Governor Thomas and the International Special Olympics director Octavo Aguilar along with a number of local officials and politicians would officially welcome the athletes and declare that the games were open. The presidental motorcade would lead the half-marathon runners out of the park at noon. And from that point for the next ten days there would be more Secret Service and police activities here than at any other place or time in U.S. history.

Grounds crews were busy making sure everything was set up the way it should be and that the field was in good shape. Workmen were putting the final touches on the stage, and technicians were testing the sound and lighting systems. Some of the coaches and athletes were already starting to drift into the stadium for their workouts, and the newsmedia were busy setting up their equipment. There was an air of nervousness among just about everyone except the athletes. Something was going on. Everybody knew it because of the increased security. The President was here, but nobody had ever seen such stringent measures. It was as if the entire world had suddenly gone nuts.

No one was saying anything out loud about the precautions, but it was clear that bin Laden was on everybody's minds.

"Hi, Daddy," Elizabeth said, dropping into the seat next to him.

McGarvey looked up and gave his daughter a smile. He was glad to see her. " 'Morning, Liz. Did you get any sleep?"

"Not much," she said. Her eyes were red, but she looked bright. She was dressed in sweats with a dark blue ISO warmup jacket and cap. "I stayed in the dorm with Deb last night, and those kids are wired. Most of them didn't get to sleep until a couple hours ago." She gave her father a critical look. "How about you? Are you okay?"

"I'll be glad when this weekend is over," he replied tiredly. "Where's Todd? I haven't seen him since I got out here."

"Neither have I. He's been busy with Deb's Secret Service people. They're putting a blanket around her."

"Won't help if the bomb goes off."

"They know that. But if we get some kind of a warning, even a hint, Todd's worked out a way to get her out of here within a minute or two. They've got a souped-up golf cart that can top eighty, and a chopper to pull her out."

McGarvey looked away. How to tell her what he was thinking? What any father in his shoes would be thinking. If there was an opposite end of the earth from bin Laden's mountain camp then this was it. But McGarvey was finding that he didn't belong in either place. Especially not here. It seemed as if an evil pall had followed him from Afghanistan and had settled over this stadium. It was his own dark mood, he understood that. But he had to ask himself how he would have reacted to the death of his own daughter. If he were bin Laden what would he have done?

One of the previous deputy directors of Operations had told him once that he was an anachronism. Shooters like him were a dangerous breed out of the past. In fact they had become indistinguishable from their targets. The lines between the good and the bad had blurred somehow. Progress.

He'd wanted to tell the smug bastard how wrong that was, but he couldn't. Maybe the man had been right after all. But he sure as hell hadn't formed that opinion while sitting next to an Osama bin Laden. He had not felt the man's anger and religious zeal. He had not felt the man's dedication of purpose, his—for him—high principles.

God save us from the self-righteous, for it's them who'll likely inherit the earth, not the meek.

"Anything I should know about?" Elizabeth asked.

McGarvey focused on his daughter. He reached out and touched her face. "Are you happy, sweetheart?" he asked.

The question startled her. She started to give him an answer, but then hesitated for a moment, embarrassed. Finally she smiled wanly. "Not right at this moment, I guess. I'm a little scared." She looked up, her shoulders back a little. "But overall things couldn't be much better. I have a job that I love, I have you and mom back together—and that's a dream come true—and I have Todd. I think that I'm in love with him, and—"

Someone shouted her name from down on the field. They turned in time to see Deborah Haynes and her coach and Secret Service detail coming out onto the field. Deborah had spotted Elizabeth and was waving wildly. Elizabeth waved back.

"I have to go," she said.

"You started to tell me something."

"It'll keep."

An overwhelming wave of love surged through McGarvey. "I'm very proud of you."

"Thanks, Daddy."

"I'll do everything I can to stop the bastards."

"When haven't you done your very best?" she asked. She kissed him on the cheek and then headed down to the field.

"Damn," he said softly. A very large hollow spot ate at his gut watching his only child taking the steps lightly, two at a time, as if she didn't have a care in the world. If there is a God who isn't indifferent, he prayed softly, please watch over her and help me stop the monsters.

FEMA Operations Center

"There were no concrete pours that big in the past eight weeks. In fact there was no work like that for the past six months," Andrew Stroud said. He was the chief engineer in charge of the Golden Gate Bridge. He and Jay Villiard were flipping through a thick sheaf of bridge blueprints.

"What about new steelwork? Someplace he could have hidden the package." Villiard asked. He was starting to get frantic, he could hear it in his voice.

"Nothing like that. We just finished our MMRs in July, I'm telling you, and this time our biggest problem was the turnbuckle pins on the Marin Pier main cable saddles."

Villiard was tired and a little cranky, but he held his impatience in check. "What exactly is a MMR, Mr. Stroud?"

"Major maintenance routine," the engineer explained. "We check all the major systems annually, of course. But every ten years we go through what we call a MMR cycle. We check every single rivet, every cable, every connector, every square inch of plate steel and concrete. The roadways, the piers and fenders, anchorages, cable housings, the lighting and electrical systems, elevators, the suspenders, even the approach roads, sidewalks and railings. Everything."

"And there were no major repairs?" Villiard asked again.

"Like I said, just the turnbuckle pins."

"What about the piers themselves?"

"The underwater parts?"

"Yeah. Do you check those as well?"

"All the time. Same as every other part of the bridge." The pinch-faced engineer shook his head. "I'd really like to help you guys, but nothing's gone on out there in the past couple of months that fits what you're talking about. I mean there's a million places to hide something like that, but you've already checked it out. All I'm saying is that the bomb is not buried in the structure."

"Could someone have snuck out there in the middle of the night?"

"And opened a hole in the bridge, dumped the package and resealed it without us knowing about it?" Stroud asked. "Not likely."

"You mean that it's possible?"

"No, I mean that there's not a chance in hell. We would have spotted the fix," Stroud assured him. "Look, I've been working on this bridge for twenty-five years. I know it better than I know my wife's body, and I've got five kids. There's nothing out there."

It was the same message he'd gotten from the divers that Dave Rogan had sent down at first light. He glanced up at the clock. It was coming up on 8:00 A.M. In three and a half hours the President of the United States and his wife would drive into the stadium at Candlestick Park for the opening ceremonies. Thirty minutes later their motorcade would head for Sausalito followed by 1,837 handicapped runners including Raindrop, the President's daughter. And at this moment the Secret Service was no further ahead in its efforts to assure their safety than they had been eight weeks ago when this first became an issue.

Villiard closed his eyes and ears for a moment, blocking out the sights and sounds of the busy operations center. Tried and true. Maybe that was a crock of shit after all.

M/V *Margo*
Golden Gate Holding Basin

A thin sheen of perspiration covered Bahmad's forehead as he picked up the radiotelephone and depressed the switch. "San Francisco Harbor Control, this is the Motor Vessel *Margo* with Charlie at the holding basin, requesting a pilot." *Charlie* was the latest Notice to Mariners about the holding basin and bridge approach closure.

"Good morning, Capt'n, Russ Meeks is your man and he's on his way. But you'll have to stay put until the Coasties give us the all clear. Should be around two."

"That's fine. Gives me a few hours to catch up on some paperwork I was going to do when we docked. I might as well get it done now."

"I hear you, Capt'n. Have a good one."

"Thanks. *Margo*, out."

Four other ships, all of them container carriers, were anchored in the holding area just off Seal Rocks Beach. The wind was unusually light, but the *Margo* still rolled a little with the incoming Pacific swells. Five miles out Bahmad had raced down to the engine room where he'd powered down the big diesels, and then had rushed back up to the bridge to steer the boat to the holding area. Except for all the running around it was ridiculously easy. The huge cargo ship was steered with a wheel that was smaller in diameter than the saucer for a tea cup. When the ship's speed was down to practically nothing, he hit a switch that released the starboard bow anchor. When it hit bottom it dug in almost immediately and the vessel swung ponderously around so that its bow faced a few points off the wind and seas and came to a complete halt, portside to seaward.

From here he could see the Marin side of the bridge a little more than three miles away. He studied it through binoculars. Traffic was heavy, and he could make out a lot of police cars and official vehicles, lights flashing, crossing and recrossing the bridge. Hundreds of people had gathered at the rails, and hundreds more on foot were streaming onto the bridge to wait for the race.

There were at least four helicopters in the air passing back and forth directly over the bridge, and a pair of Coast Guard cutters patrolling the waters on either side of the center span. Their bow guns were uncovered, the barrel caps off, and the three crewmen who he could make out on the nearest cutter wore their Kevlar helmets. They meant business. No ship would be allowed anywhere near the bridge until the runners were safely over.

He continued to study the waters on either side of the bridge until he spotted a small white powerboat, some sort of a pennant flying from a whippy mast, passing the Coast Guard cutter on the seaward side of the bridge.

The cutter did not challenge the little boat, which continued straight out toward the holding basin.

Bahmad lowered the binoculars and allowed a faint smile

to crease his lips. It was the pilot boat and it had a free rein in the harbor.

He pocketed a walkie-talkie, set to the standard VHF channel 16 and went to open the port quarter gate and lower the ladder. It was too bad about the helicopter. But there was more air traffic than he had counted on. Someone was bound to see the chopper lift off from the *Margo*. What wouldn't be so easy to spot however, would be the Zodiac and powerful outboard motor that he'd found in a deck locker last night. At the time he'd merely noted that it was there, along with the lifting tackle to put it in the water. But now he was glad he had gone looking out of curiosity and had found it.

Soon, he thought. Very soon now and the United States would be a very different place in which to live. He would also have to get back to the chart room to do a final bit of navigation, but that part was easy compared to what he'd already gone through.

Candlestick Park

The presidential motorcade, lights flashing, sirens screaming, swept down the Candlestick Park exit off U.S. 101 a couple of minutes before 11:30 A.M.

"Thunder is clear, seven," the Secret Service officer riding shotgun in the President's limousine radioed softly.

Crowds had gathered along the half-marathon route over the bridge. Thousands of them waved small American flags, but there were many along the route who waved the flags of the several dozen participating countries.

"It'd be nice to think that they turned out for us in such numbers," Governor S. Howard Thomas commented. His complexion was florid. He'd drunk enough Chivas to float a battleship at last night's AP managing editor's dinner. But he had given a creditable speech this morning to the San Francisco Downtown Rotary Club that surprised even Haynes.

"Your being here won't hurt, Howard," the President said. "The talk will get around."

The governor shot him a sly look, not sure if the President wasn't being sarcastic. It was no secret that Haynes disliked him. But Thomas was the party favorite; he had done a reasonably good job in his first term, and the ass running against him was a total flake.

"I can see him hitting the Pentagon, or Wall Street, even the Congress, but not here." The governor gave the President's wife and his wife the famous Thomas reassuring smile. "Not here, not today. Too many of his own people would get hurt. They'd tear him apart back home. Limb from limb."

"I'm still nervous," Mildred Thomas admitted.

The President's wife patted her hand. "We would have canceled the games if there was a possibility that something was going to happen. Our own daughter is here."

"I know. And I think you're so brave," Mrs. Thomas said sincerely. "But I'm not."

The President gave his wife an appreciative look. What they didn't need right now was a nervous or even hysterical woman on the stage at the opening ceremonies. It was difficult enough keeping the truth from the public though the media had started to put it together. A few calls to the presidents of the networks had put the lid on the story for a little while, at least through this weekend. But the dam would break soon. Then they would be faced with conducting an investigation in the face of a frightened nation. At that point even if the bomb were never to be used, bin Laden would have already won. The idea of a terrorist act was to terrorize. Well, just the threat of this attack was going to be enough to set the average American off. Nobody would ever feel safe in their homes so long as bin Laden was alive. It was the argument he had used on the TV execs.

"Nothing to be brave about, Mildred, unless Deb wins the race in which case they'll say that the fix was in and scream for our blood," the President assured her.

They slowed down as they passed through the stadium entrance directly onto the field. The stadium was filled to capacity. All the athletes were lined up in ranks and files behind their national flags. Most of them wore white blazers and dark blue slacks or skirts, but the marathon runners were decked out in their shorts with their numbers pinned on the backs of their shirts.

The stage was decorated with red, white and blue bunting and the pennants of all the participating nations.

A huge cheer went up through the stadium as the President's limousine crossed the field and stopped in front of the stage. ISO director Octavio Aguilar and the other dignitaries all rose, and as the President and first lady got out of the car the band played "Hail to the Chief."

The President searched for his daughter's face in the middle of the American delegation. He thought he spotted her, but then he wasn't sure as he and his wife started slowly up the stairs with Governor and Mrs. Thomas, shaking hands as they went. Two of his Secret Service agents were already on stage, four flanked the President and First Lady, and a dozen others ringed the platform. There were even more in the skybox and at other strategic positions in the stadium. Everyone was alert, no one was asleep on the job this morning.

It was a poor defense against a nuclear weapon, the fleeting thought crossed the President's mind, but then he was shaking hands with the tiny, birdlike Octavio Aguilar and his even more diminutive wife Marianna.

"International Special Olympians," the announcer's voice blasted through the stadium. "Coaches, trainers, ladies and gentlemen, the President of the United States of America."

The crowd cheered as the President stepped to the microphone to make his remarks and declare that the games were open. He prayed to God that this would be the beginning of a completely uneventful week.

M/V *Margo*

Bahmad reached the bottom of the boarding ladder as the pilot boat rounded the *Margo*'s stern. One man was in the cabin at the wheel, and another was at the rail on the aft deck. He would be Russell Meeks, the pilot, who was supposed to come aboard to guide the *Margo* to her berth after the race. Bahmad raised his hand and waved. Meeks waved back as the man driving the pilot boat expertly brought her alongside, throwing the transmission into neutral at exactly the right moment.

Bahmad passed a line across to Meeks, who seemed to be surprised, but took it. The usual procedure was for the boat to come alongside and for the pilot to simply jump across.

"I'd like to talk to you for a minute before you come aboard, Mr. Meeks. If you don't mind," Bahmad said.

"What's going on?" Meeks wore a San Francisco Harbor Pilot cap and jacket. He carried a walkie-talkie in a holster in his belt like a gun. If he reached for it Bahmad would kill him on the spot.

"It'll just take a minute, sir. I need to talk to you and your driver. I have to show you something."

Meeks was an older man, white hair, deeply lined face, but he was built like a linebacker. He'd probably worked on or around boats all of his life. He was suspicious now. "Who are you?"

"I'm Joseph Green, first officer. I've really gotta talk to you, man. There's nothing wrong, I mean, but this is important. Believe me."

Meeks turned, leaned into the cabin and said something to the delivery skipper that Bahmad didn't quite catch. He turned back, nodded, cleated off the line and stepped aside.

Bahmad jumped aboard and stumbled as if he had lost his balance. He reached out to Meeks with his left hand to steady himself, while he reached in his jacket for his pistol with his other. He turned toward the delivery driver who watched from his high seat at the helm, a calm but curious look on his narrow, dark face. Bahmad got the impression that he might be Hispanic.

"Easy," Meeks said.

Bahmad pulled out his pistol, thumbed the safety catch off and fired one shot into the delivery driver's face.

Meeks reacted immediately, batting Bahmad's hand away. But he wasn't quick enough. Bahmad swung the pistol around and pumped two shots into the pilot's chest, the second destroying his heart. He fell backward and nearly pitched over the rail before Bahmad managed to grab a handful of his jacket and haul him back. His body slumped to the deck in a spreading pool of blood.

The day was suddenly very quiet except for the cries of the seagulls overhead.

Bahmad holstered his pistol and dragged the pilot's body out of sight inside the cabin. Back on deck he found a bucket and sponge and quickly cleaned off the blood. Once again inside the cabin he cleaned the blood off the windshield, then propped the pilot boat driver's body up against the wheel. He cut a couple of pieces of rope from a heaving line and tied the man's arms to the wheel and his back up against the back of the seat. From the air everything would look normal here. The open deck was clean and the pilot boat driver was at the helm where he belonged.

Bahmad studied the instrument panel long enough to find what he'd hoped to find. Because of the frequent fogs in the bay the pilot boat was equipped with a pair of GPS navigators tied to an autopilot with a hundred programmable waypoints. With the right settings the boat could practically thread its way through a maze without anyone touching the wheel.

He took out a piece of paper on which he had jotted down two pairs of latitudes and longitudes that he had worked out at the chart table aboard *Margo*, and entered them as waypoints one and two in the autopilot. The first would take the pilot boat well clear of the *Margo*'s bow and the second would take it directly under the center span of the Golden Gate Bridge.

Candlestick Park

The Secret Service agent riding shotgun in the President's limousine turned around. "The starter is ready, sir."

The President looked out the rear window. The motorcade of six cars was poised at the fifty-yard line exit from the stadium. The runners were massed behind where the fifty-yard line would be if this were football season back to the end zone. People in the stands were on their feet, most of them waving flags and cheering. The noise even inside the bulletproof limo was thunderous. Somewhere back there was his daughter, and the President of the United States could not remember a time when he had been more frightened.

"Tell him to start," he said.

The Secret Service agent relayed the message. A few seconds later the runners surged forward and the President's motorcade headed out.

FEMA Operations Center

The security team watching the television monitors had the best seats of all. ESPN was televising the half-marathon live from the MetLife blimp that would pace the runners from the park across the bridge to Sausalito. One of Villiard's men was aboard as crew, and he kept up a running commentary over one of the tactical radio channels the Secret Service used. The view from about six hundred feet was spectacular.

They received more than a dozen other television images from Coast Guard, San Francisco PD and National Guard helicopters aloft, as well as from a half-dozen security cameras on the bridge.

Six radio operators were busy monitoring on-the-site reporting from more than one hundred Secret Service and FBI agents. In addition they monitored all the frequencies used by the county and local police, the National Guard, Coast Guard, San Francisco Harbor Control and the FAA's air traffic control units and flight service stations within the entire San Francisco and Oakland Terminal Control areas.

They had direct radio links to the presidential motorcade, including to the President's Secret Service detail as well as to the president himself. They could talk to Kirk McGarvey and Todd Van Buren as well as to Elizabeth McGarvey who planned on keeping up with the President's daughter for at least the first half of the race. If need be she could be picked up by one of the SFPD motorcycle cops and leapfrogged ahead. But she'd told Villiard that she would keep up until they were across the suspended part of the bridge. After that they would probably find her dead body fallen alongside the road.

Villiard had to smile thinking about her. She was a hell of a young woman. A chip off the old block. Tried and true.

He glanced up at the images from the blimp as the presidential motorcade emerged from the stadium followed by the first of the eighteen hundred runners and his heart began to pound in his chest.

Candlestick Park

Elizabeth had never run a marathon or any other big race in which she was in the middle of hundreds of runners. The experience now bordered on the surreal. Deborah was on her right and slightly ahead, and they were surrounded by a sea of white muscle shirts, arms and elbows, heads bobbing and weaving. Already she was beginning to smell sweat and running shoes and some unpleasant unwashed body odors. Some of the runners limped or hopped because of their disabilities; others took huge bounding leaps and still others ran flat-out, pushing their way through the mass of human flesh. They probably wouldn't even last until the highway, and she was sure that their coaches had tried to drum into their heads the notion of pacing themselves. But this was the Special Olympics, and most athletes here were so enthused for the moment that they could hardly contain themselves.

The President's daughter, however, and perhaps a hundred other runners like her who had received good training, were pacing themselves for the long haul, something over thirteen miles. For at least that much Elizabeth was grateful, although the pace Deborah was running was not going to be easy to keep up with. She would be doing the half-marathon in under two hours.

Elizabeth saw the blimp overhead and the helicopters crisscrossing the sky. Somewhere still well out ahead was the presidential motorcade, lights flashing. Once they got out onto U.S. 101 there would be spectators cheering them on, and a mile and a half out, when the field would be spreading out, there would be the first of the water stations.

Somewhere in the pack behind them Tod Van Buren and whatever Secret Service agent he'd been assigned to this morning were drifting through the field on the souped-up golf cart. They were looking for any sign of trouble, and they were keeping up with Deborah.

Elizabeth resisted the urge to look over her shoulder to see if she could spot them. It was hard enough keeping up without making it more difficult for herself.

She pulled up even with the President's daughter. Deborah's long blond hair streamed behind her, there was a thin sheen of perspiration on her face and there was a look of absolute joy, even rapture, on her sweet face.

Deborah turned and gave Elizabeth a huge grin. "Isn't this just so cool?" she shouted. She wasn't even breathing hard yet.

"Cool," Elizabeth said. She caught a glimpse of the highway in the distance, and settled back for the long haul. For the *very* long haul, she told herself as she took several clearing breaths.

Golden Gate Bridge

McGarvey bummed a ride across the bridge from an SFPD cop. As they passed under the Marin side tower he directed the officer to pull over and he got out.

The wind was down, which would make it a lot easier on the runners. There weren't even any whitecaps on the bay or in the Golden Gate. Directly below the bridge an eighty-two-foot Coast Guard cutter was making its turn back to the south. In the distance, at Seal Rocks Beach, McGarvey could see five big cargo ships at anchor waiting to come in after the race.

He pushed his way through the spectators sitting on beach chairs and on the curb, and went to the rail. He lit a cigarette and stared at the ships, allowing the urgency that had gripped him for the last twenty-four hours to ease up a little.

There was no other activity in the Golden Gate. Nothing moved except for the cutter. Even if the bomb was aboard one of the cargo ships, there was no time for the anchor to be pulled up and the ship to make it to the bridge by the time the runners arrived. The Coast Guard cutters would intercept it long before it got close. If need be, the Coast Guard jet that was standing by at the Oakland Airport could be scrambled.

All the bases were covered.

He turned and gazed down the length of the bridge. Thousands of people lined the roadway. Police units, their lights flashing, seemed to be everywhere. Overhead, he counted six helicopters and in the distance to the south the MetLife blimp was heading this way. It meant that the race was underway.

There were sharpshooters atop both towers in case someone tried to bull their way onto the bridge. Salted in and among the eighteen hundred runners were two dozen Secret Service agents plus Todd Van Buren and Elizabeth.

He turned again to stare at the five cargo ships. What was he missing? What were they all missing? Most of them, from the President down, didn't really believe that an attack would come here. It was against bin Laden's interests. Yet everyone was frightened. It was bizarre.

M/V Margo

A radio on the bridge was tuned to ESPN, and the minute-by-minute commentary on the Special Olympics half-marathon was being piped over the *Margo*'s PA system.

Bahmad had horsed the inflated twelve-foot Zodiac out of its locker on the port quarterdeck just forward of where the now-useless helicopter was lashed down, and had attached the lifting sling to the three heavy D-rings on the dinghy's gunwhale line.

The runners were off, but he had plenty of time. From everything that he'd read and knew about this type of event, a woman runner would make a full marathon in a bit over four hours. The President's daughter was an excellent athlete so it was no stretch of the imagination to believe that she would do a half-marathon in two hours, barring any delays or accidents.

Bahmad looked up at the other container vessels in the basin. There was no movement on their decks. The crews were below eating their midday meal.

Deborah Haynes would run the thirteen miles in two hours, which meant that she would average a little more than nine minutes per mile. The middle of the Golden Gate Bridge was about nine miles from the stadium at Candlestick Park. Eighty to eighty-five minutes after the start of the race Deborah Haynes would be on the center span.

Bahmad powered the Zodiac off the deck with the hand controller, and then swung the boom out over the side of the rail. When the dinghy had stopped swinging and was clear, he quickly powered it forty feet down to the surface of the water within reach of the boarding ladder.

The pilot boat would make fifteen knots easily, and the center span of the bridge was three miles away. Allowing time for the boat to clear the *Margo*'s bow and make the turn, Bahmad estimated that twelve minutes after he cast off the pilot boat's lines it would be under the bridge.

The timing could be sloppy, several minutes off either way, because of the blast radius of the nuclear device. If the pilot boat were somewhere in the vicinity of the bridge at the same time the runners were on the bridge or very near it, the President's daughter and a lot of other people would die.

He walked aft to the stern rail where three fiberglass containers, each about the size of a large suitcase, were bracketed to the deck. Each was marked LIFT RAFT EIGHT PERSON MADE IN CHINA. He undid the fasteners for the cannister on the left and lifted it off its cradle. It was very heavy, more than forty kilograms. He imagined that he could feel heat coming off it, which was nonsense of course. Nevertheless he handled the container with a great deal of care as he awkwardly brought it forward to the gate. He set the package down at the head of the boarding ladder so that he could catch his breath. It wouldn't do to drop the damn thing halfway down the ladder in the rolling swell. Not after all this. Not when he was this close.

The runners were fifteen minutes into the race on U.S. 101, and according to the ESPN commentator they were already beginning to spread out with Deborah Haynes near the lead as expected.

She would be on the center span in another sixty-five to seventy minutes. He would have to send the pilot boat off twelve minutes before then. He had nearly an hour. Twenty minutes to put the bomb in place and make the final settings. Another twenty to get his things, put them aboard the dinghy and make sure that the outboard worked. And the final fifteen minutes or so to fine-tune the timing based on the ESPN blow-by-blow.

Once the pilot boat was off he would take the dinghy around the sound end of the point, which would afford him protection from the blast. In the confusion afterward he would make his escape.

Plenty of time, he told himself, as he hefted the bomb and started down the ladder.

The MetLife Blimp

Secret Service agent Hugh Gardner had seen a lot of stuff in his five-year career with the service, but he'd never seen such a mass of humanity spread out over four miles of highway as he was seeing right now. Some of the runners had given up before they had gotten out of the Candlestick Park parking lot, while others, among them the President's daughter, were within a hundred yards or so of the lead.

"Lead One, this is Baker Seven, they're coming up on delta," he spoke into his lapel mike. Delta was the Mission Dolores just beyond where U.S. 101 made its jog to the west.

"Copy, Baker Seven. How's it looking from there?"

"No problems that I can see," Gardner replied. The view from up here was fantastic. He could see the bridge up ahead, the city and the bay to the east, including Alcatraz Island, and the outer stretches of the Golden Gate to the west, the hazy Pacific Ocean stretching off to the horizon.

He sincerely hoped that nothing would go wrong today to spoil the shear beauty of it. His fellow agents razzed him for being so overly sensitive in such a demanding job. But, as he had explained to the guys on his detail last week, the quickest, easiest and cheapest way into a woman's knickers was reading poetry. Sensitivity, gentlemen. Try it, you'll like it.

The Pilot Boat

Bahmad unsnapped the life raft's latches and opened the outer cover. He had a little trouble with one of the inner latches, but when it finally popped he prised up the lid to reveal the bomb's control panel. As he huddled inside the cabin there was nothing to be seen except for the *Margo*'s rust-streaked hull rising like a shear cliff, and no one to see what he was doing.

He entered the activation code on the keypad and the numerical display and warning lights came to life. The impression that heat was radiating from the device was even stronger now than it had been up on the *Margo*'s stern, and it was just as foolish. The bomb did not leak.

One last time Bahmad was struck with the notion that what he was doing could and should be stopped. Even now. There was no need to go through with this thing. No need for the killing and the suffering. No need for him to become the most hunted and the most reviled man in all of history. No need for revenge. Not his revenge for his parents and not bin Laden's for his Sarah.

He closed his eyes. He could see Beirut as it had been when he was a child. It had been called the Paris of the Mediterranean. He could see beautiful gardens, laughing happy people, family meals. But then he could hear the Israeli jets, feel the earth-shattering pounding of their bombs, smell the burning flesh.

Bahmad opened his eyes, focused on the control pad and entered another series of codes that set the bomb's moment of detonation fifty-five minutes from now. At that instant the bulk of the runners would be on the Golden Gate Bridge. For them there would be no pain, not like the pain his parents had suffered, not the pain that Sarah had endured. For the runners there would be a blinding flash of light and then nothing.

He entered another series of codes that activated the antitampering circuits. If anyone tried to stop the bomb it would explode immediately.

Finally his finger poised over the start button. For one moment he questioned his sanity, but then he pushed the button, closed and relatched the inner cover and closed and relatched the outer cover.

The countdown had begun.

Golden Gate Bridge

McGarvey's cell phone rang. The number on the display was Rencke's private office line. He'd been on the computers continuously for four days and nights. But when he had the bit in his teeth nothing could stop him.

"Have you come up with something new?" McGarvey answered.

"It's there, and I know how it got there," Rencke rasped. It sounded as if he was on the verge of cracking up. "From Karachi, disguised as a life raft made in China. Oh, boy, it was right there in front of me all the time. Purple—"

McGarvey gripped the phone. "Where is it, Otto? Specifically!"

"San Francisco. The coast. Came by ship, Karachi, Red Sea, the Med. It was laid up for two months in Tampa. That's what threw me off."

McGarvey was on the center span of the bridge. He spun around and looked out toward Seal Point, but from this angle he could only see the bows of two container ships. There were four or five of them out there. He'd spotted them earlier when he was on the Marin side. "What ship? When did it come in?" he demanded.

"The *Margo*, Cyprus registry, home office PKS Shipping, Ltd., Paris. Ties to bin Laden, ya know. It all fits. It was right there."

"Okay, calm down, Otto. When did the *Margo* get here? When?"

"It should be coming in right now. Went through the big

ditch where it picked up a helicopter. The Coast Guard spotted her yesterday off Baja California, and I got satellite pictures this morning. It's there, Mac. You're probably looking right at it."

McGarvey pushed his way through the spectators and raced across to the other side of the bridge. "How do you know that the bomb is aboard that ship?"

"It was delivered to the dock in Karachi. We got the delivery man last night. Traced it back to a flight from Peshwar. Chinese life rafts in Peshwar, Pakistan?"

The only ship moving on the bay side was the second Coast Guard cutter. No cargo vessel. At least none near enough so that if the nuclear device were to be lit off it would damage the bridge or kill anyone on it. They would have to deal with radioactive fallout, but that would come later.

"No chance that it could have come in late last night or early this morning?"

"I don't think so, Mac. It's gotta be right there."

"Good work, Otto. We'll find it." McGarvey broke the connection. He was still missing something, goddammit. Bahmad would not have come this far to fail. He radioed Villiard at the FEMA Operations Center as he walked back across the bridge to the oceanside.

"Villiard," the Secret Service agent came back.

"The bomb is aboard a Cypriot-registered cargo ship. *Margo*. Find out if its come into port yet, and where it is."

Villiard was enough of a pro not to ask questions right now. "Stand by."

Nothing was changed in the Golden Gate. The cargo ships were still parked just around the point, waiting to come into port. Delayed because of the shipping restriction.

He checked his watch. The first runners would be on the bridge in less than thirty minutes. There wasn't enough time for one of those cargo ships to pull up anchor and get here. Villiard was back and he was excited.

"The *Margo* showed up about an hour ago. She's anchored in a holding basin at Seal Point."

"I'm on the bridge. There're five ships out there, two that I can see right now. Neither one of them is moving. Anyway they'd never make it here in time to—" McGarvey stopped in midsentence as if a spike had been driven into his skull.

"You still there?"

"The bomb's on the *Margo*, but she's also carrying a helicopter."

"Sonofabitch."

"Scramble the jet and tell the pilot to splash that chopper the moment her rotors start to turn. Do it now while we still have time."

"I'll alert the President's detail."

"Scramble the jet first, Jay." McGarvey pushed through the crowd at the curb and ran out into the middle of the roadway. "I'm right in the middle of the bridge. I want a chopper down here right now to take me out to the *Margo*."

"I'm on it," Villiard replied tersely, and he was gone.

McGarvey grabbed a passing cop and had him start clearing the road for the helicopter to land.

M/V *Margo*

Bahmad tossed his leather bag into the dinghy, then turned around and looked at the pilot boat not quite certain that he'd heard what he thought he'd heard. The radio was on, tuned to the San Francisco Harbor Control working channel. He jumped aboard and had to step over the bodies in the cabin to get to the radio, his eyes going instinctively to the bomb wedged between the driver's seat and the bulkhead. The radio was silent for the moment. He turned down the squelch.

"Negative, she's off Seal Point. The Coasties, are scrambling a jet."

"Meeks is out there, but I've not been able to raise him."

Bahmad stepped back, staggered by what he was hearing. They knew! Somehow they knew.

"I haven't been able to reach him or Iglesias."

Bahmad looked at his watch. The runners wouldn't be on the bridge for another twenty-five minutes. The bomb was set to go off then. But if the authorities came out here they would discover the dead pilot and his driver. The bomb would go off here, killing a few people instead of thousands. He would have failed again. The thought threatened to send him over the edge.

"Maybe they have radio problems."

As had happened many times before, the solution came to Bahmad all in one piece. He knew every step that he would have to take, including the diversion he would have to create if he was going to have the time to make his escape.

He went out to the starboard rail and yanked the six-foot whip antenna out of its mount. The radio went dead. Anyone looking when the pilot boat approached the bridge would see that the antenna was down which would explain their radio silence.

Back at the helm he started the inboard, activated the autopilot and put the transmission in forward, setting the throttle to a few hundred RPMs above idle. It would take the pilot boat at least twenty minutes, maybe a little longer to get to the bridge at that speed.

The boat strained at the line holding it to the *Margo*'s boarding ladder. Bahmad had some difficulty jumping across because the pilot boat was pitching and hobbyhorsing, pulling at its leash like a puppy dog wishing to run free. He pulled out his stiletto and cut the line. The pilot boat immediately headed away.

He pulled the dinghy over, jumped aboard, lowered the outboard, connected the gas line and pushed the starter button. It roared into life instantly.

The pilot boat still hadn't cleared the *Margo*'s bow by the time Bahmad climbed out of the dinghy and raced up the boarding ladder, but he didn't bother looking. That part of the operation was now completely out of his control.

On deck he ducked through a hatch and took the stairs

two at a time up to the bridge. He hurriedly set the main autopilot to steer the same course as the pilot boat, then hit the switch to bring up the anchor.

The pilot boat would take care of itself. And just maybe when the authorities saw the *Margo* heading for the bridge it would keep them busy long enough for Bahmad to get clear.

Once the bomb lit off no one would be coming for him, the survivors would be far too busy trying to stay alive.

He headed down to the engine room, a smile on his plain, round face. Even in disunity there can be unity. Even in disharmony there can be harmony. And even in the face of my enemies there can be victory.

Insha'Allah.

Over the Golden Gate

"What boat is that?" McGarvey shouted over the tremendous roar of the Coast Guard's SH 3 Sea King helicopter's two turboshaft engines.

The chief petty officer who was studying the container ships at anchor out ahead of them lowered his binoculars and looked where McGarvey was pointing.

"That's the pilot boat," he shouted back. He took a quick look through his binoculars. "Their antenna is down." He handed his binoculars to McGarvey. "You'd better check out the *Margo*, sir."

McGarvey picked out the big container ship. It was the only one with a helicopter on its crowded decks. But the chopper was still tied down, and there was no activity around it. "What is it?"

"Her anchor, sir. It's up."

McGarvey switched to the bow. The anchor was definitely dripping water. It had just been pulled up. But there was no possibility that the ship would get anywhere close to the bridge in time.

He was still missing something, goddammit. But his

headaches were back and it was hard to think straight.

"Tell your pilot I have to get aboard on the double, chief," McGarvey shouted. He set the glasses aside and took out his Walther to check the load and the action.

Bahmad had not planned it this way. There was something else.

The MetLife Blimp

"Lead One, this is Baker Seven, they're coming up on Primary," Gardner radioed. Primary was the code name for the bridge.

"Copy, Baker Seven. Do you have Thunder in sight?"

Gardner could hear the strain in the radio operator's voice. Something was going on. "He's on the approach." Thunder was the President.

"Okay, we're closing down the race. Tell your pilot to get you on the ground right now."

"What's going on, Lead One?" Gardner asked, but there was no reply.

The ESPN reporter and pilot turned and looked at him. They'd caught the urgency in his voice.

"Problems?" the pilot asked.

"We have to get on the ground right now," Gardner said.

"What the hell are you talking about—?"

"Right fucking now," Gardner shouted. "If you want to save your life, put it down!"

FEMA Operations Center

"Flagler, Lead One," Villiard radioed to the Secret Service agent riding shotgun in the President's limousine. The Ops center was in full swing, but stopping the race without getting anyone hurt was going to be next to impossible. These were handicapped runners, some of them mentally handicapped. And there were eighteen hundred of them. It would be a nightmare.

"Lead One, Flagler."

"We're closing down the race. Do not take Thunder onto the bridge. Get him out of there."

"We're on the approach road. There's no way in hell we can turn around. It's wall-to-wall runners behind us."

Villiard made a snap decision. "Get him across the bridge then. I want him behind the hills ASAP."

"He's going to want his daughter with him—"

"Go now!"

Villiard switched channels to Chenna Serafini's. She was on the golf cart with the CIA officer shadowing the President's daughter. "Raindrop One, Lead One."

"Raindrop One."

Villiard recognized Chenna's voice. "Do you have visual contact with Raindrop?"

"Not continuously. She's in the middle of a bunch forty yards ahead of us."

"Okay, listen up, Chenna. I want you to go to her right now and get her off the bridge. You don't have much time."

Villiard could hear Chenna say something away from her lapel mike, and then she was back. "What're we facing?"

"They might hit the bridge. We're closing down the race. Thunder's already on the way out. I'm giving you a head start."

"We're on it."

Villiard switched channels again and began issuing orders to the local and state cops to start shutting everything down and clearing the bridge, with almost no hope whatsoever that they would be in time.

Coast Guard Cutter
WMEC 907 *Escanaba*

Lieutenant Gloria Sampson braced herself as the *Escanaba* came around hard to starboard. This was her first command

and she was too excited to be nervous. Yesterday at the briefing on nuclear terrorism she'd been frightened, but there was no time for that today.

She spotted the small boat well out into the Gate heading directly toward them at the same time her XO looked up from the radar.

"It's the pilot boat, their radio's out," Ensign DeLillo told her.

"Forget it, the *Margo*'s already got her anchor up."

M/V *Margo*

So far as McGarvey could tell, the wheelhouse was empty and the decks were devoid of any life. It could have been a ghost ship, except that an army could have hidden in the containers stacked eight deep. But they had finally run out of time. It was only him at this point; a situation he neither liked nor disliked. It was just the way things had worked out.

"Put me down on the afterdeck as close to the helicopter as you can," McGarvey shouted to the chief.

The chief said something into his helmet mike, and the Sea King, which was just off the container ship's starboard quarter, slid to the right and dropped directly for the two stacks of containers on the portside.

"The skipper wants to know if we should stick around," the chief shouted.

"You know the score, it's up to you."

The chief spoke into his mike, then grinned and gave McGarvey the thumbs-up. "We'll hover just off your quarter. Good luck."

"Thanks," McGarvey said.

The *Margo* was moving around in the swell, so the helicopter did not attempt to touch down. It hovered a couple of feet above the stack of containers until McGarvey jumped out, then peeled off directly aft.

As soon as he was out of the rotor wash, McGarvey

scrambled to the end of the container to look for a way down. There were no handholds except for the chains that held the stacks tightly to the deck. The helicopter was tied down and the rotors still secured. It would take at least twenty minutes to get it ready to fly. McGarvey stared at it. Goddammit, this wasn't making any sense.

He holstered his pistol and started down the chain, the links greasy and dirty with rust, shackled at intervals with big jagged U-bolts. He was at his most vulnerable at this moment. If Bahmad or one of his crewmen took a potshot at him they wouldn't have to actually hit him. A near miss might be enough to dislodge his tenuous grip and he would fall the fifty or sixty feet to the steel deck. If it didn't kill him, he would certainly be out of action for the duration.

But it was useless to think about that possibility, or any of a hundred other things that could go wrong. One step at a time. It was all he could do.

On deck finally, McGarvey pulled out his gun and ran around to the left side of the helicopter. It was definitely not ready to fly. The controls were still secured with their locks, and the engine exhaust and intake caps were still in place. It made no sense. Why had Bahmad carried the machine all this way if he didn't intend on using it. And where the hell was the *Margo*'s crew?

McGarvey's eyes strayed aft, to the stern rail, and his breath caught in his throat. Two fiberglass life raft canisters were secured to the deck on aluminum brackets. The brackets for a third canister were empty.

He took a step forward. The bomb had been right there, and now it was gone.

He felt a sudden, deep-throated rumble and vibration through the soles of his feet. He turned and looked up as a thick plume of black smoke rose from the *Margo*'s stack. The water at the stern began to roil, and the ship started to move forward.

McGarvey started around the chopper to find a hatch into the superstructure when a mind-numbing roar swooped

down on him, blotting out all sounds, even those of the Sea
King hovering just off their port quarter.

He turned back in time to see a Harrier jet slide into
place not more than a couple of hundred feet aft of the
stern. He could see the Coast Guard's diagonal orange
stripes on the fuselage, the Sparrow III and Sidewinder missiles on the wing racks and the determined look on the
pilot's face.

McGarvey slowly raised his hands in the air. Destroying
the chopper while it was still on the *Margo's* deck was one
thing, but he did not want to be mistaken for one of the
bad guys.

VS-31, McDonnell Douglas AV-8B
Harrier II

"Base, Victor-sierra-three-one. I'm in position aft of the
Margo. There's a Cuban military chopper on deck, and one
possible bad guy standing next to it with his hands up.
Advise."

"Base, Three-One, is the chopper ready to fly?"

"Negative. It's still tied down, and her rotors are secured.
But the ship is getting under way. Request permission to
go weapons free."

"Permission granted—"

"Negative, negative," someone overrode his primary
channel. "This is Victor-tango-one-seven, the Sea King just
off your port wing. That is one of our people on deck.
Copy?"

Lieutenant Bill Dillard had spotted the Coast Guard helicopter as he came in, of course. But he had his mission
orders. Splash the chopper on the *Margo's* deck if it so
much as twitched.

"Stand by One-seven," he radioed. "Base, Three-one, did
you copy that last transmission."

"Roger, stand by."

Lieutenant Dillard had no idea what the hell was actually

going on, except that it was a possible threat to the President, and the *Margo* was picking up speed. Somebody had put the pedal to the metal.

"Three-one, Base. Confirm that is a friendly on deck. But stick with the ship. If someone, I don't care who, tries to get that chopper ready to fly you have authorization to splash it before it gets off the deck."

"Roger, copy that." Dillard backed up and waggled his wings.

Golden Gate Bridge

Elizabeth pressed her earpiece closer. Something was going on. There was a steady stream of chatter on the radio. She was catching snatches of orders. Something about the bridge being closed.

"Raindrop Elizabeth, Lead One."

"This is Elizabeth, Lead One. Go."

"Are you on the bridge yet?" Villiard demanded.

"We're just coming up on the tower. Do we have trouble?"

"Chenna and Todd are on their way. Get Raindrop off the bridge."

Elizabeth's gut tightened, but then a calmness came over her. "Copy," she spoke into her mike. She shouted for Deborah who was a few yards ahead of her to hold up.

Halfway across the bridge the President was stunned. He'd been saying something to his wife when John Flagler gave the order to their driver to bug out, and the limousine suddenly shot forward like a shell from a cannon.

"What the hell—?"

"I'm sorry, Mr. President, but there is a possible threat," Flagler said sharply. He said something into his radio, then looked over his shoulder past the President and First Lady out the rear window.

"We have to get Deborah," the President told him.

"Her detail is picking her up now, sir."

"We're going back for her, John, and that's an order."

Flagler said something else into his mike. He had an Ingram MAC 10 out. He looked the President in the eye, his expression devoid of anything other than professionalism. "I'm sorry, Mr. President, but that's not possible. Your daughter is being taken care of. In the meantime we're getting you off the bridge."

On the opposite side of the bridge Chenna Serafini and Todd Van Buren were bogged down. The runners were bunching up again. Van Buren jumped out of the golf cart and ran ahead to make a path for Chenna. The President's daughter was somewhere out ahead of them. Chenna was sick that she had let them get so far ahead. The girl had to be up around the tower by now. Hopefully she hadn't left Elizabeth McGarvey behind.

"Raindrop Elizabeth, this is Raindrop One," Chenna radioed.

Van Buren was bodily shoving runners aside, knocking some of them to the pavement. He made a hole and Chenna sped up. As she passed he jumped aboard.

"Liz, you copy?" Chenna spoke urgently into her lapel mike.

"This is Lead One, she can't hear you," Villiard radioed back. "I'll patch you over."

The runners ahead cleared another path, and Van Buren spotted Deborah and Elizabeth about thirty yards away at the side of the road. "There," he shouted.

Chenna spotted them too. They had stopped at the edge of a big pileup of runners just across from the oceanside leg of the San Francisco Tower. It was a security nightmare. There were runners and spectators all within arm's reach. Getting to her and then getting her back out without hurting someone was going to be next to impossible. And calling for their helicopter to pick them up would be equally impossible until they could get Deborah out to the middle of the span away from the towers and suspension cables, or back out of the crowd somewhere off the bridge approaches.

"Chenna, this is Liz, I can see you," Elizabeth responded.

"Stand by, we're getting you and Deb out of there," Chenna radioed back. She jammed the pedal to the floor and shot out around a group of six runners, missing them by inches.

Elizabeth said something to the President's daughter who backed up a step and shook her head. Even from here Chenna could see that the girl was frightened by all the noise and sirens and commotion. When she was backed into a corner she always ran. It was something that Elizabeth could not know about.

"Don't push her," Chenna shouted into her mike at the same moment Elizabeth reached out for Deborah's hand.

Almost in slow motion the President's daughter reared back, turned and jumped over the high curb onto the sidewalk. The spectators parted for her and for Elizabeth who was right on her heel, and they disappeared around the outside of the tower leg.

M/V *Margo*

The bridge was empty. McGarvey saw a puddle of congealed blood on the deck, but there was no one up here controlling the ship. There was no sign of the crew anywhere. Bahmad had killed at least one of them, but where the hell were the others?

The ship was already starting to make a wide turn to starboard that would bring it into the Golden Gate and line it up with the bridge. But the *Margo* could not make it to the bridge in time. What was he missing?

The bomb had been removed from its bracket for some reason. Think, for God's sake. His head felt like someone had driven a hot spike through his skull.

He looked at the pool of blood again. Bahmad was a brilliant man. He would have contingency plans. The *Margo* might not make it to the bridge in time, but the bomb would.

"Sonofabitch." The bomb was no longer aboard this ship, or wouldn't be for long.

McGarvey hurriedly studied the control panel, finding and disengaging the autopilot, then flipped the switch that dropped the anchor.

He tore out of the bridge and raced downstairs to the main deck. All this time they had concentrated on this ship to deliver the bomb. But Bahmad was smart. He'd been trained by the British and American intelligence establishments. Getting the *Margo* underway was a diversionary tactic. He had another boat. Maybe the captain's gig to deliver the bomb. And afterward in the confusion he would use the helicopter to make his escape. But then why move the ship where it would be exposed to blast damage? It was getting hard to think straight.

McGarvey emerged winded from the starboard stairwell on the main deck athwartship corridor as Bahmad stepped out of a hatch twenty feet away.

For a split second they stared at each other, but McGarvey raised his pistol first and fired as Bahmad ducked back inside.

A MAC 10 came around the edge of the steel door and McGarvey just managed to pull back inside the stairwell landing as Bahmad fired a short burst, and then another, the bullets ricocheting all over the place.

McGarvey immediately fired three quick shots down the corridor in the general direction of the hatch and ducked back as Bahmad fired an answering burst. This time the shells ricocheted off the steel deck and walls just outside the stairwell.

The sonofabitch had raised the anchor and set the autopilot from the bridge by himself, and then had raced down to the engine room to start the diesels. Bahmad was alone.

He had killed the entire crew and now he was trying to get out. The bomb was already on its way.

The pilot boat!

McGarvey checked his watch. If the runners were on time the bulk of them would be coming on to the bridge at any minute. There was no time.

"Mr. McGarvey, you are an inventive man," Bahmad called.

"The bridge has been closed and the Coast Guard is intercepting the pilot boat," McGarvey said. "It's over. Toss your gun out into the corridor."

"It's much too late for such a simple lie as that to work. Actually it's you for whom everything is over."

McGarvey reached around the corner and fired two shots, but Bahmad was waiting for him, and he fired a sustained burst directly down the corridor.

McGarvey fell back as a shell fragment slammed into his hip, and another into his right side. He grunted involuntarily in pain. He was starting to get real tired of being shot up.

He heard an empty magazine clatter to the steel deck, and another being slapped into the handle. He turned and limped up the stairs as Bahmad fired, ricocheting bullets filling the landing with hundreds of deadly fragments.

"McGarvey," Bahmad shouted.

The athwartship corridor one level up from the main deck was dark, although McGarvey could clearly see that the ceiling lights were on. He trailed his left hand on the bulkhead for balance as he hurried to the portside stairwell and started down. His hip was numb, but his whole right side was on fire. It was becoming increasingly harder to concentrate.

The main deck corridor was ominously silent. McGarvey closed his eyes for just a moment to gather the last of his strength, then eased just far enough around the corner so that he could see what was going on.

Bahmad, his attention on the starboard stairwell, had flattened himself against the bulkhead and was creeping forward.

McGarvey stepped out into the corridor and raised his pistol. The ship started to spin, but then steadied down. Bahmad turned, a surprised look on his face. He brought the MAC 10 around, but he was too late and he knew it.

"You lose," McGarvey said softly, and he squeezed off two shots, the first catching bin Laden's chief of staff in his chest, driving him backward, and the second under his jaw, the bullet spiraling upward into his brain.

Golden Gate Bridge

Elizabeth raced up the narrow stairs that had replaced the elevator inside this tower, taking them two at a time. Her radio was useless in here because of all the steel, though she could faintly hear the sirens and sounds of pandemonium out on the bridge deck below. There would be time later to chastise herself for allowing the President's daughter to slip away, and for the SWAT shooter who had left the tower door unlocked to get reamed. For now she had to concentrate on finding the girl, getting her the hell out of here and off the bridge before it was too late.

She stopped and cocked an ear to listen. Somewhere far above she could hear footfalls on the metal stairs.

"Deborah," she shouted, and she listened again. The footsteps stopped. The stairwell was only very dimly lit, casting ominous shadows on the honeycombed interior of the tower. There were a million places for someone to hide in here forever.

"Liz," Todd shouted from below, his voice booming in the stairwell.

"Stay back," Elizabeth warned.

"The chopper's on its way. Hurry."

Elizabeth turned and looked up the stairwell. There were no footsteps now. Deborah was crouched up there somewhere. Frightened. Not knowing who to trust or what to do.

"Deb, it's me, Liz," Elizabeth shouted, starting up. "I'm

coming up to talk to you. This is really important, so stay right where you are. Please."

The Golden Gate

McGarvey reached the port rail, blood streaming from his wounds, everything dancing crazily in front of his eyes as if he was in the middle of an earthquake. He could make out the Harrier jet a few hundred feet aft of the ship and the Sea King helicopter hovering about the same distance straight out. But he couldn't tell if the *Margo* had stopped, though it seemed to him that it had.

The bomb was on the pilot boat heading straight for the bridge and nobody but him knew about it. Even if they did now, there wasn't a damn thing they could do. Sinking the boat wouldn't help. When the bomb went off it would vaporize tons of water into a radioactive deluge. Nor would taking the boat in tow and heading it out to sea work. There simply wasn't enough time.

"Goddammit!"

The gate was open, the boarding ladder deployed. McGarvey looked down and spotted the inflatable, its motor idling. The procedure for shutting down the Russian nuclear devices couldn't be much different than that for deactivating the American bombs. Or at least it shouldn't be, but he had no other choice. Liz was on that bridge.

He scrambled down the ladder nearly falling several times. His legs threatened to buckle under him, his right hip where he had taken a hit was nearly useless and his vision kept fading in and out.

The Sea King slid in closer to see what he was doing, but its rotor wash became so strong it threatened to blow the dinghy over, and the pilot backed off.

McGarvey didn't bother to look up or wave, it was hard enough keeping in focus as it was. He managed to untie the painter with fingers as thick as sausages, climb aboard, throw the motor into gear and take off.

This is exactly how bin Laden envisioned the scenario would unfold. McGarvey had seen it in the man's eyes. Television viewers from all over the world would witness the United States being brought to its knees. The most powerful nation on earth was unable to protect itself. They would see the helicopters, the police, the military and the Coast Guard ships surrounding the bridge and the runners. And then the bright flash.

When he cleared the *Margo*'s huge flaring bows, McGarvey turned directly toward the bridge. The Coast Guard cutter *Escanaba* a hundred yards out now was bearing down on him, the Sea King had taken up position about fifty yards over his left shoulder and an outgoing tide raised a four-foot chop in the Gate that threatened to flip the dinghy over backward.

He couldn't see the pilot boat yet, but it was in the channel and it wasn't going very fast. He'd seen that from the air. He twisted the outboard's throttle all the way open and the dinghy shot ahead, leaping over the waves, nearly throwing him out each time it came down.

Golden Gate Bridge

The President's daughter was huddled on the stairs, her knees up to her chin, her eyes wide with fright. When Elizabeth reached her the girl was shivering almost uncontrollably, tears streamed down her cheeks.

"Hey, take it easy, Deb," Elizabeth told her. She sat down just below the girl and took her hands, her palms were cold and sweaty.

"They're going to kill me and my dad," Deborah whimpered.

"Don't be silly. Nobody's going to hurt you."

"Yes, they are. I heard my dad talking about them. They're all rotten bastards."

"That's why you've got us, Deb," Elizabeth said, keeping her voice calm and gentle. The girl was on the verge of hysteria. "We're not going to let anyone come near you."

"What about my dad?"

"He and your mom are okay. They're waiting for you to catch up." Elizabeth smiled warmly. "Unless you want to stay here in the dark."

Deborah shook her head, her movements tiny and bird-like. "The bastards won't hurt me if I come with you?"

"I promise," Elizabeth said. "But maybe you'd better not call them that anymore." She got up and helped Deborah to her feet.

"That's what my dad says they are."

"I know, but that's just the way dads talk sometimes. It's not the way girls are supposed to talk."

Deborah managed a little smile. "Okay," she said.

"All right then, let's do it."

Elizabeth started down the stairs, the President's daughter clinging tightly to her arm, conscious that they had just about run out of time.

The Golden Gate

McGarvey spotted the pilot boat a couple of hundred yards from the center span of the bridge, but it took another five minutes to catch up with it. There were still thousands of people up on the bridge, flashing lights, sirens and someone issuing instructions over a bullhorn. Even from here he could see and hear the mass confusion. People were getting hurt up there right now.

He could see someone at the helm of the slowly moving pilot boat. Until he got closer he thought that Bahmad had a partner after all. But as he came up from behind he saw that the helmsman was probably dead. Blood covered the back of his head and neck, and his body swayed back and forth with an unnatural looseness.

Bahmad had been the consummate professional. He'd planned for every contingency, even for McGarvey to show up in the middle of his operation. Even for his own death.

The terrorist had sent a corpse to deliver the bomb.

McGarvey came up on the pilot boat's port quarter and matched speeds. He grabbed the rail with his free hand and held there for a couple of seconds. The chop here where the Golden Gate was at its narrowest was the worst, the waves short and very steep.

He waited until the pilot boat's rail dipped, and then as it started to come back up, he let go of the outboard's throttle and heaved himself up and over with both hands, landing in the pilot boat's open deck well with a painful thump, cracking his head against the opposite coaming.

A million points of light burst inside of his head, and an overwhelming wave of nausea incapacitated him for several seconds. When he was able to raise up on his hands and knees the boat was spinning around in tight circles like a roller coaster going through an endless series of corkscrews.

He was conscious that they were very close to the bridge now. If Bahmad's timing was correct the bomb would ignite as they passed under the center span.

The *Escanaba* was practically on his stern, and the Sea King was right behind it.

No time.

McGarvey forced himself to crawl into the cabin. Besides the dead man at the helm another body lay in a bloody heap on the deck.

For another long moment McGarvey, on all fours, simply swayed with the motion of the boat. He wanted to be lulled to sleep. He wanted to go away to another safer more comfortable place.

The *Escanaba* blew its ship's whistle, the sound so loud in the confines of the pilot boat's cabin that it was almost a physical assault on his body.

McGarvey looked up out of his stupor and shook his head as he slid back into reality, into the here and now; the CD that had been playing in slow motion in his head speeded up and came into sharp focus.

The bridge was less than fifty yards away when Mc-

Garvey scrambled over to where the bomb was wedged between the helmsman's seat and the bulkhead. He pulled it free with great difficulty, barking his knuckles and wrenching his back under the weight. He undid the latches, threw back the outer cover and undid the inner latches. One of them stuck. He desperately hammered at it with the butt of his pistol until it suddenly snapped free and he yanked the inner lid open.

The LED counter switched from 00:00:20 to 00:00:19, but McGarvey's eyes were drawn to the matte black aluminum plate in the lower left hand corner.

He knew this device! Goddammit, he knew it!

The counter switched from 00:00:19 to 00:00:18 then 00:00:17.

He almost entered the ten-digit deactivation code on the keypad when he noticed that the antitamper indicator was lit and he pulled back his hand.

The LED switched to 00:00:16.

Bahmad had reprogrammed the weapon's firing circuits with an encrypted deactivation code. Unless you knew the code anything done to the device would cause it to immediately bypass its normal sequence and fire immediately.

00:00:15.

He knew this. Rencke's research program had included the operations manual for the firing circuits and encryption techniques. It was a quantum mathematical code in which the riddle of Schrödinger's cat was apparently solved. There was no *single* solution to the code; instead there was a series of correct answers that could, depending upon how they were entered, also be simultaneously wrong.

00:00:14.

McGarvey entered a five-digit code that opened the firing circuit.

00:00:13.

The center span of the bridge was almost on top of the pilot boat now. McGarvey looked up and could see people lining the rail staring down at him.

00:00:12. 00:00:11.

He entered a ten-digit code that when activated would, if it was the correct one, return the firing circuits to the non-encrypted mode.

00:00:10.

He pressed ##, and the antitamper indicator went out. He let out the breath he'd been holding.

00:00:09.

Shutting the weapon down was accomplished with another ten-digit code, this one the simple reciprocal of the firing code. Zero was nine, one was eight, two was seven, and so on until the end when nine was zero.

00:00:08.

McGarvey drew a blank. He'd had all the other numbers, but now there was a roaring in his ears, his vision was starting to go dark and the boat was beginning to spin.

00:00:07.

The pilot boat's bow cut into the shadow cast by the bridge.

00:00:06.

The numbers came to McGarvey all at once. He held onto the bomb case with his left hand to steady himself and entered the ten-digit code with his right.

00:00:05.

He stared at the indicator as the boat came under the center span.

The LED indicator read 00:00:04.

Slowly he sat back on his heels as the pilot boat came out of the Golden Gate Bridge's shadow into San Francisco Bay. The LED indicator read 00:00:04.

He turned and gave the skipper of the *Escanaba* the thumbs-up, and she started to toot the ship's whistle over and over. Other ships in the bay and out in the holding basin took up the salute, as did people on the bridge. A lot of them were whistling and cheering, though McGarvey suspected that none of them knew why.

Golden Gate Bridge

People on the bridge were cheering and clapping as Elizabeth and Deborah emerged from the tower. Boats in the bay and out in the Gate were blowing their whistles, helicopters were flying all over the place, sirens were blaring, horns were honking and someone down on the approach road was still bellowing instructions over a bullhorn.

Elizabeth's radio came alive with chatter, but it was hard to make any sense of it. Everyone was talking at once, and they all seemed excited.

A greatly relieved Chenna Serafini was holding her earpiece close and was beaming from ear to ear.

Deborah started to clap too, her tears completely forgotten, her face animated with excitement. She began to jog in place.

"You missed all the excitement," Van Buren shouted over the din.

"What happened?" Elizabeth demanded. "Did we get them?"

"It was your dad. He did it."

Something clutched at Elizabeth's gut. She grabbed Van Buren's arm. "Was he hurt? Is he okay?"

"Of course he's okay," Van Buren assured her. He was laughing. "He's your dad. The man is indestructible."

"I wish," Elizabeth said softly.

Deborah was beside herself with excitement. "Can we run now? I want to run."

"Later," Chenna said. She gave Elizabeth a warm smile. "Tell your dad thanks for me," she said.

Several other Secret Service agents had closed in on them, and a National Guard helicopter was waiting in the middle of the center span, its rotors turning.

"We'll run later," Chenna told the President's daughter. "But right now your mom and dad are waiting for you."

"Okay," Deborah said. She grabbed Elizabeth and gave

her an exuberant bear hug. "I think that you're neat," she said in Elizabeth's ear. "And I hope that it'll be a girl."

Elizabeth's mouth dropped open, but before she could say anything Chenna and the other Secret Service agents were hustling the President's daughter to the golf cart that would speed her to the waiting helicopter.

THE FINAL MOVES
FIVE DAYS LATER

> And they that take the sword
> shall perish with the sword.
>
> **MARK 26:52**

THIRTY

Khartoum, Sudan

Two canvas-covered trucks with Iranian Army markings pulled up in front of the compound just off the Sharia al-Barlaman a few blocks from the People's Palace. The back flaps were pushed aside and two dozen armed soldiers emerged.

Lieutenant Ahmed Ghavam jumped out of the front of the lead truck and began issuing orders. This was going to be done with dignity. Papa bin Laden was a friend of the state. A friend of all Islam, and neither his name nor his person would be besmirched.

When the troops were properly lined up at the front gate, a black Mercedes sedan pulled up across the street. A huge man, with tremendous mustaches and a thick beard got out of the car and shambled across the street. He had a smile on his broad face that looked as if it had been chiseled into place.

"He's not here," the huge man said amiably. He wore civilian clothes that looked very comfortable, but three sizes too large even for his impressive bulk. He was Captain Bakat Zamir, chief of Khartoum Regional Operations for the ISI, the powerful Pakistani Interservice Intelligence Agency.

Like Iran, Pakistan was a friend of bin Laden's. But the way the international climate was shaping up these days it was wise to at least pay lip service to the Great Satan in Washington, D.C., when it suited. This time bin Laden had gone too far. Even Dr. al-Turabi had tried to warn him, as had others in the National Islamic Front. But he was a head-strong man on a *fatwa*. His own daughter had been killed by the infidels' rockets. Who could blame a father for striking back?

"I suspected as much," Lieutenant Ghavam said. "But I have my orders."

"They are sensible orders."

A CNN television van came around the corner at the end of the block. Both men had been expecting its arrival.

"Do you have any idea where he went?" Lieutenant Ghavam asked.

"Switzerland, perhaps. It's a matter of his health, I believe." The Pakistani intelligence officer shrugged. "But who knows? If he lives he will certainly strike again."

"If he dies?"

"No one in the West will ever know for sure. *Insha'Allah.*"

Lieutenant Ghavam nodded. "Yes. *Insha'Allah.*"

Bethesda Naval Hospital

It was night. McGarvey stood at the window of his fifth-floor room morosely waiting for the dawn as he stared at the sodium vapor lights in the parking lot, his hands in the pockets of his hospital robe. He was being discharged tomorrow, his bullet wounds mended, the last bleeder in his head fixed and his life back to normal. For the time being no one was gunning for him and his family.

But the job wasn't over.

He turned and glanced at Kathleen curled up asleep in the easy chair next to the bed. She'd had the hardest time of all, waiting at home for the telephone call that her husband or her daughter or both of them were dead, all the while knowing that somebody could be coming after her again too.

He wanted a cigarette. But it had been nearly a week since he'd been pulled off the pilot boat and hospitalized without a smoke, and he had survived so far. Maybe it was time to give it up, if for no other reason than to get Kathleen to quit. But he felt like hell mentally and physically right now. Just maybe he needed a crutch after all, because nothing was going to be the same.

He turned back to the window and focused on his own reflection in the glass. There was only a small bandage on the side of his head, but he looked haggard. For the first time in his life he felt old. It was stupid, Kathleen would tell him. He was barely fifty and in this day and age that was definitely not old. But his career with the CIA, especially the last five or six years of it, had been tough on the body. He had the scars to prove it.

Elizabeth and Todd had come up last night to announce that they were getting married and that she was three months pregnant. Kathleen was over the moon, but the news had the opposite effect on McGarvey. He was being terribly selfish, but he didn't know if he could handle the responsibility of another life in his life. Part of his reaction was the painkillers he was on and everything he'd gone through over the past couple of months, but he'd seen the hurt in his daughter's eyes when she realized that he wasn't happy. He was going to have to make it up to her, though it seemed to him right now that he'd been making up things to the people he loved for most of his life.

A street cop had once given him the only explanation that seemed to make any sense of his sometimes perverse moods. Cops see bad guys every day so that when they're off duty it's nearly impossible to see people as good. Everybody is a suspect. It can get so bad that you even begin to wonder about your own family. Selfish or not he had trouble seeing how adding another new life into the world could do anything except complicate things.

Otto had shown up with Louise Horn from the NRO, whom he introduced as a friend. They were going to find an apartment together to sorta share expenses. The way she had kept looking at him though made it clear that they would be sharing more than just the rent and utilities. Again

McGarvey should have been happy for his friend. Kathleen was. She'd given them hugs. But what was the value of another relationship between two people in a world that seemed bent on its own destruction? Intellectually he knew that there was something terribly wrong with his way of thinking, but he couldn't shake it. Otto hadn't noticed, but Louise had and she'd given him a "screw you anyway" look that spoke volumes about how she really felt about her man.

The President and First Lady had come up yesterday too. The President had been in for his annual physical so it had been fairly easy for him to see McGarvey without alerting the media or creating a security problem. McGarvey was a dangerous man to be around. And when a President met in private with the CIA's deputy director of Operations it meant something big was up.

The half-marathon had been stopped because a gasoline tanker anchored in the holding basin posed a hazard. It had nothing to do with a terrorist threat, and thank goodness only a few of the runners had suffered anything other than some skinned knees and twisted ankles.

"I'm not going to give the bastard, wherever he's hiding now, the satisfaction of knowing how close he came," the President told McGarvey in private.

"Or the other thing," McGarvey said.

The President's lips compressed. His was a good face; honest, straightforward, without guilt. "That came as a nasty surprise."

"One that won't go away."

"No."

"I want Dennis Berndt kept out of the loop this time."

The President flinched. "You can't think that he had anything to do with this."

"No, I don't. But I want the need-to-know list kept to an absolute minimum. At least for now."

"Okay," the President agreed. At the door he turned back. "I can think of a lot easier jobs."

McGarvey smiled. "Me too, Mr. President."

"A penny for your thoughts," Kathleen said behind him.

He didn't turn. "I was thinking about Liz and the baby. I was a real shit to her."

"Yes, you were. But she doesn't think that you love her any less."

"I don't."

"She desperately wants to make you proud of her," Kathleen said. "I think she'd even throw Todd out a window if that's what you wanted."

"I want her to be happy—"

"Then tell her that, my darling. And tell Otto and Louise. They're a part of this family now too."

He heard her get up and come across the room. She put her arms around him and laid her head on his shoulder.

"Like it or not your family is back in your life and it's growing. Not only that, there isn't a thing you can do about it. Too bad for you that we all love you."

McGarvey finally turned around and took her in his arms and held her close. He was battered, but he wasn't old, and even having a grandchild would not change that. He hoped in a way it would be a girl so that he would not only have Katy and Liz, but he'd have a minature version of them running around too.

It was good about Otto and Louise because he had spent way too much time worrying about his friend's well being. Let someone else take over that duty.

And they had beat bin Laden. This time.

For the rest, he had work to do figuring out what had happened to the Russian bomb from Tajikistan, and how the bomb he'd disarmed aboard the pilot boat had gotten there. The legend on the matte black aluminum tag attached to the bomb's outer panel had been perfectly legible, even with his failing eyesight.

PANTEX CORP.
U.S.A.

PROLOGUE

Water was rushing somewhere, the sound hollow and frightening in the confines of research Chamber Gamma. A very slightly built man dressed in striped pajamas, the Star of David patch sewn on his left breast, stopped to cock an ear. Rows of beakers and chemicals and bunsen burners, two gas chromatographs and six powerful microscopes were arranged as final, silent, terrible witnesses to the horrors that had gone on down here since 1943.

The other sound he'd been hearing since early this morning came again; deep throated, almost below the level of hearing, in that place where you can only feel it. A thudding, like a pile driver. Distant. Somewhere above.

Manny Goldfine went back into the connecting tunnel between labs and shined the weak beam of his dying flashlight on the rough concrete ceiling. The thump came again, and dust filtered down. Explosions? He'd been trying to locate the exact source for three hours, and the sounds were bringing him, as he feared they would, toward the main elevator shaft. They were trying to get in. But that way was blocked for now. He and Sharon had seen to that last night. Then around two in the morning, he wasn't exactly sure of the time, he'd held her frail body in his arms and watched her die like the others, with long, wheezy gasps as she fought to bring air into her blood-filled lungs. In the end she'd looked up at him with love, and somehow managed to reach up with claw like fingers to brush at the fleck of blood she'd coughed up on his shirt. She'd been fastidious all her life.

"I'm sorry, my darling," she whispered, and then she'd died.

For a long time Manny sobbed because of the life he and his wife had never had; for the children they'd not been allowed to conceive and raise; for the picnics, and plays, and concerts they'd not seen; for the trip to Paris she'd talked about since they were kids together in Berlin.

Then he had gone on a berserk rampage against the bastard Nazis who had done this horrible thing not only to them, but to all their friends and relatives, and to their beautiful country. He'd raged against the bodies of the German scientists and SS guards, especially *Lieutenant* Grueber, whose body lay in corridor B. He'd kicked the heartless bastard until its skull was crushed.

Afterward he'd lain in a heap in the corridor near his wife's body, and waited for his own merciful death to come. The Germans would never again reach this place. He and the others had sealed off all the passages leading to the surface one hundred meters above. They were on the shores of Lake Tollense, so water had always been a problem, now it would be their salvation. They'd sabotaged the pumps and placed explosives against the west wall, on the other side of which was the bottom of the lake. When the wall went this place would flood instantly with no way of pumping it out short of draining the lake.

For some reason he had lasted longer than the others. He'd been alone with the bodies of five hundred jews, some of them test subjects, some of them like him, scientists, and one hundred Nazis plus the SS guards. During the night he was sure that he could hear them crying out in anguish; crawling toward him, seeking help, or revenge. Do research or die, they had told him. Do it *well* or your wife will die in front of your eyes. And their souls were coming for him now; for the terrible things he and the others had discovered and perfected.

Something in his heritage, he supposed, made him survive while others died. *Grossvater* Goldfine had lived to his hundreth birthday, and uncles Benjamin and David were both in their nineties when the Nazis came for them. They'd probably still be alive if they had not been murdered. Gassed, cremated. They'd all heard the stories, even down here. He was weak from hunger and overwork, but he was not sick. No heaviness in his chest. No blood in his stools, in his nostrils, none on his handkerchief.

Another much heavier thump came, and this time small pieces of the ceiling rained down on his head, the dust so bad now that it made him cough. He hurried to the end of the corridor and opened the heavy steel door. It was the last one of the complex. All the others, down every interconnecting tunnel all the way back to the dormitories that butted against the west wall, were in the locked open position. When the waters came the bunker would flood in seconds. Nothing would live down here. Nothing would *ever* live down here; the horrible secrets would be buried forever.

Looking back the way he had come he could just make out the detonator switch lying on the floor next to Sharon's body where he'd spent the night. Wires led all the way back to the explosives on the west wall. He could have turned the switch last night. He should have done it. He certainly wanted the peace; to be with his wife; no pain, no suffering, and especially no sorrows or loneliness. But something inside of him, some curiosity about how the end would play out had gotten the better of him. And then the explosions had begun. The SS was trying to get back in to save its own, or to reclaim the weapon hiding down here. Use it against innocent women and children. The indescriminate killer. He had to see, to make sure.

He stepped through the doorway into the arrivals and security hall as an even larger explosion came from directly overhead. He was shoved back by the concussion as a big section of concrete ceiling caved in; tons of rubble, dirt, stone, concrete, reinforcing bars half buried the room and knocked him off his feet.

"It's our responsibility to ourselves to live, Manny," Sharon had told him. But she was wrong, God bless her. They had a greater responsibility to the human race. But she didn't understand, and she was frightened, so he had comforted her at that moment.

Goldfine picked himself up and staggered back to the half-buried doorway. He'd lost his flashlight, but the tunnel was no longer in darkness. For a second or two he thought that he was hallucinating, but then he realized that he was seeing daylight for the first time in more than two years.

Mindless of the sharp rocks and jagged steel that tore at his hands and knees, he crawled up the pile of rubble so that he could look outside. There was light streaming down through the thick dust.

Something moved above. Figures. He could suddenly feel a cool breeze, and then he saw them. Soldiers. Two of them; no, three or four. Peering down from twenty or thirty meters up the jagged shaft the explosions had opened.

Soldiers, the thought solidified in his mind. They were SS. He was sure of it.

Scrambling backwards, he hit the rubble strewn floor of the tunnel running. They were coming. He was already too late. God in heaven, forgive him.

Someone was shouting at him from above. His ears were still ringing from the last explosion but he didn't think they were speaking German. It was another language. Polish, maybe. He couldn't be sure. Possibly it was a trick. The bastards did that sometimes.

He stumbled and fell, smashing his face on the floor so hard that he blacked out for a moment. When the fuzz cleared he was lying next to Sharon's body. Her mouth and chin were bloody, the front of her striped pajamas black with crusted blood. Her eyes were half open, and milky; her hair was matted, and her skin was deathly white. But he loved her. She was the most beautiful creature that God had ever put on earth. Kind, gentle, understanding.

The shouting was much louder now, and there was more light. Goldfine tenderly kissed his wife on the lips, then without further hesitation picked up the detonator, raised the handle, and twisted it sharply to the right.

A huge explosion rocked the fundations of the bunker. Goldfine looked up as a solid wall of water raced down the tunnel directly toward him at the speed of a freight train.

"God have mercy—," he said, and he joined his wife.

Captain-Second Rank Aleksei Konalev, standing in the turret of his tank twenty meters from where the Special Bunker Demolitions Squad had been working all morning, felt, rather than heard, the deep underground explosion. His first instinct was to duck, he'd been fighting without leave for nearly three years. But then he thought that something terrible had gone wrong, and the team had either had an accident with their exposives, or they had run into another booby trap.

"*Yeb vas*," he swore. It was the goddamn Nazis. The war had been over for more than a month, and yet they were still finding their deadly little surprises lying around.

They were just above the lake here, the windows in the church steeple in the town of Neubrandenburg a few klicks to the north, twinkling in the bright sun. A second after the explosion a huge depression appeared on the surface of the lake a couple of hundred meters off shore.

Konalev reached for his binoculars at the same moment a tremendous geyser of water shot out of the shaft the squad had excavated into the bunker. Mud, concrete, rocks, steel and bodies were blasted one hundred meters into the pale blue sky. In three years of war, Konalev had never seen such a fantastic sight, and his mouth dropped open. The sound was like a thousand tanks bearing down on him, and he looked up in time to see something very large and black falling out of the sky directly toward him.

"Move, move, move!" he screamed at his driver. He

ducked down into the turret and slammed the hatch shut an instant before his tank was hit with a solid, metallic bang so hard that the turret jammed on its track, and the entire tank was shoved backward at least ten meters.

But his crew had been under fire before. The driver had the engine in reverse and was racing backwards, as more debris rained down on them, hitting them like heavy caliber machinegun bullets being fired from above.

The gunner, blood streaming down from a gash where he'd hit his forehead, was peering through the periscope. "I don't see any enemy fire!" he shouted. "Where are they, sir? I can't see them!"

"Easy, Yuri," Konalev shouted him down. "We're not under fire. It was an explosion." Konalev keyed his radio, but all he was getting was static. The antenna had probably been knocked out by whatever had hit them.

The driver, looking through his periscope, backed off the accelerator, and the tank ground to a halt. He looked up, a confused expression on his battle-hardened features. "Fish," he said.

"What is it?" Konalev demanded.

"It's raining fish, sir," the driver said in wonder. "Out of the sky, fish were falling."

"Still?"

The driver turned back to the periscope. "No, sir. They're all over the ground, but they've stopped falling."

Konalev climbed back up into the turret, and he had trouble opening the hatch, but it finally gave with a squeal of metal-on-metal.

The scene was like something out of the Bible that his old grandmother had used to read to him from. Water swirled around a large depression where the bunker entrance had been. Fish lay everywhere. Huge waves raced across the lake, and debris of all kinds littered an area at least two hundred meters in diameter.

But Konalev's eyes were drawn to a steel door lying on

the front deck of his tank. It was the object that had been blasted out of the bunker and had fallen on them. A large skull and crossbones was painted on the door, beneath which was the legend: VORSICHT, danger.